hasn't yet been told in quite this way. The funny and shrewdly observant narrator won me over on the very first page."
—Stephen McCauley, author of *The Object of My Affection*

"What a pleasure, this journey from Queens to Brooklyn to Korea and back with such a smart, witty, observant insider. And have I mentioned the writing? So many times I said to myself as I read a particularly delicious sentence or description in *Re Jane* 'why can't I do that?'"
—Elinor Lipman, author of *The View from Penthouse B*

"Rich and engaging. Patricia Park writes with earnestness, honesty, and exuberance, which make the novel thoroughly enjoyable."
—Ha Jin, National Book Award–winning author of *Waiting* and *A Map of Betrayal*

"The Korean Americans of Queens find a daring new voice in Patricia Park's debut novel, as she takes a story we know and makes it into a story we've not seen before—a novel for the country we are still becoming."
—Alexander Chee, author of *The Queen of the Night*

"Jane is a hilarious, sometimes muddled, and utterly beguiling heroine. Park's surprising twists and razor-sharp writing and deep heart make the pages fly by. This story is all about what it's like being young and learning from mistakes and figuring out who you are without fear."
—Margaret Dilloway, author of *How to Be an American Housewife*

"In *Re Jane*, Patricia Park transforms Charlotte Brontë's beloved novel with her own inimitable wit and imagination. . . . A wonderfully suspenseful novel that will delight those who know the original, and those who don't."   —Margot Livesey, author of *The Flight of Gemma Hardy*

"This is a richly imagined and engrossing novel, and also an important work that marks what it means to be American now. Park's writing is remarkable for its tenderness and honesty."
—Sabina Murray, author of *Tales from the New World* and *The Caprices*

ABOUT THE AUTHOR

Patricia Park was born and raised in Queens and graduated from the Bronx High School of Science. She earned her BA in English from Swarthmore College and an MFA in Fiction from Boston University. A former Fulbright Scholar and Emerging Writer Fellow at the Center for Fiction, she has published essays in *The New York Times*, *Slice*, and *The Guardian*. *Re Jane* was named the 2016 ALA RUSA Reading List Women's Fiction winner. She lives in Brooklyn, New York.

Visit patriciapark.com

Praise for *Re Jane*

"Snappy and memorable with its clever narrator and insights on clashing cultures." —*Entertainment Weekly*

"In her delightful debut novel, Patricia Park uses the classic novel *Jane Eyre* as a template to examine very modern concepts: questions of identity and love, culture and conscience, even the hardships of immigration. But you don't really need familiarity with Charlotte Brontë's most famous work to appreciate *Re Jane*; it's entertaining all on its own, vibrant and witty and a hell of a lot of fun." —*The Miami Herald*

"A sensitive, witty tale of the search for belonging . . . Park's novel is so much more than a mere retelling of *Jane Eyre*. . . . Readers should feel free to take this 'Jane' as is—an astute, resonating, humorous, discerning, original debut." —*The Christian Science Monitor*

"[A] delightful first novel . . . Park's narrative voice is energetic, witty (the book bristles with one-liners) and thoughtful." —BBC.com

"*Re Jane* . . . drolly explore[s] issues of class, ethnicity, and women's autonomy for an unlikely heroine of the twenty-first century." —Maureen Corrigan, NPR

"Breezy, engaging . . . A truly fresh, modern take on the coming-of-age novel." —*The New York Times Book Review*

"Like her Brontean namesake, Jane narrates her tale with honesty and wit. . . . Reader, you'll love her." —O, *The Oprah Magazine*

"Be ready to mull over your own place in the world as you root wholeheartedly for Jane to find hers." —*Glamour*

"Park is a fine writer with an eye for the effects of class and ethnic identity, a sense of humor, and a compassionate view of human weakness. . . . An enjoyable book offering a portrait of a young woman struggling to come into her own in the increasingly complicated opening years of a new century." —*Kirkus Reviews*

"[Jane's] journey ripples with comic and surprisingly authentic moments. Park is a smart, engaging writer, able to capture the emotional weight of a romantic gaze as well as the complicated ties of family. . . . Most everyone who has struggled to fit in will relate to parts of Park's coming-of-age tale. . . . Reader, try not to leave charmed." —*The Denver Post*

"Breezy and accessible . . . Park offers real insight into assimilationist struggles. . . . [Her] portrait of Korean American life feels authentic and is ultimately endearing. Charlotte Brontë would be proud."

—*BookPage*

"Park's debut is a cheeky, clever homage to *Jane Eyre*, interwoven with touching meditations on Korean American identity. . . . Park's clever one-liners make the story memorable, and her riffs on cultural identity will resonate with any reader who's ever felt out of place."

—*Publishers Weekly*

"Some nerve, to take *Jane Eyre*, reconfigure it, make the heroine an orphaned half-white Korean girl, all the while mixing newfangled Jell-O shots, hipsterisms, and spicy fish stew with old-fashioned romance. Some nerve to bring it off with such energy, color, and emotional insight! Reader, you'll love it." —Daniel Menaker, author of *My Mistake*

"Patricia Park's *Re Jane* is packed with authenticity, poignancy, and humor. I was enchanted by this modern retelling of *Jane Eyre* as the tough yet vulnerable narrator captured my heart."

—Jean Kwok, bestselling author of *Girl in Translation* and *Mambo in Chinatown*

"Patricia Park displays her keen observation skills, her penchant for finding *le mot juste* (be it in English or Korean), and her natural gift for storytelling in her witty debut."

—Firoozeh Dumas, author of *Funny in Farsi*

"Even with its appealing echoes of *Jane Eyre*, Patricia Park's first novel is a true original—a smart, fresh, story of cultural complications that

PATRICIA PARK

Re Jane

PENGUIN BOOKS

PENGUIN BOOKS

An imprint of Penguin Random House LLC
375 Hudson Street
New York, New York 10014
penguin.com

First published in the United States of America by Viking Penguin,
an imprint of Penguin Publishing Group,
a division of Penguin Random House LLC, 2015
Published in Penguin Books 2016

A Pamela Dorman Book / Viking

ISBN 978-0-525-42740-7 (hc.)
ISBN 978-0-14-310794-1 (pbk.)

Printed in the United States of America
1   3   5   7   9   10   8   6   4   2

Set in Adobe Jenson Pro
Designed by Francesca Belanger

To Umma and Abba

CONTENTS

PART I

Brooklyn

*"Do you think, because I am poor,
obscure, plain, and little, I am soulless
and heartless? You think wrong!"*

—Jane Eyre

Chapter 1

Flushing

Home was this northeastern knot of Queens, in the town (if you could call it a town) of Flushing. Northern Boulevard was our main commercial thoroughfare, and two-family attached houses crowded its side streets. They say the neighborhood once contained a hearty swath of the American population, but when I landed here as an infant, Flushing was starting to give way to the Koreans. By the time I graduated from college in 2000, Northern looked like this: Daedong River Fish Market, named after the East River of Pyongyang. Chosun Dynasty Auto Body, run by the father of a girl from my BC calc class. Kumgang Mountain Dry Cleaning, owned by my uncle's accountant's cousin on his mother's side. This was my America: all Korean, all the time.

Flushing. The irony was that none of its residents could pronounce the name of their adopted hometown; the Korean language lacked certain English consonants and clusters. The letter *F* was assimilated to an *H* or a *P*. The adults at church would go *Hoo* before they could form the word, as if cooling it off their tongue. My uncle and aunt's rendition: Poo, Rushing. It could've been poetry.

Home was 718 Gates Street, Unit 1. It was my Uncle Sang's house, and I lived there with his family: his wife, Hannah, and my younger cousins, Mary and George. A few blocks away was his store. It was a modest-size grocery carrying a mix of American and Korean products, along with the usual emergency supplies—flashlights and batteries, candles and condoms. From Northern you could spot our green awning, bearing four white letters in all caps: F-O-O-D. Below it were large wooden tables stacked with pyramids of fruit.

One day in late summer, I was crouched in one of the aisles, turning cans of beans face out and flush with the lip of the shelf. I heard someone say, in Korean, *"Jane-ah. I heard about Lowood. What a shame."*

It was Mrs. Bae, the wife of the pastor of our church. I stood and ducked my head into a bow. At five foot seven, I towered over most of the women of Flushing. Her words were like salt sprinkled on the sting of being the only one in my graduating class still bagging groceries and restocking merchandise. The economy—with the exception of the tech industry—was, for the most part, still booming. I'd had a job with Lowood Capital Partners lined up since my senior year last fall, never anticipating that in the months that followed, here's what would happen: The company would be heavily leveraged in dot-com investments, the CEO would resign after accusations of insider trading, and the interim CEO would issue a hiring freeze. My job offer had been rescinded.

Mrs. Bae went on. About how her daughter Jessica worked such long hours at Bear Stearns yet still she would wash the rice and do the laundry and help her little sister with her homework after she got home. How Mrs. Bae felt undeserving of such a devoted daughter. What Mrs. Bae didn't know was that "Jessica the PK" (Pastor's Kid) had cut class every Thursday our senior year of high school to shoot pool at Amsterdam Billiards in the city.

"I'll tell our Jessica to help you," Mrs. Bae said, staring back with the usual curious expression she seemed to reserve for me. You'd think that after all these years I would've gotten used to it. I didn't. I averted my eyes, focusing on the hairline cracks running through the floor tiles.

"No, no, that's too much trouble for you." That was Sang, approaching us.

They had the usual exchange—*"No, no trouble at all, you and Mary's mother must be so worried."* "*Eh, what can you do?*"—before my uncle turned his head sharply, shooting me a look. I thanked Mrs. Bae. He shot me another look—that was my cue to go get her some fruit, on the house. And none of the cheap stuff.

That was the power of *nunchi*. There's no word for it in English; perhaps its closest literal translation is "eye sense." My friend Eunice Oh sometimes likened *nunchi* to the Eye of Sauron: an all-knowing stink eye that monitored your every social misstep. Other times she said it was like the Force, a way of bending the world to your will. But Eunice had an annoying tendency of bringing everything back to *Star Wars* or *Star Trek*, Tolkien or Philip K. Dick. For me *nunchi* was less about some sci-fi power and more about common sense. It was the ability to read a situation and anticipate how you were expected to behave. It was filling your elder's water glass first, before reaching for your own. The adults at church always said that good *nunchi* was the result of a good "family education."

On my way to the fruit stalls, I was intercepted by Mrs. O'Gall, a petite Irish granny who frequented Food every day. Cradling a head of iceberg lettuce, she demanded help with the Hellmann's mayonnaise: "It's too damn high."

The jars on the shelf were at hip level—I handed one to her. Mrs. O'Gall shook her head. "No, gimme the smaller one." When I told her that eight-ounce jars were the smallest we carried, she said, "Unbelievable. You people." She told me to put in a special order from our distributor.

"Yes, Mrs. O'Gall. I'm sorry, Mrs. O'Gall."

She walked away with her iceberg and mayo, leaving a trail of her particular scent in her wake. Mrs. O'Gall had that unwashed smell the elderly sometimes had, one that made you think of brown paper bags left out in the rain and chin whiskers and absentee adult children. It was the smell of abandonment.

I returned to Mrs. Bae with the fruit, but she was gone. I was making my way back to the shelf of beans when another customer stopped me. Then I rushed to man the second cash register—a line of new

customers had formed. The delivery guy from the beverage distributor cut to the front, waving a pink invoice at me. "Who checked your
cases?" I demanded. "The little guy," he said. I knew he was referring
to our stock boy, Hwan. I jerked my head, motioning him to the
back of the line—we were *his* customers, so he could very well wait—
and when I reached him, I paid him with the dirty twenties we kept
at the bottom of the cash drawer, the crisper bills reserved for the
shoppers.

I was just about to leave the register when Mrs. O'Gall returned; I
processed her mayonnaise refund, even though she'd opened the jar
and removed one teaspoon. Then it was over to the wooden stalls, to
pick out the bruised and dented fruits from their unblemished counterparts.

I was making my way back to the bean cans again when I saw Sang.
His was a harried gait, and it always struck me as less a rush *to* his
destination than a hasty departure *from*—like he couldn't get out of a
place fast enough.

He frowned when he arrived at where I stood. "You do this?" he
said, handing me a pink invoice—the soda delivery I'd just signed off
on. My uncle usually spoke to me in English, even though it was his
weaker language.

I could hardly expect him to clarify. Sang had a very specific organizational system for running Food; he knew that store and its many
intricacies like the back of his chapped hands. The problem was, that
knowledge was all in his head and none of us had access to it. And he
expected you to read his mind.

Sang had other rules, too, that I'd had to learn over the years:
No chew gum.
No back-talk to customer.
No act like you so special.
No ask stupid question.

"Go to office get last week invoice," he ordered. I rushed past the
aisles of produce and dairy cases to the back corner of the store. This
was our "office"—cardboard boxes flattened into walls and duct-taped

to leftover PVC pipes. The desk was a slab of scrap wood suspended by L-brackets drilled into the concrete wall. The chair was an upended milk crate. As I rummaged through the banana box on the floor—our version of an accounts-payable/accounts-receivable department—I thought of my interview at Lowood on the 103rd floor of the World Trade Center. My cubicle would have had walls of sleek frosted glass, overlooking an office that overlooked the river.

I found the soda invoice. In my haste to get back to Sang, I tripped on the cinder block propped against the door of the walk-in refrigerator box. I would have pitched forward if Hwan hadn't dropped his hand truck and rushed to break my fall.

"You okay, Miss Jane?" he said, steadying me to my feet.

"That stupid door," was all I managed, my cheeks flushed with embarrassment. The problem with the walk-in was that unless you knew how to jiggle the handle a certain way, the door failed to latch. The refrigerator kept things cold as it was, but if it was sealed properly, its contents would stay preserved for up to three days, even if the power blew out. The door, as it stood, was a liability. But whenever I brought the subject up to Sang, he'd wave my words away. *If not broke, why you gotta fix?* For Sang the inverse was also true: Everything broken could be jerry-rigged to working order. It was his own special form of madness—he never stopped trying to salvage the unsalvageable.

"Why you take so long?" Sang said when I returned with the invoice. He jabbed a finger at the offending signature. *My* signature. Apparently we were supposed to receive credit for two more soda cases, but the new invoice didn't reflect that credit. I realized, with sinking stupidity, that I should have called for my uncle on the spot, instead of taking the deliveryman's word as a given. Things like this happened every now and again—the delivery guys would do a bait and switch, "pocketing" the extra pallet or two—but the store had been busy. I knew what Sang would have said if I'd paged him over the loudspeaker—*Why you ask stupid question? Where your* nunchi?—as though it were something I'd carelessly misplaced somewhere, like a set of keys or a receipt.

"Why didn't you just tell me about the credit?" I asked. "Then I would've known—"

"*Don't talk back to your uncle,*" my aunt interrupted, walking toward us. Then, to her husband, "*It's Mr. Hwang, from Daedong Fish.*"

Sang rushed away, and it was just Hannah and me. Her eyes studied mine. "*Are you trying to make his high blood pressure go up?*" she continued in Korean.

I toed a loose floor tile. Yet one more thing that needed to be fixed. I made a note to grab the contact cement and putty knife in the office.

"*Don't you know how lucky you are?*" she said. "*You should be grateful.*"

Hannah was echoing what everyone in this tangle of Queens thought about my situation. They knew all about my dead mother—I could see it in the way their eyes have fixed on me these past twenty years. Just as I knew who borrowed money from whom to start a business and which of those businesses were flourishing and floundering. I knew their children's SAT scores, their college acceptances and subsequent job offers, but I also knew who was dating whom, who was cheating on whom, where they went to get drunk or high.

In Flushing your personal business was communal property. Such intimate knowledge was stifling. I tapped a hand to my chest, seeking relief. I felt *tap-tap-hae*—an overwhelming discomfort pressing down on you physically, psychologically. When the walls felt as if they were closing in around you, that was *tap-tap-hae*. When the strap of your bra was fastened too tightly across your chest, that was *tap-tap-hae*. When you were trying to explain to the likes of Hannah how to turn on the computer, let alone how to operate the mouse, that was unbearably, exasperatingly, *tap-tap-hae*.

I must have been frowning because suddenly I felt a harsh rap on my forehead: my aunt had flicked a finger at me. "*Stop that,*" she snapped. Hannah had a theory that scrunching your face led to early aging. "*You of all people need to worry about wrinkles.*"

Then don't touch me, I thought, but if I spoke the words aloud, I'd only set off the cycle anew. *Don't talk back. You should be grateful.* It was easier to comply silently. So one by one I loosened the features of my face. I became expressionless, unreadable.

Then Hannah pointed down the aisle to the shelves of beans. *"Why'd you make such a big mess over there? Go finish."*

As I reshelved the beans, I thought once more about that job at Lowood. Flushing and Food would have been an indistinguishable speck from the office windows. I'd have had the chance to see how a real business was run. Not Sang and Hannah's mom-and-pop operation: decidedly rustic, with none of the homespun charm.

I tapped my hand once more to my chest. *Tap-tap-hae.* All I wished was for this feeling to go away.

Chapter 2

Uncanny Valley

Every Sunday we went to church. On the way you passed the American Roman Catholic church, the Korean Roman Catholic church, the Chinese Buddhist temple, the Pakistani mosque, and an ever-expanding assortment of Korean Presbyterian and Methodist churches. (The Korean Protestants, unlike their Catholic counterparts, seemed to multiply like Jesus's five loaves and two fishes.) Service was held in one half of a two-family house. After Pastor Bae gave the sermon, the mothers prepared *bibimbap* in the kitchen for the entire congregation.

Every Sunday, for as long as I can remember, Eunice Oh and I would find each other after the service. She'd always been the same Coke-bottle-glassed girl since childhood. In truth she and I were bound together less by common interests than by our differences from *them*, the more popular kids in our year: Jessica Bae—Pastor Bae's daughter, who just graduated from Columbia. James Kim, who went to Wharton and was about to start at Lehman—his parents owned a deli downtown. John Hong, who was at Sophie Davis—his father's herbal-medicine practice was down the block from Food. Jenny Lee, who went to Parsons and now did graphic design for *CosmoGirl!* magazine—her mother owned a nail salon on the Upper East Side, but her father graduated from Seoul National and, according to my Aunt Hannah, "was too proud to get a menial job."

But this was our last Sunday together. Eunice was leaving again, this time for good. First it had been for MIT, where she'd majored in something called "Course VI." Now for San Francisco, where she'd gotten an offer from Google. Eunice had had her pick of offers—including one from Yahoo!—but she went with Google. Why she would take a job with a dot-com immediately after the dot-com crash, no one could understand, but I suspected it had to do with her American boyfriend, a guy called Threepio. He'd also accepted a job in Silicon Valley. They were heading out the next day.

"The job search, how goest?" Eunice asked, pushing up the nosepiece of her thick glasses with a chubby finger.

"It goest—" I started, then stopped. You never knew what you were going to get with Eunice. One day she spoke like an Orc, the next like Shakespeare. Sometimes I found myself imitating her without even realizing I was. "It's going. Actually, it's not. There's nothing on the market."

She waved one hand in the air and rummaged through her bag with the other. The other girls from church carried purses, but Eunice had had the same Manhattan Portage messenger bag since the seventh grade, which I knew was filled with its usual jumble of stubby mass-market paperbacks, a well-thumbed C++ pocket guide with some chipmunk drawing on the cover, magazines ranging from *Scientific American* to the *501st Daily*, assorted highlighters, and German mechanical pencils (.5-mm thickness) and their lead refills. Eunice Oh could not wait for the day when paper went digital.

She pulled out a copy of the *Village Voice;* its circulation in our part of Queens was nonexistent. The page was opened to the classifieds, her finger pointing to one of the listings.

I peered down. An ad for a fertility clinic. "You want me to sell my eggs?"

"*No.* This one." She jabbed again. And there, wedged between the clinic's posting and one from an escort service offering "discreet and seXXXy services" was the following:

BROOKLYN FAMILY DESIRING AU PAIR

We wish to invite into our family an au pair (i.e., a live-in "baby-sitter," although n.b., we take issue with such infantilizing labels; seeing as the term has yet to be eradicated from the vernacular, we have opted—albeit reluctantly—to use it in this text for the sole purpose of engaging in the lingua franca) who will foster a nurturing, intellectually stimulating, culturally sensitive, and ultimately "loving" (we will indulge the most essentialist, platonic construct of the term) environment for our bright (one might even say precocious) nine-year-old daughter, adopted from the Liaoning province of China. In these postmodern, postracial times, we desire said au pair to challenge the existing hegemonic . . .

The ad cut out, exceeding its allotted space.

Eunice knew I was supposed to be looking for a job in finance, not a nanny gig. It was insulting that she thought so little of me. I might not have gone to a name-brand college like MIT or Columbia (even though everyone at church thought that Columbia was one of the easiest Ivies to get into), but I'd still gotten an offer from *Lowood*. I wanted out of Flushing, but not so badly that I'd be willing to change diapers or the equivalent in order to do it. I had spent enough of my lifetime watching my cousins Mary and George walk all over me because they knew I had absolutely no power over them. I had a plan. Baby-sitting was not part of that plan.

"Don't you want to get out?" Eunice asked, looking at me. "A very sheltered existence you lead."

She was one to talk. "So you're telling me to go live with a bunch of total strangers. Who can't even write normal English."

"What do you expect? They're probably academics."

"They live in *Brooklyn*." The whole point was not to trade one outer borough for the other but to upgrade to *the city*. We had spent countless rides on the 7 train, watching as the Manhattan skyline bloomed into view. As kids we used to imagine living in deluxe condos that overlooked Central Park.

I sighed. "A bunch of places have my résumé on file. If something comes up in the next year—"

"Much can happen in a year," she interrupted. "Just apply. Worst-case scenario, you hate them, they hate you, you part ways. But I have a *good* feeling about this. Their daughter's Asian, you're also Asian"— she glanced up at my face, revised—"*ish*. And you can play up your whole epic sob story: uncle, grocery store, orphan. Everyone loves a good orphan story." (Technically I was only half an orphan.) "Jane. Your ticket out, this could be."

Eunice extended the paper anew. Reluctantly I took it from her.

We made our way to the line for food. Eunice's father was standing in front of us. I bowed; Dr. Oh and I were nearly the same height. "Eunice-ah," he said, after I greeted him. "Make sure you mail letter to Jane after you leave home." Dr. Oh spoke a fluid, gentle English, a far cry from the choppy waters of Sang's speech.

"Abba: letter writing is obsolete."

"Yes, well . . ." He fumbled for words; finding none, he patted a warm hand on his daughter's back. But instead of leaning into her father's embrace, she pointed ahead. "Abba, the line. It's moving." Eunice Oh had no *nunchi* whatsoever.

The mothers heaped rice onto our Styrofoam plates, and we loaded up on bean sprouts with red-pepper flakes, spinach and carrots drizzled in sesame-seed oil, ground beef marinated in a sweet soy sauce, brown squiggles of some *namul* root whose name I didn't know in English, fried eggs with still-runny yolks, shredded red-leaf lettuce, a spoonful of red-pepper paste, and of course squares of cabbage kimchi.

We headed to the kids' table. Jessica Bae dabbed at her mouth with a napkin and said, "So, Eunice, you're, like, leaving us. That's so sad!"

"Yo, Eunice, isn't that, like, mad stupid? Working for a dot-com right now?" James Kim said.

"A good company it is. A greater company it will be." When she spoke, she looked at no one in particular, which gave the impression that she was talking to herself. Sometimes I wondered how Eunice Oh had ever managed to get a boyfriend.

Jenny Lee tittered into her napkin. Jessica Bae turned to me. "So . . . Jane!" she said brightly. "That, like, totally sucks about Lowood. How's the job hunt going?"

"..." I hated when it was my turn.

"My mom said she saw you at your uncle's store yesterday." Jessica paused. "It must be really tough to get a job when, like, you know ..."

"You know" meant "*You only graduated from CUNY Baruch.*"

I could feel Eunice studying my face. "Jane *has* a job she's considering. An au pair job."

I shot her a look of *nunchi*, but Eunice pretended not to see me.

"A *what* pair?" said John Hong.

"Isn't that, like, a housemaid?" said Jenny Lee.

"That doesn't look good *at all*," Jessica Bae continued. "Do you know about our rotational internship? At Bear Stearns?" She repeated the name of her firm, as if I could forget. "You should apply? It's, like, for college seniors, but I can *totally* put in a good word for you?"

Did I mention Jessica Bae only got into Columbia off the wait list?

Then my cousin Mary came to our table with a plate full of just vegetables (in public she was perpetually on a diet) and took the seat next to John Hong. She smiled brightly at him. She smiled brightly at everyone, except Eunice, at whom she curled her lip and said, "*Eunice.*" When her eyes fell on me, they grew round. "Omigod, Jane," she said, pointing at my face.

Everyone's eyes followed the direction of her pointing.

"You've got ... on your forehead ..."

I swiped at my face, thinking red-pepper paste had splashed me. My fingers fell on a tiny bump. I saw James Kim feeling his own face for pimples. He'd had horrible acne since the eighth grade. When I looked at Eunice for confirmation, she just shrugged. "Darker matters have come to pass," she said.

Jessica Bae began rooting through her tiny purse. She pushed a travel-size bottle of astringent and a Baggie of cotton pads into my hand. "Here. Go to the bathroom."

Since everyone expected me to drown my pimple in purple-tinted salycylic acid, I got up, dreading how their eyes would once again latch onto my face when I returned. On the short walk to the bathroom, I ran into Pastor Bae and his wife, Jenny Lee's parents, James Kim's, John Hong's, Eunice's, and of course Sang and Hannah. I forced myself to go bow, bow, bow to each and every adult I met.

I finally reached the bathroom, and leaned all my weight against the locked door. My neck was sore from the rapid succession of bowing. My cheeks hurt from all the strained smiling. I lifted my eyes to the mirror. What I saw was limp black hair. Baggy brown eyes. Sharp and angry cheekbones, pasty skin, pointy chin, and—like a maraschino cherry on top of the whole mess—a furious red pimple smackdab at the center of my forehead, the same spot where Hannah's finger had jabbed me the day before. At first glance I looked Korean enough, but after a more probing exploration across my facial terrain, a dip down into the craters under my eyebrows, or up and over the hint of my nose bridge, you sensed that something was a little off. You realized that the face you were staring into was not Korean at all but Korean-*ish*. A face different from every single other face in that church basement.

* * *

After lunch Eunice offered to give me a ride home. Staring down the expanse of Northern Boulevard through the windshield, she let out a long, low sigh. But soon she would leave Flushing and slip back into her world, the one where each *ping* she volleyed forth would be met with its appropriate *pong*. I was glad for her. Sad for me, but glad for her.

She gripped the steering wheel and drove off.

When we pulled up to 718 Gates, I said, "I guess this is it."

Eunice's eyes were still fixed on the road ahead. "That's right."

I reached for the door handle, paused, and blurted, "I'll miss you."

"I know." Her words sounded canned.

I jerked open the handle. "Well, don't get all mushy on me." One foot was already out the door. "See you, Eunice."

"It's 'So long, Princess . . .'" Eunice's tone changed to the one she used when enlightening the unenlightened, but there was a hitch in her throat. She stopped, started again. "Good-bye, Jane Re. I wish you well. May the Force be with you."

"And also with you," I found myself saying.

We shook hands.

"Lose the *nunchi*, Jane," Eunice said. With these words she drove off and we each went our separate way.

Chapter 3

Bridges and Tunnels

The next day I boarded the 7 train leaving the Main Street–Flushing station. There was an unmistakable rattle whenever you stepped aboard the 7, as if the train cars were hinged together by a single loose pin. We passengers accepted this precariousness with not much more than a sigh before slumping into our seats.

But I wasn't heading for the city, the way Eunice Oh and I always imagined when we were growing up. I was on my way to *Brooklyn*. There was a geographical irony of leaving Queens for Brooklyn—two outer boroughs that abutted each other. The fastest route was to make a right angle through Manhattan, crossing both bridge and tunnel.

It's not that we had beef, per se. We acknowledged our kindred scrappiness to Manhattan. We were, after all, Bridge & Tunnel: all our roads led to Manhattan. It was the borough that blazed in its own violet light and threw scraps of shadows on the rest of us.

I had been to Brooklyn only a handful of times in my life. Whenever we drove through, Sang would make us roll up the windows and double-check that our car doors were locked. He'd written off the entire borough after a fruit-and-vegetable he owned on Smith Street went up in flames during a blackout. According to Hannah, Sang had stumbled home that night with burnt clothes, a black eye, and a busted rib. Since then his mind conflated the three B's: Brooklyn, black people, and the blackout. Add to that one more B: a baby. A bundle of joy. Me. When I arrived not one year later, he was still picking up the pieces of his broken store. He took to carrying a metal baseball bat on the passenger side of his car. His wife was budding with her own pregnancy. I was a burden, the daughter of his dead younger sister—and a *honhyol* bastard to boot.

My mother was one of four children: two boys and two girls. First was Big Uncle, a man I'd never met, who still lived in Korea. Sang was second. Then my mother only two years later. Emo, the youngest, trailed behind them all by more than a decade. I had never met her either. Sang spoke little of the family in Korea and even less about "that stupid thing" my mother had done as a college student up in Seoul: she fell in love. It was an indulgence at a time when most marriages were arranged. Worse, she fell for an American man, a GI, or so the story went. My grandfather kicked my pregnant mother out, or maybe she left of her own accord; Sang was stingy with the details, and Hannah filled in patches of the narrative of the sister-in-law she had never met, colored with her own perceptions. (*"Your mother was a wild fox-girl. Don't you dare grow up to become like her."*) In any case, my mother had me—a *honhyol*, a mixed-blood. Then she died of carbon monoxide poisoning from the fumes of cheap coal briquettes used for cooking and heating—an all-too-common occurrence in Korea back then. Rightfully I should have died, too, had not Providence, or maybe it was the police, saved me from the wreckage.

After my mother's death, the responsibility of dealing with me defaulted to my grandfather. The way I pictured it, was he was stepping outside one morning to get a drink from the well and there I was, swaddled on his doorstep. He stared down at me and thought, *Oh, shit.*

There was no question I would have been stigmatized if I'd stayed in the motherland—a society where the slightest physical differences were scrutinized like a genetic anomaly. Where my dubious lineage would have undoubtedly come to light. So perhaps my grandfather was benevolent in sending me to live with my uncle in America, when he could have carted me off to an orphanage instead. Either way, he rid himself of an inconvenient problem. But here's another geographical irony for you: I traveled nearly seven thousand miles across the globe to escape societal censure only to end up in the second-largest Korean community in the Western world.

We were stuttering our way out of Queens. The 7 train was like that: Tourettic. The lights blinked on and off; the rickety train cars jerked from side to side as much as front and back. I stared at the other slumped passengers. The faces repeated in a pattern: Korean, Hispanic, Chinese, Chinese again, Indian. You could always tell by their worn expressions that they were going from home to work. You could always tell by their worn shoes: sometimes high-top sneakers with the backs cut out to form makeshift slippers, sometimes pleather platforms or paint-splattered construction boots—all sharing the same thick rubber soles, designed to absorb the work of the day.

The train emerged aboveground, the windows opening to the sprawl of Flushing. First you saw a beautiful clock tower sitting on top of a concrete storage warehouse with loud capital letters: U-H-A-U-L. Then the Van Wyck, snaking its way through heaps of sand and ash, through auto-body shops and junkyard lots. Wood and steel beams had lain in abandoned stacks for as long as I could remember; whether they represented the start of construction or the aftermath of demolition was anyone's guess. There were rows of brown, frayed, tarped storefronts with Korean lettering. Then the view of Shea: a stadium the shade of working-class blue with dimly lit neon figures at bat. On game nights you could barely make out the halfhearted roars in the half-empty seats—a smattering of loyal fans in blue-and-orange satin jackets. Ahead, the silvered peaks of the midtown skyline glinted in that violet light. This was our Queens wasteland.

Then the lights flickered off.

In the expansive darkness of the tunnel between Queens and Manhattan, the 7 stalled and let out a low, hesitant sigh that echoed inside the train car as one passenger after the next breathed out with exhaustion. It was the same sigh Eunice had let out on the drive home. We were frustratingly close, yet so far from where we wanted to be.

Then the lights flickered back on and we surged forward, Flushing falling away behind us.

Chapter 4

Brooklyn

In the row of brownstones between Clinton and Henry Streets in Carroll Gardens, Brooklyn, 646 Thorn Street was the only house on the block with a string of red paper lanterns hung in the doorway. To the left of the door was a hooded bay window, and from where I stood it gave the impression that the house was winking at me, as if we were both in on the same joke.

Brownstones were not part of the indigenous Queens architecture. Our houses were sometimes clapboard, redbrick, or concrete, more often than not aluminum-sided. The single-family detached houses lay farther east, in the neighborhoods jutting into the Little Neck Bay.

I was in Brooklyn for my interview for that nanny job. I couldn't tell you exactly what had compelled me to apply, except that I was being practical. I took a hard look at my situation: financial firms usually recruited in the fall for summer hires. The soonest I could start a new job would be one year from now. Temping or bookkeeping—my other options in the interim—was not all that attractive on a résumé; babysitting wouldn't look *that* much worse. (Not that I would dare put "nanny" under "work experience"; I'd have to explain away the time off with the excuse that I was studying for the GMATs. Or skipping about Europe with a backpack.) But maybe the real impetus had been curiosity. Who was this family with an adopted daughter from China? They were willing to hire and shelter and feed a whole other person, just for their one daughter. And Hannah used to say *I* was the lucky one. She let me tack on my piano lessons at the end of Mary and George's. (By the time that piano teacher got to me, she'd heave a *nunchi-ful* sigh, so I'd let her wrap up our sessions after a hasty set of Czerny exercises, my fingers tripping over the scales.)

When I called the ad's box number at the bottom of the paper, someone named Ed Farley answered. Over the phone he was clipped, his voice gravelly, with a Brooklyn accent. After a few basic questions, he rattled off a date and time, along with his address. But he did not pass the receiver to Mrs. Ed Farley.

I knew the Ed Farley type. He shared the same raspy tone as the older Irish men from the neighborhood who shopped at Food. Someone like Mrs. O'Gall's son. (Once a year, the day after Christmas, her son would take her grocery shopping and Mrs. O'Gall would parade him around the store. Then he'd return to his Greek Revival four-bedroom in Westchester—she'd shown us pictures—until the next year.) By the end of that phone conversation, I had outfitted Mr. Farley in a short-sleeved button-down yellowed with pit stains, brown polyester pants hemmed a few inches too short, and black orthopedic shoes with thick cushioned soles. I went ahead and added a middle-aged paunch, fading tufts of yellow hair, and sagging jowls, smattered with liver spots.

When the door swung open, the man standing behind it looked *nothing* like the Ed Farley I'd imagined. He was past the youthfulness of his twenties but too boyish for middle age; he was probably in his mid- to late thirties. He had a full shock of blond hair—the kind of natural blondness I used to see more as a kid but these days rarely made an appearance on the 7 train. His deep-set eyes were the same shade of blue as Shea, but instead of the stadium's flat, matte color, Mr. Farley's eyes were bright with vigor. He had a square forehead, a straight nose, high cheekbones, and a strong jawline. He shared the same conventionally handsome features of the male models in the Polo ads, but there was still something a touch too Irish, a touch too hard-worn about his face to be considered all-American.

Then I realized that while I was exploring his face, this man had also been probing mine. It was not in the same parsing way Korean eyes looked at me, trying to discern the percentage of my genetic split. Judging by the tight line his lips made, I could tell that mine was a face that displeased him. I grew self-conscious; I took a step back.

He spoke. "You Jane Re?" he said. There was that thick Brooklyn accent.

I nodded, too shy to trust my own voice. Our family name, in the original Korean, was pronounced "Ee"—less a last name than a displeased squeal. "Lee" was its most common Western perversion, but there were others: Rhee, Wie, Yee, Yi. Re was a bastard even among the other bastardizations.

"Ed. Ed Farley." He stuck out his hand. I expected it would be rough to the touch, but my fingers glided over the smooth skin of his palm.

I followed Ed Farley down a dark, narrow hallway, lined with carved African masks. Mr. Farley was not tall—maybe only two inches taller than me—but under his buttoned-up shirt I could tell he was broad-shouldered and lean. He had the kind of natural muscles that made you think of hours spent not at the gym but on construction sites, lifting beams of wood and steel, or warehouses, loading pallets of merchandise onto trucks.

I adjusted my suit blazer and pulled down the hem of my skirt. If something happened to me, I knew what Sang would say: *Telling you so.* I'd had to pretend I'd gotten an interview with a bank.

After a seemingly endless hallway, we finally turned left and entered the living room. We'd just made a loop around the house, only to wind up right back at the front. The bay window down at the far end of the room, draped in crimson velvet curtains, was the same hooded window that had stared out at me from the street. Dark wood bookshelves, crammed with books, floated on the walls, with more books heaped in piles on the floor.

There was a rustling of the curtains; I saw a small foot poking out, then a little leg, then a little girl. An Asian girl. She had a tiny frame but a large head, its largeness further emphasized by the unfashionable bowl cut of her stick-straight black hair. She didn't look stereo-typically Chinese—I might even have mistaken her for Korean. She jumped down from her window perch and bounded toward me with purposeful strides. She looked like a colt: half trotting, half tripping. One arm was sticking out in the air, ready to receive mine. The other held an oversize newspaper.

Her outstretched hand reached me first. "You must be Jane Re. My name's Devon Xiao Nu Mazer-Farley, and next week I start the fifth grade. It's a real pleasure to meet you." By the time she finished speaking, the rest of her body had caught up to her hand.

We shook; the girl had a surprisingly tight grip.

Devon Xiao Nu Mazer-Farley's face was so different from Ed Farley's: it was shallow, like swift strokes on a sheet of clay. On a scale of increasing facial three-dimensionality, things would look something like:

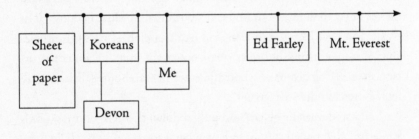

I heard light, scampering footsteps, like a mouse's. I turned around and saw a woman hurrying toward me, arm outstretched, frizzy gray hair streaming behind her. She squeezed my knuckles. "You must be Jane. I'm Beth, Devon's mom. It's a real pleasure to meet you."

This was Mr. Farley's wife? She looked a decade too old for him. "A real pleasure to meet you, too, Mrs. . . . . Farley."

"*Mrs.* Farley!" she laughed.

"That kind of has a nice ring to it," Mr. Farley said from the couch, but too softly for the woman to hear.

"Please, call me Beth," she said to me. "But for the record, it's Dr. Mazer."

I apologized for my error, but with a swipe of her arm Beth waved it away.

"Please, excuse me. I must return to my reading," Devon said to no one in particular, returning to her window nook, disappearing altogether behind the curtains.

Beth gestured to the seat next to Ed Farley. "Make yourself comfortable."

I looked at the wicker love seat where he was sitting—there was maybe a foot and a half of clearance. It would be a very tight squeeze. "Dr.—Beth, please, sit—"

But Beth insisted. "I've been parked on my ass all day." She said "ass" right in front of her daughter and didn't bother to censor herself. Only Mr. Farley cleared his throat.

I was made to sit. I pressed my knees together, so they wouldn't knock into Ed Farley's. I could feel his tense thighs against mine. Beth began pacing around the room, swinging her arms vigorously. Hannah did the same thing to increase circulation. Black, wiry sprouts of hair peeked out from under Beth's arms through her sleeveless, shapeless tunic top.

I couldn't picture a more mismatched pair than Beth Mazer and Ed Farley. Beth looked like she was well into her forties: her face was gaunt, with yellow circles under her large, dark eyes. Blackheads studded her nose. Perhaps if Beth dyed her hair or blow-dried her frizzy strands straight, she might have minimized the age gap between them. Still, she seemed to carry herself with the confidence—and entitlement—of a younger, prettier woman.

"Jane!" Beth said. "We are thrilled to meet you. Tell us everything."

Everything? I reached for the file folder in my bag. "Here is my résumé—"

Beth waved it away. "We want to get to know *you*. Let's have a conversation."

Weren't we already? "Um, okay."

"You just graduated from college, right? What was that experience like?"

Beth's question was oddly open-ended.

"It was good, I guess. I double-majored in finance and accounting."

"Isn't that a shame, Beth." It was Mr. Farley who spoke.

"Ignore him, Jane. That comment was more about me than about you." Over my head they exchanged a look. Beth went on. "I suppose the cat's out of the bag, Jane: I have something of a predisposed bias against banker types. They *are* my mother's people! *Clearly* I'm a self-hater. So it goes, so it goes." Clearly Beth was an oversharer. As she spoke, her cheeks did not flush red, the way most normal people's would when they realized they were divulging too much information.

She went on. "But frankly, Jane, I'm surprised you're applying for this kind of job. You seem like a bright, sensitive young woman, despite your degree."

It wasn't a question, so I didn't answer it.

"Tell us where you're from."

"Queens. Flushing."

Beth called out to Devon, "Remember, sweetie? The last time we were in Queens? When I took you to see the Mets play the Giants?"

Devon turned from her window perch. "And the Mets *lost*," she said, scrunching her nose. "They *always* lose."

"You've got to believe, sweetie."

People only ever have two stories about Queens: bad times at JFK and bad times at Shea Stadium.

"And what do your parents do out there?" Beth backpedaled hastily. "That is, if you're comfortable talking about it. I know *I* hate it when people are always like, 'And what do *your* parents do?' God, look at me! I'm turning into my mother." Beth made an exaggerated shudder, presumably for comic effect, but when she finished that routine, she stared down at me, waiting for an actual answer.

"My uncle has a grocery store in Flushing."

"Your . . . uncle?"

I found myself craving the sterility of corporate-finance interviews.

"I live with his family. They— My mother died a while ago."

The curtains parted, and Devon came bounding across the room. She put her face right up to mine. "How did your mother die?"

"Devon!" Beth said sharply. I exhaled a sigh of relief. But then she said, "It's not polite to ask that. It's better to say, 'How did your mother pass away?'"

Devon corrected herself, her small hand giving my shoulder a reassuring pat. Then her mother began patting my *other* shoulder. The two exchanged a conspiratorial look of shared pity. This interview was starting to make me feel *tap-tap-hae*. I turned my head away, because I couldn't trust myself not to contort my face with displeasure. You *of all people need to worry about wrinkles*. I caught Ed Farley's eye.

"If she doesn't want to talk about it, she doesn't want to talk about it," Mr. Farley muttered before picking up the newspaper. I was surprised by his display of *nunchi*.

Thankfully, the conversation moved on to other topics. Beth settled to the floor and crossed her legs. She lectured, and I listened. She told me she was a professor of women's studies at Mason College. ("Up for tenure next year!" she added in a strangely anxious, high-pitched tone.) I remembered seeing their ads on the subways—WHERE POETS BECOME PARTICLE PHYSICISTS . . . AND VICE VERSA!, the tagline read—above a set of multihued youths leaping in the air. Mr. Farley taught high-school English at a prep school downtown. They had met at Columbia as graduate students in the English department. She talked about Devon's adoption process—"We're trying to revise the adoption rhetoric by calling it an 'alternative birth plan'"—as well as the responsibilities that came with the au pair position.

"I don't want someone who's just going to clock in and out each day. We want you to grow and become part of our family," she said. "We want—"

Devon, peeking out again from the window, called out, "Ma, I need your help. What's the author mean by this?" Devon had completely interrupted our interview, but Beth did not tell her it was rude. Sang and Hannah always used to wave me away when they were with other adults, until I was old enough to learn not to bother them at all. Instead Beth turned her full attention to her daughter. "Let's have a look, sweetie." Devon brought the paper to Beth and inserted herself into her mother's lap.

Beth studied the page. I mean, *studied*. At first I'd thought, based on the thick white paper and colorful illustration on the cover, that it was some sort of children's newspaper. I was wrong. The text inside was chunky, with little white space. Four minutes ticked by. (I kept making not-so-subtle glances at my watch.) I thought of what Sang would say: *You think time like some kind of luxury?* But Beth was so absorbed in her reading it was as if the rest of us weren't even there.

Finally she looked up. "Okay, sweetie, let's break it down. The author refers to a 'cultural investigation.' What do you suppose she means by that?"

"I already *know* what that means," Devon said impatiently. But her mother was still looking expectantly at her. "*Fine.* 'Investigation.' It's like when a detective goes around and starts looking for clues to solve a crime. Like this one time on *Law & Order* they were interviewing the murder victim's parole officer—" She clamped a hand over her mouth. Beth shot her husband a look. "Ed!"

I don't know how I thought Ed Farley would react. But he just gave a boyish shrug of his shoulders and said, "She wandered in while it was on TV. What, you wanted me to turn our daughter away?"

"And Daddy made me do muffin ears and face the wall whenever they did the shooting scenes," Devon piped up, thinking she was helping their case.

Beth shook her head. "Sometimes I don't know what to do with your father." She sighed. Given the rather jocular tone of the family moment, I thought she would leaven her words with a smile, but instead she shot her husband another angry look.

Beth and Devon continued to discuss the article. There was an exhaustive thoroughness to Beth's explanations, so much so that she generated little forward movement. She seemed to circle in place, hovering over each word as she unpacked its meaning, before she moved on. She was, I could tell, a dogged perfectionist—she took all the time in the world to belabor each and every point. It was exasperating to watch. Yet Beth never seemed exasperated. She continued looking intently, tenderly, at her daughter until it was clear that Devon understood the whole piece.

When they were finished, Beth folded her daughter into her arms. "*Wo ai ni*, Devon."

"*Wo ai ni*, Ma," Devon said, her arms wrapped in a choke hold around her mother's neck.

Then, perhaps so she wouldn't leave her father out, she yanked on his hand. "*Wo ai ni*, Daddy."

He put down his paper. "I love you, too, Devon," he said, and gathered her into a bear hug. Then the family reconfigured into a group huddle.

Devon exchanged another conspiratorial look with her mother. *Should we?* she seemed to say. Beth nodded. Their circle parted. Ed Farley was opposite me at the far end of that circle, flanked by his wife and daughter. Devon and Beth each entwined their arms fiercely around me.

It would have been so easy to write them off. Beth Mazer, with her hairy armpits and her complete lack of social grace. Ed Farley, gruff and a little cold, and probably ten years her junior. Their daughter, Devon, a half-pint-size imitation of her mother, even though she was Chinese. And now they were *touching* me. Sang and Hannah never hugged me. They didn't even hug their own children. We were not a touchy-feely kind of family. I could have chalked up the whole strange experience to potential cocktail-party fodder: *This one time? When I interviewed to be a nanny?* They were a family of freaks.

And yet.

Something in that moment shifted for me; I can't explain why. On a rational level, I recognized the corniness of the moment. I recognized the inappropriateness of their behavior, of the job itself, the underutility of my college degree. Yet I also considered the way Beth had explained the article to Devon, saw the way she was holding her now. I suddenly pictured myself living with them, being taken into the fold.

It did not seem so far-fetched that I could be Devon's au pair. My tense shoulders began to loosen. Slowly I returned Devon and Beth Mazer's embrace. I took care not to brush hands with Ed Farley.

And then, just as immediately, we broke free and something shifted again.

"I know what you're thinking. My Mandarin's terrible," Beth said.

"It's true! All the kids at Chinese school make fun of Ma's *bakgwai* accent," Devon said.

I didn't know exactly what *bakgwai* meant, but I recognized it as a not-nice way the Chinese kids sometimes referred to the American kids at school. Beth blushed. I was surprised by how deeply her cheeks flushed red, for a woman who seemed to have no sense of shame. She said, "Be honest, Jane. Just how bad is my accent?"

Did she think I was Chinese? If Beth Mazer hadn't waved away my résumé, she would have found, listed under "Skills," a proficiency in Korean, not Mandarin.

"I'm . . . um, Korean—"

"You're *not* Chinese?" Beth interrupted. "You mean, Ed didn't . . ." I didn't think her face could get any redder, but it grew redder still. Her eyes darted to her husband. "Ed!"

While Ed Farley took his time composing his response, Beth whipped her head back to me. "*Please* don't think I'm one of those people who just assumes. God, I'm mortified! You must think I'm a culturally insensitive *boor*. But it's just . . . we advertised for a Chinese au pair."

"The ad cut out," was all I could manage. *Nunchi* forbade me from saying anything more, such as, *Why didn't you write a shorter ad?*

"Ed. Could I speak to you in the kitchen? Please. Now." Beth's questions fell flat at the ends, like statements.

Ed Farley let out an exasperated sigh. "If we must."

The two got up and left the room. I wondered if I should just see myself out. While I puzzled over what to do, Devon bounded across the room and took her father's seat next to me.

I heard indecipherable murmurs coming from the other side of the house.

"It'll be okay," Devon said, patting my hand, as if our roles were reversed.

I looked over at her, her face contorted into the kind of scrunch that Hannah always yelled at me to fix. Did it bother Devon that she looked nothing like her parents? When I was her age, my hair was much lighter than the black it eventually settled into, and a smattering of freckles spread like wings on either side of my nose. People were always pointing out the differences. It made me grow awkward and tentative in social situations. Yet Devon seemed so assured of her place in the world. She was just like her mother.

I heard a burst, from Mr. Farley. ". . . about to ask if she's Chinese over the phone!"

Beth murmured, ". . . our daughter's development."

Devon put on a bright smile. "Let's read something." When she said, "Let's," she'd actually meant "I'll." She snapped open her newspaper and began to read, in an even, eloquent voice, tripping over fewer words than I would have if the paper had been placed in my hands.

I heard Mr. Farley's voice again. "Then I guess you can't hire her!"

"But she's . . ." Beth trailed off.

Ed Farley walked briskly back into the room. I stood up. Then, standing close enough for me to smell his clean soap smell, he said, "We'll be in touch."

I'd heard those words repeated from enough HR departments to know what they meant: Thanks, but no thanks. I'd bombed—for being the wrong kind of Asian. I couldn't even land my backup plan, a job that up until a few moments ago I hadn't even wanted in the first place.

Devon looked up at me and squeezed my hand. "Best of luck," she said.

"You, too," I said, though she didn't need it. I squeezed back.

I told Mr. Farley I'd see myself out. I retraced the circuitous route to the front door. Beth Mazer stopped me in the foyer, breathless.

"I am *so* sorry about that," she said, taking my hands in hers. "It was just an awful miscommunication. . . ." She studied my face. "You seem like *such* a special young woman."

With that she folded me into her arms. It was unexpected. I fell against her with my whole body. "Good-bye for now," she said.

When I left the Mazer-Farley house, I still carried the scent of Beth's touch; she smelled of lavender and fermenting onions. An unpleasant smell, but also oddly comforting.

Chapter 5

Food

I wouldn't say my earliest associations with Food were pleasant ones. Sang first opened the store when I was around eight years old. According to Hannah, it took him several years to have enough confidence to start another business, post-blackout. But this time he retreated closer to home, instead of opening in Manhattan like so many of his peers.

Sang was especially irritable in those early days. All of us—Hannah, Mary, even little George—lived in fear and trembling, never sure of what small thing would trigger his too-quick temper. It might have been the way the toilet paper hung from its dispenser, making the user have to inconveniently search through the roll to find where the trail began. He'd come bellowing out of the bathroom. Sometimes I was the last of the family to scramble, and I'd be left to bear the brunt of his wrath.

It was always just him and me. I was the oldest of the children, so after school Sang would pick me up and take me to work on the store, while the others stayed home. He climbed up a ladder to remove the drop-ceiling panels, and he'd pass them down to me. They were stained and moldy on the underside. When the ceilings were done, we put down new flooring. I remembered struggling with the math, trying to figure out how many tiles would fit across the length and width of the store (*"Report card say you good at math. Why you not show?"*), which only made the sums that much harder.

Then it came time to mark the grids across the floor. We each grasped either end of a piece of string, and Sang ran the line on a solid block of chalk he held in his hands. (Later I would learn this was his cheap alternative to buying an actual chalk reel.) How my hands shook as I backed away from Sang! When he snapped the line, the string whipped my fingers and I let go. Sang was furious. We had to redo the line several times before it was perfectly straight. Whenever I stare down at the floor tiles of Food, I can still feel the sting of Sang's words from that day. When all the construction was done, we cleaned the floors—Sang swept, I mopped. The mop was too big and unwieldy for my hands. When I was older and we'd learn about child-labor laws at school, I'd get angry at Sang. *That was against the law! You should go to jail!* Then he'd snap back—*Then who gonna buy your food? Who gonna pay your clothes?*—which would always shut me down.

But through all that, one memory in particular emerged. *Jane-ah! Come here!* Sang had shouted. I hurried toward him, bracing myself for a scolding. Sang was crouched over a ceiling panel; something was stuck to its underside. I crouched next to him. He poked the thing with a Phillips-head screwdriver: it was a dead mouse, fused to the panel and fossilized. A few tufts of hair poked out from the bones. Empty shells that looked like the skin of popcorn kernels studded the mouse's chest cavity. Fly larvae. "I wonder whether he getting eaten alive or he die first," Sang said. He clucked his tongue. "Either way, I guess he not go to waste."

After we finished for the day, Sang took me to McDonald's next to the public library. As he ate his Big Mac with gusto, I stared at my Chicken McNuggets and thought about the dead mouse picked clean. Nothing ever went to waste.

* * *

When I arrived at Food after meeting with the Mazer-Farleys, Sang asked me how my "bank" interview went. I told him they'd "be in touch."

Even my uncle understood what that meant. "Because you not try hard enough," he said.

"Yes, Uncle. I'm sure that's the reason."

"You back-talk me?" His nostrils flared, the way they always flared with annoyance. I mumbled no.

Sang ordered me to go change out of my suit. Because, as he'd lectured me many times, the customers might think you were showing off with their hard-earned money. That was one of the reasons he drove a *ddong-cha*, a poop car. Yet Pastor Bae drove a Mercedes-Benz S-class—apparently he wasn't afraid of the congregation seeing what he did with the weekly collections. Hannah, who faithfully wore her darned sweaters and hole-ridden pants at the store, didn't see why we also had to live in a *ddong* house, when other families at church—like the Ohs—had years ago left Flushing for Long Island.

It was busy that day at Food, and the walk-in box was being particularly temperamental. I caught up with my uncle and told him the door was acting up again.

Sang gave me a look—*And so?*—and said, "How long you work here?" Releasing his hand truck, he did the jiggle-slide-shuffle routine with an ease that never came naturally for me. "See? You act like problem when there's no problem." He slammed the door shut again.

If I hadn't just come back from the interview with the Mazer-Farleys, I might not have opened my mouth right then (it was hard to believe that interview had taken place only a few hours ago). "I think we should have . . . a *conversation* about it," I said, repeating Beth's words.

"A what?" Sang jerked his head toward the front of the store, and through the rubber flaps of the doorway I could see the growing line of customers at the register, where Hannah was now. "Who got time for conversation? You think time like some kind of luxury?"

With that he pushed aside the thick plastic strips hanging in the doorway and wheeled off.

I stared at the door with a rising anger. I tried it again. *Fuck this.* I grasped the handle with two hands and yanked it free.

The first thing I heard was a *pop!* Then a crunch. The door handle pulled free and clattered to the floor.

Sang heard the commotion and rushed back to the walk-in, immediately followed by Hwan. They both surveyed the damage. Then
Sang looked at me, his eyes blackening.

"You . . . nothing . . . but . . . the . . . careless!" Once he wrenched
those first words out, the rest poured forth quickly. "What, you do on
purpose? Show off how you right? You no idea how much it gonna
cost?"

When Sang grew excited, his already tenuous command of English grammar fell in inverse proportion to his rising anger. I always
found it odd that he stuck it out with English rather than simply
switching over to Korean. But in the house he spoke in Korean only to
his wife and in select moments of tenderness, like when he was talking
with his daughter.

Hwan was crouched at the door with a can of WD-40 and a pock-
etknife, trying to pry it open.

"You know why this happen, right?" Sang went on. "Because you
act like wild girl!"

But each person has a breaking point. I had reached mine. I
shouted, "That door's been like that my entire life!"

There was another *pop!* and crunch between us, but it wasn't the
door handle. Then Sang's voice grew eerily calm.

"Okay. Go to office call Mr. Hwang. His brother the repairman.
Get the brother number and tell him come to Food right now. But
after that you just go home. Today you causing more trouble than you
help. *Ga.*" That last command—Go—was issued in Korean. Then he
turned on his heel and walked away.

When Sang was gone, Hwan said, "I hate this damn door, too."
With a twist of his knife, he set the door free. He dragged the cinder
block against it, leaving it a crack ajar. He fixed his steady gaze on my
face; I looked away. "Your uncle, he get angry now, but, eh, you know
he always cool down quick. You no worry, Miss Jane."

I looked up. But before I could say, "Thank you," Hwan was already gone, the plastic strips in the doorway flapping closed behind
him.

* * *

The week wore on. At work I measured out my life with cans of Spam, with apples and pears and boxes of Napa cabbage, with milk and honey and D batteries, with dimes, nickels, pennies, and food stamps. With each passing day, my thoughts would turn to the Mazer-Farleys. I took their silence to mean they'd moved on.

One night, almost a week after my interview, the five of us were sitting around the flimsy card table in the kitchen. The remains of our dinner were spread before us: a picked-apart fried mackerel, its shredded skin glinting like flakes of gold leaf; cubes of *kkakdugi*-radish kimchi (a name, I was certain, that derived from the sound you made—*kkak!*—as you bit into it); garlic stems, smothered in red-pepper paste; cold beef chunks and hard-boiled eggs, stewed in soy sauce; shriveled-up baby sardines.

The window fan whirred but offered little reprieve from the late-summer heat, barely moving the air that was thick with humidity and the smells of fried fish and Hannah's fermented bean paste. George left the table for the family computer in the living room. He did not clear away his bowl and chopsticks. Mary left the table to practice piano for church service. She carried her bowl and chopsticks to the sink but did not wash them. Each time someone got up, the table wobbled, despite the folded-up magazine pages wedged under one leg.

After Hannah and I cleared the table and washed the dishes, Sang asked me again whether I'd heard back from my interview. When I told him I hadn't, he shook his head with disappointment. "You want something happen? You gotta make happen. When other people sleeping, you suppose to be digging well."

Abruptly I rose from the table. The backs of my thighs made a squelching sound against the plastic seat. I opened the fridge to the usual assortment of bruised fruit. We took home the rejects from the store, and that night there were Asian pears, which were my favorite.

When I returned to the table with the most banged-up of pears, Sang was fanning himself with a Con Ed bill. Hannah was boiling water for tea. (She thought that eating hot foods on hot days was good for the system.) I set to work on the pear, slicing away its sores, the card table all the while rocking unsteadily. Then I began to peel.

Sang stopped me. "Look, you waste." He held up the pear peel and pointed to the white flesh on the underside. I'd cut too thick a peel. He shook his head in disappointment. Asian pears cost us around four dollars each at wholesale. Hannah picked up my too-thick peel and put it in her mouth, scraping off its flesh as if it were an artichoke leaf.

Sang launched into one of his stories that were always the same: the business of Flushing. Which of his friends were making money and which were not. In this case Mr. Hwang and his real-estate deal.

Sang's eyes, seeking an audience, darted through the doorway to his daughter at the piano, but she was immersed in her Bach. Mary always started her piano sessions with warm-up scales, then a couple of Bach two-part inventions, which you could always tell from their utter mathematical symmetry, then something more erratic and swelling: sometimes Beethoven, sometimes Rachmaninoff. Sang's eyes moved on to his son at the computer. George was clicking furiously on the mouse with one hand while punching a key with the index finger of the other. Sang sighed, his story barely started. It felt rude to leave him hanging. "Which deal is this again, Uncle?"

My uncle ignored me. "*Ya!* Georgie-ah!" Sang said. "Your *abba* talking to you!"

George looked up from his computer game and groaned. Reluctantly he trotted back to the kitchen table. Mary stopped her piano. "George! Did you log off? I'm expecting a phone call." George returned to the computer and replugged the cord into the phone jack.

Sang began his story again. "Hwang just buy house in Great Neck. Kings Point! When he suppose to buy business building instead. Now he have Chinese landlord. Every morning ten, fifteen Chinese people coming up from building basement. They just living there. Those people, willing to sacrifice anything. Where they go bathroom?"

The phone rang as my uncle went on about the Chinese. Mary rushed across the living room to answer it. "Jane, it's for you." She held out the receiver.

"Jane!" a voice cried out. "It's Beth Mazer. We've been trying you all night, but the line was busy!"

"I'm sorry, my cousin was on the computer." I glared in George's direction, but he was engrossed in his pear. His eyes went blank whenever he chewed, as if he were gazing across the pasture. I envied his ability to escape.

"Jane, my *sincerest* apologies for the delay. I was away at a conference and then et cetera, et cetera, et cetera. I'm calling to offer you the au pair position with our family, and I'm crossing my fingers that you haven't already been snapped up—i.e., if you even still *want* the position. . . ." She named a figure that would have been one-third my starting salary at Lowood, before factoring in annual bonuses. Of course, her figure included room and board. I wondered whether I'd been her first choice or if she'd made similar calls to others and was forced to move further down her list.

"And," she continued, "we really loved you—Devon especially. We'd be *honored* if you joined our household."

"But I thought"—I cupped the receiver with my hand—"I wasn't what you and Mr. Farley wanted."

I could see Sang pretending not to listen.

"*Please*, we're on a first name basis in this household. Call him Ed. And again, my utter apologies for that miscommunication." Her tone was breezy. "While we did *initially* want an au pair who spoke Chinese, we've since had some conversations. Devon's getting quite a lot of exposure through her Chinese school, and . . ." Beth trailed off. "So what do you think? Will you join us?"

I knew I should not have taken that job. I should have held out for a better offer. At the very least, I should have asked for a day or two to think it over. And I definitely should have asked Sang and Hannah's permission.

But sometimes you don't always do what you should do. I wanted that job.

I found myself blurting out, "I'd love to. Thank you for this opportunity."

"Fantastic! We are so thrilled," Beth said. We made arrangements for me to start the next morning.

Sang's eyes studied me when I hung up the phone. "Who that is?"

"I got a job."

His eyes narrowed. "What kind of company calling you night-time?"

"It's . . . different. I'd be helping a family."

"Helping family *what*?"

"They have a daughter. And . . . I'd be living with them."

"What!" Sang dropped the paring knife; it clattered on its chip-proof plate. "This is like bad dream."

"It isn't," I protested. "They're a good family. They're *teachers*. The wife is a professor at a college. Imagine how much I'd learn from her." I tried to speak Sang's language. "It'd be like . . . like getting a free education."

He wasn't having it.

"So you just want to throw away your everything? To become like indentured servant?"

Sometimes the range of Sang's English surprised me.

"Never this happen you go to Columbia."

My uncle did this every so often: trace back all my recent failures to my not attending Columbia. I'd gotten in, only to find I didn't qualify for financial aid. I couldn't ask my uncle to spring for my tuition (blame *nunchi*), nor could I justify saddling myself with all that debt. I turned down Columbia and decided on Baruch, which I'd applied to as a safety school. When Sang learned this after the fact, he'd been furious. We fought and fought, our fight devolving into a litany of piddling resentments we'd each harbored over the years. The time the septic tank burst and my profligate use of paper towels (*Use rag and bucket!* he'd shouted) as I helped him clean up. The time I accidentally locked the keys inside the car and made the damage worse with a mis-directed coat hanger. Each and every time he favored Mary and George over me. But it had been too late to reverse my decision; I was bound for this "lesser" path. And with that, Sang had swiped the air, taking an eraser to the plans charting my future.

"Uncle know this family?" he demanded. "They Korean?"

"No. American."

"American!"

"Uncle: *I'm* half American."

Sang looked stunned, as if the words had hit him square in the face—furious that I'd brought up the side of me he'd been trying all these years to forget.

He reached a point where the English language could no longer contain his uncontrollable emotion, where he had no choice but to switch over to Korean. *"Do you want to end up like your mother?"*

On any other day, the invocation of my mother would have had the power to cut right through me, making me shrivel with shame. But that evening was different. I was going to leave Sang's house forever, and now his words flew past me. In my head I was already bolting through the door and out on the street. I was already on the Q13 to Main Street, then down to the subway platform, bound for the next 7 train stuttering out of Flushing.

Chapter 6

The Mazer-Farley Household: A Primer

I wasn't even one foot in the door when Beth folded me into her arms, overwhelming me with her particular aroma. "Welcome! Jane, you have no idea how happy we are."

"Thank you for hiring me," I said. The words felt stiff; I had no natural vocabulary for receiving compliments.

Beth surveyed my clothes. "Don't you look nice today! Doesn't she, Ed?" she said. I was wearing dress slacks, a button-down shirt, and sensible heels. Her husband didn't look over at me, though. "But . . . wouldn't you rather change into something more comfortable?" *Dress for the job you* want, *not the job you have,* they taught us in the Career Services office. I wasn't about to show up on my first day in the kinds of clothes I wore at Food.

Devon pushed her mother out of the way. "Jane!" she cried. "Your room's next to mine. I'll show you!" She tugged my hand, leading me toward the stairs, but Ed Farley stopped her. "Later, kiddo. She just walked through the door."

"Come *on,* Daddy." Devon used that same pleading tone Mary used when cajoling her father, the same tone I'd once tried, too, but it only made Sang snap, "Why you act like baby?"

"Oh, come on, Ed." It was Beth who spoke. They exchanged a private look—I could see only Ed's expression, and he looked exasperated.

As Devon bounded up the stairs with me in tow, I heard him mutter to his wife, "You know you're spoiling her."

Upstairs we stopped at a door marked DEVON XIAO NU MAZER-FARLEY with Chinese characters below. "Xiao Nu's my Chinese name," Devon explained, tracing the lettering across the paper sign.

"We wanted to honor the name Devon was given at her orphanage," Beth explained. "It's the closest connection we have to . . . to . . ." She faltered.

Ed looked uncomfortable at his wife's outburst, but then he placed a hand on her back. Beth had a strange expression on her face—I swore it looked like entitlement. If I were her, I'm certain I would have stared up at Ed Farley with grateful eyes instead.

"And that's your room!" Devon said suddenly, pointing to the room next to hers, marked JANE RE. Below my name was handwritten Korean lettering. "We looked it up on the computer," Devon announced. As a child I took Korean lessons after Sunday school, and though my Korean wasn't strong, even to my eyes the letters looked misshapen— I could tell that all the strokes were in the wrong order.

"You did a *wonderful* job, sweetie," Beth said, now recovered from her earlier emotional slip. "How *thoughtful* of you to welcome Jane in both English *and* Korean."

Now Ed Farley *was* looking at me. He raised his eyebrows as if to say, *Your turn next.*

"Wow, thanks, Devon. This is so . . . thoughtful," I said stiffly, repeating Beth's word. It seemed I lacked a vocabulary not only for receiving compliments but for bestowing them as well.

At any rate, Devon beamed.

Beth's fingers stalled at the doorknob of my bedroom. "I feel like I should explain. Your room's a touch . . . rustic. But hopefully in just a matter of days it'll cozy up and start to feel like home—"

"There's nothing wrong with the room," Ed said. His interruption sounded more defensive than rude.

Now it was Beth's turn to give me a look: *Men!* she seemed to say, shaking her head in mock exasperation. And with that, she opened the door.

The room was cavernous, almost double the size of the room I shared with Mary back in Flushing. That room made all too efficient use of space with the effect that the whole room—the whole house, really—was closing in on you. *Tap-tap-hae.* But this room was an airy departure from all that. Rustic, yes—but there was something appealing about its sparseness. The bed, for one, was marooned at the center of the room, when my bed back in Flushing was pushed right up against the wall. When we went back down to the kitchen, I saw that the master bedroom was to the right of mine. I was wedged between all the Mazer-Farleys.

* * *

In the kitchen Beth pointed to the index cards affixed to each cupboard and drawer. "It might be a confusing system here," she said, "but if you're ever not sure of anything, just ask."

The family began to prepare for breakfast. Beth asked Devon to set out the place mats. She asked Ed to get the muesli and bowls. She would take care of the beverages. You would have thought these exchanges would be routine at this point—each Mazer-Farley knowing his or her tasks without the need for words. Hannah's least favorite question was "How can I help?" To which she'd always counter, *"Don't you have eyes?"*

The family bustled about, but I was made to sit at the kitchen table. It was a large, solid block of unvarnished wood. It looked handmade. A bowl of gnarled fruit, riddled with dents and pockmarks, sat on top. I felt uneasy not being put to work—*they* were the employers, and *I* was the employee.

Guided by Beth's labeling system, I located a paring knife and cutting board. Back at the table, I set to work skinning a pear, just the way Sang had taught me.

Beth was carrying a tray of cups and what looked like a patch of lawn to the table. "Oh . . ." she said, surveying my handiwork, "did you just peel that fruit?"

"Yes," I said, gathering the paper-thin peels into a neat pile to throw away. "It just . . . looked a little funny."

"Oh, sweetie. It's supposed to look like that. It's *organic*." Beth picked up a shaving and stared down at it like it was a wounded bird.

Ed Farley came to the table. "You just peeled away a dollar's worth of fruit," he said. But he was looking at his wife as he spoke.

"Ed, she didn't know," Beth said. Then, turning back to me, "It's just because all the nutrients are in the peel. If you're ever not sure of something, just ask. There's no such thing as a stupid question."

There's no such thing as a stupid question. We settled around the block table. It did not shake, the way the flimsy card table back home always did. *Lose the* nunchi, Eunice had said to me. It was becoming increasingly apparent that the Mazer-Farleys' way of doing things was exactly the opposite of Sang and Hannah's.

"We might seem like an odd family at first," Beth said, snipping green stalks from the tray of grass she'd carried over to the table and feeding them through a silver machine I'd at first mistaken for a meat-grinder. No—Beth was making wheatgrass juice. Opaque liquid poured out one end, and a thick, dense trail of grassy by-product was extruded from the other. She passed thimblefuls of the liquid around the table. "But I can assure you there's a method to the Mazer-Farley madness." As she chuckled, I took my first sip of wheatgrass. And blanched. It tasted like liquefied lawn clippings. Devon blanched, too, and was backwashing the wheatgrass into her glass of orange juice. I was the only one who noticed. When she caught me looking at her, a flash of panic flooded her face. But before I could say a word, she was tugging on her mother's arm, asking for a story.

Beth, oblivious to the whole wheatgrass exchange, immediately brightened. "Oh, I know! We should tell the Tale of Mei Lin." Beth turned to me. "That's Devon's birth mom—or how we imagine her anyway. It's just a little narrative we've come up with over the years." Then her voice took on a singsong quality and she began the tale.

"A long time ago, in a land far away . . ." Beth started, stopped. "That's always been a problematic beginning for me. Asserting 'nearness' and 'farness'"—her fingers crunched into air quotes—"just *screams* cultural imperialism. As if *our* geographical locale is somehow the normative? Although, I suppose, a counterargument could be made that the Chinese—"

"Ma, just tell the story!" Devon said. "Forget it, *I'll* tell it. A long time ago, in a land far away, specifically in the northeastern Chinese province of Liaoning, in the city of Dandong, there lived a *beautiful* young woman—"

"A smart woman," Beth jumped in. "Remember what I always say, Devon: Beauty is a social construct that forces females to pander to the male gaze—"

"A beautiful and smart woman named Mei Lin," said Devon. "And every year villagers from all over would gather in the square to behold her with their own eyes."

The tale went on. As I would soon come to learn, tales like these were a fixture at the Mazer-Farley breakfast table. Beth and Devon had a whole repertoire of interactive stories, like a call and response.

Stories of the past were never a part of the dinner fodder at 718 Gates Street. Sang had not been there when that "bad thing" happened; he'd left Korea for America years before. All he ever offered up about my mother's life was contained in three terse sentences: "Long time ago she use to listening your grandpa. Then one day she stop. Now she dead." He'd always pause before adding, "Is why *you* specially better listening your aunt and uncle." A whole world of meaning could have been unpacked in those sentences. But no matter what the true story had been, there was one constant the whole family seemed to agree upon: my mother had brought that shame on herself.

Beth went on. "All her life Mei Lin dreamed of having a little girl. A daughter so bright—"

"—she'd make Phi Beta Kappa! And write her dissertation on Victorian conduct books!"

"Or labor rights in China. Or women's empowerment in India, Devon," Beth said. "The world is truly your oyster."

"It was with a heavy heart that—right, Ma?—Mei Lin left her baby girl in the care of Happy Fortune Orphanage."

"That's exactly right, Devon," Beth said. She made no mention of the culture's preference for boys—a protective shielding from the truth that I found touching.

And what was Ed's role in the storytelling? He had gotten up to leave the room. He returned holding a thick set of bound computer pages. He cleared his throat. "Ladies, look at the time."

Beth looked annoyed. "Ed, you know I hate that word."

"And lose the alliteration?" Ed said. "Females, look at the time." He shook his head. "It's not nearly as poetic." His voice assumed a soft lilt.

Beth took the book from Ed's hands and handed it to me. The cover page read THE MAZER-FARLEY HOUSEHOLD: A PRIMER (LAST UP-DATED SEPTEMBER 2000). "Just a little something I typed up, to help you get acquainted. You'll find a map to Devon's school. It was page fifty-four of the old edition, but now I can't remember the new paginations. Any questions—just ask! My office number is listed in Appendix C."

Beth kissed the top of Devon's head, fluttered her fingers at Ed and me, and flew out the door.

After his wife was gone, Ed suddenly drew closer, and my nostrils filled with his soap smell; I tensed up. But he was only leaning across the table to tap the cover of the primer in my hands. "Better get cracking. That book's not going to read itself."

And just as abruptly, he left for work.

Then it was only Devon and me. "So!" I said, flipping through *The Mazer-Farley Household: A Primer*, trying to find the map. "Are you excited about your first day back?"

"I don't know," Devon said. "Ma and I weren't really impressed with the summer reading list this year. I'm going to have to have a conversation with my literature teacher about it."

The map was not on page fifty-four, or anywhere near it. "Well, what about your friends?"

Devon frowned. "My best friend in *fourth* grade was Carla Green-Levy, but over the summer her family moved away to *Park Slope*." Devon's tone made it sound as far away as Siberia. "I only saw her once since school ended, and now she's starting a brand-new school."

"Maybe you'll make a new best friend this year." Thanks to the index in the back of the primer, I finally found the map, on page ninety-seven.

"Maybe," Devon said. "Maybe not."

Beth had drawn a fuzzy map with a smudgy felt marker. A stick figure with a bowl cut was standing in a grassy field, holding either a lunch box or a suitcase. A dotted line swerved past X's indicating landmarks (their names illegible through the ink smears), leading to an isosceles triangle sitting on top of a square marked "Carroll Prep." There were no street names or mile markers. The map was not at all drawn to scale; if it had been, then Devon's head would've been bigger than the roof of her school, for one thing. There was little hope that this map was oriented to true north. There was even less hope of my finding the way to Devon's school.

Devon stared down at her mother's drawing. "I don't even know why it's called Carroll Prep when it's technically in Cobble Hill."

"Devon, do you know how to get to your school?"

She gave me a look like, *Duh.* "For the next edition, I'm going to ask Ma if *I* can draw the map." Then she lowered her voice to a whisper. "Ma's *terrible* at drawing. But can we keep that a secret between you and me? I don't want to hurt her feelings."

Devon led the way down Thorn Street. Number 646 was the only brownstone on the block with no wrought-iron grates on the ground-floor windows. The look of Brooklyn was still so new to me. My eyes kept anticipating the aluminum-sided, wood, or redbrick two-families of Flushing. It was hard to believe I'd left Queens only a few hours earlier.

We turned onto Court Street—a street lined with low commercial buildings. The storefronts read CENTRELLO'S BAKERY. BARBUTI'S MEATS. FRATUCCI'S IRON WORKS. Clearly Italian. The pedestrians regarded one another with a certain familiarity. Despite the difference in architectural façades, Carroll Gardens had a quaintness that reminded me of Flushing.

"Daddy says the neighborhood's changed a lot since he was a kid."

"Your father grew up here?" I asked.

Devon gave a knowing nod. "Daddy was *born* in our house. And when Grandma Francesca died, she gave it to us. But then Ma had Daddy fix it up, and afterward he said it looked nothing like when he grew up there."

And then I started to see: Peppered among the older Italian storefronts, there was an upscale-looking coffee shop. A clothing boutique that looked like it belonged in SoHo. A yoga studio.

When we reached her school, Devon said, "The final bell rings at two twenty-eight. The parents and nannies usually wait here in the lobby." She pointed to the smudged map. "If you want my advice, I wouldn't follow that if I were you. It'll only make you more confused."

When I retraced my way back to 646 Thorn, I pried off my heels and undid the confining top button of my blouse. Beth was probably right—I'd have to get some comfortable clothes. Then I flopped onto the bed. I expected to be met with the same firm resistance of my mattress back home, but this bed absorbed my impact. I opened *The Mazer-Farley Household: A Primer,* and I was only on chapter two by the time I had to pick up Devon.

Devon took me on a different route home, through a quiet residential stretch with the occasional pop of a commercial storefront. I passed a candy store, a faded pharmacy. I passed old men sitting in aluminum chairs outside an unmarked building. Then a grocery store that looked like an old Gothic church. A distinctly Korean-looking man was talking into his cell phone, pointing at the store's roof. I wondered if he knew Sang.

Devon was brimming with news of her first day back. She was not the only fifth-grader to "take issue with" the summer reading list, and the literature teacher would now compile a supplemental list for the winter break.

Devon pulled me along by my arm. "This is Gino's," she informed me. We were standing in front of a hybrid pizzeria–coffee shop. "It's where we get our Italian ices after school. My favorite's rainbow. What's yours?" She looked up at me with sweet, adoring eyes.

"Mine's rainbow, too," I said. It was. The last time I'd had an Italian ice was at the place on Roosevelt that served kimchi pizza. But that had been more than ten years ago. I indulged each of us in a treat.

That night I lay in my new bed listening to the unfamiliar sounds of the house settling. Suddenly I heard a squeak from Beth and Ed's room next door—a telltale squeak, like the springs of a mattress. I willed the sound to go away, hoping it was just one of them shifting in the bed—but no. It was followed by another, then another. *Please don't let them be getting it on.* How would I ever look them in the eye the next morning? And then I heard Ed murmur, *"My wife . . . my wife."*

I placed a pillow over my head, trying to drown out their sounds. Eventually, long into the night, the squeaks ebbed. Reader, one thing seemed certain: Ed Farley was really into his wife.

*   *   *

With each passing day, I tried to learn the rhythms of the Mazer-Farley household. My once hyperactive *nunchi* dulled, grew disoriented. At 646 Thorn it was *do* ask stupid questions. *Do* act like you're special. Instinct was becoming overridden. *Lose the* nunchi. Maybe Eunice had it backward; maybe the *nunchi* loses you.

Slowly I made my way through the primer. Its opening pages detailed the backstory of Devon's "alternative birth plan." She was three when Beth and Ed had adopted her. *"When I think back on that first day in that Beijing hotel lobby, this little girl scared and shivering in my arms, it breaks my heart,"* Beth wrote. The other pages of the section were filled with official documents in both English and Chinese.

But it was hard to make much headway through the book—it was bloated with information. In some chapters the footnotes took up more than half the page; I had to squint to read the tiny text.

I took Devon to her daily roster of after-school activities. Mondays she had art club. Tuesday was violin. Wednesday was swim team. For so young a person, Devon had a very busy schedule.

On the fourth day of my Brooklyn sojourn, the phone rang. Sang's voice blasted through the receiver. "Why you not come home!"

"How did you know I was here?" No one had any way of calling me—I had not included a phone number in the note I'd left on the kitchen table. That note had read, *"I'll call when I'm ready."* It did not read, *"Call me when I'm not ready."*

"What that matter? Uncle keep waiting you come back. But you too stubborn to know you doing stupid thing."

"I *told* you that *I'd* get in touch with *you.*" My tone was tinged with a whine; I sounded like Devon.

"Why you act like baby?"

"I'm *not* acting like a—"

"Fine," Sang interrupted. "Uncle come get you. Even though is inconvenience. Where you are?"

"I'm not telling you."

"I already know. You in Brooklyn." His tone became quieter, more solemn. I could hear his mind conflating those three B's.

"I'm not coming home, Uncle," I said.

"Why you throw away everything to be nothing but the babysitter? Make no sense!" he said. "What kind of people they are, getting stranger to watching their child?"

Sometimes Sang had a way of putting things so plainly it only made you feel stupid to try to defend yourself. But he was always black and white, with no gray in between.

Then I remembered what Beth had said the night before at dinner, about wanting to do a tour of Queens neighborhoods. She found Flushing in particular *fascinating*—and not only because she was a Mets fan. I'd demurred, not wishing to risk running into Sang and Hannah, or anyone else in Queens.

"What if I introduced you to the family I work for?" I said to Sang. "I can bring them by the store. That way you can see them for yourself. The parents went to *Columbia.* They're *professors.*" Well, really only

Beth was the professor. But my uncle was such a sucker for name-brand colleges.

I heard him softening over the phone. "When?"

We made plans for the coming weekend. But after we hung up, the rest of the day felt a bit off, thrown from its natural rhythms. That afternoon, when Devon and I returned home from our now-routine Italian ices, I finally reached a chapter of the primer called "In Matters Vegetable, Animal, and Mineral." And there, under the subheading "Forbidden Foods," was the following entry:

Devon is absolutely forbidden to eat refined sugar; artificial sweeteners, colorings, or flavors; products with high-fructose corn syrup; and others (see footnote). They are toxic to the system. Such "food" products are permitted only on weekends on a case-by-case basis (e.g., a classmate's birthday party).

And that was the afternoon Ed Farley came home early from school. He spied my mouth, stained with artificial everything; then he spotted his daughter's. "What's going on here?" Devon let out a guilty yip before scurrying up the stairs. Then Ed and I were alone.

For the past four days, Ed had been polite but curt with me. I couldn't tell if he was just a distant and somewhat sour man or whether my particular presence irked him. His temperament was such a contrast to his wife's, whose effusiveness made you feel instantly welcome. In the rare moments when it was just Ed and me—when we were passing in the hallways or on the stairs—his cold eyes would alight on me for an instant before dismissing me. In short: Ed Farley made me uneasy. I took to bowing my head to the floor, averting his (however brief) gaze.

"Are you responsible for this?"

"Yes," I said. It was my fault that I hadn't finished the primer. And if I blamed his daughter for tricking me, it would just sound like I was making excuses. My uncle *hated* excuses. An ax murderer could have chased you out of the house, but still Sang would punish you for not turning down the thermostat on your way out.

"How long has this been going on?"

"Since . . . I started." I couldn't bear to look him in the face.

"You're telling me four days?"

I froze; Ed Farley's tone was exactly like Sang's. We could have been back at Food, standing in front of the broken walk-in.

I braced myself for a heated outpouring. The lights streaming from the hallway struck his cheekbones at a severe angle and glinted off his set jaw. He could have been carved from granite—cold, unfeeling. But when our eyes met, his flickered, softened.

His tone thawed. "It's just . . . it'll ruin her appetite for dinner."

"I'm so sorry, Ed," I said.

"Just make sure Devon brushes her teeth. *Thoroughly.*" Then he lifted his finger, pointing to my mouth. "You might want to as well."

I nodded, heading to the stairway. Just then I heard Beth enter the kitchen. She, too, had returned early.

"Why is Devon's mouth that *abhorrent* shade of purple?" she said.

I paused at the foot of the stairs.

I could tell that Ed was stalling for time. "Relax, Bethie. I've got it under control."

Beth chuffed. "Just like you have everything *else* under control, too, don't you, Ed?"

I froze again. Beth was using a tone of voice I had never heard before. It was a sharp departure from her usual warmth.

Ed's voice boomed. "She's just a kid! If I can't treat my daughter every once in a while, then I don't see the—"

"*Your* daughter?" Beth interrupted.

"Whatever, Beth." Ed stalked out of the kitchen, his heavy footsteps reverberating through the house. I heard the rattle of keys, then heard the front door open and slam shut.

When I returned to the kitchen—teeth and mouth freshly scrubbed—Beth was unloading vegetables from a cloth bag. Ed was gone. She looked at me and smiled. I could tell, by the way her laugh lines strained, that it was forced. "I swear, my husband insists on spoiling our daughter. God only knows what goes on around here when I'm not home."

Chapter 7

The Feminist Primer

That Saturday I took Devon to her Mandarin lessons in Chinatown. Afterward we planned to meet Beth at Forty-second Street to ride the subway to Flushing. Ed was staying home to do work—he was, as Beth called it, "ABD"—All But Dissertation.

I'd decided to have a talk with Devon after the Italian-ice incident. She'd tricked me into buying her the ices, had done it only for me to get in trouble with Ed, and Ed to get in trouble with Beth. (I still didn't understand why he took the blame for me.) It was a problem to be nipped in the bud. *Set the precedent early,* they'd taught us in Career Services, when "managing down." "Listen," I said to Devon the next morning. "You *knew* you weren't allowed to eat those Italian ices." She played dumb. I went on. "If you ever, I mean *ever,* try that again—"

There was a moment of true, genuine fear that flooded Devon's eyes. But then it quickly dissolved. "But you ate one, too!"

She was right, but that was beside the point. "I'm an adult. I'm allowed to." I could feel myself breaking into a sheepish grin. I bit down on my lip.

She pointed to my face. "See? You went behind Ma and Daddy's back, too!"

I forced my face to go straight, stoic. "They're not *my* ma and daddy—"

It was too late. Devon was already overcome with a fit of giggles.

Sang thought *I* was "wild girl," but look at her! I knew what he would do. He'd tell me to show her who's boss—

But a burst of laughter escaped from my lips. Then another. I could not maintain my stern front. I let go. We had both erupted into peals of laughter.

I'd like to think that with that moment something shifted for us; it brought us closer together. Without anticipating it Devon and I had formed a new alliance. Or maybe it was simply that we became friends.

Devon's Chinese school occupied the top floor of a squat building on Elizabeth Street. Below the school was a Chinese herbal-medicine doctor, and at first it reminded me of John Hong's father's herbal-medicine practice down the block from Food. Both had the bitter aroma of burning herbs, but Mr. Hong's place smelled spicier and sweeter. This one gave off a muskier, staler odor.

Some of the children were dropped off by their parents: women in mismatched, bright-colored synthetic clothes and men in white button-downs and black polyester pants. Both wore the same thick-rubber-soled shoes. Other children were accompanied by their grandmothers. But a surprising number of students would file in un-accompanied—pint-size Chinese children with enormous schoolbags strapped to their backs. They reminded me of baby turtles, toddling their way to the ocean.

The grannies and I sat in the waiting room. One pointed to Devon as she slipped into her class. She asked me something in Mandarin or Cantonese or some other dialect I didn't know. When I told her I wasn't Chinese, she switched into English, in a heavy, almost unintelligible accent. "Sister?"

I shook my head and answered, in overenunciated English, "Babysitter."

Devon had taught me the Chinese character for "Korean," so I scribbled it on the back of a receipt and handed it to one of the old ladies. (I did not know the word for *honhyol*.)

The granny shook her head and smiled, waving a hand away from the receipt. I figured my character strokes were too messy for her to understand. But another granny took the paper from her and studied the character. She nodded. Then she said something to the other grannies. They all nodded and smiled, and I nodded and smiled back.

Then the first granny held out a greased paper bag filled with some kind of herbal candy. She smiled again and shook the bag at me, offering me one. I bowed my thanks, figuring that the gesture was some kind of universal one between our two cultures. The candy tasted of bitter ginger; we sat there chewing in comfortable silence.

When the students filed out of the classroom and into the lobby, their grandmothers rushed at them, smoothing down their mussed-up hair, their rumpled clothes. There was something so sweet about these fussy gestures. When Devon emerged, she frantically scanned around the room. "Devon! Over here!" I called. Her eyes alighted on me, flooding with relief. She hurried toward me. The air was filled with excited chatter. Devon and I were the only ones not speaking Chinese.

We met Beth on the 7 platform as planned and boarded the subway. The other passengers were slouched in their seats, with their bags placed in their laps or carefully suspended between their ankles, so as not to touch the floor. But not Beth. Beth sat with the straight posture of a yogi, one hand clutching Devon's, the other the straps of her WNYC tote bag. She let her load spill carelessly into the empty seat next to her despite the standing passengers. Either they were too polite or they lacked the English to shout, *Hey lady, move your stuff!* The only sounds were the rickety racket of the train grating against its tracks and Beth's chatter.

The row of old Chinese ladies across the aisle looked from Devon's face to her mother's and back again. They looked like the grannies in the school lobby. Between us Devon squirmed under their gaze, but Beth remained oblivious, prattling pronouncements to me over her daughter's head—"My colleague's doing some *fascinating* research on Queens. She'll just ride your trains for *hours*." *Your trains*, I thought. *Your trains*. The Chinese grannies, clutching red plastic bags brimming with bitter greens between their ankles, regarded Devon with amused curiosity. They watched as she freed her fingers from her mother's grasp and wormed her arm through mine.

* * *

When we got to Food, Hwan was out front restocking fruit. Beth marched up to him with an extended hand. "Beth, Beth Mazer. A real *pleasure*."

Hwan tentatively took her hand with his own, and Beth proceeded to squeeze the life out of it.

"Jane's told us *so* much about you."

"Eh, about me?" Hwan's face broke into a funny grin.

I realized Beth had mistaken Hwan for Sang. "Beth, that's Hwan, not my uncle."

Hwan smiled wider with embarrassment. He had one of those compact bodies that radiated entirely whatever he was feeling—this day it was nervous energy. Beth looked mortified. At that point I knew her well enough to guess what she was thinking: that we all looked alike. It was the same expression she'd made during my interview. "I didn't mean to—I mean . . ."

Flustered, she looked at me helplessly.

"It's okay, Beth. It happens all the time," I had the *nunchi* to say, even though Hwan was much younger than Sang. I led Beth and Devon inside.

Hannah was at the register. We exchanged a brief hello—there was a long line of customers, and they didn't like it when you chitchatted. I felt a pang of guilt for not helping out. Beth and Devon oohed and aahed, as if they were staring at dioramas in the natural history museum.

Sang was over by the refrigerated beverage cases with Mrs. O'Gall. He'd abandoned his hand truck, loaded with boxes. Sang did not like to be interrupted when he was with customers, and Mrs. O'Gall, shaking a head of iceberg lettuce at my uncle, did not like to be interrupted period.

Beth looked tentatively at me, and perhaps thinking I'd given her the go-ahead, she once again charged forward. "*You* must be Sang Re!

Beth, Beth Mazer." Beth inserted her hand over the head of wilted iceberg.

Sang blinked at her. "Who you are?"

Beth took a literal step back. "I'm Jane's . . . well, the mother of the family Jane works *with*. You know, *Jane*, your niece."

"Lady, get on line. I was here first." Mrs. O'Gall shooed Beth away with her lettuce. "Like I was saying, Re. You won't get away with selling this rotten stuff in your store."

"My dau— Jane gonna help you out, Mrs. O'Gall." Sang jerked his head at me, while he slid over to talk to Beth.

"How are you, Mrs. O'Gall?" I jumped in. "Did you bring your receipt this time?"

This was part of Mrs. O'Gall's routine—she plucked a few leaves of lettuce from a head before returning the whole thing. I once asked Sang why he didn't try to fight her, but he just shrugged his shoulders. *She not do like this if she not have to.* She fished in her pocketbook and handed me a crumpled receipt dated two weeks back. "Here. You happy?"

I couldn't fight her either, and I ran to get a new head of iceberg. Behind me Beth introduced Devon to Sang. I heard my uncle's voice ring out: "But she not look like you!"

"Because we developed an 'alternative birth plan.'"

"What that means?" Sang said.

I hurried to finish up with Mrs. O'Gall.

When I returned to Sang and Beth, my uncle was saying, "Then you near Mr. Park. He own grocery Henry Street. But he not my friend." Sang peered over Beth's shoulder, keeping watch on the store.

Beth's eyebrows pinched together, the way they did when she explained—or rather tempered—the news headlines to Devon at the breakfast table. I was coming to learn her gestures, her coded expressions. "Sorry, I'm not *terribly* familiar with it. . . ."

"You not say you living right there?"

"No, we do, but . . ." Beth stopped to gather her thoughts. "I usually shop at the farmers' market in Union Square. They have *quite* the selection of organic produce."

Sang frowned.

Beth had the *nunchi* to see Sang's displeasure. "Support local!" she said, shooting her fist in the air.

"They getting produce same place everybody else. Hunts Point Market in the Bronx."

Beth drew her lips into a tight smile. Then, as if groping for words, she looked up and around the room. "What a . . . nice store you have."

Sang again glanced over her shoulder. "I be right back."

Suddenly I saw it all from Beth's eyes. Our faded green awning. The shabbiness of the wooden carts out front. The perfunctoriness of the products we carried. The non-organicness of our produce. How humble Food must have looked to her. How utterly Queens.

Sang returned, carrying a bag of fruit. Through the plastic I could see he'd selected strawberries, raspberries, and Bing cherries. All the fruit he never brought home.

"Please take," he said. "Because our Jane is like burden for you."

Beth bristled. "Mr. Re. Jane is *not* a burden. She's become part of our family." She squeezed an arm around my shoulders.

A look of disapproval flickered across my uncle's face. "Either way, I feel so sorry for you. You take while still fresh."

"Beg your pardon?"

I realized why Beth had shifted her tone. What Sang had said about feeling sorry for Beth made sense in the Korean. It did not translate into English.

Since Beth was rummaging through her WNYC bag and not accepting the proffered fruit, Sang handed it to me.

Suddenly Beth held out two bills—both twenties—to Sang. "At least let me pay you for it." With her other hand, she pointed not at the bag of fruit itself but at me, holding the bag of fruit.

Sang's face broke into a deep frown. "I say just take! Is gift!"

There were many things I could have—should have—done, like jumping in sooner. I should have acted as a simultaneous inter-

preter—*No, Beth, in Korean culture a person's expected to refuse an offer a few times before accepting it. No, Uncle, she felt bad taking your fruit
for free.*

Lose the nunchi, *Jane.* It was tiring, straddling the two cultures.

"Stop *forcing* the fruit on her, Uncle," I said. "She doesn't want it!"

Devon, who'd been quietly watching the exchange, looked up at
me, eyes wide with disbelief at my outburst. My uncle looked away. I'd
embarrassed him in front of everyone.

Beth relented. "You know what? Thank you, Mr. Re. I'd be honored." She took the bag from me. "Devon, thank Jane's uncle for the
fruit." Devon did as she was told. Beth squeezed my shoulder, staring
at me the way she'd stared down at her organic fruit peels on my first
day. "Jane, we'll wait for you outside."

When Beth and Devon left the store, Sang returned to his abandoned hand truck. He took a box cutter from his breast pocket and
sliced open the top carton. I moved to help him, but he waved me
away. "That woman making Uncle high blood pressure go up."

I didn't say anything. I felt a pang of guilt for not taking my uncle's
side.

"You, too," he added.

The guilt was immediately replaced by irritation.

"So you met them," I said impatiently. "Aren't you going to tell me
to come home now?"

Sang put down his box cutter. He spread his arms wide, palms up,
as if the matter were out of his hands. "You want to make mistake,
what I care? Is your life now." He jerked his head to the back office.
"And don't forget your clothes."

I had asked Sang to ask Hannah to pack some of my old jeans and
T-shirts. Later, when I would unpack the bag at the Mazer-Farleys', it
would burst with the smell of 718 Gates, of the plasticky linoleum
tiles, of Hannah's *dwenjang* bean paste and toasted barley tea.

On my way out of Food, I passed Hwan. He gave me a knowing
look, tapping his temple. It was a small exchange we'd shared for years,
a way of commiserating about the fussiest of customers. At first I

thought he was referring to Sang. But he whispered, *"Loca." Loca,* not *loco.* Then I realized: He was referring to Beth.

* * *

The next morning, after breakfast, Beth asked me to come up to her office for a "conversation." The unspoken rule of the house was that Beth's office on the fourth floor was off-limits; it was where she went "to retreat from the nonsense of the world" (her words). As I followed her up the steps, I wondered whether I'd done something wrong again.

Beth unlocked the door, and we walked into a cloud of dust. Cardboard boxes were stacked everywhere like partitions. There were a series of workstations, as if each represented a different period in the writing process. Right by the door was a large Victorian desk, on top of which sat a manual typewriter and a green banker's lamp. In the middle of the room was a white drafting table, covered in handwritten pages. At the far end was a desk made of glass and steel, with two side-by-side computer monitors. There was a podium against the wall, and taped above it were typewritten pages covered in four different colors of ink in Beth's loopy handwriting. There were also floating bookshelves on the walls. They were probably cherry or mahogany—none of the cheap stuff. More books were heaped on the floor like piles of rubbish. Light sliced through the tall windows, highlighting particles of dust floating in all directions. Her top-floor office was essentially an entire floor-through apartment—full kitchen and bathroom and everything. I wondered how much rental income they were forgoing on the unit. But I supposed they could afford it.

Beth led me to a low table next to the refrigerator, and she gestured for me to take the seat opposite her. I sank to the floor, knowing that when I stood up, the seat of my pants would be completely covered in dust. Hannah would have had some choice words for Beth's housekeeping. I could hear the low hum of the fridge, the grate below blowing up miniature tornadoes. Beth reached for the cast-iron teapot on the table and poured barley tea into two small cups.

"Jane, I have to admit I'm a little concerned about you. What I witnessed yesterday at your uncle's store was extremely disconcerting."

I accepted the cup from her and took a sip. I hoped the steam would hide my flush of embarrassment. Beth's tea tasted similar to Hannah's.

"I want to reiterate that this is an environment where you should feel *completely* comfortable. You should feel free to open up to any one of us."

Sang told us never to air our family matters outside the house. *Why other people gonna care about* your *problems?* he would say. Not only because they were personal matters but also because it was a burden to unload all your emotional baggage onto another person.

I thanked Beth for her concern, hoping to end the conversation there.

But she persisted, reaching across the table and squeezing my hand. "I want to help you."

She looked up at me with her large hazel eyes. I had never noticed how long her lashes were and how they curled up and made the pupils appear brighter.

"The wonders a women's-studies course would have done for you," Beth mused, shaking her head.

I saw an out. "That's what you teach, right?"

Beth embarked on a discussion of her discipline. (At least Sang had been right about one thing: *Americans, never they getting tired talk about themselves.*) About how formally she was a Victorianist—"You know, your Dickenses, your Shelleys, your Brontës." What had started with a study of period conduct books for women led to an examination of "unsavory 'heroines' "—misunderstood and demonized characters in nineteenth century novels. She hoped to revise the traditional, canonical perspective on these characters. Eventually Beth found a home in Mason College's women's-studies department, a cross-disciplinary department cobbling together literature people like herself, along with media-studies and cultural-studies folks. She was writing a book about these "heroines." Beth had written a first book that was "merely a superficial treatment" of the topic (I got the sense that it hadn't been well received by her colleagues), so she hoped this second book would launch her to the forefront of her field. At the very least, it would make or break tenure for her.

Then she slid across the floor with the litheness of a cat and plucked a volume from a nearby stack. "This book will do great things for your development," she said. "Consider it a continuance of your education."

She handed me the book—*The Feminist Primer: A Constructive Critique of the Feminist Movement* by Stanley Obuheim. "*TFP* is a seminal work. You really *must* start here."

I thanked her for the book. As I got up from the floor, Beth called out, "Oh, Jane? Have you noticed Ed acting . . . well, different lately?"

"Different?" I'd known Ed Farley for all of one week.

"Oh, it's just . . . well, never mind." She tapped the cover of *The Feminist Primer* in my hands. "I can't wait to have a conversation about this soon."

*   *   *

Later that week Devon and I were sitting in Gino's café doing homework and eating Italian ices. (The two of us had struck a deal—Devon would be allowed one Italian ice a week, as long as she promised to brush her teeth immediately afterward. It would be our little secret— the first of many I would come to keep from Beth.) Devon was studying her Chinese characters while I was struggling with *The Feminist Primer*.

"Alla Peters is *such* a snob," Devon said, looking up from her textbook. She spoke endlessly about Alla Peters. Alla was the new girl at school, who had just moved to the neighborhood from the Upper West Side. Based on Devon's stories, I pictured the fifth-grade version of Jessica Bae the PK: beribboned hair, puffy white dress, arms perennially akimbo, an irritating know-it-all voice.

Devon was holding up a flash card for the Chinese character signifying "big." It looked like a headless stick figure about to do a cartwheel. Chinese was proving easier than Beth's book. "Do you know what she said at lunchtime today?" Devon asked. "She said it's like the countryside here, compared to her old neighborhood. Well, if she feels like that, then she should've stayed put where she *belongs*."

She shifted the flash card up, blocking her face. "Ugh, that's her! Quick. Act like we don't see her."

I did exactly the opposite. Alla Peters was a tall girl, and if I didn't know better, I would have thought she was in high school. She had long, wavy dark hair pinned to one side, and she wore a flowing skirt that skimmed the floor, with little tiny bells sewn to the hem. Bangles shot up and down her arms. She was accompanied by a girl who looked like her older sister—both shared the same dark hair and dark eyes.

"Devon, she's waving at you."

"Jane!" Devon whispered, sinking deeper into her seat, still holding the flash card up to her face. "I *told* you not to look."

Alla Peters, seeing that her greeting was not reciprocated, lowered her hand. I expected her to shake her head haughtily; instead she looked embarrassed by Devon's slight. Her hand stopped to tuck a tendril of hair behind her ear, as if she were pretending never to have raised it in the first place, before dropping to her side. The older girl whispered something to her, and they moved to a table across the room.

"Devon, that girl doesn't seem snobby at all. She's new to the neighborhood. Maybe she's lonely."

Devon rolled her eyes. "She acts like she's better than everyone."

"Aren't you the one being the snob?"

I braced myself for Devon's indignant reaction—*Who are you to say that to me? My mother* pays *for you!*—but instead she looked thoughtful, as though she were considering the comment.

I glanced over at Alla Peters, sitting with the older girl at their table. Alla was staring into space, her schoolbooks opened in front of her. She looked friendless and alone.

When I went to the counter for more napkins, I heard a voice behind me. "That your kid?"

I turned around—standing behind me was the older girl with Alla Peters. She looked about my age. She had the same thin-yet-curvy build as Alla, but they were dressed differently. This girl wore large gold hoop earrings, a tight cotton-stretch top, and jeans that flared at the ankles. She reminded me of the white girls who would hang out after school at the pizzeria on Roosevelt.

"Yeah. Why?" I replied cagily.

"'Cause she just totally ignored Alla," the girl said, shifting her weight to her front foot, as if she were assuming the offensive.

"Devon didn't see her," I said.

"Please." She shook her head side to side as if to say, *Nuh-uh.* If this girl weren't so Brooklyn, I'd guess she was from Queens. "She think she's better than Alla?"

For the most part, people read me as meek. But sometimes all it took was a few words uttered a certain way to set off a trigger inside me. Suddenly I'd grow as impatient and irate as the customers at Food. My tone rose up. Later friends would joke, *Watch it—Jane's busting out her inner Queens!*

Who did this girl think she was, anyway? "*She* think she's better than Devon?" I said, shifting *my* weight toward the girl.

We stood there like that, at a standstill for what felt like a whole minute. Finally the girl broke the silence with, "You, like, that kid's big sister or something?"

"No. Why, are you?"

"Nah, I'm just Alla's baby-sitter."

"Me, too."

The girl shifted her weight to her back foot, and her tone softened. "What'd you say your kid's name was?"

"Devon. Mazer-Farley."

"She *Ed* Farley's kid?" The girl shook her head. "She looks different."

"She's *adopted,*" I said, my tone growing defensive.

"Nah, I didn't mean it like that. . . ." She trailed off. "I just haven't seen him around in a while. Only when his kid was real little."

"So you know Ed?"

"Yeah, I know him." The girl let out a guffaw. "My dad did the wiring on his place, back in the day. And my cousin Rosie went to school with him. Before he went off to Columbia."

"Small world."

"'Specially in this neighborhood," she said. "Well, uh . . . see you around, I guess." The girl started to walk away.

For some reason I felt compelled to call out to her. "Hey!"

She turned around. "Yeah?"

"Devon and I're just doing homework. So if you and Alla, like, want to join us . . ." My confidence was trickling off and, with it, the end of my sentence.

Her response was quick. "No, yeah, let me check with Alla." She held out her hand. "By the way, my name's Nina Scagliano."

"Jane Re." I expected her to have an aggressive handshake but was surprised to find that it was actually gentle.

"You did what?" Devon cried when I returned to our table. "Jane, how could you?"

"Calm down, Devon. You don't even know if Alla will say yes."

"Watch her say no. Then it'll be even *more* humiliating."

"Or she'll say yes, and she'll become your new best friend now that Carla Green-Levy has moved away."

"You remembered that?" Devon looked genuinely surprised. "Ma, like, never remembers *half* the stuff I tell her."

A few moments later, Nina and Alla were hovering over our table with their pizza slices and sodas. Devon instantly tugged on her shirt.

"Got room for two more?" Nina asked.

"Devon, scooch," I said. Reluctantly she cleared away her books for Alla. The girls exchanged greetings, Devon surprisingly shy and staring into her cup of water.

"Nice shirt, Devon," Alla said. Her voice had a soft lilt, with a hint of an accent I couldn't quite place.

Devon looked up. "Really?"

Alla nodded.

"I made it myself." Devon's T-shirt had a puff-painted bird design on the front.

"It's really quite unique," Alla went on.

The two girls quickly fell into chatter.

I looked over at Nina, who was pulling a book from her bag. "What's that?" I asked.

She held it up: *The 411 on New York Co-Ops and Condos.* "I *should* be doing my management class homework, but instead I've got my nose in this," she said.

"Just some light reading, huh?"

"Ha," she said. "I was kind of thinking about getting my real-estate license. But not before I graduate. My *nonna* would kill me if I didn't get my college degree."

"Where do you go to school?" I asked.

"Brooklyn College. I would've graduated this year, but I'm part-time. Got two more years." She let out a tired sigh. "You still in school?"

"Just graduated. From Baruch."

Nina's eyes didn't flicker with the judgment I saw in the eyes of the kids at church. "So're you from here, too?" she asked.

"Yeah, kinda. From Queens. Flushing."

"My cousin Rosie lives in Astoria," Nina said. When I asked her if she'd been there, she shook her head. "Nah, I don't really do Queens."

I bristled. "I said the same thing about Brooklyn."

"That so?" Her tone grew sharp, and I felt the fragility of the moment.

"But here I am," I said.

"Here you are," she repeated, her tone loosening.

We were quiet for a moment, and I overheard Devon, her eyes widening when she looked at Alla's tray. "My mom says pizza's got enriched flour and stuff, and that's bad for you."

"Mum's not much bothered by my food choices," Alla said. "Her concerns lie elsewhere."

Devon's eyes went wider with envy.

"So what do you do when you're not baby-sitting?" I asked Nina. "Or going to school, or studying for real-estate broker's exams?"

"Or saving up to buy a condo in the city?" Nina shrugged. "You know, same old. Bars. Clubs. Like last Saturday we went to this new place called Twine in the city. My cousin Tony's dating this girl whose little brother bounces there. He got us on the list when—get this— DJ Stixx was spinning that night."

I wasn't hip enough to know who DJ Stixx was, and I wondered if I imagined the flicker of judgment in Nina's eyes. As she launched into her retelling of last Saturday, I couldn't help but feel a pang of envy. Same old stuff people our age were *supposed* to do. After she wrapped up, she asked, "So what do you do on the weekends?"

It was my turn to shrug. It used to be Food. Church. Dinner at 718 Gates Street, followed by fruit peels and tea. Occasionally I'd go to the movies with Eunice Oh. We used to go to the Quartet on Northern, and afterward, on the walk back to her car, we'd hurry past the Galaxy Café, making sure not to be caught peering in. That was where all the Korean kids hung out, when they weren't sneaking into clubs in the city. But I had never been inside.

If I shared those details, Nina would have thought I was a complete loser. Instead I pointed to Beth's book. "You're looking at it."

"Well," Nina said, "if you ever need to be saved from it all, give a holler."

We both laughed, but Nina didn't know just how close to the truth my comment actually was.

*   *   *

Late that night, after the whole house had gone to sleep, I crept down to the kitchen with Beth's book and a stack of index cards. I knew that Beth expected me to read *The Feminist Primer* and would be very disappointed if I didn't make *some* effort to finish it. Why did I do it? Well, for one—she was my employer. But there was something else. After I'd left her attic, I remembered the way her eyes flooded with concern. It seemed genuine. Sang and Hannah never had "conversations" about my feelings. And in truth—I wanted to impress her.

I sat at the unvarnished table, staring into the book's pages, the text growing blurry before my eyes. All was still, until I heard a creak of the floorboards. This old house was still unfamiliar to me, its groans and utterances so foreign from the sounds of our house in Flushing.

But then I heard that creak again, followed by another. I tightened. It wasn't just the house settling; something or someone was definitely roving about.

Quietly I got up from the table and peered through the doorway down the darkened hall. I could just make out a slight movement. It stopped in its tracks, turned toward me. I flattened myself against the wall. When I peered again, the light streaming from the kitchen struck the figure. I saw a glint of golden hair, the chiseled cut of cheekbones. It was Ed.

I breathed out with relief but drew in my breath again as he strode toward me.

"Jane!" he cried. "What are you doing up?"

". . ." I faltered. Ed had that effect on me, especially after he took the blame for the Italian ices. I preferred it when we would simply pass each other wordlessly in the hallway.

I started again. "Beth gave me a book to read."

"How you liking it?"

Beth's book was terrible. But I didn't want to insult his wife's reading taste. And I didn't want to lie either. Then I noticed the pile of papers, file folders, and books in his arms. So I deflected. "What are *you* doing up?"

Ed looked sheepish. "Heading downstairs."

"To do laundry?"

To my surprise, Ed laughed. "To work," he said. "Hey, apparently that's how Stephen King did it." He stared down at his load of books. "Not that Stephen King's ever written a dissertation."

There was an ease with which he spoke—more relaxed than the way he crafted his words around Beth.

He peered over my shoulder, at the mess of papers and index cards spread across the kitchen table. "You still didn't answer my question. What do you think of Beth's book?"

"To be honest . . . I'm having a little trouble understanding it."

"I can give you a hand." Ed paused. "If you like."

"But I don't want to hold you up. . . ." I gestured to the pile in his arms.

"I could use a little break," he said, taking a seat at the kitchen table. He picked up one of my index cards. "'Metaphysicality,'" he read. He flipped it over; it was blank. He rustled through the others. "They're all blank."

"So what I actually meant was, I'm having a *lot* of trouble understanding it."

Ed laughed. It was a rich laugh, with a heft and a boom to it. It was an interesting counterpoint to Beth's high-pitched titter.

As Ed talked me through the various vocabulary words ("intertextuality," "hegemony," "post-structuralism"), their meanings began to untangle. He was not like Beth, who spoke in obsessive, inefficient circles. Nor was he like Sang, who barked one-word explanations, expecting you to read his mind. Ed's tutelage was somewhere in between. He spoke to me in terms I understood; I felt encouraged by his guidance.

"Don't let this stuff intimidate you, Jane," Ed said. "I had this one tenth-grader who was just daunted by *Gatsby*. He got the book—or so he thought—until he read all this critical theory, and it kept tripping him up. The theory completely shook his confidence. So we went back to the novel. Delved in, did close readings of his favorite passages." He beamed. "Just last week I got an e-mail from him, out of the blue. Little Wesley Smith just landed a book agent."

As he spoke, his eyes lit up. It seemed to stir a passion I hadn't seen in him before. "That's so great, Ed," I said, but he waved my compliment away. "My point, Jane, is that academics love bandying their own language about. You just have to learn to speak it. That is, *if* you choose to."

Ed got up from the table. I thought he was going to leave me for the basement, but instead he offered to make us a hero.

"You like prosciutto and figs?"

"Who the heck puts fruit in a hero?" The words flew out of my mouth before I could stop them. I hadn't meant to sound so judgmental—or so ignorant, for that matter.

"I first thought it was weird, too." It was a very gracious thing of him to say. "But actually the sweetness of the figs brings out the saltiness of the prosciutto. Their contrasts, Jane, are what make them all the more delicious."

I let Ed's words sink in.

"Beth doesn't like it when I bring meat into the house." I knew that according to the primer Beth had been a lacto-ovo vegetarian since 1983, before converting to veganism with lacto-ovo tendencies three years ago. "But we compromised." Ed offered a rueful smile. "I get one drawer."

He was rooting around in that refrigerator drawer now. He held up a bag of fruit, smushed and rotting. Sang's fruit. "I swear, the things that end up in here . . ." Ed dumped the bag in the trash.

As he set about making the sandwiches, I studied his movements. Most mornings I tried not to look in his direction, for fear of being caught staring at him. But his sharp contours were now growing familiar. I watched as he sliced a baguette lengthwise. He scooped out the bread's fluffy innards and split the halves, forming two hard-shelled boats that he layered with prosciutto and fig slices. Then, using a paring knife, he shaved off peels of parmesan as if he were whittling away at a block of wood.

Ed returned to the table with our heroes, open-faced. "I meant to tell you this earlier, Jane. I know we have a lot of rules here. They might seem arbitrary, but they mean a lot to Beth." I told him I understood. Ed went on. "She's working on a very important book while gunning for tenure. It's enough to make anyone a little loopy. And"— he cleared his throat—"I'm not one to tend toward hyperbole, but Beth . . . is brilliant."

I couldn't speak. My mouth was full of the first bite of Ed's hero. He was right: the combination was perfect.

Chapter 8

Thanksgiving

Late summer had given way to a chilly autumn, and I was falling into the rhythms of daily life in Brooklyn. Which included weekly chats up in Beth's fourth-floor office. She must have been so pleased with my understanding of *The Feminist Primer*, because other books, articles, and journals followed.

What Beth didn't know was that at night, long after the remains of dinner were scraped off our plates and into the compost, long after the whole household had retired, Ed and I would meet for a snack. Either he'd wander into the kitchen and find me there with Beth's articles or I would walk in on him slicing the bread, creating rafts for the filling. They were never the same sandwiches, and they were always the most unlikely combinations—to my provincial palate anyway: gorgonzola, honey, and basil; pork sausage, endive, and Rome apple slices; mozzarella and mint with a drizzle of balsamic reduction. A considerable departure from the original Italian hero, but Ed, he told me, was not a purist.

We'd sit at that same table where we'd just eaten Beth's dinners and pore over her articles while Ed peppered his explanations with funny anecdotes from his private school, making the experience of slogging through the scholarship that much more bearable.

Gradually I began to open up to him. One night I was talking about my uncle's store and found myself describing our cardboard-box excuse for a back office. That office—all of Food, really—embarrassed me. I'd made it a point not to show it to Beth and Devon when they came to Queens.

Ed's reaction? "Cardboard! At *least* get some foam core or something—that would've been sturdier. Though I'll grant the PVC pipes are a nice touch."

"Sounds like my uncle should've hired *you* to fix up the place." Ed had mentioned he came from a family of contractors. He said he probably would have continued down that path if it hadn't been for a volume of *Leaves of Grass* and a certain high-school English teacher.

"Well, that's nothing," Ed said. "When my brother, Enzo, and I were doing work on this house, you should've seen. We broke through the walls and saw—"

"Mice?" I interrupted. I thought of the ceiling panels with Sang.

"Worse!" Ed shook his head. "Mold. It was a nightmare—you couldn't salvage a thing."

For all of Beth's attempts to get me to open up to her, it was actually Ed I felt more comfortable confiding in. I didn't need to *explain* things the way I did with Beth. He just got it. It was uncanny how two and a half months ago I'd been terrified of him; now I was divulging stories I wouldn't dare share with his wife. Pretty soon we spoke in our own comfortable shorthand. We both came from decidedly unglamorous worlds, steeped in the language of vermin, water damage, building codes. What part would Beth have wanted in any of these "conversations"?

* * *

Besides my day meetings with Beth and my night sessions with Ed, Nina and I were fast becoming friends. Not only were we hanging out in the afternoons with Devon and Alla, but the two of us also would occasionally meet after dinner, when I was technically off-duty. We usually went back to Gino's, where we'd open our books in front of us—Nina with her schoolwork, me with Beth's assignments—and talk. Nina would tell me about her friends in the neighborhood. There was Angela Fabbricari, Nina's best friend, majoring in business at Brooklyn College (her father was a contractor and was—according to

Nina—loaded). Adriana Panificio, who worked at her family's bakery on Henry. Marie Macelli worked as a day trader, and her father was a butcher. Valentina Francobolli, a paralegal whose parents owned the notary public/stamp store on Court. From what I could tell, Nina's life paralleled that of my cousin Mary and her Korean friends back in Flushing: everyone lived at home with his or her parents, and on the weekends they headed into the city to the bars and clubs. Whenever I'd run into Nina and her gang on the street, we'd only exchange a quick hello; she'd never stop and introduce me to her friends. I knew it was because I wasn't part of the in group.

One night at Gino's, Nina looked across at my book. "What you got over there this time?" she asked. That week's reading was written by a scholar named Sam Surati, Beth's adviser at Columbia, who'd since been wooed away by Stanford. Its title was *Could You Please Pass the Smelling Salts?: An Examination of the Victorian Faint.*

"You know," I said, "same old."

Nina snorted. "I don't know what's more unbelievable—that your boss gives you homework or that you actually do it."

I shrugged my shoulders like, *Whattayagonnado.* "Want to trade?" I said. Nina was reading yet another book on real estate. "Sure, why not." She took the book from me and began to read aloud.

"'We cannot discourse on the faint without first beginning our discussion with constructions of the feminine. What *is* "the feminine"? To liken it to, if you will, the lapping tides of the Long Island Sound on a breezy afternoon in the heart of the North Fork wine country would merely perpetuate stereotypes of female subjectivity (mercurial, as moody as those shifty waves, as intoxicating as a cabernet franc), as well as to objectify the female form entirely. Nor can we discourse on the feminist movement—in all its wrought history— without first discoursing on the problematic tradition of desire and the male gaze (cf. Surati, *A Thousand Times "I Do!": Commodification of Female Chastity in Nineteenth-Century Puritanical England,* p. 147).'"

"The hell is that shit?" Nina said, putting down Sam Surati's book.

"My uncle's English is better than that," I said.

"So's my *nonna's*! Why's a dude writing about feminism?" She looked at the book's cover. It was pink, featuring a picture of a tulip with quivering petals. A knowing smile spread across her face. "Oh, I know why. *Bom-chikka-bow-wow!*"

I let out a hearty laugh. "Ed says Sam Surati likes to think he's quite the authority on *every* subject."

Actually, Ed Farley thought Sam Surati was "a self-quoting, womanizing, pompous ass." That I learned over tuna, red-pepper flakes, and shredded jicama.

"You've been quoting a lot of Ed Farley lately," Nina mused.

I stopped laughing and quickly added, "And *Beth* says Sam was her greatest mentor."

Nina tapped the cover, her finger aimed at Sam Surati's name. "Just watch. You're totally gonna have a pop quiz waiting for you tonight."

* * *

Nina wasn't all that far off. It would be more like an oral examination, with the author himself—Sam Surati was coming to New York. "He's here on his lecture circuit, and I've invited him over for dinner a week from next Thursday," Beth said at the dinner table that night, clapping her hands together. "Isn't that wonderful?"

"But, Ma," Devon said, "that's Thanksgiving."

According to the primer, the Mazer-Farleys spent their Thanksgivings getting vegetarian dim sum in Chinatown, because the family didn't want to impose a Western reading on an already exploitative Western holiday.

"It was the only day he was free, sweetie," Beth said. "Plus, I know he's dying to meet you."

Ed pushed his plate away. It was Bitter Greens Casserole Night. (On BGCNs, Ed was always doubly hungry at our sandwich sessions.) "Doesn't the man have his own family to spend the holidays with?"

Beth bit her lip, as if she were about to hold back on making a retort. Then her voice went light, airy. "Jane! What a wonderful opportunity this will be for you. You'll finally meet the man behind the words. I hope you have some good questions planned!"

I hadn't made it much past those first few pages of *Could You Please Pass the Smelling Salts?*

Beth got up from the table and returned with a legal pad and a pencil. "If I'm remembering correctly, Sam is allergic to garlic...." And she set about sketching a holiday menu plan.

That menu plan consumed Beth both day and night: thick cookbooks showed up in all corners of her office, opened to recipes for spice rubs and purees marked in different-colored pens, a million tiny Post-it flags waving from their pages. Crumpled legal-pad sheets overflowed from the recycling bin and littered the floor of her study. Beth's attic was becoming a madhouse.

On Thanksgiving morning Devon and I were dispatched downtown to the Chinese bakery. "So I guess you really like moon cakes, huh," I said as we boarded the subway into the city.

Devon wrinkled her nose. "I *used* to," she said. "I've only told Ma like a thousand times I don't anymore. But Dad says it's just because she's up for tenure next year. Then after that she'll be back to normal."

What kinds of conversations did she and Ed have when Beth wasn't around? Just as Ed and I were meeting for late-night sandwiches, Devon and Ed must have had their own set of secrets they kept from Beth. I felt a pang of something inside—jealousy? selfishness? I shook my head clear of such petty thoughts.

We got off the subway at East Broadway and joined the jumble of pedestrians on Canal Street. We dodged men pushing hand trucks stacked with boxes of produce. In the restaurant windows, hanging duck carcasses glistened from their hooks. We cut through the shouts and murmurs of shopkeepers and customers mid-negotiation.

"It always feels weird to be walking around here," Devon said, clutching my arm so we wouldn't get separated in the crowds. I thought of Northern Boulevard and the Koreans spilling out of shop doors and churches. "All the real Chinese kids live here."

"As opposed to fake?" I said.

Devon looked sheepish. Yet we both knew there was a difference. "It just doesn't feel the same with my CAAA-NY friends." CAAA-NY was the New York chapter of the Chinese-American Adoptee Association, to which the family belonged. "It's like we all go to Lion Dance class and we meet for Lunar New Year, but sometimes it feels like we're just doing it because, like, we're supposed to."

"Have you tried talking with your mom about it?" I asked.

"Ma's already got so much on her plate right now, I don't want to bother her." She hesitated before adding, "Plus, she's so *clueless*."

I wondered if, for Devon, "clueless" was synonymous with "lacking *nunchi*."

As we continued down Canal, Devon told me that a bunch of the kids from her Chinese school—the "real" Chinese—were going to apply to Hunter College High School. "Have you ever heard of it?"

Eunice Oh had gone to Hunter for junior high. She'd attended Chwae-go After-School Academy since the second grade to prepare for Hunter's entrance exam. Your fifth-grade standardized test scores determined whether you were qualified to take the exam, and you had your one shot in the fall of sixth grade to pass the exam. The school was grades seven to twelve.

"You're thinking of applying?" I asked Devon.

She nodded slowly, the way she did when she was in serious mode.

We'd reached the bakery at that point, and the bell chimed as we pushed the door open. "&%$*%#@," the shopkeeper said to us.

"Sorry, I'm not Chinese," I said. My automatic response whenever I was greeted in Chinese.

He looked over at Devon.

"& . . . % . . . $*% . . . #@," she said haltingly.

The man then let out a fast string of words, punctuated with a lot of *sh* and *wuhr* sounds, and based on the growing look of confusion on Devon's face, I could tell she didn't follow. "I'm not . . ." she started, but therein lay her dilemma: She *was* Chinese. At least in the man's eyes she was. She didn't have the luxury of saying otherwise. My heart ached as I watched her standing there—embarrassed? humiliated?— her eyes now glued to the floor.

"Do you have moon cakes?" I asked quickly.

The man threw a last confused look at Devon before turning his attention to me. "We got many kind. What your favorite?"

I was about to ask Devon, but her body was doing a one-eighty, her toes pointing toward the door. Her tiny hands curled into fists. "Whatever's most popular," I told the man hastily.

After we left the store with the cakes, I turned to Devon. "Hey. What happened back there?"

"Nothing," she mumbled, eyes fixed to the pavement.

"Come on, tell me." Beth would have said, *Let's have a conversation.*

She kicked a bottle cap on the sidewalk. "You don't understand."

"*I* don't understand?" The words just came pouring out; I couldn't stop myself. "I got the opposite problem from you. I grew up half Korean. In *Flushing.* You saw what that place was like. I stuck out like a sore thumb."

Growing up, I often felt I would've been treated better if I were a hundred percent one or the other. If I were all Korean, I could have just blended in. If I were all white, I wouldn't have been met with the same curious stares—*What* are *you?*—the same assumptions about my mother's past. To be *almost* seemed to be worse than being *not at all.*

"I didn't know you were only half!" Devon's eyes went round with disbelief.

"*Only*" half. "Well, now you do," I said.

I thought of Carroll Prep, where most of Devon's classmates had hyphenated last names. All white or white and something else, like Alla Peters. One or two other adoptees like Devon. Her subset of Brooklyn looked very different from Nina's and her father's.

Devon held tight to my arm as we approached East Broadway. The sidewalk was lined with hefty trash bags filled with who knew what—fish guts and rotting fruit peels from the smell of it. It was a foul scent, with a sweet finish that followed us until we ducked down into the subway station below.

* * *

Sam Surati was one hour late for Thanksgiving dinner. By the time he did arrive, the family had devolved into various sour moods. Ed had been making snide comments all morning about Sam. Beth was frazzled; her "feature entrée" was not "taking shape" the way she'd hoped, and both oven and stove were "in cahoots" against her. When I offered to help, she shooed me out of the kitchen. Devon harbored an unarticulated annoyance at something—the moon cakes, the whole trip to Chinatown. I was somewhere in between—after hearing the man built up by Beth (and knocked down by Ed), I was actually pretty curious about meeting him.

I met Sam Surati's cologne first. A thick, spicy, boozy scent—like something one of Mary's boyfriends would wear—rolled in through the front door like a red carpet announcing his arrival. And there he stood: a tall man with a full head of salt-and-pepper hair that crested over his right eye like a schoolboy's and ruddy skin that looked as if it'd been scrubbed too vigorously with one of Hannah's red washcloths. Sam Surati looked around Sang's age, maybe older, but he dressed like a much younger man. He wore a fitted gray blazer and a blue-striped button-down shirt that attempted to draw attention away from what was clearly a protruding belly. His bottom half was outfitted in stylish dark-rinse bootcut jeans. On his feet were a pair of what looked like expensive brown bowling shoes.

He looked at me over Beth's shoulder. "I thought you told me you'd adopted a little girl from China. Not a *woman*," he said, jerking a thumb at me. It was an inappropriate comment; my cheeks burned with some mixture of embarrassment and indignation. Mostly indignation. I wished I had enough nerve, like Nina, to call him out on it.

But Beth laughed, pressing her tapioca-flour-coated, aproned chest to him, her oniony lavenderness mingling with his cologne. She did not notice him brushing off the streaks of flour from his blazer when they pulled apart. "That's Jane. She helps us with Devon. But this"— she pushed Devon forward, as though she were offering up a gift— "*this* is my daughter, Devon." Sam and Devon shook hands.

What was most interesting was Sam and Ed's greeting, or lack thereof. There was no "Hello, how are you, happy Thanksgiving."

They simply stated each other's first name. There was a tense hand-shake. Ed's lips were drawn into a tight line.

"I'd apologize for being late," Sam said to Beth, "but I blame the remoteness of your fair borough. It's simply *impossible* to catch a cab to Brooklyn. I had to tip my guy an extra five bucks."

"Or you could've taken the subway," Ed said.

Beth shot him a look. "Well, never mind that. You're here now. Come, come, let's eat."

She led the way to the dining room. As Sam walked to the table, the loose denim fabric around his thighs and calves bunched up around his spindly legs.

Beth's Thanksgiving meal seemed to really embrace the colors of fall: orange, brown, and green were heaped onto clay serving platters. But it was hard to believe that the endless bags brimming with grocer-ies across the kitchen counter had been reduced to these pureed mounds, uniform in texture and consistency. If I hadn't known how much work had gone into the meal, I would've thought Beth had un-screwed a couple dozen jars of Gerber's baby food and dumped them onto the platters.

But all those side dishes seemed a foil for the true highlight of the meal: Beth's Thanksgiving turkey. It was a tawny, speckled lump of glazed tempeh resting on a white blanket of silken tofu. It had a walnut-shell beak and slivers of black olive X's for eyes, and a peel of Red Delicious apple dingle-dangling from its chin. Alternating raw zucchini and carrot spikes poked out from its backside, and below that were fresh cranberry droppings. From where I sat, the tempeh turkey looked as if it were cowering behind the wall of moon cakes, piled high like bricks on a plate, and had soiled itself from fright.

"That's quite a sight," Sam said.

"Isn't it?" Beth said, carving the "turkey." "White or dark?" she joked as she passed plates of the tempeh around the table.

"My God, Beth," Sam said, swirling his glass of wine. "I don't even want to think of how many pages of your manuscript were forgone in the making of that . . . that centerpiece."

"About that, Sam," Beth said, "did you have a chance at all to review those chapters I sent—"

"Yes, I did. And I mentioned them to Jennifer at see-you-pee yesterday." Devon and I exchanged a look across the table and started to titter. Only later would I learn he'd meant CUP. "She had some concerns about its crossover appeal—you know it's *all about the market* these days—but follow up with her early next week. Tell her you and I talked. And how's everything else looking? You're serving on how many . . . ?"

"Five," Beth said immediately, and Sam nodded with approval. They spoke in a shorthand, finishing each other's sentences as they volleyed words across the table.

"And how are your student evals?" he asked.

Beth wrung her cloth napkin. "My students either love me or hate me."

"What did I say about going easy on them, especially now?" Sam said. "Offer to drop their lowest grades."

"Or you could just focus on doing a good job. Less scheming, more teaching." It was Ed who broke in.

But then Sam Surati let out a strange laugh. I recognized the tone—it was the same tone Beth had used with Ed when they fought about the Italian ices. It was condescension. I thought about how delicious it would feel to fling my plate of Beth's murky foodstuffs at his face.

When his laughter subsided, he said, in a tone that matched that laugh, "By the way, how *is* that dissertation coming along?"

Beth nudged her husband eagerly. "Yes, Ed, what a *great* opportunity for you to ask Sam for his advice."

"Beth, I really don't think now's the time to discuss this." Ed put down his napkin.

"Sam," Beth said, "what'd you at least think of Ed's intro chapter?"

"You *sent* him my manuscript?" Ed said.

"I thought it'd be helpful for you to have a second set of eyes on it," she said breezily.

Sam put down his wineglass. There was a flicker of *nunchi* in his eyes, as if he, too, thought the most diplomatic thing was to drop the subject.

But Beth egged him on. "Who *knows* when next we'll see you, Sam! My God, Ed, the man's so busy. He very generously took the time to look at your work. Now, Sam, be honest. What did you think?"

"I thought . . ." Sam was, for the first time, flustered. "To be brutally honest, I thought your argument felt a little . . . familiar. A bit déjà vu–ish, if you will."

"See, Ed? Wasn't I telling you the same thing?" Beth cried, delighted to be in accord with Sam Surati. "You state things like you were the first person to discover them. Meanwhile there's a whole body of work that posits the same theories you're claiming as your own."

Sam Surati receded from the conversation as Beth went on to list a mountain of the dissertation's other faults: its failure to engage with past scholarship, to anticipate counterarguments, and, what seemed to be its most egregious offense, its "far-too-readable" language. She chewed out Ed the same way Hannah worked her teeth over a piece of pear peel, scraping off all traces of flesh. Was Beth, as Devon might have put it, truly so clueless? Couldn't she see *she* was the reason her husband was pulling away?

If I couldn't save Ed, then I could at least distract everyone else from his growing humiliation. "So . . . Dr. Surati," I said. "I find your . . . dialectic on . . . femininity . . . um, interesting."

Sam Surati tittered, corrected himself. "You mean my discourse on 'the feminine,'" he said, his eyes snapping away from Beth and Ed and onto me. He clearly found my verbal slips more entertaining than their fight. "Yes, yes, and what facet of it exactly did you find *interesting*?"

"You had this part about, like . . ." The way Sam Surati stared at me intently made the words even harder to get out.

"Please—take *all* the time you need," he said. Then he reached over to pat my hand. This made both Beth and Ed stop in their tracks.

"Oh, Sam," Beth called out in a *yoo-hoo!* voice. "Don't be too hard on her. Before Jane met us, she'd never once been exposed to this kind of material."

"Is that so?" Sam said. He tried to pat my hand again, but I'd already withdrawn it to my lap.

As Beth and Sam went on, talking about me as if I weren't there, I recalled an article she'd made me read about how Victorian men gangbanged women with language. They'd "thrust" and "parry" words over the female body, while the body in question was forced to just sit there in silence and take it. The article was called "Wanting a Piece of Fanny: Male Dominance and Violation in Jane Austen's *Mansfield Park*."

Devon, who'd been uncharacteristically quiet during the meal, suddenly interrupted her mother. "Ma, I want to apply to Hunter for seventh grade."

"Devon!" I whispered, nudging her. I was grateful to her for diverting the attention from me, but she should have had the *nunchi* to see that now was a bad time to be pleading her case.

Beth disengaged with Sam and turned to her daughter. "No. Absolutely not," she said. "Carroll Prep is an excellent school, and you'll be staying put till college."

"But Hunter's a good school, too! And it's free!" Devon offered, to which Beth scoffed. "Devon, that's the *last* thing you should be worried about. I'll not put a price on my daughter's education."

"Beth, it's not a bad idea," Ed said. "I agree now's not the time to talk about this, but we should at some point—"

"And have my daughter romp about in the city on the subways all by herself? Do you have any idea how *dangerous* that is?" Then Beth fixed her dark, dark eyes on me. "Was this *your* idea?" Before I could answer, she added, "*Don't* encourage her. Please. The matter is settled."

"You always tell us to think for ourselves, but you're a hypocrite and a tyrant!" Devon squealed, rising from the table. "You're worse than . . . than Mao!"

Beth gasped. Her fork dropped onto her plate; it would have clattered if its fall weren't softened by a bed of brown puree. Devon stormed from the table. I could hear her footsteps clomping up the stairs. I wasn't sure whether to stay put or follow after her.

"Do you know that's the meanest thing she's ever said to me?" Beth said. "Not only the meanest but also the most uninformed. If it weren't for Mao's Cultural Revolution, half a billion women never would've gained equal rights." She stared at her daughter's empty seat and blinked, fighting back tears. "I swear I must've told Devon that at least a dozen times."

Sam Surati cleared his throat. "Yes, well . . ." He glanced at his watch. "Anyway, I should be off. I'm meeting Stanley for drinks, and who knows how long it'll take to get out of these far-flung regions."

"With . . . Stanley?" Beth dabbed at her eyes. She looked hopeful, as though she, too, might score an invite. Even I recognized the name: Stanley Obuheim of *The Feminist Primer* fame. He was a scholar oft quoted by Beth, second only to Sam Surati. But she had never actually met him.

"The one and only." Sam turned to me. "Have you been to the Campbell Apartment? There's nowhere else in the city that makes a better old-fashioned. In my humble opinion, that is. Perhaps we could continue this 'dialectic on femininity' there." His fingers fluttered into air quotes.

I almost said yes. Not because I wanted to spend another second with Sam Surati, but out of retaliation against Beth for the way she'd treated Ed. A little *booyah!* if you will. But then I'd lose my job.

I should have demurred, politely. I should have averted my eyes or *tee-hee*d into my hemp napkin, to let him down easy. But I'd been holding back the whole evening. Sam Surati was insufferable, and my mounting anger was making me *tap-tap-hae*. I couldn't stop my face from contorting with disgust. I couldn't stop myself from blurting out, "But you could be my *dad*." (And for all I knew, he very well could be.)

Never before had my words had the power to cause a man to shrivel so quickly into himself. Like that, Sam Surati's arrogant puff deflated. His cheeks flushed with more than just too much wine. Male desire was at its most problematic, according to one of Beth's articles ("The Hottie in the Granny Panties: Cindy Sherman and the Reversal of the Male Gaze"), when it was mixed with disgust.

"Ah, yes, well. Another time, then," he mumbled. "Beth, you've been wonderful, as ever. And thank your family for suffering me on their day off."

With that, Sam Surati collected his things and left, his sickly-sweet cologne lingering in his wake.

"At least that's over," Ed muttered, throwing down his napkin. He got up to start clearing the dishes.

"It wouldn't have killed you to make *some* effort," Beth said.

Ed looked like he was about to burst with anger, but then his voice became muted, like a piano when you press down the middle pedal. "Beth, another time. Really."

"That's almost becoming a cliché with you," she muttered.

It was this that finally set Ed off. "It's so ironic," he said, his tone escalating. "For all your talk about your daughter getting a good education, you and Sam Surati *sit* there plotting in plain sight! What is he, your Lady Macbeth?" His Brooklyn accent thickened with anger.

"Ed, you're projecting." Her tone was calm.

"Devon's right. Maybe you *are* a hypocrite."

"And you're just above us all, then, aren't you? And where *exactly* has that gotten you?"

It was only Ed whose voice crescendoed, rising with emotion, while Beth maintained her even-keeled tone. At first the contrast made *Ed* seem like the irrational one, immature for not keeping his cool. But then I realized it was something else entirely. It felt mean, the way Beth did not deign to raise her voice. It was patronizing—it kind of made her seem like a phony.

Sang and Hannah did not hold back when they fought. Their fights were loud and quick, like bursts of compressed air. But later Hannah would cook up the spicy fish stew that Sang loved, or he would bring her an unblemished Asian pear. Sang and Hannah, I knew, had *jung* for each other—a deep-seated regard. *Jung* was the kind of bond that formed equally between a mother and her child, a student and his beloved mentor, a woman and the dreadful mother-in-law she grows to cherish over time. Maybe Americans—er, white people (Beth was constantly on my case about correcting that: *You're American, too*)—expressed their *jung* in a different way. But it seemed to me that Beth and Ed had not an ounce of *jung* between them.

I took one last look at the two of them before I slipped away. And this much I knew: If Ed and Beth continued like this, she'd work him down, like the pureed heaps left over on our Thanksgiving plates.

*   *   *

A few hours later I heard the front door slam, then movement above me: Beth pacing the length of her office upstairs. Dull thumps back and forth, until finally the sound tapered off.

That night I wondered whether Ed would want company or if he'd prefer to be by himself. I sat on my bed trying to read (not Sam Surati's book; I couldn't stand the sight of it), but my thoughts kept returning to him. Ed was fast becoming a comforting presence. I longed to see him, I craved the reassuring sound of his voice. Should I venture downstairs? Or should I stay away?

I heard a knock on the door. It was Devon; Ed stood behind her. "Ma's asleep. Daddy says we're going on a secret road trip!"

"Kiddo, it's not *secret* per se," Ed said.

I reached for my coat. "Oh, I am *so* in."

We walked to the car. In the dark we heard a voice call out, "Ed Fawley? That you?" A man in a dark coat was walking toward us. "How you doin'? Lawng time no see!"

"Sal Mastronardi. Happy Thanksgiving," Ed said. "Hope you've been well."

Ed and the man had an awkward embrace—the man had his arms spread wide while Ed held out a hand.

The man and his wife were having company over on Sunday after Mass. Did he . . . did we—he looked questioningly at us—want to come over?

Ed shook his head. "My wife—she has to work."

The man was shaking his head. "That wife a-yours still locked up in her awfice? Whatta shame."

Sal Mastronardi knew how to take a hint. After a few more words, they parted. We walked on to the car.

It was clear from dinner that night that Ed Farley did not belong in Beth and Sam Surati's world. But he also no longer belonged to the one he was from.

We drove down Court Street until we reached the expressway overhead and the neighborhood shops and brownstones gave way to abandoned warehouses, bodegas, and auto-body shops. We were not far from Sang's old store, the one from the blackout. I looked behind at Devon, seat-belted in the back. Was this weird for her, the three of us together without her mother? She didn't look as if it bothered her at all—she was bouncing in her seat, sharing a joke with her father— "Da-ddy, you already told us that one!"—and laughing. Her face glowed. Devon had been three when Beth and Ed adopted her; she might have been just old enough to remember the feel of her own mother's touch, but she said she had no memories of her life back in China. Did she feel any pangs of wistfulness, or did she have so much *jung* for Beth and Ed that a heavy emptiness never swelled in the pit of her heart, the way it did in my own?

Up until I was Devon's age, I used to fantasize—of all mundane things—car rides with my mother and father. They'd pull up in a convertible in front of 718 Gates Street and whisk me off. I had only one grainy picture of my mother. She was looking away from the camera and smiling up at someone—my father?—her thin, graceful arm shielding her eyes from the sun. In the passenger seat of that imaginary convertible, my mother looked over at my father with that same shy hint of a smile.

The picture of my father, sitting behind the wheel, was always hazier. When I was a child, my hair was so much lighter and my face was covered in freckles, so I made the back of my father's head a chestnut brown, same as all the dads' on TV sitcoms. From that backseat I could make out only a sliver of his profile, but he was strong-jawed and

chiseled, with his eyes fixed adoringly on my mother. Although that
was before he had cast her aside.

Kids always knew I was different, but it wasn't until the summer
after fourth grade that they started to say things. *Your dad was a mi-*
gun—a GI! Your mom was so crazy for Hershey's chocolate bars. She was
willing to have a weirdo baby like you! You're worse than an orphan 'cause
your parents didn't even want you. By the time I started fifth grade, I
forced the forged memories of my parents, and those joyrides, out of
my head. After that I started to regard my mother the same way
everyone else did: as a loose, foolish woman who'd been abandoned by
her no-good American boyfriend.

Ed pulled in to a McDonald's. The fact that Beth would have hy-
perventilated if she knew where we were (cf. the primer, "Forbidden
Foods," subsection "McDonald's = Satan" footnote, p. 166) made our
illicit trip all the more delicious. The only other patrons were a couple
of men in stained Hanes T-shirts and black pants, hunched in a booth
and tucking into their own version of Thanksgiving dinner. I remembered my first meal at McDonald's, with Sang. The mouse picked
clean. *I guess he not go to waste.* I tried to shut the memory out of my
mind.

Ed and I ordered Big Macs and Devon the Filet-o-Fish. We toasted
our cups of soda water and dug into our meals. I was squirting ketchup
onto my fries when I looked up and caught Ed staring at me. He
leaned across the table and ran a gentle thumb over my cheek. He'd
never come so close to me before. The smell of his clean soap gave way
to a different scent—a deeper, muskier one.

"You have some mayo on your face—there, I got it."

He licked the sauce from his finger, then reached over and tousled
his daughter's hair. My cheek still tingled. *No,* I thought. I didn't want
the moment to be over. Devon was absorbed in recounting a story
from school— ". . . and then during gym, Sasha Siegler-Chen was
like . . ."—but my ears tuned her out, my whole body fixed on replay-
ing the sensation of Ed's touch. I felt something in my chest—a dull

aching. A longing? *Forget it,* I thought. *He's your boss.* I placed my hand to my chest and pressed down, hard.

But then Ed looked over at me again, locking his blue eyes on mine. The meal, the rest of McDonald's, faded away, and it was just the two of us. He smiled. It was so unlike the sour smile he seemed to wear daily at breakfast and dinner, where one corner of his mouth lifted up while the other twisted into a frown. It was a rare, real smile.

Sang would not have approved of the unabashed way Ed Farley was staring at me in that McDonald's. And he would have been downright ashamed by the unabashed way I was returning that gaze.

Chapter 9

The Male Gaze

It went on like this, through the descent into winter, the rise to spring. Ed and me eating more heroes that Beth didn't know about. Devon and me studying in secret for her Hunter exam. The morning after our clandestine McDonald's run, Devon had asked me for help; I did not even hesitate before saying yes. I'd e-mailed Eunice for some tips, and she'd e-mailed back attachment after scanned attachment of practice tests supplied by her cousin, who taught at Chwae-go After-School Academy. I was now colluding with all the other members of the Mazer-Farley household against Beth Mazer herself.

Beth and I were still meeting in her top-floor office. We'd sit at the low table on the dusty floor drinking toasted barley tea. I didn't mind being the sounding board for her theories. Whenever she talked about Foucault or Obuheim or Sam Surati, her tired eyes would grow bright with life. But it was when she would venture away from the theoretical—into the realm of her real life—that I would grow uncomfortable. One of the other mothers in CAAA-NY was sending her daughter to a child psychologist specializing in transracial adoption. Beth was thinking of sending Devon, too, but Ed was opposed. "She's coddling Devon. Back in my day, a kid needed some scrapes and bruises to toughen up. She keeps this going, Devon's going to grow up like a hothouse flower." I could see it from both of their perspectives. "Transracial adoption" child psychologists didn't exist in the world of

Flushing either. But maybe if they had, things might have turned out differently for me.

"Jane, what do you think?" Beth asked.

"Well . . ." I started, ready to give a noncommittal answer, but Beth was already launching into an account of her own "shitty relationship" with her mother (a Boston socialite, from what I gathered), who was "more intent on grooming me into the world of debutante balls than developing my mind," according to Beth. Thankfully, she found solace in her father—a political science professor who was from the Bronx— as well as therapy. God yes, therapy.

But it was when she'd segue into concerns about her husband that I felt the most uncomfortable—and also the most indignant. "We can talk, woman to woman, right?" Beth asked one afternoon. She never referred to anyone as ladies or girls—we were all women or young females. Even Devon.

What could I do but shrug yes?

"I think Ed secretly wishes I won't get tenure. To make himself feel better about his *lack* of success."

"He's still a high-school teacher," I pointed out. As if that were such a failure.

"I think he's trying to punish me. Sometimes he can be so petulant. And now he's withholding *sex*. We haven't slept together since . . ."

My eyes swung from the clock to her dusty workstations, looking for something—anything—to use to change the subject. I knew exactly how long it had been—I stopped hearing the squeaking bedsprings through the walls after my first day. My eyes alighted on the bare bookshelves that framed the fireplace. They were floating shelves—suspended in the nook of the walls without the aid of L-brackets or other visual impediments.

"Those are beautiful. Is that mahogany?"

"I think. I *guess*." Beth's tone was dismissive. "If Ed had spent *half* as much time on his dissertation as he did making those—"

"Ed *built* them?" The shelves were perfectly fitted in their nook—

no gaps, no puckering, no uneven lines. I thought of the trial and error of cutting the boards to size, and getting them just right. "I swear, the way he tinkers around the house . . ."

I wanted to shout, *Then why are you together?* I was surprised by the force of my own thoughts, but the words grew louder and stronger in my head with each passing day.

And just as she was about to send me off with the next week's readings, Beth would look intently at me. It was a look of pity.

I didn't need her pity.

In fact, I was starting to pity *her*. It was as if Beth had no girlfriends she could hash out all her problems with. She was the one who needed to go back into therapy. But I could never hope to express those thoughts aloud. So each week I'd endure our sessions up in the attic as Beth rattled on and on, caught in an endless loop.

*   *   *

Nina was my escape from the respective dramas of the Mazer-Farleys, and over the passing months our coffees at Gino's progressed to mixed drinks at bars. When it was just the two of us, we would volley words across the table—every *ping* met with its return *pong*. But when we were out with her other friends—they joked they'd been friends since the womb—Nina and her little circle felt impenetrable. It was the same dynamic Mary had with her friends, who'd known one another for so long that they spoke in a kind of exclusionary shorthand.

But Nina and her friends taught me what girls our age did with their nights off: They got drunk on candy-colored cocktails and tried to pick up guys. She'd take me to bars along Second Avenue on the Upper East Side, bars named for boatloads of every free-flowing spirit imaginable. With each Jell-O shot or Jäger Bomb came the promise of true love. We'd go out in a gaggle of plunging necklines and stacked platform heels—Nina would lend me the clothes—and nurse our one cheap drink while trying to catch the eyes of men wearing shirts with their collars popped up, the front tips of their hair gelled into stiff peaks that called to mind the crown on the Statue of Liberty. Eventually the men would sidle up to us with neon shots that were literally on fire or fishbowls with two-foot-long straws.

The men didn't really talk to me. They focused on Marie, with her frosted highlights; or Adriana and Valentina, with their huge Bambi eyes; or Angela, whose boobs were so big and bouncy they threatened to bust an eye out; or Nina herself, who had the enviable twin traits of slimness *and* curviness. I'd always end up with the drunk bozo who'd make it clear he was "taking one for the team" by talking to me. I never knew if it was because I wasn't pretty enough, because I was too Asian, because I wasn't Asian enough, or because I lacked charm. I wasn't good at the bar: I couldn't think of flirtatious zingers over the blaring music (mostly rap, occasionally classic rock); I didn't know how to hold my body in any other position but ramrod straight; I didn't know how to execute a playful slap to a man's arm or toss a teasing smile over my shoulder. In short, I possessed exactly none of the feminine wiles.

Don't get me wrong: I was grateful. Nina didn't have to invite me out. Not that her friends exactly offered me a warm welcome. The second that Nina stepped away to the bathroom or to the bar to ask for a cup of water, the girls would turn away from me and talk amongst themselves. In those settings I was shy, painfully shy; I felt I had nothing meaningful to insert into the conversation. But then Nina would return with a crack about the frat boy trailing a piece of toilet paper underfoot and we'd all laugh, and I'd almost feel like I belonged again.

And where, reader, did Ed Farley factor into all this? By this point I felt a very strong pull toward him—it tugged inside my chest and made me feel dull and empty when he wasn't around. But it was stupid to be infatuated with your boss. At best, Ed regarded me as someone to talk to. Perhaps I fulfilled for him the joint role of nanny and therapist, just as I did for his wife. So I soldiered on, hoping that on one of those lonely nights on the Upper East Side I'd forget all about Ed and meet someone else.

* * *

And that would happen, on an unusually muggy night in late spring. Not at an Upper East Side bar but a club in the desolate stretch of the

West Twenties. DJ Stixx was spinning again at Twine, and Nina's connections got us onto the list. She insisted we go shopping in the Village for new outfits. "We're not going for fancy here," Nina had advised, "just something cheap and—"

"Cheerful?" I butted in. Nina shook her head.

"Cheap and slutty." As we flipped through the racks at Bang Bang, Nina asked, "So, like, what's the deal with Beth and Ed? I don't get it."

I never felt I could bullshit Nina. I admitted that at first I thought it was weird, too.

"No one in the neighborhood can figure those two out. They're the mystery of Carroll Gardens."

"He thinks she's brilliant," I said. At least I knew he *used* to. I suddenly became very engrossed in the clothes on the racks.

But Nina would not let up. "She could be fucking Einstein. But look at her. Would he still want to hop into bed with that?"

"Is that all that matters?" I looked up sharply. "So what if she doesn't want to play to the male gaze?" I couldn't believe I was aping the words of Beth's articles.

"Arright, arright, don't kill the messenger." Nina held her hands up. "I'm not saying it's not fucked up. I'm just saying it how it is."

I ran my fingers through the rows of bright polyester dresses. Their cheap fabric felt rough to the touch.

"Also, since when do you start talking like Beth? What, are you now her mini-me?"

I didn't answer. Then, perhaps to lighten the mood, she added, "Also, my cousin Rosie's been wanting to jump Ed Farley's bones since they were in tenth grade."

I took her comment as the peace offering it was and let out a little laugh.

Nina held up one of the dresses. It was short and bright red, made of a stretchy fabric. "This is so you."

I let out a *pshaw*. "It is so *not*."

"It *could* be," Nina said. "You'll never know until you try."

In the fitting room, the dress was so tight I couldn't breathe. The material clung to my entire body, revealing the flatness of my chest and my jutting hip bones.

"You look hot," Nina said.

"I look like an idiot," I said.

"Stop fishing, Jane," she said. "We can't all be waify like you." She examined her backside over her shoulder in the mirror. She was wearing the same dress in black, but it looked like it was actually built to fit her. "I figure I got a few more good years before this ass"—she gave her bottom a firm slap, and it didn't even jiggle—"turns fat and saggy like Ma's."

"Look who doesn't even *bother* to fish."

I laughed when I said it, but I was a little taken aback by how blatantly Nina admired her own form, almost *celebrating* it. Hannah would have said that Nina had too *much* of a healthy ego. The young women she hated most at church were the ones who held their heads up high and their shoulders back when they should have been hunched over, lowering their eyes modestly.

Nina raised a hand. "I think you look good. Bangable. So you're either blind or in denial. You think I look good, and I *know* I look good. So let's just be done with it already."

I gave myself another glance in the mirror. Would Ed think I looked hot? It was an awful thought, I knew, but the harsh lines of me in the dress were already softening.

I let out a feigned sigh. "*Fine.* I'll buy you yours if you buy me mine."

"Done and done."

Each of us $19.99 the poorer, we returned home to get ready for the night.

*　　*　　*

It was one thing to wear a stretch minidress—in fire-engine red—in the privacy of a fitting room. It was quite another to put it on knowing I was going to leave the house in it. Nina warned me not to bring a jacket so I wouldn't have to pay for coat check at the club. She also told me not to bring a bag unless I wanted it to get stolen, so my left breast was bumped up to a B thanks to the keys, MetroCard, driver's license, and two twenty-dollar bills I'd shoved into the cup of my bra.

Beth was reading in the living room when I made my way down the stairs. She must have caught the glint of red out of the corner of her eye, because she lowered her book and frowned. Forget making it to the street—maybe I wasn't even going to make it out of the house.

"Oh, *sweetie*," she said, shaking her head. "Are you leaving the house . . . like that?"

I wrapped my arms across my chest. "I'm meeting Nina."

She shifted her reading glasses to the top of her head, like a pair of pilot goggles. "I hope you're not dressed that way out of peer pressure." Sometimes Beth talked to me as if I were her fifth-grader daughter. "You don't need to pander to the male gaze." Wasn't the choice to wear whatever I wanted being an empowered female? "You are *not* an object of desire." For once I *wanted* to be. (Too bad the male gaze I'd hoped to elicit was out on his nightly five-mile run.) "Men think they can take advantage of attractive, impressionable young women like you."

Maybe compared to *you*. Immediately I chastised myself for being smug. But then I chastised myself for chastising myself. Who did Beth think she was, trying to craft me into a duplicate of herself, a "mini-me," as Nina had pointed out? And then I was out the door.

*   *   *

When we arrived at Twine, we cut to the front. The people behind us on line shot dirty looks; Nina shot an even dirtier look back. The bouncer—Nina's cousin's girlfriend's little brother—checked our names off a list and lifted the velvet rope to let us pass through.

The club was a large warehouse with three floors of different music. DJ Stixx was spinning on the first floor. The bass beat pounded in my eardrums. The strobe lights throbbed, making the crowds on the dance floor look like a series of snapshots. We fought our way to the bar and ordered drinks. I was now down to just one bill in my bra cup.

Nina gripped my arm. "Holy shit," she whispered, "there's Joey Cammareri."

Nina would occasionally mention Joey Cammareri, the guy that she, along with her whole gang of friends, had harbored crushes on since the seventh grade. His father owned Cammareri Stone Works.

He'd gone off to an art school in Rhode Island. Nina had heard from her mother, who'd heard from the cashier at Winn Discount, who'd heard from *his* mother, that Joey Cammareri was living in some converted barn in Vermont. He was walking toward us now. Unlike the other guys in the bar, with their slick clothes and wet-looking hair, Joey Cammareri wore a thin T-shirt with a faded print, paint-smeared jeans, and Converse sneakers. His tousled hair was ungelled. He wore a self-satisfied expression on his face that immediately put me off.

"Nina Scagliano. Long time no see," he said, addressing not her face but whatever it was behind her right ear—the row of top-shelf liquor bottles, the other female patrons—that seemed to catch his interest.

"Joey! Wow! It's been . . . years!" Nina almost dropped her pink drink. She'd mistakenly thought his gaze had been directed at her, checking her out.

"Actually, I go by J. now," he said.

"Right! Jay. My bad." Nina let out a nervous trill.

Joey—Jay—J.—surveyed the room again and rolled his eyes. "This your usual jam?"

"Wha—? Huh?" Nina turned strangely self-conscious. She tucked her neck in like a turtle and her fingers touched her right ear, as if she were trying to caress the droplets of his exhaled breath.

Joey Cammareri glanced over in my direction and gave me a half nod, like it wasn't worth the full effort. So I half nodded back.

"But I thought, 'cause I heard from my mom, that like . . ." As Nina sputtered, I kept willing her to return to proper form. To make a crack about how he looked as though he'd just fallen out of bed. But the Nina I thought I knew was shrinking fast.

When she squealed—a notch too eagerly—it caught the attention of Nina's other friends. They all turned around and began to smother Joey Cammareri in hugs, double kisses, and *omigawd!*'s. Angela, with her big boobs, chest-butted me to the periphery of their circle. Then Marie elbowed me out entirely. A goofy laugh—Nina—punctured the air. The group drifted to the dance floor.

I was still standing along the perimeter of the bar, three people deep. I suddenly became very engrossed with the red straw poking out of my glass of rum and Coke. Then, as the ice melted, I turned my attention to my shoes, then the shoes of all the other people in the club. Each time I glanced over to the group, Nina seemed to fall more and more out of character. As she swayed from side to side with the music, she kept tucking the tendrils of hair behind her ears, head cocked awkwardly, which only made her hair pitch forward again.

I was down to the last swirl of my second drink. The dress had done nothing to attract anyone's attention. I was debating whether to order another or just go home when a clean, soapy smell cut through the throng of sweet colognes and fruity shampoos and gels. Ed's smell. I entertained the briefest fantasy that he was here in this club and would whisk me away.

What's a girl like you doing in a place like this? Ed would say. We'd exchange a hearty laugh.

Unconsciously I had drifted toward that soap smell—it was coming off a guy leaning against the slate bar. From his sideways profile, he could have been Ed: same broad shoulders, same narrowing at the waist, same blondish hair and strong jaw. But when he turned around, his face was unlined, boyish, different. Ed had the look of a man who'd weathered his youth. He'd had a whole life before we ever met. I wondered whether he'd spent his twenties in Chelsea clubs or fratty Upper East Side bars? Would he have offered up a round of Flaming Dr Pepper shots to a gaggle of girls like Nina? To me? I turned my attention back to the guy. He was looking me up and down, the corners of his mouth lifting in something like approval.

You want something happen, you gotta make happen. I smiled back.

"You want me . . . to buy you a drink?" I said, my voice shaky. Nina was the kind of girl who could walk up to a guy and demand that he buy her a cosmo, but I wasn't.

I thought for a second the guy was going to laugh in my face. But then the corners of his mouth were curling up again. "Sure," he said. "But only if I can get your next one." I had just enough money left for our two drinks. I was glad I'd loaded my MetroCard before going out.

Over the blaring music, he told me his name was Evan (or something that sounded like Evan), and as he spoke, I let myself grow intoxicated on both my rum-and-Cokes and his smell, a smell that made me feel like I was back at the kitchen table with Ed. I looked over at Nina. She was dancing close to Joey, a boozy glaze in her eyes. By the way he refused to make eye contact with her, I could tell he wasn't that into her.

Evan was drawing closer to me. It was flattering—terribly flattering—the way he kept looking at me, and was now touching my arms and the small of my back. This was what being young and in your twenties was all about, wasn't it? Going out in tight dresses, getting drunk, and letting random guys feel you up.

Evan drew even closer and whispered in my ear. "You're real pretty, you know that?"

His words cut through the fog of my inebriation; I'd never been called pretty before. Girls like Jessica Bae were pretty. Mary, despite her yo-yoing pudginess, was cute and petite and had her fair share of boyfriends. But I was never considered attractive—people thought there was something a little too unfamiliarly *ish* about my features. Eunice had a name for me: "the uncanny valley," what Beth would've labeled as "the Other."

So all my crushes were invariably one-sided. At our high-school graduation party in the church basement, James Kim had showed up drunk. He'd sidled over to me and said, "No offense, Jane, but sometimes when I look at you, I feel . . ." His beer-laced breath coated my face, and my heart skipped a beat. He was going to tell me he thought I was pretty. He was going to confess he'd nursed a long-standing crush on me all those years, too. "I feel like I'm looking at something from *Willow*. Like, kinda human but not really."

As the blow of James Kim's words sank in, Eunice appeared at my side. "I believe the 'nonhuman' creature in *Willow* that you're referring to is the Eborsisk," she said, crunching her fingers into air quotes. "Actually, the Eborsisk is an inside joke that George Lucas—"

"Okay, whatever," James Kim said, and walked away.

"Ignore him, Jane," Eunice said after he'd left. "We'll deprogram all thoughts of these losers once we start college."

It was almost five years later, and she had learned to forget. But I could not.

Now Evan said those words, and suddenly I was placing my lips on top of his. "Well, hello!" he mumbled out of the side of his mouth before pushing his tongue against mine. He tasted of whiskey and breath mints. My nostrils were filled with that smell of soap. This was not the first time I'd ever kissed a guy (we'd played versions of spin the bottle at church retreats), but it was the first time I was actually enjoying it. His hands were again at the small of my back, pulling me closer to him, pressing me firmly against his growing hard-on. I could see myself going home with Evan and returning early the next morning to the Mazer-Farleys', no longer a virgin.

We drifted to the dance floor. Evan's hands were still all over me. Out of the corner of my eye, I saw that other couples had formed, all locked in some kind of embrace. DJ Stixx's music went *untz-untz-untz*. I didn't see Nina, but I did see Joey Cammareri, this time pressing up close to Angela.

Just as I was about to run my fingers over Evan's cheekbones, I spotted Nina. She had rejoined the group, and from where I stood, it looked like she was winding back, about to launch herself—literally— at Joey. She would've been humiliated, and her other friends seemed to lack the *nunchi* to intervene.

In the way that drunken nights like these tend to happen, time moved both quickly and impossibly slowly. I was extricating myself from Evan's mouth, wiping my own with the back of my hand. He might or might not have been reaching out for me, unwilling to let go. Soon I was pulling Nina's arm, drawing her away from Joey Cammareri. "Time t'go," I said. My words were sluggish. "Leggo! Leeme-lone." *Her* words were sluggish. She fell backward, and I righted her in slow motion. I somehow managed to wrestle her from the group, Evan and the club fell away, and Nina and I were once again on the train home.

"I was having fun back there," Nina said, drifting out of the fog of her drunken stupor just long enough to form a coherent sentence.

I touched my lips, remembering the sheer pleasure of kissing Evan. My ears still rang from the music of the club. "You weren't the only one."

"Then why'd you drag us out?" She slumped down, her legs spreading apart, oblivious to the middle-aged man across from us, who'd just perked up in his seat.

I slapped her legs shut. "You were acting like a fool."

"Thanks, *Mom*," she said. "Dint I tell you Joey Cammareri's mad cute? Hewuzlike *totally* inta me." Nina was slurring again, as she seemed to lose focus on reality.

"He was, like, totally into everybody," I said, but Nina was already fading out. Her eyelids drooped.

We were starting to attract attention in the almost empty train car. The man across from us had his hand in his pocket. My eyes caught a jerking motion; I dared not lower them. Two other men at the far ends were sliding across the benches toward us. Nina leaned her head back and started dozing, while I was conscious of the pack of eyes drinking us in. I folded my arms tightly over my chest. I kept blinking and pinching the skin of my forearms, willing myself not to pass out. *You don't need to pander to the male gaze.* Well, here we were, on full display. So desperate had I been for male attention. But right now it felt as cheap as the dress.

*   *   *

After I dropped Nina off at home, I walked back to the Mazer-Farleys'. Light beamed out through the bay window. Beth was probably still up. I knew what she'd be thinking when she saw me: *Told you so.* I fished the key out of my bra. If I could ease open the door slowly, quietly, perhaps I could avoid detection—

But the door swung open, and the hallway light switched on. I blinked rapidly, my eyes adjusting to the sudden brightness. Ed.

"Now, *that's* not what you were wearing earlier today," he said, taking off his reading glasses.

I couldn't tell if it pleased him or not. I crossed my arms over my chest again. "S'Nina's."

Ed laughed. Was I slurring? Swaying? "Sounds like you had a good time. Go sit down. I'll get you some water."

He returned with a large glass of water and a plate of toast. "To soak up the alcohol," he explained.

I took both from him gratefully.

He sat on the floor by my feet. "So . . . you have fun tonight?"

Toast was crammed in my mouth. "Wuzzatta club."

"A club, huh? I remember those days." Ed looked into the distance, as if a wave of nostalgia were washing over him. "How many hearts you break?"

I flashed back to earlier—Evan's hot breath at the nape of my neck. The whole night was designed around this stupid dress. I hated my naïveté, my stench of desperation.

My face crumpled. "I'm so . . ." *Ashamed.*

"Hey, what happened?" Ed's voice went soft, and he moved to the wicker love seat and put an arm around me.

I wiped away my tears. Apparently I was a sad drunk. "Sorry, I'm stupid."

"No you're not. You're not at all," he said, stroking my back.

"It's just, every day of my life I feel . . ." *Mot-nan. Bad-born.* The word didn't translate.

Ed must have filled in my words. "Nobody thinks that." Ed smoothed my hair. "You know what I see when I look at you? I see a beautiful young woman."

No one had ever called me beautiful before. Earlier that night Evan had called me pretty, but all he saw was an easy girl in a tight, low-cut, crimson dress. I felt like an acquired taste: a raw fish, a funky cheese.

"If I were your age, I'd be too intimidated to talk to you," he said. "You'd be way out of my league. You've got this beautiful dark hair and those dark eyes. . . ."

I stared across the room, at the hooded bay window that looked out onto the street. The rest of the family was just upstairs, yet in that moment they seemed so far away.

Ed inched closer, running his fingers over my cheek and tucking strands of hair behind my ears. I grew self-conscious; I could still feel Evan's dried saliva along the perimeter of my mouth.

And suddenly Ed was pulling away. "Good night, Jane." His tone had gone chilly. He bit his lip. Abruptly he left me.

What had I done to turn him off? Maybe Ed had smelled the other man on me and thought I was a slut.

Rejection has a numbing quality. I sat like that in the wicker love seat for a minute, an hour, I couldn't tell you how long.

And then it was dawn. The morning sun slivered through the windows. I'd been dozing on the couch, covered in an itchy woolen blanket. Someone had draped it over me while I was passed out. I stole away upstairs before the family could stir from their beds.

Chapter 10

Windows on the World

A little later that morning, I awoke from a rum-and-Coke-induced haze—in my own bed—to the sound of the upstairs telephone ringing. I tripped from the tangle of sheets and out the door. When I picked up, a familiar voice blasted through the receiver.

"You come home right now. Grandpa coming from Korea. Not look good, you living outside house."

I tried to hide the sleepy mumble from my voice. "I have a *job*, Uncle. With *responsibilities*."

"What exactly you do all day?"

I launched into a vigorous explanation of Devon's rigorous schedule. Chinese school. Art lessons. Violin lessons. *Tutoring* sessions for the Hunter—

"You not say your bosses professors? They not have vacation right now?" Sang interrupted. "Why they need three people watching only one child? Should be other way around. Grandfather arriving Friday. You be home before then," he ordered, and hung up.

Later that afternoon, once I'd showered off the remains of last night that still clung to my body (making sure to scrub my mouth especially with extra force), Beth knocked on my door. "Ed and I were talking," she said, sinking onto my bed and patting the seat beside her. "And I realized we haven't exactly been the most benevolent of employers. You haven't taken vacation or *anything* since you started."

I sat. Usually we sat across from each other. This was the first time we were sitting side by side. "That's okay. I don't need one."

"Actually, it was Ed's idea. Typical of me. I'm in a daze from everything with the department and my book. . . ."

First last night's rejection. Now Ed wanted me out of his house. It was as if all those late-night heroes had meant nothing to him.

"Also, it sounds like your grandfather's coming to town, and you're expected home on Friday?"

"You overheard that?" I hoped that was the only other conversation she'd heard echoing throughout the house.

"So I thought, perfect! The timing is just *perfect*," Beth said. "I'll have just finished off edits to my next chapter by then and will need a break before diving back in, so your absence won't be a problem. Take the week off and return home to your family. I mean, we'll still pay you and everything."

Then she lowered her voice. "Actually, I was kind of hoping to . . . you know, rekindle things with Ed." A strange almost girlish grin spread over Beth's face. The way I'd imagined Ed's female students smiling up at him as he stood in front of the classroom.

On the one hand, Beth was still clueless. I breathed a sigh of relief. But on the other, my heart *burned* at the thought of her doing anything with Ed. I chastised myself anew. As if I had any claims on him. *He's not yours, Jane.*

And so it was decided—whether I liked it or not. I would leave for 718 Gates Street and bid 646 Thorn, and Ed Farley, a temporary farewell.

Ed was stiff in the days leading up to my departure. His earlier kindnesses, his continued thawing, had reversed. If anything, there was a coldness in his movements and gestures toward me. Needless to say, there were no heroes consumed in the middle of the night. On the day I was to leave, I had packed my bag, ready to take the subway back to Queens, when Beth volunteered Ed to drive me home.

He looked put out by Beth's offer, and I told her I didn't need the ride.

But Beth insisted. "You've got a heavy bag and everything." Devon clutched me and made me promise I'd return. Then Ed and I set off. And indeed we spent an awkward, uncomfortably silent ride whisking down the BQE, the Manhattan skyline blooming before receding from view.

We turned off Northern and pulled up in front of Sang's house. Ed cut the engine. He nodded in the direction of my hand, which was still gripping the handle of the door. "Dying to see your old gramps, huh?"

I loosened my grip. "I don't know how I'll make it through the week," I found myself saying. *Without you*, I added silently. I could not keep my eyes from tracing over his face, trying to commit his features to memory.

"Well, if you need an SOS . . ." He trailed off. His tone resumed its distance. "I'll help you carry your bag inside."

Sang answered the door. In their brief exchange, my uncle did not feign politeness the way he did with even the most disgruntled customers at the store. Instead he was gruff, treating Ed with the same dismissiveness he adopted when regarding the sales reps that came to Food.

After Ed shook my uncle's hand good-bye and left, Sang said, "I thought old lady who come to Food your boss."

"She is," I said. "That's her husband."

"*Husband!*" He worked his jaw, attempting to right his face. In a smoother tone, he went on. "You get call from Lowood Company. Sounding like they want you back." He held out a scrap receipt with a phone number jotted on the back.

I took the paper from him. "What you waiting for? Hurry up, you call! Before they changing mind about you again."

My uncle watched as I punched in the phone number. He listened as I left a voice message. Just as he would watch and listen when Lowood called back, asking me to come in again. I would go through the motions in front of Sang. Last summer—last fall, even—I would have died to work at Lowood. It would have been my ticket out of Flushing. But that was before Ed Farley.

* * *

The whole family stuffed themselves into Sang's station wagon to meet Re Myungsun at JFK. When my grandfather stepped through the gates, we formed a procession to greet him, bowing one after the other like dominoes falling in his wake. My grandfather wore a dark suit. He had a slight build, shriveled with age. His jaw was perpetually clenched, his eyes shone with disapproval, and his silver hair swept smugly across his forehead. To Sang he said, in Korean, *"You've aged."* He said the same to Hannah, but he didn't linger to see her displeasure. He gave George's fleshy shoulder a severe squeeze and said, *"You alone carry the family name."* He softened when he got to Mary, touched the air next to her cheek and said, *"You got prettier. Round-faced, like a lotus blossom."* And when he reached me, the last in the line, he offered the perfunctory, *"You came."* It was a standard enough greeting in Korean, but after my time living with the Mazer-Farleys where each member's comings and goings were met with much fanfare, the words felt distancing.

Over the course of the week, we were expected to wait on Re Myungsun hand and foot. He, for his part, seemed to appreciate none of these efforts and pointed only to our flaws. When we returned to the house and Hannah had tea and sliced fruit waiting for him, he complained of the tea's tepidness. Sang apologized for her carelessness. Re Myungsun complained about the humble furnishings, the threadbare slippers he was offered, the loud rumblings of buses drifting through the windows from Northern Boulevard. When George pounded away on his computer game, Re Myungsun complained about how Hannah's unhealthy cooking had let the boy expand to unruly dimensions.

Sang left Hwan in charge at the store so he could take his father to the Statue of Liberty, on a Circle Line cruise, and on a horse-drawn carriage ride in Central Park. Yet another steady stream of criticisms emerged from Re Myungsun's lips: This ferry ride was too slow—they should market an express route. This carriage smelled like a pigpen. This hotdog was too greasy—no wonder the American people were so fat. With every such comment, a look of exhaustion would flood over Sang's face. It almost made me feel sorry for him.

When Re Myungsun was out of earshot, Hannah said her father-in-law was no better than a baby who could neither wipe nor feed himself. It was a rare moment when Hannah took me into her confidence. "*I never understood why my friends complained when their relatives came to visit. But now I do. They come here thinking they can just sit back and relax, like kings. Everything fancy-fancy, so they can go show off back home. Like they think we don't have businesses to run or bills to pay?*"

In the days away from Thorn Street, everything I learned at the Mazer-Farley household began to disappear. And yet, back at Gates Street, there was a hitch to my herky-jerky movements, as I'd stop myself from asking a *nunchi*-less question while helping out in the kitchen or slicing fruit without peeling it first. Shedding newly acquired customs and reassimilating to a former way of life is a painful transition. I could not beat against the forceful current of Sang and Hannah's ways, and as the days passed, I had no choice but to acquiesce—borne back to the rhythms of the past.

Each restless night under Sang's roof, I endured Mary's snores and the sounds of the house settling uneasily into place. I remembered my first night at Thorn, tossing and turning as I heard the springs in their master bedroom squeak and creak. *I'm hoping to rekindle things with Ed. Beth . . . is brilliant.* I ached with jealousy. I would return to Brooklyn only to find I'd become nothing to Ed.

In those small hours of the night, whenever some particular memory of Ed would flare up—the way he'd smiled at me at McDonald's or how he'd tucked my hair back from my face the night after Twine— I'd force some corresponding memory to override it: Ed stroking Beth's back, the look they'd exchange across the breakfast table in the early days, those damn bedsprings. On the chart I'd created in my mind, Beth clearly ranked so much higher than me:

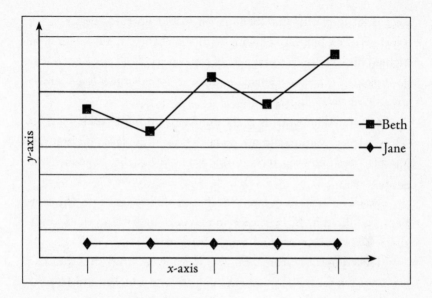

As if I stood a chance.

Falling in love with Ed Farley had not been part of the plan. But, reader! I did. Try as I might, I could not stop my feelings. And never had I loved him so well.

* * *

Because (according to Hannah) Re Myungsun was expecting fancy-fancy, Sang took the family to dinner at Windows on the World. I thought for sure my grandfather would be impressed, as everyone at church had been. Even Nina had remarked, "Look at you, all high class," when I'd mentioned it to her. (While Beth and Devon checked in just once in my absence, and I had no communication with Ed, Nina and I spoke on the phone almost every night.)

We drove into the city, traffic all the way. When we stood at the foot of the Twin Towers, Hannah pointed up to the buildings. *"Father-in-Law, isn't this amazing? Sometimes I can't believe man can build something like this."*

Re Myungsun said, *"How can you compare anything man-made to the pure beauty of nature? This will never be as amazing as Kumgang Mountain."* His tone was oddly philosophical, his expression uncharacteristically placid. But then, as we soared up the elevator of the North Tower, our ears popping with the change in air pressure, he righted his voice to its usual note of superiority. "*And anyway, Sinnara Incorporated is breaking ground for a skyscraper that will be even taller than your twin buildings.*"

Sang stared impatiently at the numbers lighting up each floor: *80, 81, 82.* The elevator could not go fast enough. He faced me and said sharply, "Isn't Lowood office inside here? What they say when you calling them?"

I was scheduled to go into the office the following week. The company had lifted its hiring freeze and was calling back previous candidates. But I had already told Sang that.

I looked over at George. He was wearing a T-shirt that read EAT MY SHORTS. Yet no one said anything to him. I looked at Mary. As usual, her clothes were two sizes too tight. She'd once managed to squeeze into a size zero after a week on a cabbage-soup diet. The next week her body rebounded, but she'd been in denial ever since, and no one said anything to her either.

The hostess greeted us when we finally arrived up at the restaurant. We must have seemed like a ragtag bunch in her eyes—George's and Mary's clothes, Sang's creased work trousers, Re Myungsun's sour expression. "How are you folks this evening?" she said, leading the way to our table. She was probably new. I could tell by the way she nervously gripped the stack of menus. Sang's and Hannah's eyes crinkled into smiles, but they didn't speak—they grew shy around unfamiliar American people. Then she looked up expectantly at Re Myungsun. But he did not answer either. I couldn't see his expression just then, but I knew exactly what face was staring back at her—cold, unfeeling, dismissive.

Suddenly she dropped her menus—they scattered across the floor. "I'm so sorry!" she said, falling to her knees to scoop them up. "I'm so sorry, it's my first day." She spoke with a flat, nasal tone. It was clear she wasn't from around here.

Just then a man across the room—her boss, presumably—gestured at her with a curled finger. *See me.* I hoped she wasn't going to be fired.

At the table Sang and Hannah insisted Re Myungsun take the seat with the best view. As he lowered himself into his chair, he grunted with displeasure. *"Doesn't this place have private rooms?"*

Hannah caught my eye and shook her head with exasperation.

"Father, enjoy the openness," Sang said. *"Closed rooms are* tap-tap-hae."

Sang ordered the filet mignon for his father and chicken for the rest of us. There were six of us and only five entrées; Hannah and I were to share. My ears were consumed with the sounds of the family eating. I watched Sang crunch down on a piece of baguette with his front teeth, chicken and potato gratin stuffed into each cheek. Eventually he swallowed the chicken-potato pulp, and the mashed baguette slid into the newly vacated space. That was how he always ate: transforming his mouth into an assembly line, the way we rushed deliveries off the truck and into the store.

Mary kept touching the tines of her fork to her mouth in thought, as schoolgirls did with pencils. She ate with her lips smacking together, her tongue shuttling food from side to side, pausing occasionally to dip into the pool of saliva. *Chyap-chyap.* It was a recently acquired habit, something she must have picked up in those Barnard dining halls. She thought it made her look cute.

Hannah scraped the bones—cartilage, too—of our joint chicken clean. When she saw I hadn't touched my pile of meat, she forklifted it onto her son's plate. George's eyes went blank as he shoved the chicken into his mouth. All the while Re Myungsun groused about his oily vegetables, his tough steak. To the other diners, we must have looked like *chonnom*—country bumpkins.

Just when I thought the meal could not get any more *tap-tap-hae,* Re Myungsun stopped chewing his subpar steak and said to me, *"You look different from when you were a child. Your poor Emo. The looks people gave her when she took you out."*

"My Emo?"

Emo was Sang and my mother's younger sister, their junior by
more than a decade. My cousins and I had never met her, and it must
have been more than thirty years since the last time Sang had seen his
baby sister. After Sang immigrated to the States, he never went back.

But Re Myungsun was studying me again, with the same scrutiny
with which he'd examined his dinner plate. "*But you look more Korean
now. How fortunate.*"

When I didn't say anything, Hannah nudged me. "*Say thank you,*"
she whispered.

But instead of forcing my head into a bow of thanks, I asked, in my
tentative Korean, "*Why fortunate?*"

Re Myungsun had the put-out expression of someone who was
trying to offer a compliment. "*A Korean person should look Korean.*"

Sang put down his fork and knife and shot me a look: *nunchi.*

I proceeded all the same. "*So that making me Korean now?*"

Re Myungsun was shaking his head. "*Your character must take after
your father,*" as though they were a binary—everything my mother was
not, my father must have been.

"*But what about—*" I ventured haltingly.

Sang shut me down with a sharp look.

Hannah shut me down with a sharp pinch to the leg.

—*my mother?* was all I had wanted to ask.

* * *

After the dismal meal, we dropped Re Myungsun on Thirty-second
and Broadway, where he was meeting a friend for a drink. One of us
was to return to the city to pick him up after he was done. On the
drive back to Flushing, Mary complained about our grandfather's
comment on her round face. Hannah pointed out that it was a compliment: she had the kind of classic face Koreans preferred. "That's
not what my friends from Seoul say," Mary retorted bitterly. Her
chubby cheeks had a rosy tint. She had big eyes that were reduced to
slivered moons when she smiled. It was a face more cute than beautiful. Hannah told her daughter to spend less time worrying about her
face and more time worrying about her body. Then George, who sat in

the passenger seat, turned the radio on to Hot 97 and mouthed along with the rapping. Sang yelled over the music to Mary, "You stop picking on Grandpa!" He took hold of the dial and switched it to AM 1010 WINS News. The view of the abandoned warehouses and the swamp and Shea and the U-Haul clock tower came rushing at us. We were almost home.

* * *

I was still thinking about what my grandfather had said to me when it came time to pick him up from the city. Hannah handed me the car keys. *"You drive for your uncle,"* she said. *"Look how tired he looks."* Sang and I piled into the car. We drove for those first few minutes with only 1010 WINS humming in the background. I remembered something Beth had once suggested to me. "Why not open up more to your uncle?" she'd said, blowing the steam (and dust) from her cup of tea. "I suspect you've never actually tried to create an intimate environment conducive to conversation."

"Uncle, about dinner," I started, lowering the dial on the radio. "What was all that stuff Grandfather was talking about before?"

Sang was staring out the window, at the storefronts of Northern Boulevard rushing by. We looped onto the Van Wyck. "How I suppose to know?"

"You know . . . about Emo. Taking me around and . . ." *The looks people gave her.* I couldn't bring myself to say the words.

Sang spoke. "Who else you think care for you before you coming to America? Your mother?"

That shut me up quick.

When we approached the entrance ramp to the LIE, he said, "Exit over there! Don't miss!"

"I *know,* Uncle. I've only been down this road my whole life." I hadn't meant to slip into sarcasm, but I hated driving with Sang—he was a constant backseat driver. After I steered us onto the expressway, we lapsed back into silence.

I broke the silence. "So you know, my bosses? They think you and I should talk about our feel—"

"What Lowood say?" he interrupted. "They gonna give your job back?"

"I already *told* you what they said." My frustration was mounting. "For once I wish you'd stop interrupting me. I'm *trying* to have a conversation with you."

"What Uncle say about sharing private family problems to outside world?"

"I wasn't *sharing* our—"

"Uncle try to understand," he interrupted, his voice softening into his rare "let's compromise" tone. "New experience for you, living American people. Such fun time! But now fun time over. Now time for you coming home."

"I'm not leaving my job," I said.

Sang raised the volume on the radio. *All news, all the time. Traffic and transit on the ones.* Two lanes closed for construction on the BQE eastbound. Congestion on the upper and lower levels of the Fifty-ninth Street Bridge westbound. Overturned tractor-trailer on the Triborough. Traffic steady westbound through the Midtown Tunnel.

"Greenpoint! Greenpoint!" Sang pointed at the fast-approaching exit ramp. As it flashed from windshield to rearview mirror, he shouted, "What's wrong you, why you not pay attention? Go right lane. Not too late. Still you can get out Van Dam, last exit." Sang hated the Midtown Tunnel. He preferred the Fifty-ninth Street Bridge, because it had no tolls.

I pointed at the radio. "Didn't you hear? They said there's traffic on the bridge."

"But Fifty-nine Street still the better way!"

"Why do you always have to yell at me?" I said.

Sang winced. I realized that my tone had taken on a Mary-like whine. "Because you going stupid way, is why!"

"You know, you could learn a thing or two from my boss. He's not like you: all criticisms, all the time. He actually *compliments* me once in a while."

I did and didn't know why I excluded Beth from my comment.

Sang chuffed. "What Uncle always telling you? Beware people giving compliments free, like water. Even *water* not free." He pointed again to the next exit. "Get in right lane, I say!"

All my life Sang barked the orders and I obeyed them. All my life I'd been expected to put aside my opinions and desires in favor of his. I felt a roiling rage—*han*—building up inside me.

I stepped harder on the accelerator. "I'm taking the Midtown Tunnel." And there was nothing he could do about it.

At the entrance to the tunnel, Sang muttered, "*Tap-tap-hae.*" He was right. The very air of the car was thick with an uncomfortable, constricting tension. Sang kept rubbing his chest—holding back an explosion of rage, I knew—and he squeezed his eyes shut. The tunnel lights flashed a sickening shade of yellow inside the car. We did not speak a word.

When we emerged on the other side, Sang barked, "Pull over." He bolted from the car—he was that furious with me—and doubled over to catch his breath, hands clenching his knees, his face white with anger.

When he regained his breathing and returned to the car, his lips made a tight, stern line. More and more he was coming to resemble Re Myungsun. He motioned for me to get out of the driver's side with a jerk of his head.

"Starting tomorrow you listening me," Sang said as he settled behind the wheel, the car still in park. "Even if Lowood reject you again, don't matter. You gonna stay home. You not going back that family."

I loosened my grip on the handle of the car door. I set my jaw. Each time I took a step forward, Sang was there to drag me back—a push-and-pull as jerky as the 7 train.

"I'm old enough to make my own decisions," I said, "and I'm *not* coming back home."

Sang looked strangely nervous, as if he were treading somewhere he didn't wish to tread. "Uncle not trusting your boss."

"You don't trust *any* American person."

"He look at you funny way!" he finally burst out. "Uncle not liking it."

A defiant little thrill ran through me. So maybe Ed did feel something for me—and Sang had picked up on it. But I played dumb. "I don't know what you're talking about."

Sang went on. *"Nunchi-do umnya?"* Don't you have any *nunchi*?

It was a rhetorical question, so I didn't answer it.

We were still pulled off to the side of the road. The car was thick and stuffy. I pried open the passenger side door. Immediately the air, though filled with car exhaust, felt sweeter.

"Ya, Jane!" Sang shouted. "Where you going?"

"Tap-tap-hae."

"Come back here!"

I started walking away.

"Come back!"

I heard the car roaring to life, and Sang pulled up beside me.

"Fine." He was speaking in Korean. He took a hand off the steering wheel and sliced it through the air, as if to say, *Not my problem anymore. "Fine."*

He lingered for just a beat—maybe waiting for some apology I wasn't going to give.

"Tap-tap-hae," I repeated.

He spoke again. *"Eat well and live well,"* he said. And then he drove off.

Eat well and live well. The closest English equivalent would probably be "Have a nice life."

*   *   *

Sang's words continued to ring in my ears as I walked south. I had the vague idea that I'd return to 646 Thorn. I reached the foot of Manhattan; I could walk no more. I found a pay phone and with trembling fingers dialed the number to the Mazer-Farley phone. As soon as I heard Ed's voice on the other end of the line, it all felt right. He would come for me.

I didn't know the feeling of relief after returning home from an absence. I had only known what it was like to return to Gates Street after working at Food—the cold dread of being scolded at the dinner table. But once I stepped into his car, all the recent chilliness dissipated. We were back to the natural rapport of our late-night hero sessions. I was already home.

"That's so like you," Ed said as we left Manhattan and crossed the Brooklyn Bridge. "You get all the way to the tip of the city before calling for help."

"I thought I could make it back on my own. I didn't want to be a bother."

"Humph," he said, though his tone was light. "A typical Janian reply."

But instead of driving us back to 646 Thorn Street, Ed got off the bridge and pulled up to the Promenade. Through the windshield the Towers, pearl gray, loomed back at us. Their reflection glinted off the surface of the East River. He stopped the car. "I used to come out here a lot as a kid," Ed said. "Long after the whole house was asleep. I'd just stare across the water into the city."

Just like my view of Manhattan from the 7 train's windows. We sat like that for several moments, gazing at the downtown skyline—its rising and falling peaks.

"I just had dinner at Windows on the World," I finally said. "My grandfather didn't take to the steak."

"No one goes there for the food," Ed said. "You should've skipped it for the bar next door. Still a little B&T, but less overpriced." His accent, which he sometimes tempered around Beth, was now unleashed.

I tried to laugh, picturing Re Myungsun perched on a barstool sipping a cocktail, but all I could hear was, *You look more Korean now. How fortunate.* I bit my lip.

"Hey, what's wrong?"

I shook my head. "Just . . . nothing."

Ed leaned in closer. He stopped laughing. "What is it?"

All my life Sang had taught us that people on the outside didn't care about your problems. All my life I'd learned to keep everything bottled up. "I'm not used to . . . having 'conversations,'" I said. "That's not the way we did things back home." I struggled to maintain my composure. Once again I bit my trembling lip.

"Hey. *Hey,*" Ed said, his voice growing tender. "Forget everything your uncle said. You're with me now. You can tell me anything."

I decided to let go. I told. About my mother. About what she'd done with my father and what that made me. And how I saw what I was reflected back in the eyes of all of Flushing, as it was in my own grandfather's gaze. Ed listened attentively.

Then he spoke. About his own family. I was struck by the parallels: how his own Brooklyn-bred, Italian mother had fallen for his father, an Irish kid from the Bronx. How her conservative immigrant parents would have kicked her out if she weren't already pregnant with Ed's sister, Frankie. How Frankie and his brother, Enzo—"short for Lorenzo Farley—talk about an identity crisis"—took after their mother. She was a woman with "beautiful dark hair and dark eyes." But only Ed came out "the fair, freckle-faced freak."

It was a new sensation to have a man opening up to me. The men back home never talked about their feelings; they spoke in only the briefest, most perfunctory of phrases.

"Jane, you can't let all that stuff define you or you'll end up a cripple," Ed said. "Believe me, I went through a whole slew of identity crises. Thankfully, there's no photographic evidence." We laughed. "Finally, I just said, fuck 'em. There comes a time where you just got to be who *you* want to be."

He leaned in closer still. "You have no idea, Jane, how much I've struggled this week. How much I've missed you. I feel—" Ed broke from me, a blush blooming over his cheeks. "God help me, Jane! You've reduced me to a blithering schoolboy."

"Keep it together, Farley," I ventured tentatively. A year ago—six months ago, even—I never would have attempted a joke like that.

Ed hesitated for a second, then burst into peals of laughter: sonorous, booming, sincere. "See, Jane? You just . . . get it. I haven't felt this way around anyone in . . ." He qualified himself. "In ever, actually." His hands, trembling, were reaching for me.

There was a sliver of a window—three seconds tops—when I could have stopped it all. I could have shifted, glancing into the rearview mirror to check my reflection, or leaned down to pick off an imaginary ball of lint from my shirt. In those three seconds, I could have salvaged the thin shreds of Ed and Beth's marriage, the thin shreds of my dignity. I could have, I should have—but I did not.

I touched Ed's face. I could feel the rush of blood pulsing beneath.

As his mouth met mine, twin warnings fired off in my head: *Nunchi-do umnya?* And from the recesses of my memory: *Do you want to end up like your mother?*

"I can't help what I feel, Jane," he said. "I love you."

Loving Ed Farley hadn't been part of my plan either, but I couldn't help it. I repeated the words back to him.

Then, ignoring those nagging voices inside me, I reached in for more. Sometimes you just had to shut off your brain and do what felt right. Reader—it was delicious.

Chapter 11

All In

I've always felt a certain wistfulness wash over me around late summer. It was the time of year when the oppressive early-August heat would taper off and by dusk a pleasing warm breeze would sweep in with the smell of cooling asphalt. The air itself tingled with possibility—a quiet possibility, more mature than the hot passion of early summer. It was the time of year I always associated with romantic love; it was when I ached most from whichever unreciprocated schoolgirl crush I'd harbored.

But this time things were different. It felt like I was finally privy to all that possibility. A giddy energy suffused the atmosphere. That summer I no longer had reason to feel wistful. Ed and I were continuing to spend our nights in the kitchen; after that night on the Promenade, our connection grew all the more deep. (I did not end up going into Lowood's office for my meeting. I ignored the voice inside that wanted me to take this seriously—but why would I do anything that might take me away from him?) I carried myself with my head held a little higher, my shoulders a little straighter. I had the gait of a woman who loved—and was loved back.

I dreaded the approach of fall.

But time ticks on, and soon it was September. The skies were cloudless and blue; the air had a newfound crispness. And Beth was leaving us, though only for a long weekend—she'd gotten a last-minute request to fill in at a conference at Stanford. "I wasn't even Sam's first choice," she complained over breakfast on the morning of her departure. "I don't know whether to feel flattered or offended."

"When's your return flight get in again?" Ed asked. I could tell he was trying to make his voice sound casual.

"Next Tuesday night. It's taped up there on the fridge."

"Sorry, Bethie. Just making sure. I'll be there to pick you up."

Beth nodded as though she expected nothing less. She reached across the table for the teapot. Over her head Ed caught my eye—her absence would mean more time for us.

Devon was beseeching her mother again about a sleepover at Alla's. "But, Ma, it's her birthday!"

"I already told you, Devon. The answer is no. Monday's a school night. Now, drink your wheatgrass."

Devon sat back in her chair and crossed her arms. She did not touch her wheatgrass.

Something in Beth's face softened. Not to the point where she was going to give in, but there was still something conciliatory about her expression. "How about one of our stories?"

Devon did not answer.

"There once lived a smart—and beautiful"—her tone was placating—"woman named Mei Lin."

Devon was getting too old for stories. Once a mainstay of the Mazer-Farley breakfasts, they had petered out over the course of the year. She was getting too old for a lot of things. The other day when Beth had tried to give her a hug and a kiss before leaving for work, Devon said, *"Ma-a-a,"* squirming away from her mother.

Beth smiled nervously at her daughter's failure to engage. She turned to her husband. "Ah, the old women's-studies conference," she said. "Remember? Where we met all those years back?"

Ed gave a faint nod.

Beth turned to Devon. "Did you know, sweetie, that your father—not to toot my own horn, but . . . he had something of a crush on me. He rushed the podium, blithering like a schoolboy, after I presented a paper on—"

"'Who Let the Madwoman Out?: Bertha Mason and Nineteenth-Century (Mis)Constructs of Female Hysteria, Madness, and the Vagina Dentata.'" Ed was dismissive. Beth gave him a steely look and resumed eating her oatmeal.

Yet Beth's anxious energy consumed the room, sucking out all the air. Perhaps if she kept her cool, she would have succeeded in reeling her daughter back in. But Beth was too effortful to be cool.

"So have you decided on a gift for Alla?" she asked Devon. The renewed mention of the birthday made Devon's face pucker. Beth, oblivious, went on. "How about a Backstreet Boys album?"

But Devon, under Alla's influence, had stopped being a fan of the Backstreet Boys more than six months ago. "They're *so* played out," Devon muttered into her oatmeal. When Beth pressed her about her new favorite band, she said, emphatically, "Evv-R-Blü."

"Ever Blue?" Beth repeated back. "I never heard of them."

Devon rolled her eyes.

It felt wrong. We were all rebelling against Beth, but we couldn't help it; her very presence was *tap-tap-hae*. When the taxi honked outside and whisked her away, all of us collectively breathed a sigh of relief. The truth was, we could not wait for Beth to be gone.

*   *   *

"So what're you going to do now that the cat's away?" Nina asked me during our usual foursome study session at Gino's. Ed had consented to letting Devon sleep over at Alla's, and the two girls were chattering about the upcoming party.

"Oh, you know," I said, trying to make my voice sound light and buoyant, the way Beth sometimes did. "Eat a bunch of Big Macs. Leave the wrappers conspicuously in the garbage." That actually wasn't so far from the truth. Devon's first request, immediately after Beth disappeared into her taxi, was, "Daddy, can we get McDonald's for dinner tonight?"

"You guys really know how to live it up," Nina said.

But there was something else, too, that was likely to happen in Beth's absence. In the kitchen the night before, with my feet hooked on the rungs of his chair, I had asked Ed point-blank, "Do you still love her?" Our conversation at breakfast and the self-assured way Beth had spoken—okay, gloated—about Ed's pursuit of her had disturbed me. It shook my confidence that *I* was Ed's and that I did not have to compete with her for his affections. Of course I was jealous of their history just as I was jealous of all the loves he might have had prior to me.

Ed had paused before answering, a pause that felt like hours, days. Then he said, "Honestly, Jane? I've been wrestling with this question myself for a long time. Beth wasn't like any of the other girls I knew from back home. You could say she was my Other. But I was only twenty-seven when we got married. The hell did I know back then? I think I was only in love with the idea of her. Not Beth herself."

He was starting to look uncomfortable, so I quipped, "Meanwhile I thought it was a shotgun wedding."

This time Ed's laugh was tinged with bitterness.

"Jane, Beth and I were never meant for each other. But you, Jane—you! You are my likeness. You're the one I want to be with." He ran his fingers through his boyish flop of hair; he grew strangely shy. "If that's what *you* want, too."

Of course that was what I wanted—that was all I wanted. The air between us was pulsing with tension, and it was obvious that at last Ed and I were going to have sex.

*   *   *

I longed to ask Nina about it—*it*. I knew that she, too, was a virgin, but she'd fooled around with a lot more guys—and had gotten further with them—than I had. But of course I couldn't tell her what was happening between Ed and me, and not just because I didn't want to betray Ed's confidence. I was scared to open up—it felt like saddling the other person with all your emotional baggage.

So I let Nina talk on—about her latest hookup with Joey Cammareri. There had been one drunken kiss, with tongue, in the back of a taxi. Nina was torturing herself with questions about what they were and where they stood. "He hasn't even asked me out on a date yet," she confided. "In fact, I've only seen him twice since that night at Twine."

"You think . . . maybe he's just not that into you?"

"You and your tough love, Jane." Nina sighed. "But I can't help it! He's so fucking hot. Speaking of which—what'd you end up doing about that guy *you* hooked up with that night?"

I looked over at Devon and Alla, who were similarly huddled, speaking in conspiratorial tones. I had told Nina that I'd found a cocktail napkin with a number scribbled on it the morning after. Either Evan or I must have drunkenly stuffed it in my bra.

"Eh, over it," I told her. "On to bigger and better."

Nina studied my face. "Okay. Well, enjoy your freedom. Things'll be quieter with your boss gone, that's for sure."

"That's one way of putting it," I said.

* * *

"I thought you'd want to wait till tomorrow night. You know, when—" Ed jerked his head, indicating Devon's room downstairs. We were on the fourth floor of the house, Beth's office, the only place in that whole huge brownstone where there'd be no risk of Devon walking in. Ed had spread a blanket and a sheet over the wood floor, with grooves that were filled with dust and grime.

I shook my head and leaned back on the sheet. There seemed no point in waiting. Sang had called me earlier that day, with the news that the whole family—myself included—was being summoned to Korea. "Grandpa dying. Not dead yet. We all flying out tonight." He did not address our fight on the other side of the Midtown Tunnel. It was as if the counter had started afresh. As my uncle rattled off the flight and hospital info, I listened absently. My uncle could tell.

"Why you not pay attention? This important!" he said.

"So's my work," I retorted. "I'm not going to pick up and leave just because you order me to."

Sang had sighed on the other end of the line. "Uncle leave your ticket open, in case you changing the mind." And with that he had hung up.

I'd already escaped what felt like the unbearable scrutiny of Flushing; what place did I have going back *there*?

"We don't have to do this if you're not ready," Ed said gently, reclining next to me and brushing his fingers across my cheekbones. He knew it was my first time.

I squeezed my eyes shut. "I'm ready. I want this."

He told me he loved me. Then, with some awkwardness, Ed peeled away my nightshirt. I shivered. I'd opted to wear a single garment for easier access (*nunchi*). He stripped himself of his soccer shorts and T-shirt and sidled up next to me. His bare chest instantly warmed mine, his fresh, clean smell cutting through the mustiness of Beth's office. His hands were on my hip bones; he squeezed them gently.

After the usual kissing, the usual stroking, Ed began inching down my body. I thought surely he would stop at my breasts, my belly button, but his head moved down farther still. I clamped my legs together. He said gently, "Relax." With his forehead he eased my legs apart. His bristled cheeks chafed the thin skin of my inner thighs. "I just want to warm you up," he murmured.

I ignored the tingles of sensation that radiated from below, because my ears were overwhelmed with sound. At first it sounded like Hannah's spoon dipping into a ceramic pot of *dwenjang* bean paste, met with a gelatinous resistance. I swear I caught a whiff of that rising fermented smell. I could hear Ed's tongue shuttling back and forth inside me, his saliva slapping the sides of my vaginal walls. *Chyap-chyap.* Shit, Mary. Now I couldn't help but picture *her* at the dinner table, licking the tip of her chopsticks in her cloyingly cutesy way, before sending her tongue lapping inside her mouth. The entire family threatened to intrude upon this moment of intimacy.

I felt bad for Ed down there. Should I reposition to ease the strain he was inevitably putting on his neck, his shoulders? Was he even enjoying this? Another panicked thought rose inside me: What if my period decided to come early? I pictured Ed's mouth covered in my blood, that faintly rancid, metallic taste. I wrapped my arms around my chest, covering my nipples, which were left out to harden in the cold chill of early September. The moonlight, streaming in through the high windows, laced shadows over Ed's back.

He resurfaced. He reached for the pile of discarded garments and fished a condom out of the pocket of his soccer shorts. Perhaps a more sensuous woman would have coyly offered to help him put it on, but not me. I couldn't bring myself to cast my eyes down there. I couldn't trust my trembling hands.

"Are you sure?" he asked again. I nodded, turning my face away from his—the smell of my vagina was emanating off him.

Ed's chest covered my whole body. I let myself run my fingers over his back, feeling his twitching muscles. He was *so* strong. An uncomfortable pressure—a finger? a penis?—teased the outside of my vagina. My whole body seized up. A certain stray odor wafted in the air. Lavender, onions. "Oh, God!" Ed cried out with pleasure. My bladder, which felt like it was being prodded inside and out, cried to be relieved. I didn't feel pain per se, but I certainly didn't feel what Ed was feeling. All I felt was an uncomfortable sensation—*tap-tap-hae.* I rubbed my chest, but the discomfort did not ease.

Ed, in push-up position on top of me, was gyrating his hips. He was still easing his way in. "You're so beautiful," he murmured. I heard the rude squelch of rubber. I kept ordering myself to relax. Then he let out another cry: "Oh, God!" This time it was a cry of panic.

Whatever feeling was starting to press inside me suddenly stopped. Ed slid away. He buried his head in the flat of my stomach. "I'm . . . sorry, Jane," he whispered. His cheek burned against my skin. He lifted his head, and in the dim light his face was red—with exertion? embarrassment? When I tried to caress his face, he brushed me away.

"What . . . happened?" I asked. I must have turned him off. I was overcome with waves of shame.

"I . . . can't," Ed said. He peeled himself off me. But as he cast a look down at me, still lying naked on the sheet in the middle of Beth's dusty office, he traced a finger down the front of my chest, as if he were marking a line in the sand or gently splitting me in two. It was that touch that would sear itself into my sensual memory, more than any of the other sensations of the night.

"You're so beautiful. I love you," he said, which only made me more confused. He picked the condom wrapper off the floor and hurried into his clothes before hastening away.

Reader, back then I was too inexperienced to understand what had just happened: Ed Farley could not keep it up.

* * *

Later, after I picked myself off Beth's floor and folded the dusty blanket and sheets, after I went to relieve my aching bladder and a single cloud of blood bloomed in the toilet water, after I showered and scrubbed the surface of my body with a rough cloth, I thought about what had happened with Ed. Had I blundered somehow? Had he wavered in his attraction toward me? *Just the tip*, I remembered hearing Nina and her friends once joke. Ed definitely dipped his toe in the waters, but how deep he had plunged I did not know, having nothing else to compare it to. Did that count? Wasn't it always all in or nothing—or was there such a thing as being half a virgin? Might as well toss that into the bin of other odds and ends: half Korean, half white, half orphan.

The next morning I awoke in my bed; the reality of what I'd done with my boss was slowly sinking in. What would Beth think of me? What would *Devon* think of me? I knew how Sang would react if he knew—*You only want fun time*—and could picture his blackening eyes, his flaring nostrils.

I rose. Showered again. Sat mechanically through breakfast, half listening to Devon's chatter about the sleepover that night, avoiding Ed's gaze across the table. I walked Devon to school, though she was getting too old for this, too. When I returned home, Ed was gone, but he'd left a note on my bed.

> *Dearest Jane:*
> *Let's start afresh. Will you meet me tonight? At 7pm for*
> *a drink at the Greatest Bar on Earth—yes, it's B&T, but*

*the view looks out to the Promenade. The very spot we
gazed out at that night. Afterward I've booked a room at the
Ash Hotel, on Hay at Church Street. This damn house is
charged with too many unsavory memories.*

I love you.
Ed

After I finished reading the note, the phone rang: it was Ed, calling from work to confirm, and to apologize, in veiled language, about the night before. "You okay?" he asked. Yes, I said, I'm okay. "Good. Love you," he whispered quickly into the phone. I repeated the words back to him. "See you tonight." He paused a beat, as if waiting for me to say something more, before he hung up.

The afternoon came and went. I picked Devon up from school and brought her home. We started on her homework. Her math, science, cultural studies, and literature textbooks and folders were piled high on her desk. Buried beneath all that were her Chinese-school worksheets. We made our way through the stack. But as we approached the bottom, Devon sighed. "Can't we just stop here?"

"No, you can't."

She got up from the desk and stretched her arms.

"Come on, Devon. The faster you finish this, the faster you can go to Alla's."

"It just feels kind of pointless." She sighed again, gesturing at the worksheets. "All the Chinese kids in my class say that stuff's all wrong, and nobody really talks like that. It's like I'm being forced to learn some old textbook version of Chinese."

"What are you talking about?"

"What's the point of learning all this when I should be learning how to speak the way *real* Chinese people speak?"

"Because your mom wants you to learn it."

"I don't care what my mom wants!" she burst out suddenly.

"Devon!"

She looked chagrined. "Sorry. But it's just . . . she makes me so frustrated! Like . . . like that stupid story we made up about my birth mother. I stopped believing it when I was a little kid. I only go along so I don't hurt her feelings. But I think she actually *believes* it. Mom's, like, so out of touch with reality."

"Since when did you start calling her 'Mom'?"

Devon ignored my comment. "For once I'd like to be around some- one who just gets the way the world *really* works. Like *you*."

My heart dropped.

"Your mom gets it, too, Devon." But I said it without conviction, and Devon knew it.

"I don't know how Dad puts up with it. It'd drive me totally crazy. Sometimes I just wish she'd leave us alone."

Devon had no idea that by this time tomorrow she would have her wish. Her family would never be the same again. Devon would have to choose between Beth and Ed, and it was all because of me—me in- dulging my feelings.

There was something about the way Devon was holding her face, creating a ridge between her eyebrows, that struck me as identical to an expression I'd seen on Beth. Mother and daughter, though they shared no actual genetics, were still mirror images of each other.

When we reached Alla's stoop, I folded Devon tightly into my arms. "Ja-ayne!" she said. Just as she was too old for fairy tales, Devon was getting too old for hugs. "Don't be too hard on your mom, okay?" I said.

She scrunched her pliable face into a ball. "Now *you're* acting like a weirdo," she said. "Oh, and Alla said her mom just surprised her with the new Evv-R-Blü album. She said she's going to lend it to me. Prom- ise me we'll listen to it when I get back?" She didn't wait for my re- sponse. "'Bye, Jane." She was buzzed in. I watched her disappear through the double doors.

I walked back to 646 Thorn Street. When I let myself in, Beth's voice was cutting out on the answering machine. After I unstrapped my bag and put down my keys, I played back her message. It was the usual string of commands, issued in her singsongy voice.

Take our vitamins and wheatgrass.

Water the aloe plants.

Fax over the results of Devon's cultural-studies quiz, so Beth could review her answers on the plane ride home.

I was about to hit DELETE when, almost as a postscript, Beth added, "Devon. Sweetie. I popped into a record store today, and guess what I bought? The newest album from Evv-R-Blü!" Beth overenunciated every syllable. "I know it'll be a day late, but you think Alla will like it? Hope so! Love you. Love you all."

But Alla already owned the new album. Beth would be more than a day late. But she'd tried.

I showered, for the second time that day, the third time in less than twenty-four hours. I packed a bag. I locked the front door behind me. From the sidewalk I looked up at the house. Its hooded bay window, framed in those thick crimson curtains, formed a single slit that stared out at me. From the street, you could not see the countless fissures breaking beneath the surface of this house.

I remembered how just earlier Devon's face had scrunched into that expression that was identical to her mother's. I thought back on all those talks with Ed. Over the course of those heroes, we had each alleviated the other's unhappiness in some small way. We were kindred spirits. I knew what I had to do.

I walked to the subway, descended to the platform, boarded the train, transferred to a bus, and bounced along with the other passengers.

Hours and hours later, as four planes took off from points along the Northeast Corridor, I was already flying west: away from a field in Stonycreek Township, the Pentagon, the Twin Towers.

PART II

Seoul

There will be time, there will be time
To prepare a face to meet the faces that
you meet.
—T. S. Eliot, "The Love Song of
J. Alfred Prufrock"

Chapter 12

9/12

I flew so far west I landed east, in Korea. My mother's homeland—
my homeland. I don't think I was fully aware of it as I crammed a
few articles of clothing into my backpack and hurried to JFK, but as I
tossed about in my too-upright seat on the flight over, it was painfully
clear: I had come back to atone. From Incheon Airport I would rush
to Gangnam Sinnara Hospital and present myself to my grandfather,
Sang sitting at his bedside. And I knew they would know. They'd
smell it radiating off me. I could still feel the burn of Ed's finger splitting me in two.

But on the other side of the custom gates, a thick, dark tension
coated the air. At first I thought it was just nervous energy, the collective aftermath of a long flight. The people in front of me stopped
abruptly in their tracks, muttering cries into their cell phones. Impatiently I weaved my way around them toward the exit. A crowd had
gathered in front of a TV monitor suspended from the ceiling. And
that was when I saw: against a clear blue sky, one of the Twin Towers
suddenly crashing in one fell swoop. It went *whoosh!*—disappearing
into ballooning clouds of ash, imploding, collapsing in on itself rather
than exploding outward, as if even in the midst of disaster it was des-
perately trying to observe *nunchi*.

What the F—

"Always inconveniencing!" I heard someone shout behind me.

It was Sang, wearing a rumpled black suit, his eyes bloodshot and pouchy with fatigue. He alighted from his spot with his usual harried gait. When he reached me, his tired eyes still mustered enough energy to flash a shiny black. "You! Why you not tell anybody where you go!" he said, gripping me by the shoulders. He whipped his head from me to the television. "Lowood," he uttered in a hoarse whisper. Lowood's offices had occupied the 103rd floor of the North Tower.

I blinked at the TV screen. The images were still not registering. "How did you know I was here?" I said dumbly.

"Uncle calling here, there. Nobody know! You alive, you not alive. Finally airline say you boarding flight Monday night. I guess you deciding listen your uncle." He tutted. Then he switched over to Korean, continuing in a more serious tone. *"Jane-ah. New York is like a war zone right now. We've been attacked by terrorists."*

My uncle explained about the four hijacked planes that had taken flight, two of which had crashed into the Towers. It had just happened, that morning, on the eleventh. My flight had left JFK the night of the tenth, and I touched down in Seoul before dawn on the twelfth. As I flew west, the day kept trailing behind me. I never experienced September 11; the day was lodged in a space-time vortex, hovering somewhere over the expanse of the Pacific Ocean. And here in Korea, 9/11 was literally yesterday's news.

In those early moments of disorientation, I could barely make sense of my uncle's words. My thoughts skittered in every direction. If I had taken that job at Lowood. If I had spent that night with Ed. *Ed.* He'd been down there—because of me. I had stood him up at the bar. Wasn't the hotel in the shadow of the Towers? What if it had collapsed on top of . . .

"Why you not pay attention?" Sang snapped me back to focus. "I say you make whole family worry about you."

"You heard from them! Is everybody okay?"

I realized my mistake. Sang, too. "That family worry, too. Uncle already call them."

"Uncle, please." I looked to the pay phones. "I need to speak to them."

He handed me a phone card. "Tell them you okay. Hurry up."

I punched in the numbers I knew by heart. I heard the foreign dial tone, then a click; someone picked up. "Mazer-Farley residence. Devon speaking."

There was an unfamiliar, grown-up tinge to her voice, as though she'd matured years in the span of half a day.

"Devon! It's Jane."

When she cried my name in response, her voice resumed its child-like tone. "Jane! Daddy and Ma are so worried! Your uncle's been calling like a million times." As Devon explained the sequence of events, starting with the first tower falling, her voice kept modulating: adult, child, adult, child. How my uncle had finally gotten through, demanding to know my whereabouts. But no one knew. How her father, coated in ash, had arrived at her school to take her home early. How they got back to the house to find Beth waiting for them—she'd caught an earlier flight and had arrived at dawn to an empty house. How Devon was relieved she wasn't going to get into trouble about attending Alla's sleepover. And finally—how my uncle had called to say he'd heard from the airline, who confirmed I'd boarded a flight to Seoul the night before.

"Where're your parents?" I demanded.

"Daddy just ran out to pick up some heroes for lunch." *Heroes.* "No one feels like cooking. Hang on, I'll put Ma on—"

"I . . . can't." Sang was gesturing for me to wrap it up, but that wasn't the real reason. "I have to go. My grandfather . . ."

"Your uncle said." Devon paused, then put on her mature voice. "My condolences to your family."

I had been too late. "Please tell your parents . . ." *I'm sorry for everything.* "I'm sorry for inconveniencing them."

"Jane, when are you coming back home?"

"As soon as I can," I murmured.

"Pinkie swear?"

"Pinkie swear." But I was lying as I said it. After what I'd done, I knew I could never set foot in the Mazer-Farley home again.

I hung up the phone. "I'm sorry. About Grandfather."

Sang tutted. "What you sorry for? You too late. We all too late." His usually impatient tone softened. "He die when Uncle flying in airplane."

The same night I was doing what I had done with Ed. My grandfather's death and my transgression in the attic—like two memories fused together.

"What wrong you? Why you look so suspicious?" Sang's everscanning eyes were reading me again; I must have been staring into space.

"Nothing." I snapped back to reality. "Uncle, you knew I was on this flight. And you left a message with all the hospital info. I could've found my way."

"Uncle not sure, maybe again something happen. . . ." He blinked, then cast his eyes upward, away from me. He stood like that, not speaking, for a few moments. Then he pointed to my backpack, voice shaking with irritation. "Why you not bring suitcase?"

If I had brought a suitcase, he probably would have said, in the same agitated tone, "Why you bring suitcase?"

He turned on his heel and clomped away from me, the thick, worn soles of his orthopedic shoes squelching against the airport's polished floors. "Hurry up!" he called out. "Everybody waiting for you."

In the cab ride from the airport, I stared out the window, dawn rising over the sprawl of Seoul. Gray high-rises shot up all around us. They stood tall, erect, and smug, oblivious to the fact that halfway around the world their counterparts had come tumbling down, down, down.

* * *

The taxi pulled up in front of Sinnara Hospital, in the Gangnam district of Seoul. "I thought you said Grandfather already die—I mean, passed away," I said.

"Here Korea funeral home inside hospital," he said. "And everybody suppose to have sleepover here until we go cemetery."

The funeral home was a separate wing of the hospital. It looked like a catering hall, hosting multiple (grieving) parties. Six-foot-tall flower arrangements bearing calligraphied messages of consolation framed the entrance to each private suite.

Sang pried off his shoes in the foyer, but I hesitated. "His body . . . is it in there?"

"They already take away. But you too late, like always." He jutted his chin in the opposite direction, indicating, *Over there.* "Go hurry up say hello Big Uncle and Emo. They still awake."

The suite consisted of several chambers. Sang led me to the dining room. A man and a woman were seated on the floor at a low table, speaking in hushed tones. I knew they were siblings of my mother and Sang. The man was Big Uncle, the eldest. Emo, my mother's sister, was the youngest of the four. "*Ga,*" Sang said. With a push of his hand, he launched me forward.

I greeted Big Uncle first, tucking my head into a bow. His cheeks were flushed red. "*You came,*" he said in Korean, pouring himself a drink from a small green *soju* bottle. Then I turned to Emo. Again I lowered my head. She shot up from her spot on the floor. At full height she reached my chin. Although she gazed up at me, her eyes did not feel intrusive but soft and almost gentle. I did not look away.

"*I have been waiting for you!*" she said. Or she could have meant "We" or "They" or "It." In Korean, subjects were often dropped, implied—the onus was on the listener to fill in the blanks.

I was not expecting Emo to take me by the shoulders and fold me so fiercely into her embrace. At first I held myself back, afraid to lean my full weight against her. But she held me tightly, her body fleshy and soft. It was as sturdy as Beth's first hug had been.

"*Look, Big Brother,*" Emo said. "*She grew up so beautiful! Just like her mother.*"

Beautiful. The only other person who had ever called me beautiful was Ed. The last time he said it to me, his face was hovering just inches above mine.

"*She looks nothing like her,*" Big Uncle said dismissively. He *hraaack*-ed a spit wad into a napkin. Then he jerked his head to the glass-doored refrigerator at the far end of the dining room and told Emo to bring over another bottle.

Emo had started toward it when Sang let out a *hssst!* of reproach. *"Jane, you go."*

"Yes, Uncle Number Two," I said. In the presence of his elder brother, Sang was relegated to second place.

As I made my way to the fridge, Big Uncle shouted, *"And grab another glass, too!"*

I placed the bottle and glass in front of Big Uncle, and he began to fill the second glass. *"Take a drink, Sangduk."*

Sang waved away the proffered glass. *"I'm exhausted. I'm going to bed."*

Emo nudged me toward the door. *"It's late. We should go to sleep, too."*

"Hssst!"

I turned around, but the hiss was not directed at me. Big Uncle was *hssst*-ing Sang. *"I said take the drink."*

Emo pushed me along. But when we reached the doorway, I saw that Sang was not following behind us. Instead he lowered himself to the floor and received the drink from his older brother.

Emo led me to the back room, where two figures—Hannah and Mary—were sleeping on the floor. Guided by the thinnest sliver of light peeking from under the closed door, I changed into a T-shirt and boxer shorts; Emo slipped into long johns. She had already made our floor bed, and she patted the mat. *"It's late, let's sleep."*

We slept. When I woke up at one point in the smallest hours of morning, I found Emo's head nestled in the crook of my shoulder. Her thick, stout arm was thrown over me. She smelled of fresh spittle and warmth.

* * *

The next morning I awoke to the sounds of people bustling about. The whole family was already up. Mary knelt down by my bed. She was dressed in a black two-piece *hanbok* dress with white trim. It strained across her bust, and the skirt's hem trailed the floor. A white ribbon was pinned in her hair. When we were little, she used to wake me up with a jab of her big toe to my ribs. Now she was touching my shoulder gently with her fingers.

"Jane," she said. "You're . . . okay, right?"

I sat up. She wasn't wearing her usual smirk. Instead she looked stricken. When I met her eye, she looked away. She tugged at her dress. Mary and I didn't really do corny moments—nothing about our family was touchy-feely. Quickly she tossed a packet of clothes onto my lap. After I folded away my blankets, I put on the black *hanbok* dress. The cold, cheap fabric—polyester masquerading as linen—chafed against my skin, a different kind of chafing from Ed's stubble grazing my thighs. The sleeves stopped short of my wrists, and the skirt's hem stopped above my ankles, exposing my socked feet. The dress was one-size-fits-all; neither Mary nor I was built for it.

* * *

I had missed most of the funeral. That morning the last of the mourners came to pay their respects to Re Myungsun's altar before we went to the cemetery. And what an altar! It was covered in long-stemmed flowers and lacquered plates of steamed meat, dried fish, sticky rice cakes, and pears and apples with their tops lopped off. Incense burned in a brass bowl. At the center of the altar was a framed portrait of Re Myungsun. His frown was forever memorialized in that photo; his beady eyes casting their displeasure across his funeral spread. Even in death nothing seemed good enough for Re Myungsun.

The mourners came and went. With each new arrival, Big Uncle and Emo let out a renewed cry or yelp of grief. Big Uncle's deep, rumbling shouts especially made a show. Tears spilled from the slits of his eyes. I had never seen a grown Korean man cry, and it was uncomfortable to witness. At some moments Emo would collapse to the floor, wailing, *"Father! Father!"* Her *hanbok* dress spilled out all around her, and she was lost in its many folds.

Their sobs made Sang's reserve seem all the more conspicuous. Unlike his siblings he sat straight in his chair: quiet, dry-eyed, and unmoving. Hannah was rubbing his back, yet his eyes remained fixed on the bowl of incense on the altar. One of the sticks was propped precariously in its bed of ash. It was tilting to the side, trailing a thin wisp of smoke. But my uncle did nothing to right its downward wake.

I lifted myself from the floor and walked to the altar. My hand stretched toward the brass bowl. But before I could right the falling stick, I felt a gentle pressure on my back; it was Emo's hand, and it had the dual effect of offering me comfort and forcing me into a bow. By the way her hand hiccupped on my back, I could tell that her tears had tapered off. Reluctantly I succumbed to the pressure, but as I bent forward, I refused to meet my dead grandfather's disapproving gaze. Try as I might, I could not muster the same sorrow for the man who had sent both my mother and me away.

Sang was equally unemotional as we drove to the cemetery. Out of the city limits, the high-rises gave way to empty stretches of what was once farmland, littered with the skeletons of new buildings.

When we arrived, we saw burial plots cut into the side of a mountain like terraces. We unloaded mats and the funeral food from the trunk of the car. With these in hand, we ascended the mountain to Re Myungsun's spot at the top.

The men driving the hearse had beaten us to the grave; my grandfather's coffin lay beside his dug-up rectangle of dirt. The men stood off to the side, smoking cigarettes and speaking in hushed tones. I watched as Sang knelt on the mat and bent over into a bow, while the men lowered Re Myungsun's coffin into the ground. Suddenly a muffled sob escaped my uncle's chest; it made an ugly sound, like a terrified cat. *Mrkgnao!* Sang clamped his hand to his mouth, rose, and with a sweeping sidestep he took refuge behind a tree.

It was just that one, sharp, quick cry before it was drowned by the sounds of the wind rushing at the empty branches—the cherry blossoms were long past their bloom. When Sang rejoined the group, he was dry-eyed. As he brushed off his wife's attempts to soothe him, I caught a glimpse of a man racked with pain. But I couldn't distinguish between his anger and his grief.

Chapter 13

Gangnam

Gangnam, whose name means literally "south of the river," is on the southern banks of the Han, the river that splits the city in two. The family apartment was in Building 404, Unit 1801, of a large complex called Gangnam Sinnara Apartments. The front door was operated by a digital keypad lock. When you punched in the number combo, the bell tone chirped a synth version of the folk song "Arirang," like a miniature karaoke machine.

According to Big Uncle, my grandfather had made a smart investment in the eighties—he bought a plot of undeveloped land in Gangnam right before the Gangnam market exploded. Everyone was scrambling to develop. Re Myungsun sold off a portion of his property and used the handsome profits to purchase more. And so on and so forth.

The first thing I noticed about the apartment was the floors—swirling white-and-caramel-colored marble. Our house in Flushing had cheap linoleum tiling. In the living room, an L-shaped white leather couch sat opposite a huge television set flanked by speakers that were as tall as Emo. A traditional low lacquer table sat beside the couch, and a terrace opened to a view of the manicured lawns below.

As Emo led us on a tour of the apartment, Sang kept shaking his head—he hated conspicuous displays of wealth. This fancy apartment had not always been the family home. When Sang had set sail for America, the family still lived in Busan. In fact, the family wasn't even originally from the South, but from the North; Sang and my mother were born in the coastal city of Wonsan. Sang, who seldom talked of the past, shared only one memory of their home in the North: that it smelled of wild rice and the sea. When war broke out, they were forced to abandon the house. They fled to the southern tip of the peninsula, to the port city of Busan where they lived in a small house—more hut than home—in a neighborhood among other *ibuk pinanja*—Northern refugees.

Suddenly there was a squeal—"*Ee!*"—from the kitchen. It was Hannah. I thought for sure she'd seen a mouse. But when we all rushed in, we found her caressing a large, flower-printed appliance that looked like a freezer chest.

"*It's a kimchi fridge!*" she said. But her excitement turned sour, then shrill. She slapped her husband's arm. "*I told you everyone's got one! How many times do I have to ask you for one?*"

"*One refrigerator's enough,*" Sang said dismissively.

Emo looked from Hannah to Sang. She pursed her lips. Then her tone went light and airy—girlish, even. "*Big Brother Number Two, I will say it does make fermenting kimchi so much easier,*" she said.

Sang shot a look at Emo before stomping out of the room.

Just a few minutes later, his voice echoed loudly from the bathroom. "*Aish!*" *Aish* was an annoyed exhalation, its meaning ranging from "darn" to "damn," depending on intonation. Looming back at us was a shiny white toilet with electronic buttons that lit up in pastel colors. It kept making a robotic chirp. Sang's turds floated in the toilet water.

"*Mwuga irukhae bokjaphae?*" Sang muttered. *Why is this so complicated?*

"*Oh, Brother.*" Emo inserted herself between Sang and the toilet. She pointed to the manual buttons on top. I leaned in to look—they were labeled with Chinese characters. In Sang's scribbled memos, he sometimes used Chinese characters as a shorthand, like how Latin symbols littered most of Beth's Post-it notes. I recognized the characters from Devon's flashcards as those for "big" and "small." I could hear Devon's voice explaining, "He's not doing a *cartwheel*, Jane. He's spreading out his arms to say, 'Thi-i-i-s big!'"

Emo pointed to the other buttons. *"This one's to warm the seat. This one's to raise or lower it. This one squirts water after you—"*

"Why can't they keep it simple?" tutted Sang. *"All you need is one lever."*

Emo pursed her lips again, forming a tight, polite smile. It was an expression I never saw Sang or Hannah make. I was coming to see Emo's role in the family: She was the mediator. Any hint of conflict and she was there to defuse it.

"There's obviously a demand for it," Big Uncle said. *"You've been out of our country too long."*

My heart tightened when I saw Sang's humiliated expression. He had left Korea at a time when the night-soil man still made the rounds to each family's outhouse. Now, more than thirty years later, he'd returned to his native land—a place with talking toilets in sky-high condos.

* * *

When Big Uncle announced he would take us out to dinner at a restaurant called Dosirak, I pictured wooden tables and chairs and a casual bustle, a place like the Korean restaurants lining Northern Boulevard. The name Dosirak, which means "lunch box," conjured up a humble affair. Taking a cue from Sang and Hannah, who wore their usual work clothes, I pulled on a T-shirt and my last pair of clean jeans—faded blue and fraying at the hems. Mary was dressed in her usual too-tight all-black, as if she were off to a nightclub. George wore cargo pants and a T-shirt that read IF YOU CAN READ THIS, YOU'RE INVADING MY PERSONAL SPACE, with shrinking type sizes, like on an optometrist's chart. Besides Mary, Emo was the only one of us who was not dressed casually. She wore a black blouse and a long, sequined black skirt. The waistband pinched at her midsection. The collar of her top was studded with rhinestones. She literally sparkled all over. She teetered on black patent-leather platform shoes that looked like they were designed for someone Mary's age or younger. Her short bob was wound into tight, permed curls, and her round face was painted white, with red lipstick coating her thin lips.

Emo surveyed Sang. *"Big Brother Number Two, are you sure you'll be . . . comfortable in those clothes?"*

He stared back at her as if she were an idiot. *"Of course I'm comfortable. Why would I wear something if it was uncomfortable?"*

Emo pursed her lips.

The six of us squeezed into Emo's car. Big Uncle was at the lawyer's office and would meet us at the restaurant. We arrived at Sinnara Hotel, in the heart of Gangnam. We rode a glass-walled elevator up and up, a view of the Han River spreading below us.

The elevator doors opened to the top floor. On the wall opposite, the restaurant name—Dosirak—was written in both Korean and transliterated English in gold lettering. The words glinted down at us.

Sang charged his way to the front. *"Party of seven,"* he told the woman behind the podium.

She blinked back at him. Her face was a blank, ageless slate—she could have been twenty or forty-five. Her hair was pulled back into a stiff bun. *"But there are only six of you, Client,"* she said.

"The seventh is on his way." Big Uncle had phoned Emo to say he was running a few minutes late. Sang pushed up the sleeves of his plaid shirt. The same plaid shirt he always wore: a wrinkleproof cotton-nylon blend, breast pocket crammed with its usual assortment of Bic pens and old receipts used as scrap paper.

The woman's face remained expressionless, but I saw her eyes tilt ever so slightly downward, sweeping Sang from head to toe. They flickered into an almost imperceptible wince. But my uncle was turning away to say something to Emo and didn't see.

I fell in line behind Sang, fixing a glare on the woman. I crossed my arms over my chest. I heard Beth's voice: *Clothes shouldn't mark a person's character.* But the woman's eyes would not meet mine.

"So sorry. I cannot seat you until your whole party arrives," she said.

Sang did a quick sidestep toward the restaurant entrance, craning his neck to peer inside. The woman, alarmed, upset her reservation book; its pages flapped helplessly in the air before the book fell to the floor. She swished sideways with surprising speed, despite her tight pencil skirt and heels, just as Sang was sliding back into place. They looked like two figures on a foosball table.

"*There's no one in there,*" Sang informed her.

"*Client, you must not be . . . from here.*"

"*What did you say to me?*" Sang's eyebrows shot into a knot, the way they did when a subordinate was being insubordinate.

The woman went on. "*You have an air about you that is not—*"

Emo, who'd been hanging back, jumped in. "*Our reservation is under Re Hoon.*" Then she added, "*They are visiting from America.*" The diamonds studding her earlobes caught the light of the chandeliers above.

When the woman confirmed our name in the reservation book—she glanced down a few times, as though she expected not to find it listed—she briskly gathered a stack of menus to her chest. We followed her down a narrow hallway. At the end there was a large and—as Sang had rightfully noted earlier—mostly empty main dining room. The walls were floor-to-ceiling windows. It reminded me of Windows on the World. Except Dosirak had private rooms that lined the hallway. We were led to a narrow, windowless room to the right.

"*That woman has too many words,*" Sang said when the hostess had barely exited the room.

"*Oh, Brother,*" said Emo.

Through the walls I could hear the flush of the toilets next door.

When Big Uncle finally arrived, red-faced in his shiny black suit, he was not at all pleased with the location of our table. He gave us a sour look before he pressed the electronic call button for the waitress.

"*Miss,*" he said when a woman—similarly bunned, similarly ageless—arrived at our room. "*There's been a mistake. I reserved one of the rooms on the other side.*"

When the woman said she would go check, Sang called out after her. "*Or the main dining room is fine, too.*" He tugged at the collar of his shirt. "*It's a little* tap-tap-hae *in here.*"

In truth, it *was* pretty *tap-tap-hae*—the room was cramped and confining. There was not much clearance between our chairs and the walls behind us. It seemed that the more desirable rooms across the hallway were built at the sacrifice of these dark interior ones.

Big Uncle looked reproachfully at his younger brother. But Sang was too busy looking down at his menu. *"At these prices you'd think they'd treat you like a king."*

Big Uncle huffed. *"People treat you how they think you should be treated."*

Sang pursed his mouth, as though a retort were about to spring from his lips, but he seemed to think better of it. He fell silent.

The waitress returned, with the manager in tow. The manager wore a black suit with an iridescent sheen, like fish scales. *"Client, the other rooms are occupied. So sorry."*

"They looked empty to me," George said, to nobody in particular. By the sudden flush of red flooding the cheeks of the manager and the nervous titter from the waitress, I could tell they understood English. Not Big Uncle; he was too focused on his anger—I don't think he understood English anyway—and was now winding back to release it.

"Do-you-know-who-I-am?" The air blasted from his mouth and hit the waitress in the face. It was almost comical, the way her hair would have whipped behind her if it weren't already pulled back in a severe bun.

The manager lowered his head. He let out a little laugh of discomfort, exposing a gold incisor. *"So sorry. It's because we have a . . . situation in those other rooms."* He did not elaborate on this "situation" before going on, *"But I hope, Client, you find this room suitable for your needs—"*

"That's right, this room is completely suitable!" Hannah jumped in, her first words of the night. *"We are so lucky to have such a fine room."* She narrowed her eyes at me, then at Mary, and soon all three of us were also nodding in agreement with enthusiasm. *"So fancy-fancy!"* we added.

The manager and the waitress stared back helplessly at Big Uncle. To my surprise he threw Hannah, and not them, an angry look.

"*Gaja*," he said curtly, rising from the table. I didn't move; I wasn't sure if he was being serious. "*I said let's go!*"

The urgency with which he'd barked the command made me think he wished us all to scramble as quickly as possible. But then *he* would be the last to file out of the room. I hovered a few inches above my chair. When Big Uncle reached me, he made a reverse hissing sound—*hssst!* Immediately I scooted my seat in, just as he was pushing the back of my chair out of his way. The edge of the table sliced into my ribs, knocking the wind out of me.

The manager and the waitress did not stop us, and when we passed through the hallway again, I saw that the windowed rooms—those coveted rooms—were now filled with middle-aged men in suits.

On the elevator ride down, Sang said to Big Uncle, "*Did you really have to make a big scene? It was so embarrassing.*"

Big Uncle scoffed. "*You want to talk about embarrassing? Just stay quiet if you don't know how things work,*" he said, shooting a look at Hannah, who was picking lint off her shoulder.

Sang's eyes flashed, but he said nothing.

I probably should have taken a perverse delight in watching Big Uncle chew out Sang. But in that cramped glass elevator, as we descended the many stories down, I thought about Thanksgiving dinner with the Mazer-Farleys. Watching Beth do the same thing to Ed at the dinner table had made me lose my appetite.

When we reached the bottom floor, George asked, "So . . . where're we going to eat now?"

Which was how we ended up in the basement food court, sitting in red plastic chairs and eating soggy burgers and fries at the Mc-Sinnara.

Chapter 14

Depreciation

The courtyard of Gangnam Sinnara Apartments had looked particularly impressive from the late Re Myungsun's terrace on the eighteenth floor. The well-groomed lawns formed tidy square rows. A large fountain stood at the center, shooting tall peaks of water. Stone sculptures dotted the lawn, and a babbling brook coursed through the grounds. But up close the greenery looked no less man-made than the gray towers surrounding it. I threaded my way through the perfect squares of Astroturf and took a seat on a wooden bench, opposite a miniature waterfall.

My grandfather had left me one hundred thousand dollars in his will. After we returned from our McMeal, Hannah all the while complaining about how she could feel the back of her head throbbing from the MSG, my uncles and Emo called me into one of the spare bedrooms that had served as the late Re Myungsun's office. They told me he had left money in the will for each of us, and I was given my late mother's share.

Share, not shame. As my mother's siblings dissected the will, I couldn't help but recall a memory from the past: a fight Sang and Hannah had when I was maybe no older than kindergarten age.

"*Why's he need our hard-earned money for?*" Hannah had said. "*What about your lazy big brother?*"

"*Big Brother's attending to his own hardships right now, with his wife. . . .*" Sang had trailed off; then, with a renewed firmness, he said, "*He's my father. It's our duty.*"

After that, my uncle had gone away for four days. I was terrified that Hannah had kicked him out and he was never coming back. While Sang was far from benevolent to me, even then I knew that my connection to him was the only thing keeping me under that roof.

It was now clear: Sang had given Grandfather the money to invest in Gangnam.

But all this—the apartment, the right to enjoy these grounds—belonged to Big Uncle now. Across the street was a FamilyMart convenience store. I watched the apartment dwellers streaming out. Men with bottles of *soju* or beer. Schoolgirls tearing open bags of shrimp chips. And then two young boys who looked like brothers eating ice-cream cones, their mother trailing behind them. The boys wore socks with plastic slippers, and their legs were so skinny you might have thought the children were war-stricken, if not for the fact that each had his own ice cream and their mother wore high heels and had an expensive-looking handbag hanging from her shoulder. The brothers chattered on animatedly, stopping only to take licks from their cones, and I wondered if they would have been as happy if there were only one cone to share between them. Would the older brother have offered his younger brother the first bite, the way Sang and Hannah had always made me share with my younger cousins? Most likely they would have squabbled. People were hardly as generous when the resources between them grew scarce.

"*There you are,*" Emo said, taking the seat beside me. "*I was looking all over for you.*"

"*So sorry. I inconvenience,*" I said, because it seemed to be the thing to say. The truth was, I was glad she had found me. Being around Emo felt the way it had that first night in the funeral home—like warm blankets and spittle. I felt a connection with her I had never felt with any of my other relatives or, indeed, anyone else before. It was a different comfortable feeling from what I felt around Ed. Was this *jung*? Even though I was only an infant when Emo had taken care of me, perhaps some sensory memory, far buried in the recesses of my mind, could still recall the feel of her touch. Beth might've called it Freudian, but Beth hated Freud.

"*You've gone through a lot these last few days, haven't you?*" Emo said, sinking into the seat next to me.

You don't know the half of it, I thought. Aloud, I said, "You, too."

Emo took my hand between her hands, as if we were schoolgirls playing a slapping game. "*It must not have been easy for you, over there.*"

I listened to the rushing sounds of the fake waterfall. It sprayed a cooling mist on my face. Silently I shook my head.

"*I always tell your uncle to lighten up! The air around him is so heavy and stern. But he's like a typical Busan man. And you know what they say: 'Men from Busan don't emote.'*"

"*The meaning, what is?*" I asked her.

"*You never heard that?*" Emo said, her hands clapping excitedly over mine. "*Then Emo will tell you a joke. What are the three things a Busan man says to his wife when he comes home each night?*"

She looked at me with bright eyes, as if she fully expected me to know the answer.

"No idea."

"*'Bapjwo. Ahnun? Jaja.'*"

Give me food. And the kids? Let's go to bed.

Emo let out a girlish trill of laughter; I followed suit. "*Emo, so fun you are.*"

She gave my hand a tight squeeze. "*We need to work on your Korean. So you can learn Seoul standard.*" She said I spoke Korean like an American—my sentence structure was reversed. "*We have a saying: You have to listen all the way to the end to know what a person's really talking about.*"

"Oh," I said, trying to hide my disappointment. It was indeed the opposite of English, where you led with the most important thing. I would have so much more to learn.

Emo examined my face. "*I had to fix my Korean, too, when we moved up to Seoul. Before that I had the thickest Busan dialect!*" She laughed.

"But now look: People even mistake me for a Seoulite. I never thought I'd see the day."

But Big Uncle still spoke with a strong Busan accent. Sang and Hannah, too. As did all the adults at church.

"But only short time left," I offered sadly. *"Well, that's the thing. . . ."* Emo paused to look into the waterfall. *"Beautiful, isn't it?"* she murmured. *"It must feel like a waste, with only one day left. How do you like it here?"*

I shook my head. *"Not how I imagining inside my head. But like in good way."*

Emo nodded with approval. *"American Uncle told us about your work situation back home. What a shame."*

My chest tightened, remembering what I'd done with Ed.

"Thank goodness you didn't take that job." Immediately it loosened. *"I was thinking. Maybe you shouldn't go back to America. Especially . . . after all that's happened. You should stay here, with us. I read there's a big demand for native English-speaking teachers."*

"But always American Uncle and Aunt say I not suppose to living here—" I stopped. I knew I was saying it all wrong.

Emo chose her words carefully. *"They belong to a different generation. Times have changed since."*

"But . . . you so busy. I get in the way." I was speaking Sang's scripted words. *"And what about Big Uncle?"* I found him intimidating; he reminded me of Re Myungsun.

"To be honest, I think Big Uncle gets sick of me sometimes," Emo said, chuckling. *"He'd appreciate having someone else around. Now that Father is . . ."* She fixed her eyes again on the waterfall, then changed course. *"We'll have so much fun together! I will take you shopping. The beauty salon. And I have so many jokes to share with you. Jokes and"*— her tone grew wistful—*"and stories."*

Stories. I was suddenly brought back to the Mazer-Farley kitchen table and the stories the family would tell. We never had that in Sang's house. I knew almost nothing of his life in Korea.

Emo pulled an envelope from her pocket and opened it. Inside was a black-and-white photograph, yellowed with age. Two children, a boy and a girl, stood in front of a small house with a thatched roof. Both children were painfully skinny—skinnier than the boys I saw earlier with the ice cream. They were holding hands.

"*I found this while going through some old things,*" Emo said. "*That's your mother with American Uncle. And that's our old house, in Busan. Not long after they fled the North. I wasn't born yet.*" She smiled wistfully. "*Sometimes I think they had all the fun before I came around.*"

I took the picture from her. Sang looked like his usual irritated self, even as a child, his mouth tilting down in its habitual frown. I focused on my mother's half of the picture. Back in Flushing we had only one photo of her, where she was staring up at the sun. But there was something about her expression in this photo that was extremely unsettling. Even though she was a child, she wore the haunted face of someone much older. The dark shadows cast under her eyes gave her an air of grave maturity. I wondered if this was her natural disposition or the trauma of war.

Times have changed since. Suddenly I knew what I would do. Emo was offering me a new home, in Korea. What did I have to return to in New York?

* * *

Sang did not approve of my decision to stay. It didn't matter that Emo had told him of the job opportunities in Seoul. He still said, "Better you come back home."

"But there's nothing for me back there," I said. I thought of the Mazer-Farleys', of that hooded bay window staring back at me. *Homewrecker.* It was a word whose literal meaning I'd never had reason to ponder before.

Sang frowned. "You find new job. Something else. Something better."

"What, like work at Food?"

His frown deepened. "What the problem with—" But he stopped himself from saying more. "Maybe you right." I was surprised by his loosened tone. "Maybe better you stay here. Safer. And Grandpa money worth more here anyway."

"What do you mean?"

"Anytime you taking something outside country, gonna lost its value," he said. I don't think I imagined the wistfulness etched in his voice. "And don't forget taxes. Always there taxes. Worth maybe only half by the end."

"I'm planning to find a job here. I'll earn my own money," I said.

"You better not stay here just for the fun time. Uncle hearing lot of story about *gyopo* who only going Itaewon nightclub." *Gyopo* is the word for a Korean raised overseas—I'd never heard it used before arriving in Seoul. His eyes narrowed. "*Never* you dare go Itaewon."

Itaewon had been shaped vividly in my consciousness, the handiwork of Hannah's stories when I was growing up. She would paint tales of nice Korean girls wandering down the wrong alleys, only to be snatched up by loutish American men in army fatigues or equally loutish Korean men working in conjunction with them. These poor girls would get tarted up and be sold into prostitution, and soon you'd see them drowning in the cheap neon light of sordid bars, spreading wide their red-lipsticked mouths in exaggerated trills of laughter.

Sometimes Hannah switched her stories: A certain kind of Korean girl—wild, wanton—would deliberately seek out Itaewon's carnal pleasures. Hannah used to curl her lip and stare into my eyes—as if she could *see* that budding wild wantonness. "*Do you want to end up like that?*" she'd warn, to which I'd vigorously shake my head and fix my penitent gaze on the floor.

Sang's default mode was to assume the worst of me. And just like that—whatever tenderness was starting to form between us instantly dissipated. "Maybe it's good I'm not going back."

There was a moment when something flashed across his face, and I thought for sure he'd fly into his usual rage. *Who you think you are? No back-talk!* But when my uncle opened his mouth to speak, his voice wavered.

"You know when Uncle first coming to America? Around same time they starting construction for Twin Tower. Every time I walking by construction site, they building one more story. Just like Uncle building up the business, Smith Street. Always feel little bit like we growing up together."

Before I could press my uncle to go on, he stopped himself. His tone resumed its usual roughness. "Anyway, here nothing like America." He reached for his pocket. "You like burden to Emo and Big Uncle."

My uncle handed me an envelope. His handouts were few and far between—I recognized the importance of the moment.

As I thanked him, his face turned red—an expression I normally would've written off as annoyance. Now I wondered if it wasn't embarrassment. Quickly Sang left the room.

Inside the envelope was a thousand dollars in U.S. twenties, their edges tired and worn from use.

*   *   *

Sang and the rest of the family boarded the plane to New York, but I stayed. After they left, I studied the photo that Emo had given me with newfound eyes.

Sang seemed to be holding my mother's hand not out of tenderness but exasperated obligation, as if keeping her from some impending danger—a mud puddle, a snarling dog. But I caught a glint of something in his black eyes that I had missed the first time. For all his inexpressiveness those black eyes seemed to shine at my mother with just the hint of a smile.

Chapter 15

Michelangelo

Eat up! You have a big day ahead of you," Emo said, pushing a plate of mackerel toward me. It was my first breakfast alone with just Big Uncle and Emo. The three of us sat around a cream-colored marble table. No Sang to shoot me *nunchi* daggers. No splitting the fish carcass with Hannah, picking off the bits of flesh clinging to its thin bones. Here Big Uncle and I each got our own whole fish.

I was planning to spend the day at an Internet café applying for English-teaching jobs—Emo had given me a list of suggestions. Mary had mentioned that the Internet cafés here were called "PC bang"—a Konglishism marrying the English "PC" with the Korean *bang,* or "room."

Big Uncle mentioned there was a PC bang nearby. *"From our apartment go through the South Gate. At the FamilyMart alley, go another hundred meters. It'll be on the left."*

"Wait—just one minute—" I ran to get a pen and paper to catch everything Big Uncle had said. *"Please one more time repeating?"*

"From the South Gate, go a hundred meters down the FamilyMart alley—"

"But, like, street names? Address number?"

Big Uncle looked at me blankly. *"No one here uses street addresses."*

Emo jumped in to explain. *"Here we usually go by famous landmarks or stores."*

As I would later learn, streets in Seoul were nothing like the streets back home, where grids were imposed on the landscape and even the shortest of streets was duly labeled. In Seoul, building numbers were assigned in the order they were built in that neighborhood. At that time a typical address might read, say, "Jung-gu, Sindang-dong 383." That was like being handed an address that read "Manhattan, Upper East Side 383" and you were somehow supposed to find the 383rd building constructed anywhere between East Fifty-ninth and East Ninety-sixth Streets. People gave directions here, but they were always relative to your shifting orientation in space.

"*But how a person suppose to finding the way here?*" I asked.

Big Uncle let out an annoyed chuff. "*Why do you have so many words?*"

My brain sometimes did that: it computed the unfiltered, literal translation of the Korean spoken around me. What Big Uncle had *actually* meant was, *What's with all the questions?*

He went on. "*A person should already know where he's supposed to go.*"

Emo, perhaps impatient that I wasn't eating the fish quickly enough, dipped her chopsticks into its belly and deposited a hunk of meat into my bowl of rice. It was something Hannah used to do—still did, in fact—with George. I thanked her and took the piece. Before I was done swallowing, she'd already replaced it with a new piece of fish. Her own bowl was left untouched.

After the meal was over, Big Uncle said he wanted something to clear his palate, so I was sent to the fridge for some fruit. I came back to the table with a pear. Big Uncle watched me intently as I carved away the skin of the fruit. I hoped he knew I knew that pears weren't cheap and that I was cutting the fruit for all of us, not just selfishly for me. My fingers became unsteady; I could sense him growing *tap-tap-hae*.

Finally Big Uncle shouted, "*You're hacking that thing into a hexagon!*" He pointed to the series of knife marks scoring the pale flesh, then to my pile of shavings. I relinquished the pear to him. He demonstrated, torquing his wrist in even, elegant motions. "*It's supposed to be round and smooth, like this. You see the difference between mine and yours?*" He held up a thick, wasteful peel. It looked nothing like Sang's. *"If you cut fruit like that, you'll never land a husband."*

This was the longest interaction I'd had with Big Uncle; I didn't know what to think. Was this a reprimand or an attempt at intimacy? Whatever it was, Big Uncle sent me to the fridge for more pears. He made me practice, over and over, until the marks scoring the flesh grew less pronounced, until soon there were no signs of knife work at all.

"There you go!" Big Uncle said encouragingly. His tone, so didactic just moments earlier, turned almost gentle. He spread his hands wide on the table. His palms were as pale and smooth as the sliced pears. They looked nothing like Sang's callused ones.

* * *

After a few missed turns, eventually I found my way to the PC bang. I signed on to a computer and was met with a chorus—a cacophony— of e-mails, calling out from my in-box. I opened Eunice's first, because her e-mail offered the least possibility of trauma, despite its subject heading: "Dark Times These Are."

> Jane:
>
> Greetings from 37.4250°N, 122.0956°W. Glad you must be you didn't get that job with Lowood: your whole office would've been obliterated.
>
> E.O.
>
> PS: Sorry to hear re your grandfather.
>
> PPS: When you get back to NY, would you mind checking in on my mom? She's been kind of freaking out about everything.

I did not click on the link Eunice had included in the bottom of the e-mail (it was to some conspiracy-theory Web site). After responding to Eunice's message, I threw myself into the job search for the next couple of hours, ignoring Ed's and Beth's unread e-mails staring bold-faced from the screen. I didn't know how other people dealt with trag-edies. In the movies people were always making grand displays of their anguish: sobbing into handkerchiefs, punching through walls. But for

me, when something was out of sight, it was also out of mind. If it was
not out of sight, then I'd force my eyes to go dead, before the violating
images had the chance to sear their indelible impressions.

I found a Web site called Dan's ESL Coffeehouse that posted job
openings for foreign English teachers. Most of the jobs did not require
certification or previous teaching experience. In the forums a number
of Americans and Canadians boasted instant success. "I didn't even
have to open my mouth, they hired me on the spot," said waegukin69.
"I got so many offers I had to beat them off with a stick," wrote
yugiyo411. My confidence bolstered, I e-mailed out my résumés and
was surprised by how quickly I heard back from the schools. Already
I had two interviews lined up for the next day.

That task completed, I returned, reluctantly, to my e-mails. I
clicked on Beth's first. She'd sent a number of messages, each one escalating in its level of alarm. I dreaded reliving her panic. Her first e-
mail, sent before the attacks, was a long missive addressed to both Ed
and me. She expounded on the conference she'd left early and her ex-
hausting red-eye flight home, only to find the house "utterly devoid of
the family I'd left the conference early to be with in the first place."
When you read between the lines, the e-mail was clearly a passive-
aggressive censure at her not being informed of anyone's whereabouts.

Immediately after the attacks, however, the tenor changed. As
she grew increasingly panicked, the lengths of her e-mails grew
shorter and tighter, as if she functioned solely on instinct. "Forget
everything said before. Water under the bridge. Just let me know
you're okay?"

Her second-to-last message was like sharp staccato notes: "Jane.
Are you alive? Please God. Answer." All extraneous words fell away;
her language was distilled to its bare essence.

Beth's final e-mail had been sent after I'd already landed in Seoul.
The tone and length resumed their normal extra-wordiness.

After being informed by my daughter of your call, I am beyond
relieved that you're safe. My deepest condolences are with you

and your family in this difficult time (i.e., your grandfather's passing). I understand the delicacy of the situation, but I do ask that should (God forbid) some similar future event occur, you please keep us abreast of said developments as they're transpiring. Frankly, I find it a touch out of character that a responsible woman such as yourself would fly off without a word of notice.

What kind of notice could I possibly have left behind? "I'm sorry I slept with your husband and ruined your family's life—here's my flight number"? I made several stabs at a response to Beth, but I found myself continually hitting the BACKSPACE key, deleting strings of words that sounded like empty rhetoric. Sang hated when we tried to explain away our apologies. He much preferred that we stare contritely at the tops of our feet, at the linoleum. Later he would expect us to piece back together the lamp we'd broken in our recklessness or scrub out the offending stain from the juice spilled on the couch through our carelessness. In other words, taking action instead of offering false "I'm sorry"s.

And I'd taken action: I'd removed myself from the Mazer-Farleys. I couldn't hit BACKSPACE on what I'd already done, but I could make certain I'd never let it happen again.

I wrote the most perfunctory of e-mails, offering my resignation.

Then I braced myself for Ed's messages. There were two from the night I was supposed to meet him at the hotel. There was a third immediately after the Towers had been struck. But the fourth e-mail, his last, had been sent just twenty minutes ago:

Dear Jane,

Let's just get one thing clear first: I'm not mad at you for not showing up at that hotel room. I understand your sudden flight. At least I'm trying to make sense of it all.

The hours, the days drag on. Without you. Sometimes I wake up in the middle of the night. Swear I hear you in the kitchen. But when I rush down the stairs and flick on the light, all I see is

that empty table. I just stand there for a moment, deluding
myself into thinking you'll appear. But you never do.

Your absence is echoed by the utterly stricken state of this city,
post-attacks. An oppressive something—sorrow? grief?—hangs
in the air. It manifests itself in the black clouds of ash that coat
the sky.

Sometimes I think I spot you on the streets. I call out your name.
But when I draw near, you've vanished in the shadows. I feel
and see and hear you everywhere.

Devon confirms that you're safe. They've reopened JFK. Jane—I
keep hoping, praying, you'll find your way back to me.

In that PC bang, as the Koreans surrounding me were completely absorbed in Starcraft or whatever computer games they
were banging away on, not one of them saw my hand shaking over
the mouse as I read Ed's e-mail. Not one saw the tears that splashed
onto the keyboard like hot drops of rain. Not one saw me raise the
back of my trembling hand to my eyes as I pressed—hard—to blot
them away.

Ed,

I've decided to stay on in Korea. I'm not coming back to New
York.

You should be with your family now.

I'm so sorry.

Love,
Jane

Before I could overthink it, I hit SEND.

Just when I thought I was done, I saw that, buried all the way at
the bottom of those e-mails, was a message from Nina. I opened it; a
burst of freshness filled the air:

yeah thanks again for taking off to korea without telling me.
but i'm really sorry about your grandfather. that's just . . .

awful. i told my nonna and she's doing like five decades of the
rosary for your fam.

all i know is they better catch those assholes responsible for
this. YOU DON'T FUCKING MESS WITH NEW YORK.

hit me back with a joke, a story, anything to take my mind off
stuff. it feels like everything's falling apart. i could use a good
laugh.

I stopped crying, calmed my trembling hands. My fingers were poised
over the keyboard, and I began to write.

If I have to explain a joke, then it probably defeats the
purpose, but here goes: What are the three things a man from
Busan says to his wife each night . . .

Just as I was about to log off, another e-mail popped into my in-
box, from EduAcademy, one of the schools I had applied to earlier.

New teacher opening we have our school. Old foreign native
English speaker teacher leave. Today afternoon for interview
you can come? Our location is . . .

I hit REPLY. I made a copy of the e-mail with the directions to the
school. As I logged off the computer, I resolved to shut out all thoughts
of New York and the people I'd left behind.

* * *

EduAcademy was in the Jongno district—directly across the river
from where we lived in Gangnam-gu. Dressed in the same black suit I
wore to the Mazer-Farley interview (the one I'd smartly thought to
pack, anticipating a funeral), with the same sneakers on my feet and
the same dress heels tucked into the same black pleather tote bag, I
headed over to the subway station.

According to the map on the station platform, the Number 2 train
made a complete loop around the perimeter of Seoul. It spun in an
uninterrupted circle, with no final destination. In New York there
was no such thing as a subway that made a complete circle—there was

always a finite start and end. Jongno was a straight shot north, but the only way to get to my destination—according to the map, anyhow—was to take this roundabout train route.

When I boarded, the subway was fairly empty, and I managed to get a seat before the surge of other passengers got on. There was an ad for an English-language after-school. LEARN PERFECT ENVIABLE NATIVE ENGLISH! Another ad shouted, BECOME THE PERFECT BEAUTY! with side-by-side pictures of a woman's face. The one to the left was a broad, kind face with slivered-almond eyes and a small pug nose—she looked like Eunice. The picture on the right had big, round, double-lidded eyes, a prominent nose, and a pointy chin. There was something off about the gaze—something a little flat, a little dead in the eyes. It did not look like a Korean face at all. It took me a moment or two longer than it should have to realize that it was an ad for a plastic-surgery clinic.

I was so focused on these ads that I nearly missed my stop. I emerged from the subway and stared at the printout of the e-mail the school secretary had sent me. The directions, written in English, didn't make sense. *Go Exit 6 walk to Provence Bakery alley and left turn second Sinnara Bank alley to Brown Chicken Hof alley and 200m on the right side school location.* Why did they keep calling them alleys and not streets? I thought for sure something had been lost in translation. Amazingly, at Exit 6 there were three Provence Bakeries: one behind, one ahead, and the other across the way. I walked up to the one straight ahead and turned down the street. But I could not find a Sinnara Bank.

I huffed and puffed up narrow hilly streets, thankful I was still wearing my sneakers. I realized that finding your way around here was just as Big Uncle had said: *A person should already know where he's supposed to go.* And if you didn't already know where you were supposed to go, you had to rely on someone who did to guide you.

The quiet back alleys offered glimpses into what I imagined was a Korea of the past. Old men carried flattened cardboard in large wheelbarrows. Grannies squatted on their haunches, selling handmade rice cakes on makeshift Styrofoam tables.

After asking around for directions and being pointed up and down the wrong alleys, I eventually found my way to EduAcademy. I was sweating, and my hair was pulled back into a flustered ponytail that stuck to the back of my neck. I, who'd always prided myself on getting to places early, was five minutes—and counting—late for the interview.

On the elevator ride up, I hastily changed my shoes. I was still balancing against the wall—one foot shod in a heel, the other in a sneaker—when the doors dinged open. An older woman passing through the hallway stopped in her tracks and stared at me.

"*Can I help you?*" she said, in a tone that made it clear she did not really wish to.

"*Here I am. For the job meeting,*" I said. I didn't know the Korean word for "interview."

"*You're not . . . the foreigner candidate, are you?*" the woman said, studying me.

"*I am Jane Re.*" Maybe she didn't recognize Re as Korean. I told her I wasn't a foreigner.

The woman hesitated for a moment before saying, "*Follow me.*" She led me to her office. She took a seat at a sleek white desk and gestured for me to sit opposite her.

"*What are you? Gyopo? Or one of our people?*"

Weren't they one and the same? I paused, not sure I had claims to either word.

"*And how long have you lived in the States? Were you born there?*"

"*No, I born here.*"

"*Here!*" She looked up suddenly, surprised. "*But how old were you when you left?*"

"*When I was a baby.*"

The woman turned her attention to my résumé. "*You went to college . . . at Baruch? I never heard of it.*"

It never heard of you either, I thought.

She asked a few wrap-up questions before handing my résumé back to me. "*We'll be in touch.*"

"*In touch?*" The same as Ed Farley's words to me.

The woman busied herself with a stack of papers. "*I have some work to attend to, so if you will please . . .*"

The elevator ejected me onto the street. The woman wouldn't have brought me into her office for an interview if the school weren't truly hiring. Something about me had put her off. I shuffled into the bustling masses. Pedestrians scurrying behind me pressed sharp elbows into my back, forcing me out of their way. Dejected, I leaned against the side of a high-rise, pried off my heels, and shoved my tired feet back into my running sneakers. What choice did I have but to trudge on?

Just then I saw a withered, hunchbacked granny, struggling to open the door of the building. She was as shriveled as Mrs. O'Gall. In one hand she carried a cloth-wrapped bundle, in the other a cane. When I held the door open for her, she looked at me with kind, grateful eyes before slowly passing through. I was about to let go of the door and continue on my way when four curly-permed *ajumma*— middle-aged women—rushed through without a word of acknowledgment. Back in New York, people at least nodded or offered a curt "Thanks." Not here. The women were immediately followed by three middle-aged men in hiking clothes, two twenty-something men in business suits, and a girl in a miniskirt chattering into her cell phone. I could have stood there for hours; it was impossible to stop the endless gush of people. It would have been comical—"How many Seoulites can squeeze through one door?"—if it hadn't been so soulless; each person after the old woman regarded me with cold indifference, as if I were no more human than a door wedge. Then a brigade of preteen girls in school uniforms trundled in. Where was their *nunchi?* I was their Big Sister; they should have held that door open for *me.*

I released the door and watched with perverse delight as it bounced off the shoulder of the last girl. Momentarily disoriented at being on the wrong side of the glass partition, the girl gathered her strength and yanked at the door. But she fell backward, weighed down by her large, turtle-shell-like backpack. She could have been Devon. Her friends on the other side pointed, laughing. Flooded with guilt, I hurried away.

* * *

By the time I boarded the subway back home, it was rush hour and the trains were packed. The first thing that struck me was how every single face on that train was Korean. You'd think that, coming from Flushing, I'd be used to being around all Koreans. But I kept expecting other ethnic faces to pepper the masses, the way they did on the 7 train. Here there were none.

Standing near the door, I stepped momentarily off the train to let the other passengers out. Back home the unspoken rule was that I'd have first dibs reboarding. But here the rules were different. The new passengers waiting on the platform behind me pushed me aside to make sure they boarded first. They came in endless waves, and I was rocked farther and farther away from the doors—a lone raft drifting from shore. As I fought my way back to the train I'd just stepped off, the doors slid shut. In New York one karate chop to the subway doors would have forced them back open; here the heavy doors looked like they would clamp over your arm and drag you away. I let them close and waited for the next train. But when it arrived, I again fought unsuccessfully against the current. I couldn't breathe.

I gave up and scrambled out of the station. I was at Sinchon, near Yonsei University, my mother's alma mater. But after a few minutes of walking, I did not see the campus. Exhausted and thirsty, I popped into a coffee shop called Café Michelangelo.

I bowed at the barista behind the counter—just as I'd bow to all the shopkeepers back home—and ordered a bottle of water. *"Your total is three thousand won, Client,"* she said in a robotic voice, not acknowledging my bow. I asked to use the restrooms, and she stared back at me with the kind of funny face we reserved for fanny-packed tourists clogging the city sidewalks.

I tried again. *"You know, the* byunso.*"*

"..."

"*Where . . .*" I felt like I was reduced to a four-year-old's speech. "*Where you doing* shee-shee *and* ddong."

"*You mean 'hwajangsil'!*" The barista burst into giggles. In Sang's house we'd always used the word *byunso*. Later I would learn that the word connoted an outhouse. "*You are very awkward-sounding!*" she told me.

"*Thank you,*" I said.

"*You must not be one of our people,*" she added. I snatched the keys from her, and when I got to the *hwajangsil*, I found a porcelain hole in the ground.

I returned to the main café area and took a seat toward the back. The chairs were leather, the tables a rich, gleaming wood. At the table next to me was a group of girls around my age and all dressed in black. Back home the girls also dressed in black, but there was something different about the Seoul girls' polish. They were hyperfeminine, like the rhinestones that sparkled from their collars and cuffs. Their shiny black hair was fastened with ribbons or a headband. Despite the early-September heat, these girls wore pantyhose, in shades of beige, coffee, or black. Their black patent-leather shoes had silver buckles. I wondered if they carried a change of shoes, the way New York women did. But their leather purses, which were draped on the backs of their chairs—something you wouldn't do at home unless you wanted to get your bag stolen—were too tiny to fit anything. I wondered whether Beth would have accused these women of pandering to the male gaze. Or maybe they just dressed up for themselves.

I wished I had brought a book, a newspaper—anything so I wouldn't look like I was staring at them conspicuously. I pulled out my cell—Emo had given me her old one—and pretended to be engrossed in the phone's golf game.

They were soon joined by a stamping of high-heeled feet; a girl carrying a blue cake box limped toward them, panting heavily. She was met with a chorus of:

"Ya, *you're like ten minutes late!*"

"Ya, *why didn't you pick up your* 'handy'?"

To which she retorted, "Chuh! *Like I was gonna pick up. I'd never hear the end of it from you guys.*"

The girls spoke in a kind of Korean I had never heard before: young, female, modern. It was both high-pitched and slurred; it rose and fell in different waves from the Korean that the adults spoke back in Flushing. Their laughter, too, was also high-pitched, peals ringing out like the electronic chime of Emo's front door. When Nina and I laughed, we'd toss our heads back and let out deep, unseemly rumbles. Nina would sometimes slap a hand on the table. Devon and Alla laughed like us, too—clutching their stomachs and gasping for air.

"*Excuse me, by any chance . . .*" a voice said.

I looked up. One of the girls from the table was standing before me. I straightened my shoulders, ran my fingers through my half bun, half ponytail.

She tapped her palm against the back of the chair opposite me; my sneakered feet were hooked on the bottom rung. "*Could I . . . ?*"

At first I thought she was inviting me to join her group for cake. I lowered my feet from the rungs of the chair—I even offered to walk it over to their table. Then I saw the expressions that flashed on the girls' faces: the pinching of the eyebrows, the curling of the lips. It was almost too quick to catch.

I returned to my golf game.

When the girls weren't looking, I continued to sneak glances their way. They set about opening the cake. It was a group effort: one freed it from its box, another pried off an envelope taped to the side and plucked out candles and a matchstick. Together they poked the candles into the cake and lit them. Then they sang "Happy Birthday," but with Korean lyrics. When the candles were blown out, the girls did not cut the cake. Instead they each reached for a silver fork and speared it directly into their mouths.

"*Delish!*"

"*Ya, it's way too sweet. Didn't we decide on cheesecake?*"

"*Ya, you know how far that cheesecake place is? Next time you go get it.*"

"*Ya, it's not sweet, it's stale. They totally sold me yesterday's leftovers.*"

Their chatter and *chyap-chyaps* filled the air. I envied their intimacy, their back-and-forth volley containing years' worth of inside jokes. As I watched them eat, I wondered whether I would have been part of a group like this, had my grandfather not sent me away.

But I knew the answer to that. Hannah's stories—the ones she'd let slip when she was angry with me for misbehaving—had made it clear to me. Had Re Myungsun not sent me away, I would have ended up in an orphanage. Then serving drinks at a bar, or clinging to the outer gates of the military base, calling out "Yoo-hoo!" in broken English to the passing soldiers.

Suddenly my cell phone rang; it was Emo. *"Where are you?"* she shouted into the phone. I told her. *"Good! I'm on an errand nearby. I'll come join you."* She clicked off before I could say good-bye.

When Emo breezed in, her sturdy heels clipping behind her, she frowned. She looked me up and down. *"Why are you dressed like that?"*

"Job meeting," I explained.

"Why didn't you tell me!" she cried. *"I thought you were just hanging out at the PC bang all day."* Thankfully, the girls next to us were too busy eating cake to pay attention to Emo's outburst. She studied me again. *"How did it go?"*

"Not so good. The lady not liking me," I said, trying to mask my disappointment.

Emo pinched the fabric of my suit. *"It's worn,"* she said. But it was good-quality wool and a designer name at that—I knew because only part of the label had been cut away when I'd bought it at Filene's Basement. *"And your face,"* she went on. *"It's raw."*

"Raw?" I repeated. Maybe I had misinterpreted the word. I stared down at my half-empty water bottle.

"Why would they give a job to someone who looks like she just rolled out of bed?" It was a rhetorical question, so I didn't answer it. *"Gaja,"* she said. *Let's go.*

Emo pulled in to the parking lot of Sinnara Department Store. *"You need new clothes,"* she informed me. When we entered, my sneakers squeaked conspicuously on the marbled floors. Then the salespeople were immediately on top of us. They shouted and shrieked; they held up blouses and sweaters and skirts at us. It was a frenzy—and Emo just grabbed, grabbed, grabbed. She steered us to the cash wrap before I could even try anything on. Emo waved away first my protests, then my offers to pay. As she lay down her credit card, I was too afraid to look at the register total.

Next it was on to the makeup counter, Emo once again refusing to take no for an answer. The saleswoman yelped as she took in my features. *"Her skin is so pale! I'm so jealous. She probably doesn't need this, but . . ."* She applied a cream to my face, and as she waited for my skin to absorb it, she turned again to Emo. *"Client, this is the best whitening cream on the market. I can give you a sample if you'd like to try—"*

"I already have it," Emo snapped.

The woman mixed different pastes and creams and spread them across my face. She showered me with a continual stream of compliments—my eyes were so big that she was skipping the eyeliner. My lashes were so thick that I could do without the fake extensions. My face—she held up a fist—was *this* tiny! (I didn't see how that one was a compliment.) There were huge gaps in my Korean; the language of praise was one of them. The words felt strange. They rang hollow in my ears.

The saleswoman applied the final stroke to my face. *"Older Sister, you look so pretty!"* She called me Older Sister even though she looked at least ten years older than me.

"Emo, what you think?"

She nodded with approval. *"You did a not-bad job on my niece,"* she told the woman.

"Oh, you're her emo! I was wondering . . ." the woman said. *"She must take more after her father's side."*

Emo squared her shoulders as the woman's eyes glided up and down her. What had struck me more than anything about Emo's face was that it exuded warmth. Before that point I had no reason to evaluate her for her prettiness. But now I found myself seeing my aunt through this woman's scrutinizing gaze.

Emo's face was a wide, flat, square plane, like a griddle pan. Foundation coated her skin like pancake batter. Her eyebrows were tattooed in blue-black ink, forming a harsh arc above her crescent-moon eyes, with eyelids sewn into double creases. (It didn't look natural—Emo must have had work done.) The effect was that Emo looked a little *too* alert, as if she were taking in everything around her a little *too* greedily. Her bob, curled into a tight middle-aged-lady perm, was tinted—no doubt at the behest of her hairdresser—with a reddish orange dye. She was short and compact—Eunice would have described Emo as "hobbitlike" (though Eunice Oh was built not unlike a Tolkien hobbit herself).

Then the mirror was turned to me. Impenetrable foundation caked my face. My lips were painted an unnatural shade of pink. I knew that Sang would not have approved. He *hated* when Mary or Hannah left the house wearing makeup. *What's wrong what God give you?* he'd demand. *You not suppose to cover up!* Once he told Mary she looked like a bar hostess. And of course Beth hated makeup, too—she'd once likened it to modern-day bound feet. Emo nodded with approval. Then, to me, "*You see! You didn't make the most of your potential. If your Emo looked like you, I'd be married by now.*"

I don't know what I would have thought just one day ago if the same face were staring back at me. But I was so far from New York and everyone now. As I stared, familiarizing myself with this new face, I let the praise from Emo and the saleswoman wash over me.

*   *   *

When we returned home, Emo made me parade my new clothes. She clapped with glee as I modeled one outfit after the other—"*You look just like Ahn Jaeni!*" she said, referring to some celebrity—and I couldn't help but think she derived a little vicarious pleasure at watching me fit into clothes she herself could not (dared not?) wear. She ordered me to wash off my face and reapply the makeup so I could practice over and over, just as Big Uncle had made me repeat peeling pears that morning. "*I hope you were paying attention when the woman did your makeup,"* she said. *"From now on, you have to look your best each time you leave the house."* Not wanting to disappoint Emo, I did as she said.

The new routine was uncomfortable at first. I had to rise an hour earlier and fix my face at the vanity table with unwavering concentration. I had to fight the urge to yank my hair up into a ponytail, even when it would stick to the back of my neck. I had to soften my New Yorker gait, because I could not move freely in my new clothes—my skirts would ride up and my pantyhose would dribble down.

Walking all day in my new shoes was difficult. The hard patent leather was unforgiving; it cut into my Achilles tendon and squished my feet into a narrow toe box. The heels made my arches ache. And there was no room in my purse to stash a change of shoes. After a few stops of standing on the crowded subway, the balls of my feet would begin to throb. My eyes continually scanned for an empty seat. But I could never seem to compete with the other young and middle-aged women who rushed for it when I found one.

Maybe I should just have given up the act.

But self-affirmation has an intoxicating quality. As the days passed, I could feel the world regarding me differently. *Confidence radiates from within!* Beth would tell Devon (and me) at the breakfast table. But for me it was the opposite post-makeover; the reactions of the people around me *generated* my inner confidence. I felt men's eyes follow me as I walked down the street, and I saw women young and old frown at me with a hint of jealousy. I was getting high off the fumes of my newfound beauty. I began to understand how girls like Jessica Bae got "gassed in the head," as we said back home.

But still the layer of foundation coating my face felt *tap-tap-hae.*

Each day I improved on my appearance, just as I worked on my Korean. Whenever my sentences threatened to revert back to their old syntax, I'd force my mind to reverse their order. I spoke all Korean, all the time. I learned that the Korean of Flushing was a holdover from the sixties and seventies; I had to replace each antiquated word or phrase in my existing vocabulary with its modern-day equivalent (*outhouse→restroom; apothecary→pharmacy*). Emo and Big Uncle were impressed with the rapid improvement to my language.

Sang had been right: Here was nothing like Flushing. How freeing it was! I did not have to go bow, bow, bow with each Korean face I passed. Here I was completely anonymous; no one knew my history.

In those early days, my thoughts involuntarily, invariably wandered back to Brooklyn. I'd do side-by-side comparisons between my old life there and my new one here. If I hadn't done what I'd done with Ed, I'd still be walking Devon to school, sitting with Beth in her office, still laughing about her articles with Nina at Gino's. But would I have spent my nights sitting across from Ed at the kitchen table?

No good had come of indulging my feelings for Ed.

But I'd come to Seoul to start anew. I was successfully doing as the Romans did, and for the first time since I'd arrived I felt I was falling into the rhythms of my new home. New York was becoming a distant memory. I nailed my next interview, for a job teaching adult conversational English. And it was there, at Zenith Academy, that I met Changhoon.

Chapter 16

Don't Throw Me Away
and Leave Me

Teaching can be a pretty thankless job. You never think to give credit to your teachers until you've had to stand in front of a classroom and do it yourself. On my first day, my legs shook, my fingers were unsteady as I wrote my name across the dry-erase board, and the simplest of facts slipped my mind under the spotlight of a dozen blinking sets of eyes. In those first few weeks I'd continually scan the room, afraid to land on any one pupil's face. No matter how many hours you spend doing lesson planning, you can never predict on the spot what direction the class will take. My energy would be shot after only a two-hour class. I'd run downstairs to Rice Dynasty and order two rolls of *kimbap*, which I'd swallow without chewing, the disks of rice-stuffed seaweed bulging in my throat on their way down. Then it was back upstairs to do it all over again.

The experience gave me a newfound respect for Ed. (I was less impressed with Beth, because she only taught seminars of two to five students, which she often held in her office.)

Public speaking did not come naturally to me—it's a skill that requires confidence and approachability. Ed possessed both, and I think this is where his Brooklyn accent worked in his favor. It lent him an air of authority, yet it also spoke of his humble roots (as opposed to the better-than-thou polished tones that Beth—and Sam Surati, for that matter—could not shake from her speech). I always imagined Ed as the kind of teacher whose good opinion you *wanted* to earn, with the implicit understanding that he was also someone you did not want to piss off.

Nina had it, too. She could command a room—or at least a tableful of her friends—and keep them engaged with what would otherwise have been a mundane anecdote. She was a natural saleswoman; she'd hit all her marks, had the crowd laughing along in all the right places.

There were always two friendly faces I searched for during each lesson. One belonged to Monica, another staff member at Zenith. She was taking my class at the behest of Principal Yoo, who told her she needed to work on her conversational English. Monica was a sweet, agreeable girl who sat ramrod straight at her desk—eyes alert, pink pencil scribbling furiously as I spoke. Her English was not strong, but she knew the most arcane rules of English grammar and had a memory that captured everything, like the strips of packing tape, weighed down by batteries, that dangled from the ceiling at the back of Food.

Unfortunately, Monica came as a pair with a haughty girl named Rachel. They were best friends from Ewha Womans University, where they'd both majored in business management. Rachel, who had the full checklist of prized beauty features, carried herself like she knew it; the sense of entitlement that came with that checklist made me ache with irritation. I could only imagine how it must have felt for Monica, who had to live in her shadow.

The second face smiling up at me each night belonged to a student who went by the English name Chandler. (He, along with the rest of my students, had named themselves after characters from the TV show *Friends*.) He had what was called "windblown hair"—a tousled, side-parted style favored by most of the young men I saw on the subway. Chandler came to class each evening in a slim-fitting black business suit and a crisp white dress shirt, carrying a patent-leather briefcase. He had the same lanky frame as the guys at church who played volleyball, but the tallest of them still capped out at five-ten. Chandler was easily six feet.

When Chandler first learned I was from New York, his whole face turned grave. "I feel so sympathy your whole country tragedy," he said. After a sufficient moment of silence had passed, he added, "But also jealous! 'Big pimpin' up in NYC.' I am Jay-Z *big* fan." I recognized the line immediately—I'd once walked in on George rapping it to himself in front of the bathroom mirror.

Chandler possessed an impressive range of vocabulary. (He knew terms like "ROI," "defibrillator," and even "hotboxing.") Unfortunately, this knowledge was coupled with no grasp of connotation. As a result, his diction was an awkward pastiche of the *Wall Street Journal*, Hot 97, and *Clueless*.

Monica spoke the same way. (Rachel not so much—she favored simple, unadorned prose and took few linguistic risks.) Monica asked endless questions about English grammar, seeking rules governing irregular forms. More often than not, I'd have to shrug and say, rather stupidly, "I don't know why, it just is." English is a punishing language for foreigners—it has been tainted by so many outside influences that the one constant is that every rule has an exception.

Each week the students submitted their vocabulary log notebooks, and the first time I flipped through Chandler's, it felt eerily like stumbling around inside his mind. Each entry, in precise mechanical pencil print, had been cross-referenced three times: first giving its unwieldy English definition from the dictionary, then a slightly shorter translation into Korean, and finally its one-word Korean distillation. There was a column showing its phonetic pronunciation and another listing its part of speech, and the last contained three sample sentences using the English word or phrase. Take, for example, his entry for the slang word "whipped," which I had taught them:

When wife whips at husband, we say she gives him hard time.

I am so low self-esteem because my girlfriend say I am hideous. I whipped.

Our army friend Yongsu, because he do whatever Mom say, we say he is whipped.

And so on.

Taped to the notebook's back pages were cutouts of newspaper articles in Korean and English, annual GDP tables from the World Bank, and a curiously named "Development of Myself Schedule"—a chart with a list of goals on one end and dates on the other. At the bottom of the chart were the culminating letters: CEO. I had a feeling that if Sang were peering down at these pages, he would have approved.

I had brought my grading home with me one night and was staring into Chandler's notebook at the kitchen table when I felt Emo peering over me. *"That student looks diligent,"* she said. *"Who is it?"*

"A boy named Chandler," I said.

"Let me see that." She took the notebook from me. She was looking at the inside cover, where his business card was taped. *"Kang, Chang-hoon. He's a sales analyst for Sinnara Bank."* Emo pursed her lips. *"How tall did you say he was?"*

"Emo!"

"What? I'm just trying to look out for you. Maybe our pretty Jane will snag his attention." Emo spoke with the gusto of the mothers from church scheming to marry off their sons and daughters. They'd run down the laundry list of desirable traits: academic pedigree, career pedigree, eugenics. In the end, though, it always came down to what families they were from.

"You don't know him, even," I pointed out to Emo.

Emo tapped her finger on Chandler's business card. *"It doesn't hurt to keep your eye on him."*

* * *

Emo and I were now on different schedules, and we overlapped for only a sliver of the mornings. She worked a pretty standard eight to six at her late father's office (from what I gathered, she was something of a glorified office manager), returning straight home to cook the evening meal for Big Uncle and herself. I taught in the afternoons and evenings, and when I came home at night, Emo was always waiting for me with a plate of food, eager for me to fill her in on all that had transpired during the course of my day.

And, as promised, Emo told me stories. There were stories of her childhood in Busan. Stories of her school days. And stories about my mother. At first I could hardly stop myself—my questions came pouring out in an endless stream. What did my mother look like? *"She was beautiful!"* So she had natural double-folded eyelids? *"No . . . but she had the pretty kind that folded inward."* (But I had thought that having the double fold was what Koreans considered pretty.) Was she tall? *"Yes, so tall! Well . . . maybe not as tall as you."* What was her favorite subject in school? *"She was good at everything."* But did she like one more than the other? Emo frowned. *"You know, I'm not so sure. . . ."* The more I pressed on, the more she was at a loss for answers.

Emo's stories read at first like the fairy tales passed around the Mazer-Farley breakfast table: beautiful, smart heroine, impoverished childhood. When you're starved for any taste of the past, you bolt down what little is rationed your way. But after a while Emo's stories started to taste tinny, like tuna sitting out too long in a can. Whenever I pressed her for more details, her face would go blank. My mother was but a hazy portrait: a composite of Emo's fuzzy adolescent reflections. She could have been anyone: the co-ed laughing with friends at Michelangelo. The schoolgirl sitting alone on the subway, spinning her way back home. After a certain point, your palate begins to long for something fresh. Eventually Emo's stories began to peter out—I stopped asking, and she stopped telling.

But the most interesting picture to emerge from all of Emo's tales was that of *Sang.* Before she had placed that photo of him as a child in my hands, I'd never had reason to ponder his own backstory. *"Your uncle used to be so funny,"* she said. *"Okay—maybe more like corny. Okay—maybe more like a troublemaker."* Emo had spent much of her childhood skipping home from school only to find her big brother kneeling in front of the house, arms raised high in the air as punishment for his latest mischief. The time he and a friend had swiped melons from a local farmer's patch. Or when he was sent to the fish market for some fresh mackerel and blew all the money on *boong-uh-bbang,* toasted carp-shaped cakes filled with red bean paste, for all his friends. Or the time Sang made a quip about Re Myungsun's short-lived pompadour.

These stories had me bursting with laughter—Sang would make George, Mary, and me do the same raise-your-hands-in-the-air punishment when we were little. (We'd always lower our sore arms whenever Sang had his back turned.) Yet they formed a very different portrait of the Sang I knew: stern, militant. But what did we know of his childhood? There were no framed snapshots of him as a little boy back home—the literal film reel of his life began in New York. How was it possible for Emo to have such specific memories of Sang when the age gap between them was even wider than that between her and my mother?

When Emo wasn't telling me stories about the family, she was watching soap operas. She never spoke of her friends, and no other plans seemed to occupy her evenings. (Whereas Sang and Hannah were always darting off to some church function. Or *gye* gathering—a money-lending club they joined as an excuse to get together with their friends.) Emo *loved* soaps. Apparently Big Uncle did, too. One night we sat down to watch a new show, a Chosun-dynasty court romance called *Don't Throw Me Away and Leave Me.* The title came from a line from the folk song "Arirang"—*The beloved who threw me away and left me / Will get no farther than ten* ri */ Before he injures his foot.* It was the same melody as the front-door chime—a cheerful tune with a spiteful message. Emo and I sat on floor cushions with our backs propped against the white leather couch. Big Uncle sat in a leather massage chair. We passed a bowl of squid-flavored rice crackers back and forth.

"*The main lead is Eun. He was lowborn, but he studied his way into the scholar class,*" Emo explained between animated crunches. "*So the king arranges a marriage for him with a nobleman's daughter named Bora. She's an 'Old Miss,' just like your Emo.*" Emo often used the Konglishism "Old Miss" to refer to herself—it meant spinster. "*That is, until he meets a beautiful young courtesan named Jihae!*"

I think she expected me to gasp, so I said, "*No he didn't!*"

Big Uncle went *"Uh-uh-uh"* as the chair's tiny electric fingers jabbed his back and the undersides of his legs.

Emo ignored him. *"Do you see Eun's dilemma? Will he choose his duty? Or throw it all away for love?"*

The plot of this soap opera hit eerily close to home. I tried to change the subject. *"So yesterday in my class, that funny boy Chandler, he was saying—"*

Big Uncle cut me off. *"You always focus on the wrong stuff,"* he said to Emo. *"The most important part is how our people will outsmart the Japanese. Those warmongering bastards. The highlight's gonna be the tale of Nongae."*

Emo explained. Nongae was a courtesan who lured a Japanese general onto a romantic boat ride in the Nam River. Then she threw her arms around him, fastened jade ring locks around her fingers, and tipped them both overboard. They drowned.

"Nongae is one of the finest ladies in our people's history," Big Uncle said. *"Now, what Japanese geisha would do that for her country?"*

The mood between all of us was so relaxed that I ventured a joke. *"Very funny how Big Uncle's also enjoying soap operas, like middle-aged housewives,"* I said.

But Big Uncle didn't appreciate my joke. *"It's called 'drama,'"* he corrected me, his tongue tripping over the English word and rendering it into three syllables: *duh-rah-mah.* It was one of the many foreign loan words that had become embedded into the language. *"And it's not just for the ajummas."*

The festive mood instantly dissipated. *"Sorry, Big Uncle,"* I said. I instantly focused on the television screen.

The "drama" was about to start. Eun, the male lead, had thick, strong eyebrows and a square jaw. He was supposed to be a young lad, but he looked almost as old as Big Uncle. He walked around the set with a pained expression, as if he had to relieve his bowels. But whenever his eyes alighted on Jihae, the young courtesan, his whole face broke into a smile. Eun's smile reminded me of the unabashed way Ed had smiled at me at McDonald's. It had been one of his rare smiles, the one he deemed too good for everyday use.

"If only I were half the beauty Jihae is!" Emo sighed wistfully. But I did not find the actress playing Jihae attractive at all. Her face was pale and pointy. The bright TV lights washed her out. She looked like the "after" shots in plastic surgery ads on the subways.

Eun, staring longingly at Jihae in the distance, failed to notice the gang of Japanese samurai charging behind him with raised swords. The episode ended and was immediately followed by a commercial for a kimchi refrigerator.

Big Uncle pointed to the television screen in disgust. *"See? That's what happens when you get caught up in silly romance."*

But Emo was lost in her own thoughts. *"I'm such a sucker for romance,"* she said with a dreamy sigh. *"My head says Eun should follow his duty, but my heart wants little Jihae to succeed. Jane, what do you think?"*

There were infinite reasons their union was all wrong. Eun was way too old for Jihae, for one. He should have focused on securing his future—being with Jihae would only have set him back. And frankly, Jihae wasn't all that.

"Jihae should show some nunchi *and just going away,"* I said. Then I promptly excused myself for bed.

* * *

Don't Throw Me Away and Leave Me only seemed to stir up the feelings I'd been trying to push down since leaving—fleeing—New York. During those first few months in Seoul, as the pleasant chill of fall gave way to the early frost of winter, I found my thoughts turning continually to Ed Farley. In the mornings, when I crossed the river on my commute to work, I pictured him sitting at the block wood table carving out shells of baguette. In the evenings, when I crossed the river again, circling my way home, I thought of him sitting at that same table opposite the woman he did not love. The two of them could hardly "have a conversation" without disagreeing. Whereas Ed and I spoke the same language.

That was the other thing I missed as the months wore on—conveying all the subtleties and nuances of language. My Korean had stalled, despite the exponential leap I'd made early on. I grew frustrated at my inability to move beyond the most perfunctory speech. I could feel myself making mistakes—the clunky sentence constructions, my stunted vocabulary. At the same time, my English grew stagnant. Despite the fact that I spoke English every day in class, I repeated the same phrases over and over, like a scripted reel. The simplest of expressions were beginning to elude me—my brain growing dull as I tried to conjure them up.

I was caught in a no-man's-land—the gulf between English and Korean felt wider than the East River and the Han combined.

I was lonely, my linguistic loneliness echoing the dull ache that tugged continually at my heart. That loneliness was amplified by the swift chatter of the subway passengers surrounding me and by the ads blaring from the walls of the Number 2 train as the Seoulites and I spun round and round its endless loop.

Chapter 17

Friends

A *Don't Throw Me Away and Leave Me* craze swept over the land. The drama was all that Emo and Big Uncle talked about at mealtimes. My students chatted about it endlessly in labored English during class and rapid-fire Korean during breaks. Then a new character arrived on set—Chulsu, a young nobleman making a play for Jihae the courtesan. The love triangle reconfigured into a quadrangle.

That winter there was a popular ad for a brand of kimchi refrigerator. A bride in a white wedding gown and a tuxedoed groom stood on either side of the pink-and-white flower-printed appliance. The bride was the actress who played Jihae. The groom was Chulsu, and he had the same windblown hairdo and jaunty lankiness as Chandler. Their faces glowed; their arms formed a heart shape over their heads.

The slogan, written in English, read FRESH ... MOIST ... WELL-BEING. WHEN ONLY #1 MATTERS. The first time I read it, I snorted; the passengers on either side of me glanced over and inched away. It was only when I stopped laughing that I noticed the two parents in traditional *hanbok* dress, tucked away in the corner of the ad. *"Our child deserves only the best for a perfect life!"* said the balloon blowing out of their mouths. They stared with approval at the newlywed couple.

The news about *Don't Throw Me Away* even spread to Flushing, where, of all people, *Sang* learned about it. Imagine my surprise when an e-mail arrived from him. Well, not from him directly (to this day I still don't think Sang knows how to operate a computer). It was sent via George.

"Yo, Jane Nuna. Abba made me write to you. He says, 'Your aunt like drug addict for *Don't Throw Me Away and Leave Me*. But they not have yet in New York. Church mothers, they say you buy VHS tape in Itaewon. But I say, NO WAY. Aunt say maybe you find someplace else, safe place, like Dongdaemun Market. When you coming back home, you give to her. But only after you bargaining down price.

"'You not forget, Jane: you living there still burden for Big Uncle and Emo. No making mess. Once a week you buy something, say thank you. You not be cheap. Right now Jeju *hallabong* orange in season. Use money Uncle give you.

"'Yesterday Uncle get call from your old lady boss. "What we gonna do Jane's stuff?" she say. So now Uncle have to go all the way Brooklyn. Why you not taking care your stuff *before* you leave?'"

I shuddered thinking of Sang entering the Mazer-Farley house. Would he be able to sense what had happened between Ed and me? Hurriedly I read through the rest of the e-mail.

But Sang had no more words for me. George had taken over. "P.S. Jane Nuna, I heard H.O.T.'s coming out with a new album. Can you pick it up for me before you come home? I'll totally pay you back."

And then the last postscript: "Abba didn't tell me to write this, but at dinner last night he said, 'I'm glad Lowood rejecting her.' I just thought you should know."

Sang's e-mails, by way of George, were not the only reminders of home. Nina and I continued a regular correspondence. It was she who narrated the aftermath of the attacks, the utterly downcast spirit that shrouded the city. And it was she who sent updates about the Mazer-Farleys. Interwoven with these accounts was the latest in her own love life: Joey Cammareri had finally asked her out.

I scrolled down through her e-mail. Joey (though Nina was now calling him "J.") had taken her to a gallery opening in Chelsea. Nina couldn't follow any of the conversations that swirled over toothpicked cubes of smoked gouda and water crackers flecked with black pepper, so she quickly downed three Grey Goose and tonics instead. She spent the night gazing at the floor tiles that lit up to a neon pink until Joey packed her off in a cab with the promise they'd do something again "real soon."

I braced myself for the next paragraph, one undoubtedly chockablock with Joey Cammareri effusions. But instead my cursor landed on the word "Ed."

The morning after that first "date" with Joey, Nina was stumbling hungover down sunny Court Street in search of ginger ale when she ran into him—them.

"Ed and Beth were out buying their bagels and coffee, and—get this—they were holding hands."

In my one year with the Mazer-Farleys, I had never seen Ed and Beth hold hands, in public or in private. (I had also never seen Beth eat bagels or drink coffee.) They never displayed any affection at all, except for that one time I'd overheard them having sex.

"I was going to say hi but the two of them looked totally lost in their own world."

Ed and Beth. Holding hands. Ed and Beth. Holding hands. The words glowed in pairs from the screen, flaunting their union.

All this time I'd taken a silent comfort in knowing that we were both suffering, respectively, even if on opposite sides of the globe. I *loved* him. I gave him (sort of) my virginity. And apparently it had all meant nothing. As soon as I'd left, Ed went right back to Beth. Her! Parading Beth down Court Street, for all the neighborhood to see. There was an expression they used a lot here: *There's no tree trunk that doesn't fall after it's been struck with an ax ten times.* It sounded much more elegant in Korean, yes. Couldn't Ed see? Of course I was the one who had to leave—I was the one who'd wrecked their home. But if he had truly wanted me, wouldn't he somehow have chased after me? It was a stupid thought, yet still it persisted.

"I thought things were rocky between them when you lived there. So . . . what happened?"

If Nina was hinting at something, she could just forget it. I had been reduced to nothing in his eyes. And spilling the beans to Nina would change none of it. *You did the right thing.* I should have been happy he was honoring his commitment to his family, to his wife, to his daughter.

But I wasn't happy. The ache in the cavity of my chest resurfaced. I remembered that graph I'd imagined, the one that clearly showed all the ways Beth took precedence over me. It was obvious that Ed had made his choice: Beth. Not me.

* * *

The school semester was drawing to a close. After our last class, Chandler, Monica, and Rachel invited me out to the local *hof,* or bar. *Always refuse offer first time.* If the offer was renewed, you knew it was genuine. At least this one bit of advice from Sang proved true. After two rounds of refusals, my students insisted, Chandler especially. He nodded vigorously—"We take American teacher to American *hof!*"— and led the way.

I had never been inside one before, even though I'd seen them everywhere. This one was Western-themed, with a sign in the shape of a spur and glossy swinging saloon doors. We ordered *chi-maek*—short for fried chicken (*chiken*)and pitchers of beer (*maekju*). This was also the first time I'd been out socializing with other young Koreans. It was a welcome change after spending months watching the cake-eating groups all around me while I sat alone.

Our food and drinks arrived. Rachel was frowning at Monica, whose fork was hovering in midair above the plate of fried chicken. Monica glanced up at her friend before moving her fork to the bowl of radish cubes. She speared one and gently gnawed off one corner, her mouth and tongue going *chyap-chyap.* A large sound for such a small bite.

Then Rachel's eyes flitted over to me. Was I imagining the way they explored my chin, my cheeks, the bridge of my nose? She said, "Chandler, you not say you want to see new Ahn Jaeni movie? Monica, she also want. Maybe you must go together." She was going *chyap-chyap,* too—on a large hunk of fried chicken.

Chandler busied himself with refilling my beer glass. "No, I never say."

He was moving on to fill the other glasses, but Monica took the pitcher from him.

Rachel, rebuffed, tried again. "*Ya*, Monica! What do you eat? Your skin looks so pretty!"

Monica jumped in. "Ah, no, no, no. I am not pretty. Rachel is pretty. Jane Teacher is pretty. So pretty she look like actress!" That's what they called me, no matter how many times I tried to correct them. ("You don't actually *call* your teacher 'Teacher.'")

Chandler nodded—"Yes, just like Jihae from *Don't Throw Me Away!*"—and I demurred. Rachel shot Monica a look.

That Rachel was trying to peddle Monica to Chandler was obvious; what I didn't pick up on for a long while yet was *why*. At the time I thought it was less about Monica's feelings for Chandler and more about Rachel's attempts to make me look like a *babo*, a fool, in front of him. She must have picked up on the fact that over the course of the months I'd found myself drawn to Chandler. I always perked up with a nervous energy when he was in the room. Emboldened by the alcohol, I found myself fluffing my hair coquettishly and addressing him pointedly in the conversation, sometimes to the exclusion of the others. Girls can be petty when they're competitive. Even more so when they're drunk.

My paranoid suspicions were confirmed when Rachel, her eyes once again latching onto me, cocked her head to one side. "Jane Teacher, may I ask you question? Where your parents are from?"

My chest tightened at the thought of where this conversation was leading. "My mother's from here," I said cagily.

"Your father, too?"

When I was younger, I tried to pass. It would have been easier to lie. *There comes a point where you just got to be who* you *want to be.* Ed's words were wending their way back to me.

"Yeah, they met here," I said at last. "He was an American stationed here. I'm *honhyol*."

Rachel nodded knowingly, as if congratulating herself for being right.

"Who care, someone *honhyol,* someone not *honhyol,*" Chandler said. I looked up at him and smiled, grateful to him for easing the tension. Then I threw a smug look at Rachel—but she was poking at her chicken and missed it.

"I'm so jealous!" Monica exclaimed.

"Jealous?" I repeated back.

Monica, whose cheeks were flushed with beer, started counting off her fingers. "*Honhyol* has the white skin, big eyes, big nose, small chin, long legs," she said. "You so lucky." She spoke wistfully, as though romanticizing my *honhyol*-ness.

Still, the weight of lying by omission had been lifted from my shoulders. And, thankfully, the conversation didn't linger on me. They talked of the latest episode of *Don't Throw Me Away,* and celebrity gossip.

I could not believe we went through our 3,000 cc pitcher so quickly. Chandler flagged down the waiter and ordered another. He poured our refills, and we all toasted—they taught me the word *Gunbae!*—and drank. And drank. And drank.

"So . . . why'd you guys choose *Friends* for names anyway?" I asked them. "Back home the show's kind of passé."

"What it means?" Monica said, reaching for her pink notebook.

I was getting tipsy. My tongue, without my realizing it, slipped into Korean. "*It's meaning it's played out already,*" I said, trying out a new phrase I'd overheard at Michelangelo's.

"*What?*" I said, staring at their stunned faces. "*Why's everybody looking so surprised?*"

"*We didn't know you could speak our people's language,*" said Rachel.

"*It's my language, too,*" I mumbled into my beer.

Monica backpedaled. "*No! It's just, we heard that our people raised overseas don't speak our language well. It's kind of* singihae." *Singihae*—a novelty.

Chandler said, "*You really speak our language excellently!*"

I started at hearing Chandler speak Korean. His English was endearing but choppy and awkward. With the switch to Korean, he shed his linguistically bumbling self and then some—he was so self-assured in his native tongue. I was still getting accustomed to hearing Korean being spoken by young men. The only male voices that spoke it back home were middle-aged; the language was rendered in rough, unemotive tones.

"You sound different when you speak Korean," I told him. (Of course I didn't mean different; I meant *hot*.)

And those were the last words I spoke in English that night.

Would it be too corny to say that the shift from English to Korean was accompanied by a shift in mood—one that seemed to bring us all closer together? Winter was thawing and, with it, the collective cold shoulder of the city. I imagined the other tables watching our tight-knit circle with envy while they were left out of the loop.

After we changed to Korean, Chandler—Changhoon—demanded to know our ages. Rachel, Monica, and I were the same age, but Changhoon was three years older.

"*Changhoon Oppa, since you're the oldest, you're picking up the tab, right?*" Rachel said.

"*Of course,*" he said. "*What else should I treat you guys to? Ice cream? Choco Pies?*"

"*Choco Pies? Pfft!*" I said, farting the word out of my lips. I was, at this point, pretty drunk. "*If you buy us Prada bag, I call you Oppa any day.*"

I was subconsciously mimicking the way I heard girls on the subway and in Café Michelangelo talk to their boyfriends. *Oh-p-p-pa-a-a-ah!* they'd wail—*Big Brother!*—voices dripping with *aegyo*. It was how Jihae talked to Chulsu on *Don't Throw Me Away*. And yes, maybe I was being a flirt.

And I think Changhoon kind of got off on it. "*She's got aegyo, this one!*" he said, not disapprovingly. *Aegyo*—the word for the babyish act girls put on to look cute. "*Okay, Oppa will buy you one from Itaewon.*"

"*At least splurge for a real one!*" Monica squealed, knocking back the rest of her beer.

Then Rachel said something I didn't quite catch, and they all laughed.

I couldn't tell whether they were laughing with me or at me. By the time bottles of *soju* were magically summoned, poured into shot glasses, and dropped like bombs into our glasses of beer, I didn't much care.

They asked me for stories from America. I told them about Flushing. When they asked what my uncle did, I told them he owned a produce stand. (Sang always said it was better to downplay our business than to show off that we owned a grocery store.) I told them about the Mazer-Farleys, which made our circle break into yet another hearty round of laughs. I told them about Beth's hairy armpits, and her fateful Thanksgiving tempeh turkey, and how she once tried to pay for Sang's fruit. What started as a joke at her expense was now devolving into anger the more I thought about her, and that anger overrode any pangs of guilt I felt in offering up her life as fodder for this drunken evening. I couldn't believe *she* was the one who got to be with Ed. She was so lucky, yet so ungrateful.

"*What about her husband? Surely he wasn't the same way, was he?*" Rachel asked. Her laughter, I'd noticed, was the thinnest of the bunch, as if she caught a whiff of something off.

"*He was . . .*" I was not too drunk to stop myself. It would have made a hilarious story, I knew, to go on about the oldness and plainness and academic pretentiousness of Beth, contrasting them with the youthful, hunky Brooklynness of Ed.

I opened my mouth to speak. "*He was* 'whipped.'"

* * *

Consider that night my farewell to Ed. I was officially moving on. During the subway ride home, I stared foggily at the kimchi-fridge ads, then out the windows. Frost coated the glass. Changhoon sat next to me. Rachel and Monica had spun home in the opposite direction. "*Girls can be so funny, don't you think?*" he said.

"*Mm,*" I said, closing my eyes. Changhoon smelled of cigarette smoke and sweet cologne. I breathed in deeply, filling my lungs with his scent.

"*Monica, she's nice and all, but she's just not my* 'style' " he said. "Style" was Konglish for "type."

I was drawing closer to that smell. "*Then who is your* 'style'?" My words slurred, my vision blurred. Changhoon's face loomed closer still.

"*I think you know.*"

"*Yes?*"

"*Ee Jane is my* 'style.' " Ee. My Korean name, not its Western bastardization. Changhoon's arms circled me, pulling me toward him. I lifted my chin. Right there on the train, he was suddenly kissing me. I tasted the cigarettes. I tasted the garlic-smothered chicken. I tasted the beer and *soju*. I drank him in the whole ride home.

When I surfaced from that kiss, the frost on the subway windows had thawed into vapor.

And after that, reader, let me tell you: Changhoon and I were *on*.

Chapter 18

Motherland

The spring brought a welcome shift in my responsibilities at Zenith Academy. I was in the break room with the other teachers, making some joke about Sang's banana-box filing system, when Principal Yoo passed by and said, *"What was that?"* I realized then why he had perked up during my interview when I'd mentioned working at my uncle's store. But at the time *nunchi* told me to steer the conversation away from the blue-collar toward my more "prestigious" work experience—if you could call helping a fifth-grader with her homework prestigious. Now, in flustered Korean, I rambled on about helping to manage the store's cash flow. Next thing I knew, Principal Yoo was swapping out my teaching sections for administrative work and the occasional private tutoring session. I was happy to be rid of the classroom—no more trembling at the dry-erase board in front of all those students. You would have thought I'd be daunted by Korean spreadsheets and financial statements. But the language of business— money in versus money out—is pretty much universal.

My new job set me on a more normal workday schedule, freeing up my evenings. Which left time for more dates with Changhoon.

And what dates they were! Changhoon threw himself into constructing elaborate itineraries—cable-car rides up to Namsan Tower, trips to Sinnara Amusement Park, walks around Seokchon Lake (*"Thirty years ago that lake didn't even exist,"* Big Uncle had told me)— followed by dinner, followed by coffee or drinks. He'd endlessly re-

search which restaurants had the best "set menus," and we'd join the
rush of other young couples at that new Japanese curry joint near City
Hall, or that Italian trattoria in Hongdae, or the Australian steak
house in Gangnam (which turned out to be an American chain, but
here their steaks cost almost thirty dollars a pop). Changhoon would
always stop me from spearing my food so he could snap a picture with
his digital camera first. *"I need to upload it on Cyworld,"* he'd say. I
wasn't on Cyworld—it was some social-networking site that required
a national ID to log in—but I took it as one big forum where you
could boast to your friends about where you'd been and they hadn't.

After the meal we'd nestle into a plush couch at one of the Café
Michelangelo branches, drinking green-tea lattes while watching ille-
gally downloaded videos on his laptop computer. Changhoon's favorite was a sketch-comedy called *Gag Concert.* On weekends we'd cap off
the night at the latest wine bar in the gallery district, where the som-
melier would pour our bottle of wine into a glass carafe with extra
flourish. Changhoon would also order a large platter of fruit *anju.* The
server would set before us a pretty display of sliced pineapples, melons, pears, which we couldn't even touch because we were too stuffed
from dinner. But ordering *anju* was what you were supposed to do. It
always broke my heart to see that fruit go to waste.

His was an old-fashioned courtship—refusing my offers to split
the check, endlessly holding doors open, carrying my bags. (*"You don't
feel like a girl, holding my purse?"* I'd asked him once, but either he
didn't hear me or he didn't get the joke.) Going out with Changhoon
felt like a guilty indulgence—the rich food settling uneasily in my
stomach each time the check arrived.

But wherever we went, the servers were always commenting on his
stylishness, his height. Changhoon carried himself well; there was always an extra polish—both literal and figurative—to his clothes, his
shoes, his hair. Around him I felt the need to "step up my game," as
Nina put it in one of her e-mails. Imagine if Emo had never taken me
for a makeover, I'd think while rifling through my closet in the morn-

ings. I'd stand in front of the mirror holding up one blouse or the other until resolving to buy a new one right before our date.

Beth would have labeled my behavior a "regression of feminism." But in truth, what girl doesn't want to impress her new boyfriend? The fruits of Beth's mentoring were rotting away in the bottom crisper of my mind.

In the school's break room, I would gab about my dates with Monica, who was quickly becoming a good friend. How much it must have pained her to sit there and listen as I prattled on and on about Changhoon's romantic gestures! Yet—if I may say—she always seemed to pry for more details, as if she derived some vicarious thrill from hearing these accounts.

Monica was always the last one to leave the office and the first one to arrive. She conducted her work as if not only her reputation but her mother's, her father's, her entire clan's were riding on it. "I don't want to be shame," she'd say by way of explanation. One morning I found her at the office after having pulled an all-nighter.

"Don't you get tired this routine?" I asked as I watched her splash cold water on her face. *"Maybe you should put your foot on the floor. You should say, I'm not gonna keep doing like this, Principal Yoo!"*

Monica scrubbed away yesterday's makeup. She looked confused, as if she couldn't tell whether I was joking or not. I was and I wasn't.

Monica patted her cheeks dry. "Not so easy," she said. It was at her behest that we each spoke our weaker language, for practice. "Oh, Principal Yoo? He ask me write memo? I make extra copy for you. I left in your desk."

I watched her reapplying her makeup. Through the reflection in the mirror, she smiled—a placid, unreadable smile. I wasn't sure whether I was telling her what she already knew or if she simply could not understand my imperfect Korean.

* * *

When Emo learned of my relationship with Changhoon, she shook me up and down like a party favor. *"So exciting!"* she said. *"If all goes right, you'll stay in Korea forever!*" She began fussing about me with renewed energy. It reminded me of the way the grannies at Devon's Chinese school flocked to the children. Emo would smooth a smudge of foundation from my cheek or pull a loose thread from the hem of my skirt. Smudges and threads that up until that moment I hadn't even noticed, despite having studied myself carefully in the mirror.

I'd like to think Emo was happy for me. When I came home late, she'd still be up, waiting so I could regale her with details about my date. But after a while I started to grow self-conscious—surely she'd smell Changhoon's cologne, his cigarette smoke clinging to my clothes, my *breath*—and told her she no longer had to wait up for me. Emo took it as a slight. She resorted to leaving grease-stained notes under a plastic-wrapped plate of fish on the kitchen table. Maybe it was my limited Korean, but there always seemed to be a passive-aggressive tone beneath her bright words and smiley-faced emoticons.

Emo seemed to keep better track of the progress of my relationship with Changhoon than I did, and sometime in early May she left me the following memo: "*Your 100th-day anniversary is coming up! He better plan something special for our Jane. Or else he'll get in big trouble with your Emo.*"

*   *   *

By the tail end of that spring, Seoul was a sea of red. Banners waved from storefronts. Flags flapped from streetlamps. Posters were plastered in the subways. That summer Korea was hosting the World Cup—well, cohosting, begrudgingly, with Japan, a point that Big Uncle was particularly sore about. The breakfast table conversation— once consumed with what felt like nonstop talk of *Don't Throw Me Away* and *Leave Me*—was suddenly soccer, soccer, soccer. New hybrid phrases—new for me, at least—circled the table:

Daehanminguk, Ha-i-ting! Literal translation: *Land of the Great Han People, Fighting!* Figurative translation: *Go, Republic of Korea!*

"Oh, *Pilseung*, Korea!" Literal translation: *Oh, victory, Korea!* Figurative translation: *You're going to win, Korea!*

"Be the Reds!" That slogan was in English, but it referred to the Korean fans, who called themselves the "Red Devils."

One morning Big Uncle laid the newspaper flat on the table. *"That Coach Hiddink is really something. Whipping our boys into shape,"* he said.

Emo, who never struck me as the soccer type, pushed her brother's arm off the paper and began furiously scanning the picture of the national team. *"What are you doing?"* Big Uncle demanded. She was tracing a finger under each player's face, as though reading the lines of a book. *"Looking for my favorite."*

"Your favorite should be Park Jisung. He's the one to watch." Big Uncle stabbed the chest of a player who was down on one knee in the front row. I'd seen that player before, in the posters on the subway. He bore an uncanny resemblance to Changhoon—both shared the same boyish, eager grin, their eyes crinkling into slivers, a smile that went all in.

Emo snatched the paper back from her brother. *"Park Jisung is only my favorite from the neck down."*

"What you don't know could fill the shelves of our national library," Big Uncle muttered.

Seeing Big Uncle and Emo banter sometimes made me wonder what my mother had been like around her siblings. Would she have joined in the back-and-forth? Or did she have that kind of rapport with Sang instead?

Emo's finger stopped at a young player with long hair and a delicate face. He looked like the frontman for a boy band. *"Ah, there he is! Our Ahn Junghwan! The prince of the soccer pitch."*

Emo wasn't exaggerating—that was actually what Ahn Junghwan was called, as Monica would gush to me later at school.

Emo said, *"Jane, who's your favorite?"*

I peered down at the picture of the team. I supposed the loyal thing to do would have been to choose Park Jisung. But instead my finger landed on a different face, with a square jaw and pronounced cheekbones. There was something about his face that was different from all his other teammates'. There was something about him that reminded me of the Korean guys I grew up with back in Queens.

"*Who is he?*" I said.

"*Cha Duri.*" Big Uncle shook his head. "*His father played for the Bundesliga. But I don't know, this little punk still has to prove himself.*"

Emo shook her head, too. "*He's not my style at all. His features are too harsh. You probably like him because he's a gyopo like you. But born and raised in Germany.*"

That was why he looked familiar. It was funny how the same Korean faces managed to look different depending on where the person grew up. It was like how back in New York you could spot the FOBs (Fresh Off the Boaters) in the crowd—the genetics were the same, but the expressions they wore on their faces had a foreign, confused air.

"*The first Korean match is in Busan,*" Big Uncle said. "*My company for a ticket.*" Then he sighed—a low, wistful sigh. He was staring not at the newspaper but across the room, out the glass of the terrace door, and past the courtyard. I recognized that sigh. It brought me right back to Flushing, and Food, and the 7 train.

For our hundredth, Changhoon was planning a surprise two-day trip for us. I was able to get the days off from school only because Monica had offered to cover for me. I promised I'd buy her a souvenir from wherever it was Changhoon was taking me. "Maybe he escorts you Jeju Island!" Monica mused in the break room. "Is where Pae Byun and Ahn Jaeni go their wedding honeymoon."

The actors who'd portrayed the roles of Chulsu and Jihae, respectively, from *Don't Throw Me Away.* But when I told her what Emo had told me—that the show was "played out"—Monica looked chagrined. "But I still like."

I was two minutes late meeting Changhoon in front of the ticket booth at Seoul Station. He was tapping on his watch. "*Ya, I kept calling you! Why didn't you pick up?*"

Chuh! *'Cause I'd never hear the end of it from you,* I almost joked, remembering the words I'd overheard the first time in Café Michelangelo. But it was too early to joke. I fished my phone from my purse and saw six missed calls from him. *"Sorry,"* I said instead.

He gave me the once-over and told me I looked like a student back-packer. *"It's my only luggage,"* I explained. It was either that or packing my clothes, makeup, and hair products into plastic FamilyMart bags. It was the same nylon backpack I'd brought with me from New York but hadn't touched since. When I unzipped it to pack for the trip, the insides released, strangely enough, the smell of mahogany and wheat-grass. It brought me right back inside the Mazer-Farley house. But as Changhoon took the backpack from me and examined it, I began to see its shabbiness through his eyes. Despite its overall sturdiness, it was worn here and there. And it was a rather unbecoming shade of forest green. I grew self-conscious. Probably Emo never would have let me leave the house with it.

"So where is exactly this secret place?" I asked.

"Well . . ." Changhoon rubbed his hands together. *"I'm taking you back to your ancestral homeland. I thought you'd want to know where you came from."*

"We take the train to North Korea?" I said with exaggerated effect.

I waited a beat for Changhoon to laugh along at the ridiculousness of my question. He didn't. Instead he stared back at me blankly. *"That's impossible,"* he said. He could be a very literal person.

But Changhoon was actually taking me to my mother's adopted home of Busan, the coastal city on the southern tip of the peninsula. As our train thundered southbound, I stared out the window. Large steel cranes dominated the plots of land, jaws gaping dumbfounded in the air. Wrecking balls were poised over low-rise buildings, ready to raze their old and tired façades. But then the scenery shifted, concrete giving way to farmland. Makeshift huts with plastic roofs dotted the fields. We passed trees bearing what looked like round bundles of pa-per. Later I would learn they were pears. Big Uncle said that was why they were so expensive—because of the labor of wrapping each indi-vidual fruit to protect it from the elements.

My mother had once made a similar journey southbound to Busan, during the family's wartime flight from the North. But she had been only a child. Sang, too. The few details Sang had offered up were characteristically sparse: *Train inside full. No choice but riding on top. It was little bit* tap-tap-hae. Then his tone would grow dismissive. *But those days what isn't little bit* tap-tap-hae?

Emo was the one to fill in the blanks, even though she herself had not yet been born. It was my grandfather who'd ordered the family to flee south as war broke out. *"We'll meet in Busan,"* he'd said, before the Communists came and conscripted him into their army. But all southbound trains were already bursting with women and children clutching cloth-wrapped bundles. My mother and her family had been forced to ride on top of the roof of the train car. Sang and my mother sat toward the middle while Big Uncle and their mother sat to the outer ends, their hands encircling the smaller children as if playing a game of ring-around-the-rosy. At each stop more passengers got on, but no one got off, the cars groaning with the burden of too many people. Sometimes the train stalled for days at a time. Their journey took more than a month. What the family's livelihood had been in those early years in Busan was uncertain—my grandmother had probably peddled rolls of homemade *kimbap*; the boys ran odd jobs for the neighbors. It had been a dark stretch of the family history. They were finally reunited with Re Myungsun when he was able to escape from the Northern army. He started running south and never looked back.

I gazed out the window. Our train was approaching a tunnel burrowed into the face of a mountain. The train rushed through—the whoosh of wind causing the cars to rattle—and the lights flickered off. In that darkness it felt more than just a "little bit *tap-tap-hae.*" It felt as if we were being swallowed whole.

When we emerged from the tunnel, Changhoon pulled my hand away from myself. I'd been rubbing my chest. *"Everything okay?"* he asked. *"You look pale."*

"It's just . . . I wonder if my mother's family took this same train from Wonsan. During the war."

"*That's not really possible*," Changhoon said. "*Unless they transferred trains in Pyongyang or Seoul.*"

Sometimes I wished Changhoon would just indulge me. "*Ay, I'm not talking real-life train schedules. Only imagining.*"

"*Don't say it like that*," Changhoon told me. I felt chastised. Maybe talking about the war was a no-no.

But he was referring to my Korean itself. "*Your cadence. It goes up and down too much.*" His finger drew a zigzag through the air. When I asked if he meant my accent, he shook his head and said that was fine but that my cadence was "*a dead giveaway you're a foreigner.*"

Changhoon took his hand from me and ran his fingers through his windblown hair. "*Here's what you sound like: 'The TIger GOBbled UP the BOY and GIRL.'*"

He smiled, triumphant in his ability to diagnose the problem with my Korean. "*We Seoulites stay neutral when we talk. Listen: 'The tiGER gobbled uh-UPP the boy and gir-RUL.'*"

"*But you go up and down, too!*" I pointed out. I thought this would make Changhoon laugh, just as I couldn't help but laugh sheepishly with Devon about the Italian ices.

But Changhoon bristled at my comment. "*No I don't.*"

I trained my ears on the conversations surrounding us. The other passengers' animated chatter rose and fell like lapping waves. The Busan cadence had a distinct, familiar rhythm. If I closed my eyes, I would be right back in our church basement. It felt quite different from the Korean spoken in the capital. It was only in hearing the contrast at that moment, on the train, that I realized that Seoul Korean felt unfamiliar, sterile.

"*I like Busan-speak. It sounds like music.*" Like a lullaby, I thought.

"*But that's not how you're supposed to speak Seoul standard Korean.*" He said it as if it were no big deal to ask me to fix the very rhythms of my speech.

I probably should just have left the conversation there. Why rock the boat when we could have enjoyed the rest of the train ride holding hands and watching *Gag Concert* on his laptop? Except I didn't.

"*Your cadence isn't perfect and flat either,*" I said. "*What about when you say 'why'?*"

"*What* about *when I say 'why'?*"

"*Here's Changhoon Oppa's sound.*" I unlaced my fingers from his. "*'Wah-ai-AI-yai!'*" I slashed a line in the air. It spiked like a series of murmurs on a heart monitor.

Changhoon looked nonplussed.

"*I do again: 'Wah-ai-AI-yai!' Kind of like when Valley Girls say, 'Oh-miGAWahd!'*"

He continued looking at me blankly.

"*You can dish it out, but you're not so good to take it, huh?*" I said, poking him gently in the ribs to try to lighten the mood.

"*Oppa is just trying to help you,*" he said. I thought his tone would soften, but it remained resolute. "*If all you want to do is make jokes, how will you ever improve?*"

*   *   *

We did spend the rest of the ride watching videos. But there was an uncomfortable silence between us. This had been the closest we'd come to having a tiff, and by Changhoon's stiffened jaw I could tell he was still upset. His words, too, continued to rattle uneasily within me. It felt a bit as if he'd posed a test. As if my ability to correct my cadence—or not—was like some last linguistic hurdle to surmount before achieving full assimilation.

But when we arrived in Busan, that tension was immediately defused. Perhaps it was the energy of the city—so different from the frenetic, competitive pace of Seoul. Here the air itself was alive with freshness and tasted almost salt-licked. Again we were subsumed in a sea of red: World Cup paraphernalia was draped from every post and storefront.

"*Big Uncle told me the first Korea match happens here today,*" I said. "*If only we had tickets to see it.*"

"*That would've been nice, wouldn't it?*" Changhoon said.

"*But even more than that, I want to see the ocean. Can you take me? I feel and smell and hear it, but it is so* tap-tap-hae *that I cannot see.*"

The last time I remembered seeing the ocean was through the window of the plane as we lifted off from JFK. Queens, Brooklyn, the city—all became indistinguishable specks surrounded by water. Seoul, despite the Han River splitting the city in two, was otherwise landlocked.

"*You sure you're not* bada-chulsin?" Changhoon said, taking my hand once more. *Ocean-born.* It sounded less corny in the Korean. "*You really are a Busan girl.*"

"*And a New York one, too,*" I added, wagging my finger from side to side, the way Devon and Alla used to do with each other. *And don't you forget it,* I almost added. But I was certain the expression did not translate from the English.

In a matter of minutes, there was water, water everywhere. "*There's your ocean,*" he said, pointing out the window of our cab to the stretch of beach. I tugged his arm, making my voice light like a buoy, dripping with *aegyo.* "*Can we stop? Pretty please?*" I hoped it would coax him into ordering the cabbie to pull over. I wanted nothing more than to pry off my heels and sink my feet into the cool water.

But of course there wasn't time. We drove on, smelling and hearing and seeing the sea through the windows of the cab, until it gave way to high-rise buildings and receded from view.

Changhoon had hired the taxi for the day—we'd stopped quickly at the Grand Sinnara Hotel, on the shores of Haeundae Beach, to drop off our luggage, before he crammed all the city's sights into the short span of the morning: Dalmaji Hill, Dongbaek Island, the famous "Forty Steps" staircase. But probably the most memorable was Jagalchi Fish Market. Alley after alley, stall after stall, sea creatures of all kinds writhed and wriggled in buckets and tanks. There were rows upon rows of red fish, blue fish, big fish, small fish. Prickly sea urchins, long ropes of eel, abalone on the half shell, translucent baby octopuses and their larger, purple, opaque cousins. We laughed as one particularly feisty octopus attempted mutiny, sliding out of its Styrofoam box and across the floor. It was a successful three feet into its escape before the vendor noticed and dumped it back into the box. The air was hot with notes of early summer and cool with the clean smell of fresh fish.

We ate a late breakfast in one of the restaurants lining an alley of the fish market. Women in pink galoshes and matching pink gloves scooped treasures from their fish tanks out front. *"Dine with us, brother and sister, dine with us,"* they chanted. Their voices gathered in a chorus—cadences scaling up and down, like sirens of the Donghae Sea. *"Rest your legs here. Scallion pancakes, on the house."* We were lured into the one that called out to Changhoon, *"Handsome bachelor, come in! Come in!"* The woman was old enough to be his mother.

When we were back in the cab, Changhoon squeezed my hand. *"I have a surprise for you. I thought . . . well, you might want to see where your mother grew up."*

Living in Seoul, sometimes I found myself forgetting there was a whole country beyond the capital's concrete limits. But Busan, still the second-largest city in the country, had a different persona altogether—it was suffused with a fresh energy and rhythm. To think that my mother had wandered these streets from the time she was a little girl. To think I was breathing in the same ocean air as she had all those years ago. This was the closest thing to my mother's true homeland—not Seoul.

I squeezed Changhoon's hand back. *"You're right. I was so curious. Now, thanks to you, I know."*

"No, I mean where she actually grew up." Changhoon pulled a sheet of paper from his bag. It was a printout of a map. *"You said your mother lived in one of those refugee villages in Busan."*

That had been on one of our dates—at a sake bar in Gangnam— where I'd rambled on with one of Emo's stories. After a few thimble-fuls of sake, I could barely recall what exactly I'd divulged to Changhoon.

"Well—I think I found it."

"You what!" English flew out of my mouth.

I had formed a picture of the whole neighborhood in my mind. A stretch of shantytown shacks lining the Donghae coast. The dull tin luster of corrugated metal roofs contrasting with the bright salted blue of the sea. But an abstract curiosity about a place harbored in your mind was very different from arriving at that actual place in a matter of minutes.

When the cab pulled up, however, a gaping construction site stared back at us. Whatever had been there before was gone.

"*No, that can't be right,*" Changhoon said, scanning his printout furiously. "*It's definitely supposed to be here. . . .*"

We stared at the empty dirt lot. To one side lay neat piles of wood and steel beams, primed for construction. There were the bones of a building being erected, and the hollow spaces between the framework exposed the horizon line, where blue sky met blue-green ocean. The view was both like and unlike the view from the 7 train.

A man in a hard hat and an orange vest stepped out of a truck parked on the site. Changhoon ran over to him, waving for me to follow. I was tripping on the gravel but right at his heels all the same. "*Sir! Sir!*" Changhoon called out. When he finally caught up to the man, he asked what had happened to the village that had been there before.

"*How'm I supposed to know?*" the man said, turning away. "*I just work here.*"

"*Sir, please!*"

The urgency in Changhoon's tone must have made the man soften, if just a notch. "*Yeah, there used to be villages like that around here.*" He paused to go *hraaack!* before launching a spit wad onto the ground. Big Uncle always did the same thing. "*But they could also be anywhere.*"

Changhoon looked dejected.

"*Sorry, kid. That's all I know.*"

This quest had stirred in me a longing that up to this point had been dim and hazy and inarticulate. But now that we were *this close*, it suddenly asserted itself, grew sharp in my chest. To give up now would have felt worse than never having tried at all.

I punched Emo's speed-dial number on my phone. I heard Changhoon ask the construction man what they were building and the man's gruff response: "*Take a wild guess. High-rise condos.*" Emo picked up on the first ring. I had called her before, when we'd first arrived in Busan, and she'd launched into an endless stream of questions—until

Changhoon had pointed to the phone with a *Hurry-hurry, wrap it up* motion. This time I was spared the long-winded exchange of pleasantries, and I asked immediately for the location of the house.

"Oh, that was so long ago! I just remember how down the road the carp-cakes man had his stall set up and American Uncle would sneak off to—"

"Emo! We try to find it now. Tell me where it is. Please. If you can."

Emo at first bristled. I knew it was rude to cut her off. Yet she complied. *"We lived at the foot of the old drawbridge. Follow the coastline. It was the first alley to the left. Pass the carp-bread— Pass the corner. That was always my route home from school."*

"But . . . you don't have any more details?" I asked, trying to mask my impatience when I really longed to yell, *Just give me the exact address!*

"Hold on," Emo said. I heard her shouting over to Big Uncle, and I heard him shout back a variation of the same imprecise directions, peppered with a few more details. Changhoon looked at me expectantly. I cupped the phone and repeated them to him. He stared at the map in his hands and shook his head. *"Then this is it."*

I don't think Emo quite understood how much it meant to me in that moment to find my mother's childhood home; it was a sensation that was new even to me. *"Have a great time!"* she said breezily, and clicked off.

It would have proved impossible to retrieve her imprecise childhood recollections—the exact location of the family home would be forever buried in the hazy recesses of memory.

Either that, or my mother's girlhood shantytown had been razed and was now resurrected as luxury condos.

When I got off the phone, Changhoon took my hand and led me back to the car. *"I didn't mean to put a damper on the day,"* he said. *"I just thought it'd be a nice idea."*

It had been disappointing, though; it was the pinprick deflating an otherwise perfect morning. But it wasn't Changhoon's fault. *"Good,"* he said when I shook my head and put on a bright smile. *"Because I have another surprise for you."*

Back in the taxi, Changhoon pulled something out of his bag. It was a package wrapped in pink paper and pinched at the ends, like a giant Tootsie Roll. *"Happy hundredth,"* he said, kissing me on the cheek.

When I took the package from him, it was soft to the touch. I held it to my ear and shook it with exaggerated effect.

"What are you doing?" he asked, puzzled.

"It's just . . ." A joke. *"Never mind."* I undid the ribbons; a rolled-up red cloth popped out of the paper. It was a red jersey that read, in English, KOREA, FIGHTING!

"Put it on!" Changhoon said, undoing the buttons of his short-sleeved shirt.

"What are you, Superman?" I said as he revealed what was beneath his shirt. He was wearing the exact same red jersey. Then he helped me put mine on. He straightened the shoulders and then stared proudly at his handiwork. "Couple-T's!" he said, pointing from his matching shirt to mine. "Couple-T" was the phenomenon of couples wearing matching outfits—on purpose. Monica had had to explain it to me when a gossip magazine in the break room was opened to a photo of Pae Byun and Ahn Jaeni dressed identically from head to toe: pink polo shirts tucked into the same pale blue jeans and shiny black loafers. The photo was snapped just as they'd stepped off the plane on Jeju Island for their honeymoon.

I didn't know what to say. I felt like the only person in the country who wasn't following soccer. And now Changhoon wanted us to walk around matchy-matchy. It was a sweet gesture—it just wasn't my style.

But it was a gift. And I could see that it made Changhoon happy. I thanked him for his thoughtfulness, kissed him on the cheek, then, quickly, on the lips. I could feel the cabbie's eyes in the rearview mirror, giving me *nunchi*.

But it turned out the KOREA, FIGHTING! jersey hadn't been the real surprise. Our cab was pulling up to what at first was an impenetrable ocean of red—Busanites wearing identical jerseys. When the crowd parted, I saw that we'd arrived at the World Cup Stadium.

I slapped Changhoon on the arm. *"No you didn't!"*

If his smile when I put on the shirt was bright, it grew even brighter still. *"I did,"* he said. *"I did!"*

My company for a ticket. It was Korea's first match of the World Cup. *"How on earth you getting tickets?"*

Changhoon shrugged. *"My father might've called in a favor."*

I didn't actually know what Changhoon's parents did—I always sensed he didn't feel comfortable talking about it. Since it was a sentiment I shared about my own family, I'd never pressed him for details. Although the other Korean-Koreans never seemed to have the same qualms; all the teachers at school pressed first about my MIA father's occupation until, after I offered up a few evasive answers, they redirected their pointed inquiries to the subject of my American uncle.

As we got out of the taxi, I immediately admonished myself for my earlier disappointment about the couple-T. *Why you act like baby?* And beneath that there was another nagging question that managed to surface: Would Ed Farley have ever done this for me, constructing an elaborate day in my mother's home city? *No.* He was too busy holding hands with Beth down Court Street. I had come to Korea to escape him, and I'd found Changhoon.

"Thank you, thank you, thank you!" I said, covering Changhoon's face with kisses. *Take that, Ed,* I thought with each kiss.

Changhoon laughed. *"One thank-you is more than enough."*

We grabbed hands and ran to the stadium entrance, becoming one with the sea of red fans.

If you watched any of the news coverage for the World Cup that year, you would've seen images of the South Korean Red Devils fans everywhere—an overwhelming tide of red T-shirts and painted faces. The Western media praised the Red Devils for their good manners and lack of . . . well, hooliganism. (This praise, however, did not extend to the one superfan who doused himself in paint thinner before lighting a match, with the hopes of becoming the twelfth man, the "ghost player" on the field.) But what that media coverage could not capture was the collective energy that radiated in the air of the crowd. It was palpable and pulsing; the only word to describe it? *Jung*—that deep, shared sentiment coursing through the entirety of the stadium and bursting into the streets. *Jung* for our national team. *Jung* among the fellow fans. I witnessed that overflowing *jung* for myself. A second wind pumped through my body—the exhaustion from the travel and the peaks and troughs of the day's emotions were ebbing away. The ripples of *jung* began when the Korean national anthem played and we solemnly placed our hands to our hearts and sang. Our notes soared from Baekdu Mountain to the Donghae Sea, just like the words to the song.

And then Korea scored its first goal. The bleachers were alight with life. We cried out in triumph. The woman in the red jersey next to me caught my eye. There was no flicker of hesitation as she wrapped her arm fiercely around me.

Suddenly we were all linking arms, swaying side to side and chanting cheers as one synchronized mass. *Oh, Pilseung, Korea!* I didn't know the words, but I mouthed along all the same. I looked over at Changhoon: his lips were pinched together in a tight O, his eyes crinkled with joy. Changhoon's arm was draped over my shoulders. *"Thank you, again,"* I said to him.

"Ay, no need," he said before turning back to the game.

"Changhoon Oppa," I whispered in his ear. *"Saranghae."*

I had never told anyone "I love you" in Korean. At first the word tasted . . . foreign, uncanny. It tumbled off my tongue and hit the warm ocean breeze. But its aftertaste was all freshness and familiarity. It felt like *jung* itself.

There's always a risk in being the first one to utter the L-word. In those fraught seconds before your beloved responds (or not), you're left wide open and trembling. And it's too late to snatch the word back, even if you wanted to.

But that's the thing with love, isn't it? It's not a venture for the risk-averse.

Breaking from the human chain, Changhoon clasped me and lifted me into the air. *"Jane!"* he cried, with feeling. *"I've wanted to tell you for so long. I love you. I love you. I love you."*

Patricia Park

I'd been holding my breath. Now I exhaled with relief. In the confusion of our embrace, the match, and the chanting crowds, the bag of *ojinguh* that Changhoon had been holding got tossed into the air. We spun round and round, drowning in dried squid confetti.

* * *

Korea beat Poland 2–0, and that night we celebrated on Haeundae Beach, in the red *pocha* tents that lined the shore. Curly-permed ladies served up slices of raw abalone, translucent strings of live octopus tentacles, and crab innards mixed with rice. Groups of friends pushed their plastic tables together and poured one another rounds of drinks. I remembered Sang once saying that the Haeundae *pocha* tents were where the *gangpae*, or gangsters, used to hang out. But those were the days long before ground was broken for the five-star resorts.

Every now and again, someone would cry, "*Daehanminguk!*" or "Fighting!" and that whole table would erupt into whoops. Their voices rose and fell in that familiar Busan cadence. I let their rhythms wash over me. I remembered my early days in Korea, eavesdropping on all those conversations—each one had felt like a flaunted reminder that I would never belong.

In the midst of the revelry, Changhoon teetered to his feet. It was clear he was about to make a public announcement.

"*What do you do?*" I said, tugging on his arm. "*Sit back down!*"

His cheeks were flushed and rosy. "*Don't worry,*" he said before turning to command the room. "*Attention, everyone!*" he said. The room came to halt. And then, to my utter mortification, Changhoon began dragging me to my feet.

"*You embarrass me!*" I whispered. But he was too strong; he pulled me up all the same, wrapping an arm tightly around my shoulders lest I wriggle away.

"*Don't struggle so!*" Changhoon whispered back. I could have been the escapist octopus from the fish market, writhing out of its too-tight box.

Changhoon turned to the crowd again. "*To our beautiful gyopo girl-friend, returning to our beautiful native Busan!*" He was not from

Busan—his family traced its roots back many generations to Seoul—but Koreans sometimes did that. Instead of emphasizing the individual "my" or "her," they spoke in the collective possessive.

Then, as one, his audience turned its eye to me.

The crowd did not whoop and cheer, the way they had at their own private tables. They looked from him to me—I froze under that scrutiny—then back to Changhoon.

"*Okay, drunko!*" someone shouted. With that, the crowd's attention snapped; they all turned away and resumed their tableside chatter.

Busan in that moment felt uncannily B&T.

My cheeks were still burning red from Changhoon's public outburst when the *pocha* lady weaved her way toward us. There was something in her purposeful gait that reminded me, for some reason, of Nina. "*Here,*" she said. She was addressing me. "*Took you for a foreigner at first. I didn't know you were one of us.*" She lowered a Styrofoam plate of live octopus tentacles onto our table.

She didn't linger to hear our thank-yous but instead spun on her heel and stalked off. I told Changhoon that if she hadn't just given us free *anju*, I would've thought we had pissed her off.

"*Well, you know what they say about Busan ladies,*" Changhoon said, reaching for his chopsticks. I thought of the women in the pink galoshes, calling out to us in soft voices in the fish market.

"*What, they're mermaids of the ocean?*"

"*No, they're tough.*" He lifted a still-squirming string, dipped it in a mixture of salt and sesame oil, and dangled it above my mouth. "*Here, eat up.*"

The tentacle was curling itself around the tip of the chopstick. I was fascinated and repulsed at the same time. As I chewed tentatively, the octopus tentacle fought me furiously, suctioning the insides of my mouth. "*Keep chewing!*" Changhoon instructed. Finally it relented. It let out a salty burst of sea before giving up the fight.

"*That was a little grossing me out. But kinda cool. I guess I can now cross it out of my list,*" I said, but Changhoon was turning around. A bottle of C1 *soju* arrived. It was sent by a man sitting at the next table. He looked about Sang's age.

"You'll need a drink to go with that anju," he said gruffly. We tried to thank him, but he was already turning away to quaff his own *soju*.

Changhoon poured me a drink, and then I poured him one. We toasted—first to our magnificent victory, then to our magnificent national team. We drank to the magnificence of our Busan people. The *jung* that began in the bleachers of the stadium pulsed through the *pocha* tent. It filled my lungs and made me gasp with breathlessness.

We finally stumbled back to the Grand Sinnara Hotel, to a suite that overlooked the Donghae Sea. Up to that point, Changhoon and I had never been intimate—like most Koreans we both lived at home, and the furthest we'd gone was the occasional make-out or grope at the movies or in his car before he dropped me off at home. We hadn't even gone to one of the many love motels that rented rooms by the hour, a fact that shocked even Monica. *You guys* still *haven't done it?* But I knew that our getaway trip came with the implicit promise of sex. And I was determined to give him the best sex of his life.

But Changhoon passed out before I could do it.

While he snored off the *soju*, I stared out the window. The *pocha* revelry had died down, and a stillness swept over Haeundae Beach. I slipped out of our suite and rode down in the elevator. Once I hit the outdoors, I pried off my heels and found myself half trotting, half tripping toward the ocean. My feet sank into the damp, soft sand and then the ocean itself, the ebbing waves licking my toes.

A bridge stretching across that expanse of water glittered in the distance. Later I would learn that it wasn't the old Yeongdo drawbridge, but in that moment I imagined it was. Just as I imagined I was staring out at the little cluster of shacks at the foot of that bridge, where my mother had once lived. And in all of my Korean sojourn, that moment was the closest sensation I'd ever felt to coming back home.

* * *

The next morning, eyes still blurry with sleep, I roused Changhoon, climbed on top of him. I closed my eyes, bracing myself for the waves of discomfort.

But they never came. Changhoon flipped me so he was on top, perhaps to save me from doing all the work. The second I began to wince—sex wouldn't start to feel enjoyable until much later, once we became accustomed and attuned to each other's rhythms—he'd ease up with gentler movements.

After he came, his face shone with sweat. Panting, he petted my hair. *"Jane-ah,"* he said. *"Way to end things."*

I started, then realized that my brain had blipped—it was doing that literal-translation thing again.

What I think he'd actually meant was, *That was out of this world.*

Chapter 19

Seoul for New Yorkers: The Definitive Guide

That summer our national team enjoyed a winning streak. Each victory—each draw, even—was met with an ever-escalating frenzy. We kept advancing until we lost to Germany. Our loss coincided with the anniversary of the Korean War—two tragedies twinned together, palpable in the very air of the streets. And just like that, the revelry ended, the waves of fans ebbing away.

* * *

The monsoon season came and went, followed by a thick, claustrophobic humidity that coated the city like a damp woolen blanket. But when summer reached its end, the oppressive heat lifted. As fall swept in on a cool, refreshing breeze, I received an e-mail from Nina. "So over everything here," she wrote. "Is there a Gino's in Seoul we could catch up at? That is, if your offer's still on the table."

I didn't think Nina would actually take me up on my offer to visit Korea, though it was one I renewed at the end of each e-mail. I'm ashamed to admit this, but I had dismissed Nina as too provincial. I could hardly picture her leaving the neighborhood to board the subway to Queens, let alone a plane to another country halfway around the world.

"*She's your best friend. We must show her a good time,*" Changhoon said over dinner one night, with the same dogged determination he mustered for his vocabulary logs and his daily calisthenics (something he did every morning since mandatory military service). He pulled out his phone and furiously punched keys.

"*Maybe not* best *friend*—"

"*Oh! Just heard back from my army buddy Yongsu!*" Changhoon scrolled through the message. "*He just checked with his co-worker, who checked with his foreigner English-teacher friend, who knows all the hot spots. But that foreigner friend hasn't gotten back to us yet.*"

"*You just sent that text barely one minute ago.*"

Changhoon's phone buzzed again, bearing messages from other friends. He'd gone through his entire social network in less time than it took me to compose a single text in Korean. Now I understood why Emo would get so impatient when I failed to respond to her immediately.

"*Everyone agrees: We should take her to Itaewon. She'll probably feel more comfortable around other foreigners.*"

Itaewon. Where Sang had warned me not to go. Where my mother had met my father.

"*Why Nina will want to come to Korea only to see American faces*—" I started to say when Changhoon's cell vibrated once again.

"*Fi-nally! Yongsu's co-worker's foreigner friend got back to us.*" Changhoon was working himself into a frenzy. I touched his arm. "*No need to go obuh.*"

Obuh—presumably from the English "overboard"—was another adopted foreign word that had drifted its way into Korean. It shed its extraneous second half, its harsh Western contours. As it circulated from tongue to tongue, the word grew smooth and round, like a pebble washed up on shore. Now it made its home here, assimilated among its Korean counterparts. But the word was no longer recognizable from its native form.

But Changhoon was pushing aside his bowl of rice, frenziedly typing notes on his phone with his thumbs. "*Here's where we should take her for round one. . . .*"

* * *

Nina flew in on the red eye from New York, just as I had. But I had been at my lowest point then. And now I had a new home, a new city. A family. A *boyfriend*. I was nothing like the Jane I had left behind.

"*Jane-ah*," Emo said on the drive to Incheon Airport. "*You know you're responsible for everything while your friend's here.*"

I knew what she meant: *Don't let Nina out of your sight.*

Emo took her eyes off the road to give me a stern look. "*Did you hear me?*"

"*Yes,*" I answered.

At the airport I almost didn't recognize Nina when she came through the gate. She wore dark-rinse fitted jeans, a T-shirt with a printed design, and a pair of dark leather sneakers that looked like Sam Surati's bowling shoes. The old Nina used to wear light blue flared jeans and chunky-heeled Steve Maddens during the day, spandex minidresses by night. That Nina also wore heavy makeup. But instead of the usual dark liner tracing her mouth, her lips were now nude. Gone, too, were the thick gold hoops that hung heavy from her earlobes. Her once iron-straightened hair now framed her face in loose waves.

"What the . . . !" I said, throwing my arms open to her.

"Oh, God, please don't say hipster," Nina pleaded as we hugged tightly. "I was going more for Banana Republican."

When we broke apart, she looked me up and down. "Whoa, what's with the makeup and heels at three in the morning, or whatever time it is over here?"

I spun around. "How do I look?"

"You look!" she said.

I felt a little slighted that she didn't actually offer a compliment, but Nina was already turning to greet Emo. She tucked her body stiffly into a bow as Emo held out her hand. Seeing Emo do this, Nina changed course and stuck out her hand as Emo retracted hers and tipped her head slightly into a bow. They laughed.

"Nice to meet you, Ms. Re," Nina said. I was surprised by the nervous tinge to her voice. "Thanks for letting me stay with you. I'm sorry you had to come get me in the middle of the night."

I wasn't sure how much English Emo actually understood, but she had a wide smile plastered across her face. She kept nodding and saying, "No purobohlem! No purobohlem!"

"Oh! Before I forget—" Nina reached into her backpack (Nina with a backpack instead of her usual fake black leather tote?) and pulled out a white pastry box tied with red-and-white string. It was from Gino's. "They're cookies. From a very famous bakery in my neighborhood," she said in slowed-down speech.

"You know the way to my aunt's heart," I told her.

Emo accepted the box from Nina and took a whiff. "I diet!" she said, but she was smiling.

"You? Nah!" Nina swatted the air. "You look like a woman."

Emo said to me, "*Your friend, even though she's a foreigner, you can tell she had a good family education.*"

I pointed to the Gino's box. "There better be cannolis in there," I said to Nina. My tongue found its natural footing in English—I'd forgotten how much it had atrophied during my time in Korea.

She rolled her eyes in mock exasperation. "First off, Jane, it's 'cannoli,' no *s*. Second, smuggling cannoli fourteen hours out of Brooklyn? That's just . . . *wrong.*"

"Man!" I feigned annoyance. "That's the only reason I invited you."

"I ain't your cannoli mule," Nina said, index finger swaggering through the air.

I jerked my thumb at the loudspeaker. "You hear that? That's them calling your return flight."

Nina and I both broke into laughter—deep, rumbling laughs. We hugged again.

"I missed you!" she said.

"Me, too!" But when I looked over at Emo, she was shaking her head at me. I didn't know what I'd done exactly that she disapproved of, but I could read her expression. And it said, *You, on the other hand, did* not *receive a good family education.*

*   *   *

When we arrived at the apartment, Emo insisted on heating up some
fish stew. Nina politely finished the whole bowl. After she unpacked
her things and freshened up, I took her to Café Michelangelo.

"I still can't believe you're here," I said over our cups of caffe latte.
"You've changed."

"Look who's talking," she said, fluttering a hand at me. "Jane, it's
just me. You didn't need to get all dolled up."

"Like I did it for you," I said at first. Then, glancing around, I lowered my voice. "Honestly, though—people here expect you to dress up
more."

Nina's eyes swept the room. "But that girl's not. And that one. And
that one."

I knew what Emo would have said: *Those girls aren't making the
most of their potential.*

I made my voice light and airy and changed the subject. "So what
do you want to do? Get some sleep so you don't crash later? Or power
through the day? Or . . ."

Nina fished out a book from her bag. A million little Post-its fluttered
in the wind. Its cover read *Seoul for New Yorkers: The Definitive Guide.* A
picture of Namsan Tower was sandwiched between the Twin Towers.

"What an awful cover," I told her.

"It came out right around 9/11," she said, shaking her head with
pity. "What could they do? Retract the thousands of copies after the
fact? You can't help but feel bad for whoever published it."

"So you bought it anyway."

She pointed to the orange price sticker. "It was in the bargain bin,"
she said. Then she let out a laugh; it sounded bitter. "Speaking of bins:
Joey Cammareri and me split up last month."

"What!" Nina's last e-mail—the one before she wrote about flying
over to Korea—had gushed about him. "Why didn't you tell me sooner?"

"I wanted to tell you in person."

So that was why she had come. Not to see me but to run away

from her ex-boyfriend. Nina looked from my face to the book down on the table.

"So . . . what happened?" I asked.

She scraped away the price tag with her fingernail. "Whatever, it doesn't matter anymore." Abruptly she opened her book again. "Anyway, these are the neighborhoods I want to go check out."

I flipped through Nina's flagged pages, marveling at her organization. Here were her marked entries:

MYEONGDONG:

A toss-up between Times Square and Rockefeller Center, this shopping mecca is packed with more Japanese tourists than a Hello Kitty store. Stop for lunch at Myeongdong Kalguksu for its famed knife-cut noodle soup . . . but you'll have as much luck finding the "original" as you will Ray's Famous.

INSADONG:

Combine Greenwich Avenue's quaint nod to the Motherland (think: Tea and Sympathy, Myers & Keswick) with Montague Street's landmarked charm and you get Insadong Road. Come here for the traditional teahouses, where one thimbleful of persimmon-and-herb-infused *cha* will set you back eight bucks.

SAMCHEONGDONG:

Sleek SoHo galleries mingle with ye olde *hanok* architecture in a surprising East-meets-West, yin-yang harmony.

HONGDAE:

Pratt types and Chelsea club kids alike hang in this wannabe East Village hood (read: Williamsburg). Strut down Gutgosipungil, aka The Street You Want to Walk Down. (*Really.*) You'll get some serious Astor Place déjà vu.

DONGDAEMUN MARKET:

Buyer beware: Four-for-a-dollar socks and China-made trinkets galore await in this ginormous flea market.

"So," Nina said, rubbing her hands together. "I can't wait to meet your new man! What's he like?"

"Changhoon's great," I said. "He's planned a huge night out for you featuring not one, not two, but *five* rounds of funnery! Spreadsheets may or may not have been involved." I threw my hands up in the air for added flourish. I was laying it on thick—deliberately—and Nina knew it.

"God, you're such a cornball," she said. "At least that hasn't changed."

Nina knew that about me, and I realized how refreshing it was to talk to someone with whom I had a shared history. "But seriously, Changhoon—well, you can call him Chandler—might've gone a tiny bit *obuh*—overboard—but it's all good."

"Who knew having fun would be this much work?" Nina said. "But . . . it's all stuff *you* want to do, too, right?"

I shrugged. "I'm up for whatever."

"Okay, but I'm warning you—not sure how much steam I've got left in me." She downed the last of her cup. "Coffee here's *expensive*." They had cost six dollars apiece. "This stuff better last me all day."

* * *

That evening, after Nina and I checked out some of the tourist sites marked in her book, we made our way to Itaewon. I had yet to check out the neighborhood, and not just because I was dutifully heeding Sang's warnings. The truth was, after my trip down south with Changhoon, I'd started to create a more forgiving portrait of my mother. Busan had been a time of her innocence, and I didn't want to sully that image. So I kept putting it off, putting it off, the way Devon used to push her Chinese textbooks to the bottom of her homework stack.

Here was what *Seoul for New Yorkers* had to say about Itaewon:

This "foreigner-friendly" nabe is now chockablock with the latest fusion lounges, clubs, and restaurants more multi than a Benetton ad. Recently spotted: Pae Byun and Ahn Jaeni (the Korean

Brad Pitt + Jennifer Aniston) canoodling at JJ's. Duck into the back alleys for your fake Prada fix or bootleg K-dramarama videos.

And then, as a postscript:

Those seeking carnal pleasures, worry not: Hooker Hill can still be found in the back alley across from the Hamilton Hotel.

When Nina and I emerged from the 6 train station, here was what Itaewon actually looked like: pops of white and black and brown faces, mixed into the sea of Korean. Here and there soldiers in camouflage sprinkled the crowds—rough-necked, clean-shorn, and impossibly young. African men in suits spoke softly into their cell phones. It was the first time since my arrival that I saw anything other than a steady stream of Korean people. The low, squat cement buildings were smudged with smog, and their old tarp awnings bore a mixture of Korean and English writing. The wooden stalls selling decorative fans, chopsticks, and leftover World Cup paraphernalia spilled onto the sidewalks. The occasional sleek coffee shop or bistro dotted the stretch of tired façades. There was a familiar grittiness in the air. I could have been emerging straight from the 7 train station: Itaewon looked just like Main Street, Flushing.

That moment marked something new for me. It was the moment I bundled up the very last of Sang and Hannah's words on all matters Korean and tossed them in the wastebasket. They had taught me a lifetime of misinformation. It was all, to put it in Sang's own words, *nothing but the wrong.*

We were supposed to meet Changhoon and Monica at a place called Irish Pub, which was said to have the best burgers in all of Seoul. Round two would take us to Pose, a cocktail bar where the bartenders made an elaborate show of tossing bottles in the air and setting drinks on fire. Round three: a luxury karaoke bar. Round four: a *minsokjujeom*—a folk-themed bar that served scallion pancakes and milky *makgeolli* rice wine in hollowed-out gourd shells. And finally we'd cap off the night at JJ's, a club.

After a few wrong turns, we arrived at Irish Pub. Monica texted to say she was already there. She showed up ten minutes early to everything. Changhoon was held up at work but would be there shortly. Inside, the air was thick with cigarette smoke. The bar was crowded with young Western faces, mostly men. Their eyes went straight for us. "Who are all these white guys?" Nina whispered to me. "Army?"

"No idea," I whispered back.

The walk to the back of Irish Pub felt endless. There were dozens of men staring at us or beckoning us over to their tables. "I could maybe get used to this," Nina said.

Monica waved at me from a table in the back. To my disappointment, she'd brought Rachel along. Before I could introduce Nina to them, she was already doing the honors. "I'm Nina. Good to meet you," she said, sticking her hand out at them with her usual assertiveness.

Right away something felt off between us. In general, Rachel and Monica tended toward the hyperfeminine, and they seemed a little taken aback by how easily—and perhaps presumptuously—Nina had inserted herself into the group. Where I always hemmed and hawed, never quite assured in social settings, Nina assumed familiarity with everyone. But that was what I loved most about her.

The girls offered limp hands in return.

Just as we settled into our seats and poured drinks from the pitcher of beer that Monica and Rachel had already ordered, we were surrounded by three men. They draped their torsos over the empty chairs. "Hel-*lo*, ladies!" they said. "Mind if we join you?"

Nina sized them up. They were tall, lanky, and fair, probably about our age. "Hello yourself," Nina said before turning back to me. She was not into skinny blond guys; she preferred her men dark and muscled. But Rachel and Monica tucked in their shoulders and giggled—actually *giggled*—and nodded demurely at the empty seats. The men sat down and introduced themselves. They were English teachers from the middle of America. Since Nina wasn't interested in the guys and I had a boyfriend, there wasn't much point in talking with them. While they focused their attention on Rachel and Monica, Nina filled me in on all that I'd missed out on in New York.

"I swear," she was saying, "all of a sudden every guy on the F train's wearing these dumb-looking trucker hats."

"Trucker hats," I repeated back. "What's that even mean?"

Monica's high-pitched trill cut through the air; she was laughing—it sounded forced—at something one of the guys was saying. She always tried too hard. Nina glanced over at Monica and shook her head before turning back to me.

"You know, like they're driving a John Deere tractor or something, wearing it all like"—Nina demonstrated. "What, do they think they're farming for corn in the middle of Brook—"

"Hey, *ladies*," one of the guys interrupted. "What's so funny over there?"

Nina ignored him and continued with her story.

But the guy persisted. He had the boyish air and dress of someone in his mid-twenties, combined with the hard-worn, bloated face of a forty-year-old man. "No, come on. Tell us," he said, his arm grazing mine.

"We were in the middle of a joke," I said, pulling my arm closer to me. I didn't want to encourage him.

But the guy did a double take, regarding me in a new light. "Wow, you speak English real good!" He proceeded patronizingly slowly. "How many years you been studying—"

"She's *American*," Nina interrupted, rolling her eyes. "And she obviously speaks it better than you."

The men, realizing they had overstayed their welcome, stood up and left the table. Rachel and Monica exchanged another look.

It was going to be a long night.

An hour and a half later, Changhoon finally arrived. He smelled of his usual cigarettes and sweet cologne, but as I stood up to greet him, he also reeked of barbecued-meat fumes, and alcohol coated his breath. I was furious; he was late to the very evening he had planned himself. *"Where you were? Why so late?"* I demanded. I was like Sang, my already tenuous grasp of the language deteriorating with my rising emotion.

"Ay, I told you I was running behind," Changhoon said, patting me to sit down.

"But only ten minutes!" He'd texted, in ten-minute increments, each time to say he'd be ten minutes late. *"Why you not right away say you one hour late?"*

Monica and Rachel exchanged another look; I was being unseemly. *"Hwesik,"* Changhoon told them. Company dinner. They knew—and I should have known—that these things were sprung suddenly, and attendance was not optional. They nodded understandingly.

Evening out my tone, I introduced him to Nina. He shook her hand enthusiastically and apologized for his lateness. "Nice to meet Jane's best American friend!"

I was immediately embarrassed. She *was* my best friend from America, but I wasn't hers. She had a whole crew waiting for her back home. Though Nina took it in good stride.

Monica jumped in. "Changhoon Oppa—I mean, Chandler is hungry? Thirsty? What I can get for you?" She began fussing about—frantically flagging down the waiter for a menu and another glass.

Changhoon glanced about the table and said, in a loud voice, "Tonight style is all-American! We take American friend to American Irish Pub." It was the same line he'd once used on me.

Nina didn't hear him, didn't understand him, or didn't think it was funny, because she did not laugh. Changhoon's comment hung in the air and was falling fast, so to keep it buoyant I let out a long string of laughter. *"Ah-ha-ha-ha!"* I said. *Nunchi.*

Nina shot me a look.

"So who is superior English speaker: Jane or Jane friend?" Monica asked Nina.

"I'm sorry, I don't understand your question." Nina looked at me in confusion.

"I think she wants to know which one of us speaks English better."

"Yeah, I got that, but her question still doesn't make sense."

Changhoon, perhaps out of *nunchi*-ful obligation to Monica, jumped in. "Only because Jane is like Korean and you are real American."

Real American. Like "real Chinese." As opposed to fake.

Nina said, "I've got a New York accent, but Jane doesn't. Jane talks like people from the news. I talk like people from *Goodfellas.*"

They countered with blank faces.

Nina puffed out air. "Forget about it." She took a swig of beer, and Rachel and Monica exchanged another look I didn't understand. When Nina put down her drink, she said, "Actually, Jane's also got a much bigger vocabulary than me. She picked up a lot of new words working for her last boss." Nina caught my eye, and we both laughed.

"What does it mean?" Monica said.

Nina explained. How Beth would foist her academic, feminist readings on me. As she talked, I was brought right back to the Mazer-Farleys'—to that dusty top-floor office. Beth's smell worked its way through the stale beer and cigarette smoke.

"'Nor can we discourse on the feminist movement—in all its wrought history—without first discoursing on the problematic tradition of desire and the male gaze,'" Nina said.

"I can't believe you remember that!"

Nina was a fucking genius.

She turned to the group. "This Jane you see before you now? A year ago she was *nothing* like this. No makeup, no heels, no nothing. T-shirt and sneakers every single day. Beth would never recognize you now!"

Nina also had no fucking *nunchi.*

"Really!" Changhoon said. "I cannot picture."

I'd hoped his reaction would be different, that *he* would be able to picture it—or at least accept it.

"It is because she lives with crazy feminine boss?" Monica asked. "Jane told us stories of her. She is with too much . . ." Monica fluttered her fingers under her armpits.

Rachel said, "And Jane tells us her husband is whip."

"Ed *was* whipped." Nina turned to me. "I guess he got so tired of it that he ran away to upstate New York."

"What!" I couldn't help the gasp that escaped from my lips.

"I thought I told you. Ed's left Brooklyn. He took a job at one of the SUNYs up there."

"Ed's . . . gone?"

A thousand questions swirled. Did Beth follow him? Were they still together, or did that mean they were now separated? And what about Devon?

"What he looks like?" Rachel asked Nina.

"Blond, blue-eyed, pretty built. Personally, Ed's a little too fair for my taste, but compared to his wife he was way hotter. She looked like a troll. Jane didn't tell you?"

I was turning red, redder by the minute. I looked down at my beer glass, feeling Rachel's eyes on me. "Hotter than Chandler?" she said.

How could I answer that? My face would give me away. But Nina was slapping Changhoon on the arm. "He couldn't hold a candle to you, Chandler."

Changhoon laughed. But based on the confused tone to his laughter, I knew he had no idea what the expression meant.

*   *   *

And so the evening proceeded, on to the next round and the round after that. But just as we were leaving Irish Pub, the plumes of fresh smoke gave way to a staler stench, of decades' worth of cigarettes and spilled whiskey and something else: a heavy, downtrodden spirit hanging in the air. I hadn't noticed them before, but a huddle of middle-aged Western patrons sat propped on stools at the bar. Something about their faces gave me pause. Their features sagged toward the pilled carpet on the floor, as though defeated by gravity. I stared into their dull, disillusioned eyes—all yearning and hope had long ago been extinguished from them. Had their eyes ever shone with youthful luster? Had one of these men, in his younger incarnation, once gazed at my mother with desire?

Hurry up, hurry up . . . I heard Changhoon and Rachel and Monica chanting behind me. I wanted to look away, but I couldn't. I studied each face, dreading a connection linking someone's features to my own. But I found none. I told myself I was never coming back to Itaewon.

At the end of round three in the luxury karaoke bar where we mouthed along the words to English and Korean songs, Nina let out a not-so-subtle yawn. "Jane, come with me to the bathroom?"

At the sink she stared into the mirror, prodding the bags under her eyes. "I'm completely wiped out. Mind if we cut the night short?"

"But we only have two more rounds to go." I thought of all the effort Changhoon had put into planning the night. "You sure you can't rally?"

"Honestly, Jane? Your friends are kind of wearing me out. Your boy Chandler's way too hyper. So's that girl Monica. I just can't deal right now."

"Yeah, no, fine."

"Jane." Nina's tone was pleading. "I just flew in this morning. I haven't slept in thirty-six hours. I'll have more energy tomorrow."

Nina was right. I relented. "I'll explain to Changhoon." I fluffed my hair in the mirror, then stared back at our reflections. Nina did look exhausted. We both were. "Let's head home."

We rejoined the others outside. The streets were teeming with groups of young Seoulites in various rounds of revelry. Middle-aged women worked food carts selling rice cakes smothered in red-pepper sauce and deep-fried battered vegetables. The air smelled of cooking oil and wisps of girls' perfume and car exhaust.

"*So sorry, but I think we should go home now,*" I told Changhoon.

"*But we still have two rounds left. . . .*" Changhoon trailed off when he saw Nina looking at us.

"Sorry," she said. "I'm the one being lame."

"What it means?" Changhoon asked.

Nina shook her head. "It doesn't matter."

Changhoon insisted on escorting us home, while Monica and Rachel went ahead to round four.

When our taxi pulled up to Sinnara Apartments, Nina and I got out. Changhoon was waiting in the cab, to make sure we made it safely inside.

"I owe you one," she said. "Well, technically two: that time I dragged you from Twine when you were making out with what's-his-face."

"Still holding a grudge. I might've married what's-his-face," I said. "Forget Seoul. You'd be visiting us in the suburbs instead. Two-point-five kids, Labradoodle, white picket fence."

"As long as it wasn't in *Jersey*." She let out a comical shudder. Then, "Look, I'm sorry I dragged you away from your friends."

"No biggie," I said, shrugging. But I knew that Changhoon was disappointed. He'd just been too polite to show it.

Nina studied me. "You know you can go. You don't have to come in with me."

You are responsible for everything for your friend. "I should."

"You should do what you want." She nodded at the cab. "So go."

"He *did* pull in a favor to get us on the list at JJ's. . . ." I started.

"You think he'd do that for just anyone?" Nina said. "You should go to him."

I knew that *nunchi* was why Nina insisted I stay out. *Nunchi* also told me I should renew my offer to go back home with her, but I didn't.

"He's crazy about you. You can tell just by the way he looks at you." She turned toward the entrance. "Good night, Jane."

I watched Nina disappear through the doors. I didn't follow her. Then I returned to Changhoon in the cab, and we drove into the night.

* * *

We soldiered on through rounds four and five without Nina. But all of us were flagging. At the folk-themed rice-wine bar, we slumped in our booth, our heads propped up by our arms, our gourds of *makgeolli* rice wine left untouched. At the club the pounding bass brought me right back to that night at Twine. After Changhoon and I said good-bye to Rachel and Monica, we popped into a motel that rented by the hour—it was usually how we ended our dates ever since our Busan trip. We were too drunk and Changhoon was too exhausted to perform, but we went through the motions all the same.

By the time I returned to the house, it was five in the morning and Emo was sitting cross-legged on the marble floor, awaiting my return.

Chapter 20

A Good Family Education

W*hat did I say about not being a bad friend?"* Emo shouted as soon as I bowed hello. *"Did you think I was joking?"*

My eyes were still adjusting to the glaring overhead lights. *"No, but—"*

"Don't 'No, but' me. How dare you leave your friend, your poor foreigner friend who traveled all the way from America to see you, by herself?"

When I told her that Changhoon had made all these plans and I felt responsible to him, Emo interrupted with, *" 'Responsible'? Don't bother me with 'responsible'! Who on earth raised you in this manner? Did you receive no family education whatsoever?"*

In that moment Emo could have been Hannah. She matched her tone for tone, and even the structure of her rhetorical questions was parallel—only some of the words were swapped. With Hannah it was, "Who on earth were you born to?" or, "Do you want people to think you received no family education whatsoever?"

Then Emo went on, in a softer tone. *"It's not exactly the safest time for a foreigner to be traveling alone. With all that's going on . . ."*

She was referring to the demonstrations downtown. During the World Cup, in a camp town just north of Seoul, two girls had been struck and killed while walking to a classmate's birthday party by a U.S. military tank "practicing routine drills." The news was buried as the nation cheered our successive victories. Now that the soldiers driving the tank had been found not guilty, the story bounded into the spotlight once again.

"*But that's beside the point.*" Emo's tone snapped back to its earlier harshness. "*You don't throw your friend away for a boy! She's like a sister to you.*"

I fixed my eyes to the floor. "*I'm so sorry, Emo.*"

She sighed. "*Go to bed.*"

*   *   *

Nina waved away my apology later that morning. "Your aunt was still up when I got back. So we watched some soaps."

"But still, that wasn't cool of me."

"It's really not a big deal—"

My phone bleeped; it was a text from Changhoon.

"Chandler wants to take you out for lunch today. To apologize for being late yesterday."

Nina held up *Seoul for New Yorkers.* "I was just going to do my own thing today."

"Come on, please? It'd mean a lot to me. I want you guys to get to know each other."

"Sure, fine."

It took me an hour to assemble myself while Nina waited impatiently. By the time we got to lunch, she'd decided she was going to be in a sulky mood. Every attempt to lure her into the conversation was rebuffed. Eventually Changhoon and I just resumed our Korean rapport.

When we left the restaurant, we walked through Gwanghwamun Square. "*Oh . . . we shouldn't have come this way,*" Changhoon said. "*I forgot the protests.*"

But it was too late. We were already in the thick of thousands of people holding candles in paper cups. Changhoon took hold of Nina's arm and ordered me to take her other. He wore an embarrassed smile. "I'm so sorry!" he said to Nina. "Usually our country not like this. Usually so safe. Only because this accident make our people have so much . . ."

He trailed off, but I knew that the word he wished to say was utterly untranslatable. *Han.* A fiery anguish roiling in the blood, the result of being wronged.

Nina studied him. "I'd be pissed, too. Fucking military," she said.

But as we steered Nina through the crowds, no one confronted us. Instead they looked at us—looked at Nina—and quickly parted, making way for our passage.

* * *

Through the course of the week, Nina and I diligently went to the other sights earmarked in her guidebook. But something felt a little off between us, like soda gone flat. The effervescent burst that Nina had swept in with her on arrival had dissipated.

On her last night, after a rather sullen dinner of fatty pork barbecue, we returned to the apartment, where that sullenness spread and filled the air. Nina began to fold clothes and stuff them into her bag with a quiet but tense efficiency. Then she looked up from her piles of clothes and souvenirs. "You sure you don't want to just . . . I don't know, hop on the plane back home with me?"

The forced lightness of her tone put me off. "Why would I? This is my home now."

Nina returned to folding her clothes. "Whatever you say."

"What's *that* supposed to mean?"

"Nothing, nothing," she said, backpedaling. "I'm just worried about you."

"Well, don't be. Things are going great for me here," I said. "I've got terrific friends. I have Changhoon."

Nina brushed lint off one of her shirts. She muttered, "Keep telling yourself that."

"You got something you want to say to me?" I asked, staring straight into her eyes.

"Yeah, actually I do." She put down the shirt she'd been folding and met my unwavering stare. "Chandler's all right, but I hate how you act around him. It's like . . . it's like you're on a job interview and you're afraid you'll blow it."

Her words hit a nerve. She pressed on. "If you stay, you know you'll just end up like that femmebot Monica."

"You mean Rachel," I corrected.

Nina blinked. "Nah, Rachel's all right. At least the lights are on upstairs. I'm talking about the taller one. The fake-nice one who was all up on Chandler. You just know a girl like that's gonna snap one day."

"Monica was *not* all up on Chandler. She's just a little eager to please," I argued. I had a dim awareness that Monica had *some* feelings for Changhoon, but then again she was like that with everyone—tripping over herself in order to accommodate others.

"You know what I think? I think you're not really in love with Chandler. You're just grateful he loves you. I wish you'd stop acting like a phony and go back to being the Jane I know. The Jane I *knew*."

Who did she think she was? Haranguing me as if she were the only one who'd ever experienced love and heartache.

"You nothing know." My brain unexpectedly blipped, conflating English words with Korean syntax. If Nina noticed my slip, she didn't mention it.

I went on. "Just because *I* don't feel the need to gush endlessly about my feelings"—the way Nina always did, the way she was so unabashedly, embarrassingly *open* about everything—"that doesn't mean I don't feel passionate."

"Please, Jane," Nina scoffed. "I've seen you get more excited about cannoli than about Chandler. I know what love is. And what you've got with Chandler? It isn't it."

"You're one to talk," I said sharply. "Did you see the way you acted around Joey—J.—whatever the hell his name is now? *You* were the phony! Meanwhile, anyone could see he was a total d-bag."

Now *my* words hit a nerve. She stopped, blinked. Blinked furiously, as if she were trying to shut out the words but couldn't. "H-he was . . . my everything, Jane," she whispered. "And turns out he's been hooking up with Angela this whole time."

Nina had only found out about it after the fact, when Angela accused Nina of swooping in when she had "first dibs" on Joey. She somehow managed to turn the whole gang against Nina. And just like that, in the span of a few months, two decades of friendship—gone.

"Every time I run into Angela and Mrs. Fabbricari, they just stare past me like I don't even fucking exist. And not only have I lost him, I've lost my best friend from child—"

Suddenly Nina burst into a sob. It was a sob unlike any I'd heard before from her, like a watermelon cracking in two, with a sweet, raw redness bursting forth.

I recognized that sob. It was the same sob I'd stifled in the PC bang more than a year ago as I struggled to force thoughts of Ed Farley and New York out of my head, my heart. And now Nina's cries threatened to unlock that pain again. I ached: for Ed, for Nina. *Push the pain away*, I wanted to tell her. The more you indulge those tears, the more that raw sweetness will spoil and seep into all parts of your waking life.

I opened my mouth to speak, but my brain became a confounded mix of Korean and English clichés: *There are bigger fish in the frying pan. Strike while the tree trunk's hot. The beloved who threw you away and left you will get no farther than ten blocks before he catches a foot disease.*

I said nothing.

Nina's sobs began to taper off. "Anyway, sorry," she said, hastily wiping her eyes with the back of her hand. "I didn't mean to"—she hiccupped—"make this all about me."

When she steadied her breath, she said, "Why'd you run away from New York, Jane?"

I went *pfft*. Tried to anyway. "I didn't run *away*."

Nina studied my face. "Did something happen back there? With . . . Ed?"

"Wh-what makes you say that?"

"Just a feeling I got. From e-mails. Other things. Like the way you reacted the other night when I mentioned him."

I struggled to control my face; abruptly I turned away. But how I longed to tell Nina! I'd free myself of this heavy burden, this feeling of *tap-tap-hae* weighing down my heart.

But what good would come of it? The relief would only be temporary. It wouldn't change what I'd done. And she would judge me. How could she not? I'd never be able to look her in the eyes the same way. If our roles were reversed, I would judge her as well.

"Jane, you don't have to keep trying here. You know you can just come back home."

Nina was wrong; I had nothing to go back to. If I couldn't change the past, then the least I could do was bury it far behind me. I pressed one firm, final hand to my heart.

When I turned back around, Nina looked up at me with expectant eyes.

"You're being ridiculous," I told her.

"Jane, I just poured my effing *guts* out to you right now—"

Her tears were starting up again. She reached for a tissue from the vanity table and blew her nose loudly. I cringed. That was a no-no here. When she blew again, her nose made a rude, squelching sound, like a fart. I almost laughed. Recognizing the humor of the moment, Nina almost did, too. If either one of us had broken out laughing in that moment, I suspect that things might have been salvaged on the spot.

But neither of us laughed. When she turned back to me, her eyes had gone dead. And that was when I knew: I had lost her.

Nina boarded the plane home to New York. Winter came rushing in. The condensation collecting on the subway windows grew hard and white, calcifying into frost.

Chapter 21

Cost-Benefit Analysis

In the heart of that winter, Changhoon began conversations, in earnest, about the future. *"You're not going to ditch me for America, are you?"* he said one day over sweet-potato lattes at Michelangelo. His tone was intentionally light—to save his pride, I knew. But even I had the *nunchi* to infer that he saw that future with me.

Other things were happening, too, that made staying more attractive. I got a promotion at work. Who would've thought that Food would help me become assistant CFO of Zenith Academy? It was an inflated job title, I knew, but still, it was my first promotion. Sang had never recognized me for all I did at Food. Any joy I took in my newfound success, however, came at a cost: Monica had been passed over. Success at Zenith was zero-sum; my gain was her loss. She'd been at the school for longer, and she certainly worked more hours than I did. Don't get me wrong—I took pride in my work and did it well, but I didn't *live* for it the way Monica seemed to. When the clock struck six-thirty, I shut down my computer and set off on yet another date with Changhoon. It was the classic principal-agent relationship theory, but having never been on the "agent" side, it didn't make sense to me beyond the theoretical until now. If you didn't have a stake in the business, then what incentive would you have to work harder than you had to? It was the reason Sang perennially complained about finding good workers at the store; with the exception of Hwan, he thought the rotating cast of stock boys and cashiers were all *nothing but the lazy*.

"*You deserve this promotion more than me,*" I said to Monica in the break room. "*Principal Yoo should give to you.*"

But Monica demurred, shaking her head rigorously. "No, Jane Teacher, you deserve. You speak perfect native English. Always make me so jealous!" She was really too modest for her own good.

*   *   *

At the end of that winter, Changhoon proposed to me. And, reader, I accepted. But Korean proposals were not treated with the same romantic fanfare as their American equivalents. There was no ceremonious brandishing of a diamond ring, for one. He did not get down on one knee. What he'd actually said was, "*My parents want to meet you. Want to come over to say hello?*" Emo had to decode that for me. "*That means he wants to* marry *you! But he's supposed to come to the girl's side first. Call him, quick! We'll set a date. What's his favorite dish? Never mind, we'll make him a ginseng chicken stew. . . .*" Then she sent herself into a tizzy.

When I told Monica the news, she said, "He wants you meeting his parents? You are so lucky!"

But there was something about the way she said it that felt off— the emphasis was on the "you." I chalked it up to a snag in translation. "*Ya, he's the lucky one,*" I said.

But Monica did not match my joking tone. "You know who is Changhoon father, right?"

"*I think he does something for Sinnara?*" I still didn't know exactly what his father did. I think I was mostly grateful he never pried about mine.

"But . . ." She lowered her voice. "They okay, who you are?"

My skin prickled at where this conversation was headed. I forced my voice to go light. "*If this is about my Choco Pie addiction, I swear I getting help. . . .*"

Monica's face tightened. There was a flash of something—anger? annoyance? feeling *tap-tap-hae?*—before her expression became blank and unreadable. It reminded me of the way the hostess at Dosirak had sized up Sang and the rest of us disapprovingly.

This wasn't how I'd pictured our conversation. We were supposed to whoop about the engagement, the flowers, the dresses, the honeymoon. Wasn't that what friends did?

I switched to English. "There something you want to say to me?"

Immediately a different look darted across Monica's face—fear. Then it was gone. Her expression flooded with its usual friendliness. "Ah, nothing. I was just think—" She corrected herself. "Just think*ing*, maybe Jane Teacher needs some help planning. Anyway, I'm so happy for you!" She smiled. It was painfully forced.

Monica was right: I *was* lucky. But I was also right: Changhoon was lucky, too.

* * *

Sang, too, was not exactly thrilled with the news of my engagement to Changhoon. This was a blow, because I'd taken it as a given that Sang would approve of our union. I was getting married to a *Korean*; he wouldn't have to worry about me anymore. Instead he grew quiet. Thinking the phone line had gone dead, I called out "Hello, hello!" until Sang finally said, "How long you know him?" I told him a little more than a year. "Who he is?" he asked. "What kind of character he has?"

I gave Sang a rundown of Changhoon's *jogun*—conditions and qualifications. It read like a résumé:

• He graduated from Yonsei—the Yale of Korea.
• He worked for Sinnara—the combined GM/IBM/GE/ Walmart of Korea.
• He came from an excellent family. (Apparently Emo, as well as Monica, had done some snooping.)
• He was ambitious.
• He was organized; he made prodigious use of spreadsheets.
• He was smart.
• He was kind.
• He was age-appropriate.
• Oh, and he was tall.

I added one more item, in my head: *He wasn't married*. As I ran through the *jogun*, I couldn't help but compile a second, simultaneous list. And by all objective measures, Ed Farley came up short.

"When your wedding gonna be?" Sang asked.

"I'm meeting his parents next week. Then, after that, I guess we'll figure out a date. Changhoon wants to get married before the spring." As I spoke, I remembered Nina's comment about getting the job interview. I promptly dismissed it.

"So I guess you staying."

"Looks like it."

Sang cleared his throat. "Uncle probably should sending your stuff."

"What stuff?"

"You forget already? Everything you leaving behind your old boss house in Brooklyn."

"Oh," I said. "Right. Sorry."

"I thought no point Uncle sending because waste of money, when you just coming back home anyway," he said. "But now you not."

"No," I said. "Now I'm not."

Sang fell quiet again. The rhythms of our speech were off, out of sync.

When he started up again, he said, "They ask about you. I tell them you fine."

"Who?"

"Lady boss and little Chinese girl. She getting big. The husband, he not there."

I wondered if Ed was still in upstate New York, as Nina had mentioned. But I knew better than to ask Sang.

"That neighborhood, change a lot. More American people."

I knew what he meant. American like Beth. Not American like Ed or Nina. And certainly not black.

"Uncle old store, Smith Street? Now sushi restaurant. Around the corner they building new construction. *Condos.* Who gonna buy when projects down the street?"

I was growing exasperated with my uncle's digressions. "I thought you'd be *happy* for me."

"Happy? Why happy?" He sounded genuinely confused.

Finally I burst, "Uncle, I'm getting married!"

"Why I gonna be happy, when you make decision out of impulse?" And like that, Sang's tone snapped to impassioned, angry. "Better you take more time, think responsibility. But you doing only what your heart wants!"

Marrying Changhoon is the responsible thing! I longed to shout back. Couldn't he see? That responsibility was the sole impetus behind every major decision I'd ever made: choosing Baruch over Columbia, double-majoring in accounting and finance, applying for a job at Lowood, *fleeing* Ed? If I had done only what my heart wanted, I would have chosen to be with Ed—consequences be damned. But my uncle knew nothing of my heart.

Sang went on. "You *always* like this, since you was the child. You say, 'I want to run away, becoming baby-sitter! I want to run away, living Korea!' People not suppose to do like that. What you choose not gonna be easy for you. But anyway, is your life now."

Sang seemed to have made up his mind about the kind of person I was. I knew that none of my actions—past, present, future—would ever change his perception of me. "You don't know anything about me," I told him.

Sang let out a *chuh* of disbelief. "You, too."

It was one of his classic comeback lines, his way of wedging in the last word. But whether he'd meant I knew nothing about him or that I, too, knew nothing of myself was unclear. At any rate there wasn't much left to say.

"Will you make it to the wedding?" I asked him.

"Maybe, maybe not. Timing not so good right now, Uncle business."

"Well then . . . I guess we'll be in touch."

And with that, Sang and I hung up.

"I just don't understand him!" I muttered on my way back to the kitchen, where Emo, squatting on her haunches, was pickling cabbage on the newspaper-lined floor. Ever since the proposal, she'd been intent on teaching me how to cook. She looked up at my sudden outburst, the intrusion of English.

"What's wrong?" she said.

"It's just . . . tap-tap-hae." I relented. *"So sorry. I know it's not respectful to say."*

Emo said, *"I always felt a little sorry for American Uncle. Your grandfather was always so hard on him."* Her eyes darted to the front door before continuing. *"Much harder on him than on Big Uncle, if you ask me. I used to overhear fights between your grandfather and Big Uncle. Right after Big Uncle got married to that crazy fox-woman. He said, 'Why don't you show* noryuk *like your younger brother? It should be the other way around.'"*

Noryuk. Effort. Diligence. Follow-through. *"American Uncle had gotten into Seoul National. He was all ready to go up to Seoul when your grandfather told him he was sending him to America instead. And not to study."* I asked why. *"In case everything here went belly-up, I think. You never knew in those days."*

It could have been the language of business. Re Myungsun was hedging his bets or diversifying his investment portfolio. Which meant Sang had been his father's Plan B.

"And American Uncle, he never came back. Not until your grandfather's death." Emo shook her head with pity. *"He's been away for too long."*

I asked Emo why my grandfather had sent American Uncle away instead of Big Uncle. It didn't make sense to me. Why cast off the one you thought was better and had more follow-through? Why not keep that son beside you and send the son you thought less of far away?

"Didn't you hear a word I said to you?"

Emo was still crouched as she spoke. It always amazed me how long she could hold that pose—the kids at church called it the "kimchi squat"—without tiring. I couldn't stay on my haunches longer than a minute before pins and needles started shooting through my legs.

"*It takes a certain kind of person to go through immigration. You get broken. Only the strongest can put themselves back together again. But even then . . .*" Emo, still balancing, pried open the leaves of a cabbage head and sprinkled them with fistfuls of salt. "*Even then you can never return to what you were before.*"

I asked her what Sang had felt when my grandfather had ordered him away. Again Emo gave me a look like she thought I was a *babo*. "*What could he feel? That was the way things were back then. Parents ordered and children obeyed. No back talk, no questions asked. Not like this young generation, that only seems to do whatever they want.*"

She handed a cabbage head to me, and I followed suit: packing the salt into its tender leaves.

"*But anyway! We shouldn't be talking about sad things,*" she said. "*We have much, much happier things to focus on. Like your proposal! Well, I guess it's not official-official until the parents give permission. Oh, Jane-ah! You know why I'm so happy, right?*"

"*Because you were scared I become 'Old Miss' and now no more worry?*"

"*No, no, not that. I never worried about that. I'm happy because now I won't have to guard my heart anymore, thinking you'll up and leave me for America. I'm happy because you've returned home to Korea. For good.*"

After the salt leached the excess water from the cabbage, I helped Emo drain the heavy bucket. Carefully we rinsed each wilted cabbage head three times. Her words were still sinking in. My heart was torn. Here, in Korea, I made a connection I had always felt was missing my whole life and had now found with Emo. She was the mother I'd never had. But I also knew that her *other* words also rang true: If I stayed here, I could never return to what I was before.

*   *   *

The next morning I got into my usual blouse, skirt, and stockings. I sat at my vanity table; the reflection in the mirror sighed back at me. I spun open a jar of cream foundation. Dipped my sponge in, but I was down to the last "schmear" (one of Beth's words). I'd have to borrow some of Emo's.

I reached for her vanity drawer, bracing myself for the jumble of chaos that was bound to be inside; Emo tended to hoard things, stashing them out of sight. (I learned this when I stumbled upon the bakery box of Nina's chocolate cookies in the linen closet, half nibbled and growing stale.) I pulled on the drawer but was met with resistance. I gave the drawer handle a firm yank, and instead of the *clack-clack* of glass or plastic bottles hitting wood, I heard a rustling, like the sound made by a wedged piece of paper. I got on my hands and knees and carefully removed the drawer from its tracks. Out tumbled a downpour of mostly empty tubes and bottles. They clattered to the floor, rolling off in all directions, but my attention was focused on the impediment: a crinkled envelope that had been taped to the outside of the back of the drawer. It had come loose, flapping free like a barn door.

I hesitated. This was obviously some private letter or other. Emo had gone to so much trouble to hide it—was it my right to snoop? I remembered the short-lived period in the fifth grade when I had kept a diary. *"I hate Sang and Hannah! They're so mean! This house feels like a gulag!"* (We'd just finished up a unit on the Cold War in social studies.) *"I'm going to run away and go find my real dad and live with him!"* Hannah had found the diary, which I'd hidden in a shoe box tucked under the far side of the bed, against the wall. Which meant she'd gotten on her hands and knees and reached for the box with a broomstick. *So ungrateful!* she'd boomed, shaking my diary in the air. *How dare you call us by our first names? Don't you know how to show respect?* I didn't know whether she couldn't understand the English past the first sentence or if in her anger she'd latched onto my first set of offenses. She'd handed the book to my uncle, who studied the words on the page. Then, tossing it casually onto the table, Sang turned to his wife and said, *She wants to run away? Then let her go. But she's a fool if she thinks for a second that her American father wants to take her back.*

I held the envelope in my hands, debating what to do. But it felt thicker and stiffer than a letter, like photographs. What was Emo hiding?

Curiosity won out. I pried open the flap of the envelope.

Inside was a heavy, yellowed paper that had been folded over and over, as if someone had been trying to obscure its contents. Three brittle photos tumbled into my lap. One of a young couple. Another of two girls. But it was the third photo that hit me.

The man in that photo had a shock of rich brown hair—a color I would describe as all-American, a chestnut brown like the rich crests of the dads from TV sitcoms I watched while growing up. So, too, were his high cheekbones, cracking into a smile; the full bridge of his nose; and his strong jawline. His eyes I could not see at all—they were cast down at the bundle he cradled in his arms. I turned the picture over: *Currer Bell and his daughter, Jane.*

That bundle was me.

The photo slipped from my hands. I knelt in place, motionless. What to do? Tuck the photos away, pretend I never saw them? Confront Emo? Call Sang? Demand an explanation? But I could only fixate on the strewn makeup bottles, their irritating disorder. The photo, fluttering in the air like a fraught, suspended chord, dropped suddenly into my lap.

I felt a shadow in the doorway. Emo.

"Tsk, tsk, look at the mess you made!" She knelt to a squat and began corralling the bottles with a hasty sweep of her arms. She gathered them to her breast and dumped them wholesale into the drawer.

"Why are you just sitting there? Hurry-hurry!" She looked over at me, and she must have seen my blank, faraway expression. Then her eyes fell on the photo in my lap.

Disgust shot over Emo's face, her inky eyebrows pinching into peaks.

"I know who that is," I said in a steely tone.

"Oh, that." Emo was reaching for the photo. Her face righted; she forced air into her voice. *"That's just nobody."*

I was getting tired of her act. *"Don't call my father 'just nobody'!"*

My sharpness startled her; her hand froze in the air. I wasn't good at expressing—or modulating—my anger. My *han*. It was always the first emotion that leaped from my gut and licked the back of my throat, although life—Sang—had taught me to swallow it back down.

But suppressing your emotions, forcing your face to go blank like a dry-erase board, that was *tap-tap-hae*. Why couldn't I be like Nina? I envied her ability to open up, her emotions pouring out in unbridled, if unseemly, waves.

It was tiring, being kept in the dark.

Emo knew that I knew that the jig was up. *"Yes, you're right. That's your father."* She sighed. The singsong quality had drained from her voice.

"How could you keep him secret from me?"

"Honestly, I didn't really like him. Your father had no nunchi."

"Why, because he didn't fill your water glass first?" It was an insolent thing to say, but I couldn't stop the words from coming out of my mouth.

"That was the least of it," Emo tut-tutted. She took my father's photo and stuck it back with the others, rearranging them into a tidy stack. *"I only met him once. But we could all tell his character right away—he had no family education whatsoever. And then he took Big Sister away."*

Emo began the tale of how my mother had met my father. But as she spoke, a sharp bitterness suffused her story. It felt unfiltered and raw, so unlike her usual homespun tales. For once her words felt unrehearsed.

My mother had met my father—Currer Bell—while she was on a school-volunteer work trip down in the countryside of Jeolla province. That was where my father had been stationed. When she returned to Seoul, they continued a lively correspondence—so lively that she invited him home to Busan for the Chuseok holidays.

Every year Emo could hardly contain her excitement for the harvest holiday, because my mother would play with her and her friends and help her study for exams. That year, however, her excitement was tempered by the arrival of this "foreigner friend."

"Who was this man? Big Sister said he had no family. He'd come here on some government 'voluntary peace mission' trip. Father was so busy

trying to earn a living he failed to make the proper inquiries. Big Brother was already married to that crazy wife of his. Big Brother Number Two was long gone in America."

And so my grandfather, thinking the man was just a poor foreigner with nowhere to go for the holidays, gave him a warm welcome, complete with a banquet table so laden with food that its legs threatened to collapse. This I found hard to picture. But apparently my grandfather had a soft spot for the Americans—when he fled the North Korean army for Busan, they'd helped him along the way. They were generous with their food and supplies. Perhaps my grandfather thought he could return the favor in some small fashion.

"That man was insufferable," Emo said. "He and Father began to talk politics. I couldn't follow everything they were saying—I was just a child, and also his Korean was terrible—*but I remembered thinking how he should have just sat there quiet like a proper guest. Instead he had the gall to tell Father how he would reform our country. Him! A foreigner! Who did he think he was? Swooping in and expecting everyone to treat him like he was so special.*

"I kept looking over at Big Sister, to see if she would stop it. Maybe nudge her 'foreigner friend' to shut up. But the whole time she kept staring up at him all moony-eyed. Like she was grateful. *Big Sister should have taken Father's side. It was the worst kind of betrayal.*

"Finally Father shouted at that man, 'It's just your kind of thinking that split our land in two!'

"Crash! went the banquet table. Kimchi juice splashed all over the man's pants. He ran outside—or maybe Big Sister told him to go, I can't remember. When he was gone, I thought the worst was over. At last! I was starting to tell Big Sister about the new game that Oakja"—Oakja had been Emo's best friend from childhood—*"taught me. But Big Sister said, 'Younghee-ah. Later, okay? I promise."* Younghee was Emo's Korean name. *"She turned to Father. 'He's asked me to marry him. And I've said yes.' 'Have you gone mad?!' Father shouted back. 'I'd rather you marry the worst beggar in Korea than that man.' Big Sister said nothing.*

Father went on. '*I bet even the worst beggar in* America *is better than that man. That man is the* babo *of all* babos.'

"He kept trying to stop her. Told her this was her last chance. That if she stayed, he'd forgive her disobedience. And you know what she said to him?"

Eat well and live well, I thought. The same words Sang had once uttered to me.

But I was wrong. "She said, '*I love you, Father. But I love him even more.*' Then Big Sister got up from the table and left.

"I ran after her. Told her she better stay, because we had to play that game like she promised. She lifted me up. '*Younghee-ah, do you want to come live with us?*'

"I shook my head. '*Father thinks your friend's a* babo.'

"'*But your big sister loves him. Does that mean I'm a* babo, *too?*'

"*Jane-ah. I'll never forget this.* Big Sister gave me a big hug. But I was still pouting so I didn't hug her back.

"'*As soon as we sort things out, I'll come back for you,*' she told me. '*And then you can teach me that game.*' But she never did."

Emo's last words hit me in the gut. *Promise me we'll listen to the new Evv-R-Blü album when I get back?* I had never kept that promise to Devon.

But that was the thing, wasn't it? If my mother had made the "right" choice and stayed, she would have been heartbroken. Instead she left, and it was Emo who suffered afterward. Someone was always losing out.

Later, after Emo had regained her composure, she would tell me other things. The details she'd pieced together through the years. For one: My father had come as part of some "government volunteer mission" promoting "peace and culture." *The Peace Corps?* I'd asked, to which Emo nodded and said it sounded familiar. (Beth had done the Peace Corps in Costa Rica, right after college. She was continually on my case to apply, even though it would have put me two years out of the job market, with no new skills to add to my résumé.) Emo told me how my parents and I eventually set up house in Itaewon, where they could move about a little more freely than in the other, less "foreigner-friendly" neighborhoods. How they had traveled down again to the Jeolla countryside—*"another volunteer trip—or so they claimed,"* Emo said, with some consternation, as if alluding to something I didn't understand—and it was there, in a cheap *minbak* inn, the kind heated with *yeontan,* coal briquettes, that carbon monoxide seeped into the room where my parents were sleeping. Both died in the middle of the night. I had been left in the care of friends in Seoul; had I accompanied them on the trip, I would have died, too.

For as long as I could remember, I had created a certain memory of my last night with my mother before she died. It was a constructed one, but still its images were etched into my brain. There was the cheap room with the hard earth floor, the thick blankets and mats redolent of spittle and warmth. Our last hours together. My mother swaddling me in those thick blankets to protect me from the gas that took her own life. I thought she'd given her life to spare mine, the way mothers in fairy tales died to save their children. But that's not how it had happened at all.

I knew that Emo blamed my father for my mother's death. She was performing backward induction, tracing the sequence of events that led to her death, and all those roads led to Currer Bell. If only he had never set his "insufferable" foot in this country. Who knew how far back Emo followed the thread of blame. For her the story, and that photo, changed nothing. Her Big Sister was dead, and That Man was the one responsible. But for me, for me!

"So . . . *my father* wasn't a GI?"

"*Is that all you care about?*" Emo cried.

"*Of course I care. This changes everything!*" Was Emo so clueless? Who my father was changed what kind of person my mother had been. It wasn't so much that I was the kid of a GI; it was that my mother hadn't just been his one-night stand, the way everyone back in Flushing thought of her. She hadn't been thrown away and left behind. *She's a fool if she thinks for a second that her American father wants to take her back.* But this picture, too, revised my whole history—Sang had been wrong. I *had* been wanted. *"Not fair, you keep something so big from me!"*

Emo stared at her hands in her lap. *"I'm sorry, Jane,"* she said. *"Your grandfather would get so angry if anyone mentioned your mother that I guess I got used to never talking about her. But that was wrong of me. And I only found that picture after your grandfather passed away. It was tucked inside some old files. But it still doesn't change the fact that that man should've had the* nunchi *to leave our family alone."* Emo's tone was suddenly petulant, like a child's.

But soon it grew hazy, nostalgic. *"And then—you came to me. After they died. You were my sister's best parts. Whenever I held you in my arms and looked down at your little face, I could see only Big Sister."*

Emo reached for one of the other photos from the envelope—the one of the two girls. She gazed down at it tenderly.

"This was taken right before your mother left to start school in Seoul." She held the picture of my mother up to my face. *"This is your good half. Don't ever forget it."*

That night, after my talk with Emo, I kept staring at the photos, trying to force a flood of infantile memories to rush over me. But they remained locked; the photos released not one shard of the past.

In the black-and-white, sepia-tinged picture of my mother and Emo, Emo wore a school uniform and looked no older than Devon. In her prepubescent years, Emo was painfully skinny and knock-kneed, and she gazed up at her older sister with adoration. Devon had looked up at me in the same, hopeful way, when she asked me to help her with the Hunter exam. I focused on my mother in the photo. She looked lanky and drawn—the skin was stretched taut over her pronounced cheekbones. She had the same haunted expression clouding her eyes that she'd had as a child.

I placed her image side by side with the photo of my father. Could I picture them as a pair? I squinted, comparing them to the distant, hazy faces I had created for them when I was a child. My father was pretty much consistent with the picture I'd long created for him. But my mother was different. I'd always imagined her as looking more co-quettish, in a way that would have lured men. What happened to her laughing in a convertible, hair whipping across her face? Instead she seemed bookish, serious, and introspective.

Emo had said my mother stared up at my father during that Chu-seok dinner as if she were grateful. Just as Nina had accused me of being with Changhoon. It was the same word that had echoed through all of my childhood in Flushing.

If I had stared into my mother's face one year ago, I would have pronounced her handsome. Seeing her now, though, through my Seoul-adjusted gaze, I realized this: My mother would have been con-sidered plain.

Chapter 22

High-Maintenance

I ended things with Changhoon. Reader, I wasn't an idiot; I knew he was everything on paper. Marrying him would have been the responsible choice, providing the ultimate stamp of legitimacy for me in this not-quite motherland. I would finally shed my problematic American *gyopo honhyol* ways and, with Changhoon's guidance, fully immerse myself in the waters of Korea-Korea. But you could list assets ad nauseam and still the balance sheet staring back at you would not change what your heart longed for you to do. *You only doing what your heart wants,* Sang had chastised me. He'd been right about me after all.

When I broke the news to Changhoon, he told me I was just nervous, that it was perfectly normal to have cold feet. We were sitting on a bench on the banks of the Han River, and he was taking quick puffs from his cigarette. He said we should continue going ahead with it and that later, after the rush, we could sift through my confused emotions and make sense of them. As he spoke, I scratched my cheek; a film of foundation rolled under my fingernails.

But when Changhoon saw that I was resolute, he hunched over, his hands tapping together. He wouldn't look at me. He sat like that, blinking. Composing himself. Finally he said in his deepest voice, *"I know that my feelings are stronger than yours."* He took a long, deep pull of smoke. It swirled in his open mouth before a hopeful wisp streamed out. *"But . . . couldn't you just work on it? I'll help you."*

I thought back on Changhoon's "Development of Myself" chart. I thought of each of his elaborately constructed plans, our trip to Busan. Across the water, on the banks of the Han, there was a gap in the skyline, where a stretch of old buildings had just been razed. The city was dotted with cranes and scaffolds and stacks of building materials. All of Seoul under construction—a never-ending scramble to develop and redevelop itself.

With Changhoon I felt I was trying to be someone I wasn't. Yet he'd continually reward me for behaving in ways that felt unnatural, so I kept working on the act. But I couldn't force something that wasn't there. There comes a time where you've just got to be who *you* want to be. His words were finding their way back to me.

"*You deserve someone who's all in,*" I told him. I didn't know if the words translated, but I know he understood.

Changhoon and I were over. Ever the gentleman, he insisted on driving me home. It was a slow, despondent drive, nothing like the thrill of rushing over the Brooklyn Bridge with Ed. I wondered what that view from the Promenade looked like now, without the towers. Their absence must have echoed all through that empty sky. As we crossed the Han, I took in the river's stillness, this foreign expanse of water that should have felt like home—but never did.

*   *   *

When I returned to the apartment, Emo was sitting on the floor, back propped against the leather couch, watching television. She spotted my sullen face and jumped up. "*Apologize immediately,*" she said, before I even uttered a word. "*It's not too late to salvage things. If you don't act now, you'll lose your chance to secure your future forever!*"

At first it sounded as if she were speaking the language of commerce, of infomercials. But her words were accompanied by an expression that looked utterly pained. "*Do you want to be lonely for the rest of your life?*"

"Emo, I broke his heart. But I don't—I couldn't—love him. . . ." I trailed off. I was losing confidence.

She pointed to the TV screen. It was a rerun of *Don't Throw Me*

Away and Leave Me. "*You never finished watching it with me*," she said. "*You were too busy going on dates with Changhoon.*"

"*I know. I'm sorry.*"

She waved away my apology. "*Only because you never learned how it ends.*"

"*What you talking about?*" I said. "*Eun rejects Jihae and marries Bora. The end.*" The preview commercials for the finale had told me enough, without my actually having to watch it.

"*But he only marries her because he thinks Jihae's going to marry Chulsu. And Jihae only marries Chulsu because she thinks Eun's marrying Bora. When they each find out what the other did, it's too late. And the rest is trage—* Wae wooruh?" she said sharply. "*You'll ruin your makeup.*"

Emo was right. I shouldn't be crying. I couldn't stop them, though, the tears welling up in my eyes, threatening to smudge my mascara.

But there was a flicker across her face, her expression going gentle. "*Who is your Eun?*" she asked softly.

Ed and I used to sit around the kitchen table, eating his heroes and making stupid jokes long into the night. We spoke with an ease that never came naturally to Changhoon and me. It wasn't just due to his poor English and my weak Korean.

I wiped my eyes with the back of my hand—makeup be damned—and whispered, "*Ed Farley.*" I wasn't sure how Emo would react. She'd want a name like James Kim or John Hong. I remembered the way she'd referred to my father as "that man" and the scowl that had accompanied it. "*This man,*" she said. "*Do you still love him?*"

I nodded. "*I think I still do.*" I know I still do, I corrected silently.

"*Does he love you back?*"

"*He did.*" I paused. "*I don't know if he still does.*"

"*Then you have to go back and find out. Before it's too late.*"

I knew how much Emo understood longing. She could not get her sister back, but maybe I was the closest thing. What about all that Emo had said about guarding her heart?

"*But, Emo—I would leave you.*"

Her lower lip trembled. But she bit down and swallowed. She took in a deep breath and righted her face. *"Do you want to end up like the people from* Don't Throw Me Away?"

Apparently Bora went mad and set the house on fire. Eun tried to save her, but she leaped to her death. He ended up maimed and blind. Jihae committed suicide, and Chulsu remarried. Then the network shut down the show.

She continued, in a bright voice, *"What can I say? I'm a sucker for romance."* She put the photo back down on the table. Then she shot a fist into the air. Emo could have been Beth, rooting for local produce. *"Ee Jane, fighting!"*

It was time to come home.

*   *   *

I set about making arrangements for my return. I knew I should have looked for a corporate-finance position. But I was tired of doing all the things I *should* do. Once again I found myself on the job hunt. This time, though, I changed the focus of my résumé, playing up my small-business experience. Those jobs were there aplenty—if you knew to look for them—but they were overshadowed by their flashier big-bank counterparts. I applied for an analyst position at a family-run real-estate developer. I passed the initial phone interview and was asked to come in person. I set my return date to the States accordingly. It was probably not the most glamorous of jobs, but I was familiar with the work. I took a small pleasure in corralling details into place and trimming away inefficiencies.

After I gave my resignation at Zenith Academy, Monica said, *"Must be so nice for you, sweeping in and out as you please."* She struggled to keep her voice light, but a note of resentment cracked through. I noticed her change in tone before I registered her switch to Korean.

"What's your meaning?"

Monica began ticking off her fingers. *"Looks. Boyfriend. Job. Whereas some of us have to work for the things we get. Or don't get."* There was now no mistaking the bitterness steeping her words.

"You may *think* you know me," I said tersely, switching into English, "but you don't know the other half."

"*Oh*, tap-tap-hae!" she cried. "*You just don't get it, do you? They just gave you that job because you're the only native English speaker on staff. Principal Yoo thought it'd look good. You know*"—she let out a little laugh—"*for the image of the school.*"

The words cut; they undermined the work I'd been proud of and cheapened it.

"*Then maybe good for you I leave. Freeing up the budget. Maybe now you getting the promotion.*"

"*Wow, lucky me. I get your leftovers.*"

Maybe Nina had been right after all about Monica. I was too stunned and angry in that moment to process entirely what was happening. But later, looking back on that final conversation with Monica, I realized she must have found me as insufferable as I had found Beth, perhaps as insufferable as Emo and my grandfather had found my father. All those times I'd offered my advice to her—*Put your foot down* or *The squeakiest wheel gets the oil*—when I myself didn't have a clue about the system here. Maybe Monica longed to repeat back the same words I'd used to explain to her the rules of English grammar: *I don't know why, it just is.* No matter how hard we tried, neither of us would ever master how the other's world worked.

* * *

I wrote to Nina. I told—spilled, like a gushing watermelon—about everything I hadn't, or couldn't, that last night in Seoul. I worked up the courage to e-mail Ed. "*I'll cut straight to the point,*" I wrote. "*I have not been able to stop thinking about you since the day I left New York.*" It was a burden, I knew, to unload my feelings this way, but I ignored Sang's words echoing in my head. I poured out my heart to Ed.

When I wrote to Beth, I told her that "I'm sorry" couldn't even begin to explain—let alone excuse—what I'd done. "*I did something very bad when you were away at that conference in California. But in truth my betrayal to you began long before that.*" At a certain point, I didn't even know what I was typing anymore. I just blurted out the whole truth. Then I hit SEND.

I wrote a censored version to Devon, explaining my hasty departure. I told her I was sorry for breaking my promise to return, but I hoped I could make it up to her back in New York.

I did one last thing before I left Korea. I ended up going back to Itaewon, even though I told myself I'd never return. You could say I was paying homage to the place where I was born—and borne from. But the real reason was for bootleg videos. I rescued the entire series of *Don't Throw Me Away and Leave Me* on VHS from the bargain bin.

A few hours before I was to set off for Incheon Airport, Ed Farley wrote back. *"Jane! Jane! Jane!"* Nothing more. Hastily I fired back with my flight info. *I am coming! Wait for me!* I shouted in my head.

*   *   *

At the airport Emo handed me an envelope. Inside was the picture of my father and me. But she'd also included another photo—the one of her and my mother. When I tried to give it back to her—*"Emo, this is all you have of her"*—she pressed it into my hands.

"And now it's yours. Your mother . . ." Emo was suddenly spirited away to somewhere else—a faraway look bloomed over her face.

"Emo, what is it?"

She shook her head and chuckled. *"I'm just remembering a prank your mother pulled on the school bully."*

My mother? Based on Emo's stories, I thought Sang had been the prankster. But apparently a boy in Sang's year—known as Dongho the Terrible—had terrorized every kid in the school. *"Stealing their marbles, their pocket money, you name it,"* Emo said. *"He was jealous because your American Uncle always did better than him on exams. So one day Dongho lied and told the teacher your uncle had cheated. American Uncle was devastated. You know how much of a stickler your uncle is about that sort of thing.*

"That was the last straw. Your mother hatched a plan. She saved up all her pocket money for three months to buy a jar of honey. Do you know how expensive honey was back in those days? When I saw the jar sticking out of

her backpack at school, she said, 'Oh, that's nothing for you to worry about, Younghee-ah.'

"It was school assembly day. Right before Principal Suh was about to speak, we suddenly heard a huge squelchy sound, like a fart. Then another. It was coming from Dongho! He turned bright red. Principal Suh was furious. After that, Dongho the Terrible became Farty Dongho. No one could take him seriously, not even the teachers. And your uncle's honor was restored." Emo let out a peal of laughter. *"I knew that Big Sister was the one who'd coated Dongho's seat in that honey. If she took the credit for the prank, she would've been the most popular girl at school. Not even Big Brother Number Two knows about it! But that's the kind of person Big Sister was. Quiet and polite, but ooh . . . if you messed with her or one of her friends . . ."* Emo took my hand, squeezed it. *"I see her in you, too."*

Emo's story was like a parting gift. I started blinking, rapidly. "Emo, I don't know whether to laugh or cry."

"Laugh and cry!" She placed a gentle finger on my mother's photo. *"Each time I stare at her picture, thoughts of the past come rushing back to me. I can't stop them. I think that's why I had to put it away, out of sight. If I stare at it too much, I'm afraid I'll just . . ."*

She swallowed, quieting whatever swell of tears threatened to rise up. I swallowed, too. We were both determined not to cry. We stood together like that, each of us fighting back the sobs that threatened to surge. She and I were so alike. The waves passed; calm was restored.

Then Emo wrapped a fierce, fleshy arm around my shoulders. With her other hand, she held her phone out at arm's length, aiming its lens at us. *"Say 'watermelon'!"* she commanded. *Soobak!* We opened our mouths wide. Emo snapped a photo of the two of us: she lifting herself on her tippy-toes, me crouching down. Each of us going a little out of our way to meet the other in the middle.

I touched down in New York at the very same hour of the very same day as my departure from Korea. It was, as Eunice might have said, very Narnian. It was, as Beth might have said, like "time regained."

PART III

Queens

Homeward bound
I wish I was.

—Simon & Garfunkel, "Homeward Bound"
(music and lyrics by Paul Simon)

Chapter 23

Time Regained

J ane. Jane! JANE!"
    The cry cut through the general din of JFK—of rumbling suit-
cases and passengers rushing into the arms of loved ones and security-
checkpoint bleeps.

Rushing toward me, wearing his standard work clothes—
wrinkleproof cotton-poly blend shirt, breast pocket crammed, I knew,
with its usual worn-out Bic pens and receipt slips used for scrap
paper—was a familiar face, a face I had not seen in more than a year.

My uncle, Sang. *Not* Ed Farley.

I struggled to mask my disappointment. Not because I wasn't
grateful. Only because I'd spent the entire flight picturing Ed instead.

There was no rational reason for me to have expected Ed to come.
And yet, with his last cry of an e-mail, I was buoyed with the hope
that, just maybe, he'd be waiting for me on the other side of the gate.

Nor had I expected my uncle to come. He knew that the engagement had been called off—thankfully, Emo had been the one to break
the news. He also knew I had a place to stay lined up in the city; Eunice had a friend from MIT who rented out a second bedroom like an
ad hoc B&B. *"Uncle! How did you know I was—"* I corrected myself.
"What an inconvenience for you come getting me here."

He harrumphed. "Your Korean getting better. At least you not
waste time over there." It took me a moment to realize we were each
speaking in our weaker language. It took another moment to realize

that my uncle had just offered a rare compliment. "Aunt making *mae-untang*," he continued. It was a spicy fish stew, one of Hannah's specialties. "You come home dinner first."

In the crowds I caught a glimpse of a blond head—Ed?

"What you looking for?" Sang barked.

I'd been mistaken; it wasn't him. "Nothing," I said, my tongue settling into English. *No one.*

My uncle gave me a stern look. "Why you bring so much suitcase? Hurry-hurry." Much of what I'd brought back home were the things Sang had sent me in the mail. Taking the luggage from me, he turned on his heel and strode off toward the exit.

I took a last glance through the crowds—still no Ed—before hurry-hurrying after my uncle.

* * *

We pulled up to 718 Gates Street. It's funny how you think you've known a place your whole life but when you return after an absence, you move tentatively through a now-unfamiliar space. The air, redolent of toasted barley and drying slivers of ginger and warm blankets. The utter quiet, interspersed with the occasional *putt-putts* and groans of the buses floating down Northern Boulevard. The stickiness of the linoleum tiles under the soles of your feet. This house had once felt so cramped, so *tap-tap-hae*. And now it did and did not feel like home.

I stood in the doorway of the kitchen, where Hannah and Mary bustled about. "*Where's your* nunchi?" I heard Hannah say sharply. But she was addressing Mary and not me. When she looked at me, she said, "*You came.*" But her words did not sound unkind. "*Now go tell your uncle and George that dinner's ready.*"

We took our seats around the card table. The water glass felt thick and tall in my hand. The glasses at Emo's had always been thin and squat. I sat back in my chair—its metal legs scratching against the linoleum—and listened to the waves of conversation that flowed across the table. My ears kept anticipating the back-and-forths of Emo and Big Uncle's speech. Emo, with her girlish, joking tone, and mostly "Seoul standard" cadence, a good counterpoint to Big Uncle's forceful

words and unwavering Busan accent. But I was now realizing how differently Sang and Hannah spoke—their Korean tainted by decades of
"overseas" life. Their cadences rose and fell in the same rhythms as
American New York English, their language a pastiche of all of their
adopted homes.

Even our conversational fodder that night felt different from those
earlier dinners. It had always seemed as if the picking and prodding
was directed at me. But tonight Hannah was scolding George, who
was already on his second bowl of rice, to slow down for goodness'
sake. When Mary snickered, Hannah immediately snapped that she
was hardly one to talk—Mary just swallowed without chewing. I noticed then that the air was no longer punctuated with Mary's *chyap-
chyap*-ing. I was filled with an inexplicable wistfulness. I had once been
at the center of those conversations—conversations that at the time
had felt like attacks. But sometimes you only see what you want to see.

Then Sang turned to me. "So now you decide you not living there
no more."

I readied myself for the ensuing barrage of criticism. *Why you not
follow through your engagement? Why you giving up so easy?* How could
I explain to him that Changhoon and I did not speak the same language after all? That Seoul, much as I'd wanted it to, had never felt
like home? I braced myself for a fight.

Mary picked up where her father had left the conversation dan-
gling. "So . . . I guess things didn't work out with you and that FOB
you were supposed to marry," she said.

"They're not FOBs if they're still in Korea," I said. "*We're* the
FOBs."

"You know what I mean."

I could feel Hannah's eyes reading my face. I tensed up anew. But
she said, "*You know what everyone says about* gyopos *like you? They're
too* sunjinhae *for their own good when they show up in Korea. You know
that word, Jane-ah? It means being naïve, like an innocent* babo. *Those
Koreans from Korea*"—she shook her head—"*we're a completely different breed from them.*"

I had fully expected my aunt to rail at me for my irresponsibility. But she hadn't. Hannah had had the *nunchi* to spare my feelings.

*   *   *

After the meal the phone rang. My heart jumped—Ed Farley. I just *knew*. Mary rushed to answer it. She handed the receiver to me. "It's for *you*."

I took the receiver from her, bracing myself for the boom of Ed's voice. Would he sound the same as he had the first time, when I'd answered his *Village Voice* ad—a little clipped, a little gravelly? Or would the soft, gentle tones he came to use with me over time wind their way back to me like a familiar refrain?

"Way to pull a runaway bride, Jane Re."

"*Nina?*"

I immediately cringed. Whatever disappointment I'd felt by finding it was not Ed was replaced by *embarrassment*, thinking about that e-mail I'd sent her from Seoul. In which I'd rambled unabashedly about everything: Changhoon. *Ed*. With that letter I had ignored everything they'd taught us in Career Services: *Never leave a paper trail*. But at the time it had felt liberating, like a delicious release. Now I just felt like a *babo*.

"Your e-mail was very . . . dramatic," Nina went on. "I swear there's, like, a movie or something about your life." She let out a laugh, a booming laugh. But it wasn't one of judgment; it was a good-natured one.

I couldn't stop myself from laughing, too. "There totally is."

"Before we call it water under the bridge, I just want to say . . ." She paused, started again. "Look, I'm sorry, too. I shouldn't have backed you into a corner like that, when I was there. I just couldn't stand to see you keep it all bottled up. It felt so . . ."

Tap-tap-hae. I mentally filled in the word for her.

"Anyway, if I knew, I wouldn't have acted like such an asshole."

"I acted like an asshole, too."

Nina and I quickly resumed our natural rapport. The familiarity of our bond came rushing back to me, just like the smells and sounds of 718 Gates Street wove their way into my consciousness. She told me about her job as a real-estate broker, handling mostly rentals on the Upper East Side. I told her about my upcoming second interview at a real-estate developer's office, to which she said, "Look at that. We're both kinda in the same industry." She asked whether I was disappointed not to be working on Wall Street, as I'd once planned.

"Maybe two years ago I would've been," I said. "But sometimes plans change."

"Yeah, I guess there's no guarantee you would've gotten one of those finance jobs anyway," she said. "The economy's total crap. It wasn't anything like when we started college. You kind of feel lucky to have a job at all."

Just before we were about to hang up, Nina said, "So . . . what are you going to do about Ed Farley?"

The swell of disappointment returned. "Hunt him down. Profess my undying love. Face rejection, maybe."

"Well, according to the Peterses, they definitely got divorced," Nina said. "If you say you're still in love with him, you better get cracking."

* * *

It was quite late, after the dishes, the fruit, the *yujacha* tea. When my uncle suggested I just stay home instead of venturing into the city to Eunice's friend's place, I secretly felt relieved. Back in our old bedroom, I asked Mary if I could borrow her laptop. I didn't want to check my e-mail on the family computer in the living room, in case anyone peered over my shoulder. "*Fine,*" she said, handing it to me. Sitting up in my old twin-size bed, my back against the wall, I flipped open the computer. But when I logged into my e-mail, there was no word from Ed.

I returned the laptop to Mary and got ready for bed. I lay there under the covers, until the sounds of traffic from Northern died away, Mary's snores tapered off, the floorboards beneath the linoleum tiles settled down, and finally I was lulled to sleep.

Chapter 24

A Reunion

Nina was not the only one with whom I made, or attempted to make, peace. I worked up the courage to call the Mazer-Farleys—now, I supposed, just the Mazers. Beth answered the phone.

"Hi, Beth. It's Jane Re."

"Hello, Jane." I could hear the shift in her voice, from friendly to guarded.

"..." That was as far as I had rehearsed. I knew that this wasn't some situation you could right by sending over a box of fruit. And yet some small part of me had hoped that Beth's old self would take over the conversation, flooding it with her usual ebullience. Of course it didn't.

"How is your ... work?" I asked.

"It's fine." Beth's response was clipped.

"I feel like I have a lot of explaining to do." The words came out in flustered heaps, like the books and papers piled up every which way in Beth's office. "I don't know if you got my— I'm sorry for sending such an overwhelming e-mail. But I'd love to take you out for coff—I mean, tea. Could we talk things over? In person?"

It felt so insincere to blurt out an "I'm sorry" over the phone.

"There's really nothing to talk about," she said. I recognized her tone of voice—it was light, airy; the one she used when she was faking it. It was the same voice Emo would sometimes put on. "I do appreciate your message. Good-bye, Ja—"

"Wait!" I cried. "Is ... Devon there?"

Instantly she took up her guarded tone of voice again. "Devon is not available to talk. Have a good day, Jane." And with that, she hung up.

As I stared at the phone, I saw how much I had relied on Beth's friendliness as a given. Only in its absence did I realize I'd taken it for granted.

* * *

The next time I tried calling, I picked a time when I was sure Beth would be at school and not home. When Devon came on the line, she said, "Didn't you get the message? From my mom? I'm not available to talk."

"Devon, I'm sorry—" I started, but the line was already dead.

* * *

Ed had been away at a conference. When he returned, he apologized for the delay in responding, and invited me over for dinner at his apartment in Rego Park. Because all our communication happened via e-mail, I could not pick up on either tone or intention. He made no reference to the message I'd sent in Korea. Was he open to reconciliation, or did he merely feel obligated to get together? For all I knew, he wanted to chew me out in the privacy of his own home. *You think you can just come waltzing back into my life? After what you put me through?*

"Dinner at his place? You know what *that* means. Don't forget to shave your legs," Nina had said when I told her. And while I wasn't a complete *babo*—yes, of course I had hoped the invitation meant Ed wanted to rekindle *something*—still, a lot could have changed in the course of a year and a season.

It's a little hard to dress for something when you don't know whether or not it's a date. I decided on jeans and a nice top instead of a skirt. I debated hair up or hair down, then decided on down. I did not wear makeup. Since my return home, I saved makeup for special occasions only, and most days I went out with a bare face. And I wanted Ed to remember me as I had been.

* * *

Ed lived in one of those large, nondescript apartment complexes just off the hustle-bustle of Queens Boulevard. The reddish-brown brick exterior matched the reddish-brown of the thick paint on the walls of the sunken lobby. The elevator, inconvenienced, groaned on the way up to his floor. The bottle of wine in my hands was slick with nervous sweat.

I pressed the black buzzer of his apartment door. My ears expected the honeyed electronic chimes of its Seoul counterparts; instead it let out an unwelcome *err!* The door swung open, and there was Ed.

There was a slight blip between the picture of Ed Farley I had carried in my mind for more than a year and the Ed Farley before me now. Gone were the boyish flops of dark blond hair; now he wore his hair short, which made his whole head shine blonder. His broad shoulders, his lean muscles were the same, but instead of his usual plain white T-shirt he was wearing a button-down. His once-baggy light-rinse jeans were fitted and dark-rinse, a style favored by all the twenty-something guys on the subways. I traced the once-familiar contours of his face—high cheekbones, strong jaw. When my eyes met his, I realized that Ed had also been taking me in, figuring out what had changed, and what had not. I don't think I imagined the cloud lifting from his eyes as they turned a brilliant blue.

We stood like that in the doorway—for seconds, for minutes, I couldn't say for sure. Finally I held out the bottle of wine. "I brought . . . this."

Those were my first words to Ed after more than a year's absence? Nina would tell me I had no game.

"You shouldn't have." Ed took the bottle from me, his fingertips gently brushing mine. His same soft touch.

I was overcome with a familiar sensation, as Ed led me in and I followed him down a dark, narrow hallway. It opened to a square living room with carpeted floors. The walls were plain and white and bare, whereas the walls in Brooklyn had been covered in artwork and pictures. None of Ed's handmade furniture had made it to his new home—the living room had a black leather couch and a glass coffee table, opposite a large flat-screen television. (The Mazer-Farley home had an old model relegated to the laundry room.) I don't know what I was expecting—but my heart sank a bit, noting how little resemblance Ed's new home bore to the Thorn Street brownstone.

Even the aromas were different; this home smelled of plaster and—I sniffed the air again—roasting meat. It was delicious.

"Let me go check on dinner," Ed said. "Keep me company?" I followed him into the kitchen, expecting it to look as plain and devoid of character as the living room. But I was surprised to find that it looked newly renovated. The appliances were all a sleek stainless steel. One wall was covered in pots and pans, hanging like elaborate pieces of art. His spice rack was as expansive as his bookshelves; his cooking equipment rivaled his toolbox. I ran my hand along the counter. "Is this granite?" I asked.

Ed nodded. "You don't want to know what I had to do to get the landlord to splurge on those."

"Drop trou?"

And he laughed—a hearty laugh, a genuine laugh, the laugh I remembered so well. I felt a little embarrassed—my joke wasn't *that* funny. "I forgot that about you, Jane," he said, wiping his eyes. "I haven't laughed like that in a long time." He looked at me.

We again stared at each other; I don't know for how long.

"So . . . what's for dinner?" I finally asked, taking in the various pots and pans simmering on the stove and peeking at the roasting pan in the oven.

"A cassoulet," he said. "Have you had it before?"

I shook my head. "I don't even know what's in it."

"It's like pork 'n' beans," he explained, "and duck."

"Sounds fancy," I said. "And here I was expecting heroes." As soon as I said it, I chastised myself. It was presumptuous of me to bring up memories of those late nights.

But Ed just shrugged. "I enjoy cooking," he said. There was something so luxurious and appealing about the way he moved in the kitchen. I watched as he popped open and poured the wine, as he chopped vegetables with slow, steady strokes (Hannah was always so haphazardly hurry-hurry with the knife) and added them to the pot. He was deliberate and relaxed; I was suddenly struck with an awful thought: How many other women did Ed entertain in his beautiful kitchen by cooking an elaborate dinner? How many others had stood here sipping wine, watching him work?

Ed caught me staring at his hands; he held up his bare left one. "As you can probably guess"—now he was sweeping his arm across the room, as if to gesture how all this was his—"Beth and I got a divorce."

"I'm so sorry."

"Don't be," he said. "It's a relief. And you and I both know that a divorce was long overdue."

I cradled my wineglass. "You look happy. I'm so . . ." *Happy you're happy?* It was almost too corny to utter. Also, it was and was not true. I wanted to be the source of his happiness.

"I could be happier," he said. "It's genuinely good to see you, Jane. I'm glad you came over."

"I'm glad you invited me," I said. I took a sip of my wine. "And what about Devon?"

Ed looked away. "Devon lives with her mom. But, you know, I still get to see her. Whenever it's convenient for Beth."

His smile changed, from genuine to rueful. I got the sense he didn't feel like elaborating, so I changed the subject. I told him about my new job with that real-estate developer—they'd hired me on the spot at my interview. I told him Nina and I were thinking of looking for a place together in the city.

When he asked about Korea, I told him about my first day of teaching. "I don't know how you do it every morning, standing in front of all those students," I said. "I couldn't stop my legs from shaking the whole first week."

"Actually, I'm not teaching at the prep school anymore," he said. "I'm at Queens College now. Hence the move to Queens." Ed explained how shortly after "all that had happened" (here *I* looked away), there had been an opening to teach at SUNY Rochester for a semester, to fill in for someone on sabbatical. He'd applied for the job on a whim. "I guess I was the only chump they could find willing to brave it up in Rochester," he said. He quit the prep school and moved upstate. After that, he was—"by some miracle, or fluke, or both"—hired by Queens College.

"Ed, that's fantastic! So your dissertation's all done? You must be thrilled. And relieved."

Ed took a drink of his wine. "Not exactly. They hired me as an ABD," he said. "I'm adjuncting part of the time, dissertating the other part."

"But still," I said, "that's really prestigious. You're a *professor*." But he didn't look as pleased as I was for him. "Ed, you should let yourself enjoy your success. It's huge! This is—"

I was interrupted by that buzzer—*err!* Ed held up his finger as if to say, *Hold that thought,* and ran to the door. "Devon!" I heard him cry. "What are you doing here?"

I froze. I heard the door close, and they were advancing down the hall. What would Devon think, seeing me here like this with her dad?

"You didn't get Mom's message?" There was an edge—distinctly the tone of a teenager—in her voice. "I had some *stupid* group project out here. Mom didn't want me taking the subway by myself this late, so she told me to come here and then you could drive me home."

"Why didn't *you* call me?"

"*Because.* I didn't even *want* to come, but Mom—" Devon reached the kitchen, and I froze again. "What's *she* doing here? Dad, what's going on?"

"We're just— Jane just got back from Korea, and we're catching up—"

As Ed fumbled for words, I took in this new Devon. How tall she'd grown! Her once-tiny frame was now all limbs. Gone were her usual casual jeans and soft pastel T-shirts. Now she was wearing all black. But not in a Goth sort of way—she wore a tight-fitting shirt that revealed the flatness of her chest. Her black flare pants let out a synthetic rustle. Her hair was different, too; it grew free from its bowl cut and hung past her shoulders. There were highlighted streaks in her formerly jet-black hair, as if she'd sprayed it with Sun-In. The Ko-

rean girls used to use that stuff back when I was in high school. The
product was meant to bring out the natural golden highlights in white
girls' hair. When Asian girls used Sun-In, their hair turned a cheap
brassy color. Her chubby cheeks had thinned out; the skin stretched
taut across her face. Devon looked so uncomfortable standing there in
her new body, with her new hair and new clothes. When her eyes
alighted on me, her scowl deepened.

"Is that for *all* of us?" she said, jutting her chin at the bottle of wine
in her father's hands.

"Nice try," Ed said. "Maybe in ten years. Now, go greet Jane. *Properly.* We haven't seen her in ages."

Ed pushed his daughter toward me. She did not charge forward
with one hand sticking out to shake mine, the way she'd done once
before. "Devon, I'm . . ." I struggled for words. *I'm so sorry. I know
you're angry. There's so much I want to say to you.* ". . . so happy to see
you."

I held my arms open to embrace her. But Devon just stood there,
her own arms crossed over her chest. Mine dropped back down to my
sides.

"Just like old times," Ed said with a forced lightness.

Devon looked from her father to me to the bottle of wine. Then
she rolled her eyes and walked out of the kitchen.

Devon had caught a whiff of whatever was stirring between her
father and me. But how much did she know? I kept trying to catch her
father's eye, so he could give me some hint. But he was engrossed in
his cassoulet.

Ed urged Devon to stay for dinner. As he cooked, Devon and I
were alone in the living room. I tried to make small talk with her. We
were on such fraught ground; I knew it would be presumptuous to
assume too much intimacy, as if we'd picked up right where we left off.
Small talk was our only option for now. I congratulated her on
Hunter—I'd heard about Devon's acceptance through Nina, who'd
mentioned that Alla had applied and gotten in as well. Devon met my

compliment with a wordless shrug. "That must be nice, to have a familiar face at a new school," I said. "You guys must take the train together."

Devon didn't answer. I felt myself rambling to fill the silence. "Nina was saying how Alla really likes it there. And she thinks—"

"Do you guys just, like, have nothing better to do than talk about us behind our backs?" she said.

I faltered. Devon slumped in her seat and scowled.

I tried once more with Devon during dinner. I thought back to those early days at Gino's, when she'd look up at me not with anger but with an open friendliness. Except that was *before*. "I was thinking. What if you, me, Nina, and Alla went on one of our double dates? Maybe back to Gino's?"

Devon chewed and swallowed slowly, as if she were digesting my words along with the cassoulet. She took a big sip from her glass of milk. She wiped her mouth. She seemed to relish how uncomfortable her silence was making me. Finally she spoke.

"Could you please pass the pepper?" Those were the last words Devon said to me for the rest of the night.

*   *   *

When dinner was finally over, Ed offered to give us both rides home. We piled into the car. "But, Dad, why are you dropping *me* off first?" she asked. "You should be dropping *Jane*, in *Flushing*."

"Oh . . ." Ed said. I was sitting beside him in the passenger seat, sensing that familiar blush bloom over his face and neck. He mumbled something about westbound traffic not being so bad on the BQE, then drowned out his own words by turning up the volume on the radio.

"But, Dad, it doesn't make *sense*," Devon called out from the backseat.

Suddenly Ed's tone grew stern. "You really want to have this conversation right now?" It was the same tone he had used on me when I'd first started working for him. Devon mumbled no. We drove the rest of the way in silence, the slow chatter of WNYC in the background.

As we traveled westbound on the BQE, the downtown skyline rose before us. It looked nothing like the skyline I'd stared out at with Ed on the promenade. The negative space of the night sky looked so bare without the Twin Towers.

We pulled up to 646 Thorn Street. Devon had been in such a sour mood during dinner that I expected her to fly out of the car and into her house. But she trudged up the stairs slowly, as if she dreaded what awaited her there. There was a rustling in the bay window. And there Beth stood, the light streaming out from behind her. Her eyes fell on me, and I instantly shrank into my seat. Did she know? They shifted from me to her ex-husband, before falling back on me. Then she lifted her arm, as if to wave, but instead yanked the curtains, closing them firmly shut. Darkness resumed.

We drove on, to Flushing. Whatever static had been tingling between us earlier that evening had dissipated after Devon's arrival. I directed Ed to Gates Street, but with much reluctance. When we pulled up to the house, I did not want the evening to end like this. Not on this note.

"I'm really sorry about Devon," Ed said. "She's just going through a phase."

"She's right to be upset, after what I did. Then I pulled a runner on her"—I bit my lip—"and on you." A wave of emotion threatened to overtake me, and I bit my lip again to quiet the flood. "I'm so sorry."

Ed's hand waved through the air, dismissing the matter. "You shouldn't be. I put you in an awkward position. I should be the one apologizing."

"Please don't think"—my voice caught—"that it didn't mean anything to me. That wasn't why I left. It actually meant . . . a lot to me. It still means a lot to me." My words felt clumsy, but I couldn't leave the car without telling Ed how I felt.

The streetlights cast a shadow across his face, but it remained unreadable. It was presumptuous to assume that Ed felt the same way. I took his silence as his answer; my fingers fumbled for the door handle.

Suddenly Ed's hand shot out, pulling mine from the door. "Jane. Don't you ever leave," he said with feeling. "I couldn't bear it again."

His grasp was so warm!—it pulsed with life. I did not dare let go.

Chapter 25

Astoria

When Nina called to say she knew of a great two-bedroom for us, I didn't think she'd meant in *Queens*. Nina was at best ambivalent about the borough, just as I'd once been ambivalent about Brooklyn. When we agreed to find a place together, we'd both initially hoped to live in Manhattan—only to find that our collective rental power priced us out of the city entirely.

"It's a ginormous floor-through unit. The rent's way below market value," Nina said, giving me her Realtor's pitch. "Super-safe neighborhood. Laundry in the basement. Grocery store down the block. A short walk to the N. Minutes to the East Side." I worked in the East Fifties, and Nina's office was on the Upper East Side. "Oh, and my great-uncle owns the building," she added. "My cousin Rosie's been living there the last ten years, but she just up and left for Sicily to 'find herself' or whatever."

Queens. The very borough I'd been plotting to escape my whole life. I thought about the path I was *supposed* to take, the one I'd charted out with decision trees and spreadsheets. Wall Street seemed a far cry away, like a whisper from someone else's dream.

Nina took my silence for reluctance. "Look, I'm not sold on Astoria either. It's just a bunch of Greek joints. But it's supposedly up-and-coming. Some craft-beer bar's opening up on Thirtieth Avenue. Or was it Thirtieth Street? I don't know—the neighborhood doesn't make sense to me yet." Somewhere along the way, Nina had turned into a beer snob. "Maybe it's only a matter of time before Astoria becomes the shit-show going on over here."

She had regaled me with stories of the changes to Carroll Gardens. For one, our beloved Gino's was now a fair-trade coffee shop with free Wi-Fi. New tenants were renting the ground-floor apartment of her family's brownstone. Nina described them as "Beth types. Enough said."

With our starting salaries, neither of us was in a position to be choosy. And that was how we came to live in Astoria—a short ride from Flushing, and Food, and Sang.

*   *   *

The building at 917 Helen Street was a wood-and-brick three-family house on a residential stretch between Thirtieth and Thirty-first Avenues, sitting in a row of other three-family houses, all attached. You could hear the rumble of the N train overhead from a few streets away. It had a little porch out front and a Tudor roof whose sharp peak stretched to the sky. This was quintessential western Queens architecture.

What came with our cheap rent were caretaking duties: Collecting the trash and putting it out on the curb (we would have had to sort the recycling, too, but the city had temporarily put the kibosh on that). Vacuuming the staircases and sweeping the front porch. Shoveling the snow from the sidewalk and putting down salt. The tenants filtered their problems through us before we passed them on to Nina's great-uncle, who had retired a few years ago to Florida.

After Nina and I moved in, we became aware of the apartment's many . . . idiosyncrasies. Every now and again, the plumbing would gurgle and the hot water would suddenly run cold. Sometimes there'd be a blockage in the drainpipe. We'd call a plumber, and Nina would insist on shadowing him, the two of them crouched on their haunches, as plumbers are wont to do. I could sense Nina trying not to bother him with questions, yet she watched intently all the same. It helped that she was cute; the plumbers never seemed to mind Nina's hovering. "This is such a racket," she'd say after she paid the bill and forwarded it to her great-uncle. "All he did was stick a snake down the pipe and yank a few times. Pulling up *your* hair balls, Jane." ("Sorry," I'd mutter. Nina was always on my case about monitoring the shower strainer.)

Suddenly how-to manuals from Home Depot littered our hand-me-down kitchen table—a raw slab of wood set atop sawhorse legs, from Nina's father's basement workshop. Nina's reading materials were starting to resemble the contents of Eunice Oh's Manhattan Portage messenger bag.

One night that winter, it snowed, followed by thick sheets of rain. The snow became heavy and slushy, having absorbed the full weight of the rain. Nina and I had to keep taking breaks as we shoveled the front walk. The roof above us creaked from the accumulated snow, and at some point in the middle of the night it buckled.

That was the last straw. The house hardly seemed salvageable. As Nina and I spent the next morning calling around to get estimates from contractors, I asked her why her great-uncle didn't just sell the house or do a complete demo and build anew, Seoul-style. Weren't all these "little" expenditures like throwing good money after bad? "It's got good bones," Nina insisted. "It just needs some TLC."

We ended up going with a guy I knew through work, whose rates were higher but who seemed more trustworthy than his competitors. The other contractors would patch things up in a quick fix, only to leave behind a host of other damage in the process. There was no accountability in these one-off interactions.

And so my new life with Nina was beginning to take shape. When we weren't tinkering with the apartment, we did all the things people in their mid-twenties do in New York: we went to cheap happy hours in midtown, open bars downtown (where one-or-another liquor company was cross-promoting with one-or-another luxury-branding company), birthday parties at dive bars in the East Village, or house-warmings in carved-up apartments in Stuy Town or the far eastern stretch of the Upper East Side—which, at that time, seemed to be the only Manhattan neighborhoods people our age could afford. The invitations usually came through our co-workers or Nina's clients. Our social network was growing; we'd connect with people in that glib way that happens when you're shouting over loud music in a crowded bar, over the rising yeast stench of beer, as you're shouldering a heavy bag full of work files and balancing a drink in your hands. Those evenings would culminate in the ceremonious exchange of business cards with cell-phone numbers scribbled on the back and promises to connect on Friendster. (I took it to be the American equivalent of Cyworld.) Then, in your work in-box the next day, there'd be a follow-up e-mail with an invite to another party or open bar, and it would start all over again.

Sometimes Nina and I ventured to the few bars in our neighborhood, and I'd help her try to pick up men. We'd size up the smattering of potentials—compared to Manhattan there just weren't that many young people in Astoria—and scheme ways to throw her into their sight line. But more often than not, we'd talk about the course of our days. Nina loved and hated her job. Her showings were in Murray Hill, Midtown East, and the Upper East Side. She loved the sales aspect—at her core she was a people person—but anytime she'd try to voice her ideas for enticing more clients to her superiors, she'd be met with, "Yeah, we'll look into it," followed by no follow-up. Yet she could not pilot innovations on her own without having a superior first sign off on them. She was one of hundreds of brokers at her company; it was a large, clunky boat that was slow to change direction.

I felt more ambivalent than Nina did about my administrative job. In the first month, I was completely disoriented—I was just dropped into the thick of it all and expected to navigate on my own. (My boss was the opposite of Sang—he was entirely hands-off.) I was now starting to fall into the rhythm of things, and I felt that in a year's time I would probably master everything I needed to know and could thereafter coast on a kind of autopilot. While my boss relied on me to look for cost-cutting measures, whenever I suggested we look into new ventures—doing an e-mail marketing campaign or hosting investor seminars to promote the company name—he'd shy away. He was risk-averse. It quickly became apparent that the mentality of the company was "If it ain't broke, don't fix it." Could I see myself in this job forever? No. But still, a job was a job, and as Nina had said, you kind of felt lucky to have one at all.

Some weekends I'd help Sang out at the store. It would just be for a few hours here or there, filling in when he or my aunt had to run an errand or attend a church function. Then Sang would send me off with a bulging bag of fruit and vegetables—and never the moldy stuff.

But my nights always ended with Ed. I'd let myself into his apartment—he gave me a key—and would arrive to the warm, yeasty smell of bread baking, the sizzle of garlic in the frying pan. And there was Ed—standing in the kitchen, welcoming me with one of his rare smiles.

Freed of Beth's imposing culinary restrictions, his cooking now flourished. It was uncanny to witness. Ed's heroes—no simple preparations in themselves—metamorphosed into elaborate stews and roasts and desserts. He'd make a leek soup from a broth of seared pork bones, a slow roast of pork shoulder marinated in white wine and lemon, accompanied by a salad of shaved fennel and citrus slices and finished off with a chocolate mousse that bore hints of lemon peel. The way each course was built upon the previous one reminded me of Ed's handmade bookshelves back in Brooklyn. His rich meals were a hearty comfort during an unrelenting stretch of cold.

Afterward, we'd go to bed, and it was so different from that first time; my body, anticipating his touch, rose to meet his. Then we'd lie together in the dark, our arms and legs still woven together in warm, loose braids. We'd stare up at the cracks on the ceiling as if they were a constellation of stars, until we drifted off to sleep.

"Don't let him fatten you up!" Emo would write in our e-mails back and forth. Emo being Emo, she wanted to know all about my dates with Ed. But even more than that, she loved hearing about my nights out with Nina. She found Nina's rotating cast of love interests fascinating—there was the insurance salesman, the firefighter, the disk jockey—her dates unfolded like Emo's episodes of TV dramas.

"Oh, to be young and pretty and living on your own in New York City! All the things I never got to do. After everything with your mother, your grandfather wouldn't dare let me out of his sight. This is such an exciting time for you, Jane. Promise me you'll enjoy it. Before it passes you by."

* * *

But in the middle of the night I'd wake up to the cold panic of finding myself abandoned in an unfamiliar room—Ed no longer beside me, his warm arms no longer draped over my body. He didn't sleep well— which explained all our late-night sandwiches back in Brooklyn. It always took me a minute or two to reorient myself, to realize Ed had skulked off to work on his dissertation.

There was a stack of multicolored files that occupied a prominent spot beside his computer, which Ed jokingly called "The Thing." One night I got up from bed and found Ed at his desk, scribbling furiously in a notebook. He was surrounded by a mess of newspapers and books. The radio hummed in the background. At the far end of the room, the television was paused midscene, casting a blue glow on the videocassette tapes scattered on the floor. But when my eyes fell on the bound stack of dissertation files, it was shunted off to the far corner of his desk. The same bright green file lay at the top of the pile.

"What are you doing," I asked.

Ed, startled, looked up. "What? Oh . . ." He was still scribbling; he held up his other hand to signal, *Hang on a minute*. Then he put down his pen. "Sorry, just had to finish off a thought. WNYC was doing this segment on androids. It gave me a great idea for my next class— we're doing 'The Wasteland.'" Ed was constructing a lesson plan on technology's effect on modern man, which he hoped would contextualize the poem. He gestured to copies of *1984, Brave New World, A Clockwork Orange*, which were all flagged with multicolored Post-its. As he spoke—with gusto—his eyes lit up. Ed's approach to teaching shared the same interlinking construction as his dinners, as those bookshelves.

"So that explains *Blade Runner*," I said, nodding at the TV screen. It was Eunice Oh's fourth-favorite movie. "But how's . . . The Thing?"

As his bright blue eyes fell on the file stack, they darkened. Whenever Ed spoke about his dissertation, a shadow would fall over his face. It was the same burdensome expression he used to wear whenever he spoke about Beth over heroes in Brooklyn. "Every minute I spend on that thing is another minute I can't spend lesson planning. Honestly, it's so far from my mind right now."

"But . . . don't you need to finish *that*"—*nunchi* told me to keep my tone light—"in order to get tenure?"

"If I keep working on *that*, I won't have time to build a new course prep, which *will* guarantee a teaching spot next semester. And course proposals are due in a week." Ed let out a sigh. "Believe me, Jane. I know I should keep working on The Thing. But it just doesn't feel right right now. Or maybe not ever." Recognizing the growing tension of his tone, he lifted his shoulders into a *What are you gonna do?* shrug. "*Ah!* The glorious life of an adjunct."

Sometimes Ed's dissertation felt like a holdover from an earlier life—life with Beth.

"Well, you know what the economists say," I told him. "Forget sunk costs, focus on the marginal."

"So you're saying I should cut my losses and move on?"

I shrugged. "Only if you think you're investing all this time and energy"—*and hope*—"into something that's no longer working." But I knew Sang would have disagreed with that—he could not bear to see even the most far-gone of investments to go to waste.

Both our eyes fell again on the dissertation, bound in a tight stack.

Pretty soon The Thing was relegated from the desk to the shelf, from the shelf to somewhere tucked out of sight. We never spoke about it again.

Chapter 26

A Bad Family Education

It was wishful thinking, I knew, to expect Devon to thaw toward me, yet I hoped it all the same. I asked her to tea, to the movies, to go shopping. If only I could spend some one-on-one time with her, I might have the chance to explain better and take steps to repair our relationship. Devon turned down every single one of my invitations. While she was sullen with her father as well, every now and again a flicker of her former sweetness shone through. Never with me. The three of us were thrown together quite frequently, and she made her displeasure about our relationship quite plain.

Once, when her father had excused himself to go to the bathroom, Devon and I sat across from each other in our usual strained silence. I broke it by rambling about "the good old days" back at 646 Thorn Street, to which she retorted, "I'm sure that all had to do with you baby-sitting *me*." She made no effort to hide the bite in her tone.

The next day I told Ed what Devon had said. We were spending a rare afternoon together—I had to run some paperwork downtown, and my boss had given me the rest of the day off. Ed had finished his lesson planning early and had a few hours to kill before his class that evening. He'd driven into the city to meet me. I asked him what he thought I should do. "Whenever I ask if she wants to talk, she just shrugs me off." What she'd *actually* said to me was, "Can you, like, please mind your own business?"

"Do you think she knew about us, back then?" I asked.

"She's a perceptive girl," Ed said, "but you and I were pretty good at covering our tracks."

"I think it might help things if you talked with her. About us."

Ed glanced into the rearview mirror before changing lanes. "I'm sorry. It was a nasty thing for her to say. But we just have to chalk it up to puberty."

"Is it *that* big a deal to have a conversation with her about it?"

Ed was quiet; I could tell he was annoyed. But still I pressed on.

"Well, what about Beth?" I asked. "What, exactly, did you tell her about us?"

Ed looked tired. "I came clean right after 9/11. Right after I got that e-mail from you, saying thanks but no thanks."

That shut me up. We drove on in silence.

We passed the exit for the Midtown Tunnel, then the Fifty-ninth Street Bridge; Ed continued north on the FDR. "You taking the Triborough?" I asked him.

He shook his head. "I thought we'd swing by Devon's school. She's probably just getting out now," he said, glancing at the clock.

"Does she know you're coming for her?"

"No, but I thought we'd give her a ride home. Beats taking the train."

"You think that's a good idea?" I remembered what it was like to be in seventh grade. All the other kids watching while your parent came to pick you up, like you were some little kid. Forget about it.

"Why wouldn't it?" Ed's tone was testy. "I would've been *thrilled* if my old man had bothered to show his face every now and again."

I stopped myself from saying more. Maybe he was right. Although nothing seemed to thrill Devon these days.

We pulled up in front of the school. I touched Ed's arm. "Why don't we just call out to her from here—" But he was already stepping out of the car. Since we were double-parked, I waited inside.

If Hunter was anything like my junior high, kids were starting to group off with their own kind; like hung out with like—and like only. Hispanic, Indian, Jewish, Greek, Caribbean, mainland Chinese versus Taiwanese versus kids from Hong Kong. At my school there were so many Koreans they broke off into cliques according to which church they attended, and still there was a ranking system. The groups seldom mixed, unless they banded together against a common ethnic enemy. For the most part, we coexisted independently, like self-sufficient ecosystems.

Occasionally there were those who crossed the party lines. They were given names that usually revolved around junk food. The Asian kids who hung out with the white kids were Twinkies (or sometimes, more nutritionally, bananas). Whites who hung out with Asians were Reverse Twinkies. Black kids who hung out with white kids were called Oreos or Ding Dongs. Whites who hung out with blacks were Sno Balls (or sometimes, completely un-food-related, "wiggers"). Koreans had a name for one of their own who deigned to hang out with the Chinese: *jjangkae* lover—the pejorative for the rickshaw guy who delivered your Chinese-style *jjajang* noodles. If the Chinese had a name for one of their kinsmen who ditched out for the Koreans, I didn't know it. But I suspected it might have been considered an upgrade.

Ed had indeed timed our arrival just right. At first a handful of students dribbled out of the building, and then they were immediately followed by herds, color-coded by race, hair, clothes. Everywhere were more impenetrable knots of Koreans, Chinese, Indians. I thought I saw Alla Peters firmly at the center of one of these packs, but when I looked again, she was swallowed up by a swirl of chattering friends.

I had to remind myself to look for Devon's taller, sleeker self. She was no longer a runt of a girl with a tortoiseshell for a schoolbag. After the last swell of students passed through the front doors, a few lone stragglers ventured out, the ones who couldn't keep up with the flock. And there was Devon, one of the last to emerge.

Based on the way she was dressed, she was clearly trying to fit in with the other Asian kids. But the Chinese and Korean faces around her glanced up at her, then past her. Not one in those crowds called out "Over here, Dev!" and waved for her to join them. It was painful watching her, the way she looked eagerly through the crowds. I recognized her expression: feeling desperate for a group—*any* group—to take you in. But kids can smell that kind of desperation a mile away. Devon was completely alone.

This was the exact moment Ed decided to make his presence known. "Kiddo!" he shouted. "Over here!" The nearby groups turned around at the sudden commotion.

Devon hesitated, as if debating whether to acknowledge her father's voice or to slink away.

Before she could decide, her father bounded toward her. "Dev! What are you, deaf?"

She gathered her arms up and across her chest, a barrier from her father. But Ed closed the distance between them, squeezing her into a hug.

He could not see Devon's face, but I could. It was frozen in panic. A dad picking up his kid at school: embarrassing. But a man who looked nothing like you—still your father nonetheless—embracing you in front of your whole school? Those milling about glanced from Devon to Ed before resuming their conversations. But how long those glances must have lasted for Devon! I remembered the way she had squirmed in front of the Chinese grannies on the 7 train and the man in the moon cake bakery in Chinatown. It was the same discomfort I felt when Hannah would take me in and out of the shops on Northern, and I'd sense the shopkeepers' eyes scanning from her to me and back again. I wanted to step out of the car right now and link my arm through Devon's, but I didn't want to make the situation even worse. As if her father had a particular fetish: a white man with his Asian girls.

Finally Devon broke free from Ed; she said something to him, then stalked off. He stood there, dumbfounded, arms falling helplessly to his sides. Her long strides slowed to a dawdle. Her face looked not angry but *hopeful*. She stopped, peered over her shoulder.

But Ed was already bounding back to the car.

Anger resurged across her face. She, too, bounded away.

Whenever Sang and I used to fight when I was a child, I'd try to run off. But he always ran after me, grabbed my arm, and pulled me home. One time I felt so *tap-tap-hae* that I sprinted away from him. After six blocks I thought I'd lost him. The second I stopped in my tracks, panting, he was right there behind me, not even a whit breathless. Gotcha. He had a surprising amount of endurance for a middle-aged man. Why didn't he just let me run and wait for me to return home, sheepish, exhausted, penitent? I never understood why my uncle didn't simply give up, when it would have been the easier thing to do.

I felt oddly unsettled when Ed returned to the car. "Where is she?" I asked.

"She left. Let's go," he said.

"And you just *let* her?"

"I wasn't planning to drag her back to the car, if that's what you're asking." He started up the engine.

I couldn't hide my annoyance. "I *told* you we shouldn't have stopped here in the first place."

"Jane." He used a firm tone with me, one I hadn't heard since my early days as the family au pair. "I don't need to hear it."

It was a tone that normally would have shut me up. Now it just set me off. "What'd you expect?" I said. "You totally humiliated her."

"Humiliated her? I'm her *father*."

"That's what I mean. . . ." How could I explain? "Try to see it from her perspective. Maybe not all her classmates *know* you're her father."

"Let me get this straight: First you yell at me for picking up my daughter from school, and now you're yelling at me for not chasing after her? There's a logical fallacy here."

That might have been true, but he hadn't seen the look on Devon's face. "You make this big to-do about coming all this way to see her, and then we're *here* and you just let her walk away. You can't even follow through—"

I was interrupted by my own phone ringing; it was Sang. Ed stewed while I answered.

He asked what I was doing after work that evening. "Oh, you free now? You can stop by store for few hours, while Uncle running errand?"

"Yes, Uncle. I'll head over soon."

"Good. You come home after, we gonna have dinner together."

Then we hung up.

"You're still going to Queens after this, right? Mind dropping me off in Flush—?" I stopped. Ed was letting out an angry laugh.

"That's real rich, you know that?" He shook his head. "You're telling me I need to fix my relationship with my daughter, when look at you! Do you *hear* the way he talks to you?"

I'd actually thought it was one of our more pleasant phone conversations.

"For one, he hollers at you—although that's not news to you, the way you hold the damn phone away from your ear. He wasn't even on speaker. But then he expects you to come at his every beck and call. And guess what? You come running."

"He's *family.*"

"Does he even pay you to work?"

I wasn't officially on the books—that wasn't the way we did things at Food—but Sang would always send me home with groceries when I left, and he'd give me the periodic handout. In *fact,* Ed had just eaten one of Sang's apples that morning.

"Well, *does* he?"

"Do *you* clock in and out to watch Devon?"

Maybe it was a cheap shot, but his question felt that preposterous. You don't keep a tally of expenses with family.

Ed let out an exasperated sigh, the way he sometimes did with his daughter. "I just *hate* watching the way he treats you. And don't even get me started on everything with your late mother. You know he's still holding all that against you."

I hadn't actually broached the topic of my mother—and father—with my uncle since I'd returned from Seoul. I continually debated whether to bring it up, but things had been going so well between us (okay, as well as they were probably ever going to go) that I'd held off. I didn't want to rock the boat.

"He's a man of his generation," I snapped. "*You* try working fourteen hours on your feet all day. *You* try operating in a language that's not your native—"

"Stop defending him!" Ed interrupted. His tone was so sharp that I shrank back. He must have seen my stricken look, because he softened his voice. "He should love you *for* you. Not *in spite of*. But that man talks to you like he doesn't have an ounce of respect for you."

Ed's words stung me into silence.

* * *

"You late," Sang said when I arrived at Food.

Do you hear *the way he talks to you?* I tried to shut Ed out. "There was traffic coming from the city."

"Now because you late, *I* late."

I'm the one doing you a favor, I thought.

His eyes narrowed slightly. "And why you driving from city? Who drive you?"

"I *told* you. I had to review some paperw—"

"Hurry up, you change your clothes," he interrupted, waving at my dress shirt and slacks.

We could have been back in the old days at Food.

Dinner that night, too, seemed to regress to the patterns of the past. Hannah picked and prodded at my "salty, bloated face," pointing to my "bad American diet" as the culprit. Mary, who was also home that night (she was hardly ever at her Barnard dorm; it seemed like an expensive dumping ground for her books between classes) chimed in, saying it looked as if I had eaten "like, a huge bowl of instant ramen right before going to bed." Sang jumped in about my job—"Who this company? How much business they bring in?"—as all the while George grunted. And round and round and round they went.

Maybe it was what Ed had said earlier that was making me see everything with a different slant. Or maybe the family had really directed a heightened criticism at me that particular evening. To this day I'm still not sure which is the truth—for all I knew, that dinner could have been just like any ordinary one. But it didn't feel ordinary to me.

"Why you waste time on going-nowhere company?" Sang was saying. "Better you just work at Food!"

That man talks to you like he doesn't have an ounce of respect for you. Ed's voice railed against the rising chaos of the family. I dropped my chopsticks against my bowl with a loud, deliberate clatter. Everyone looked up.

"You think I came all the way here just to get lectured by you people?"

Sang looked at me with darkened eyes. "'You people'?"

This would have been my cue to lower my eyes and murmur, *Nothing, Uncle. Sorry, Uncle.* Instead I said, "Whatever, Uncle." I could've been Devon.

"Where you learn talk like that?" Sang said. "You picking up bad habits from outside. Like you getting a bad family education." He waited a beat, as if he were giving me another chance to come to my senses and apologize.

I said, "It's always from the 'outside,' isn't it? Like 'outside' is full of contagious diseases."

Sang shook his head. "Ever since you coming back home from Korea, you acting funny. You know that? Like you some kind of big shot."

"*You* act like a big shot," I said. "But you know what? You don't know anything. Everything you taught me about Korea was *wrong.*"

I had hit a nerve. Sang's eyes went completely black. "Everybody, *naga!*" he shouted. The rest of the family scrambled out of the kitchen, but not before George rushed a chopstickload of rice into his mouth first.

Then it was just Sang and me sitting opposite each other at that rickety fold-up card table.

"Who you think you are?" he said. It was a rhetorical question, so I didn't answer it. "You go over there—to *hof,* to karaoke, you buy fancy hand phone and fancy handbag"—he pointed through the doorway to the living-room couch, where I'd left my Sinnara purse, a gift from Emo—"and now you knowing everything. But you don't know *nothing* about Korean. Only fifty percent, if you lucky!"

Fifty percent. Half. "That's real rich," I said, echoing Ed's words from earlier. "You know what else you were wrong about? My *mother*. She was never thrown away and left behind by some GI."

"What you talking about?" His eyes didn't even flicker.

I told. How my mother had not been some foolish GI lover. How my father had not been a GI at all, but a volunteer in the *Peace Corps*. And—here was the real clincher—that my father hadn't up and left her, but they'd actually fallen in love and stayed together. As I spoke, Sang just listened, neither confirming nor denying.

"Do you have any idea how this changes everything for me?" I said. I thought of the schoolyard torments. The sinking feeling overwhelming me each night as I lay in bed at Gates Street—that ineffable longing that tugged inside my heart. The rise of shame whenever Flushing cast its collective eye on me. "And yet *you* kept this from me my whole life. I could've been proud of my mother. Of myself. Instead all I felt was ashamed."

Then, finally, Sang had words of his own. "GI Corps, Peace Corps, What Corps, why I care? Still she disobeying when Father say no!"

There was something about how he uttered that line—perhaps it was the slip into "Father" instead of "your grandfather"—that made me think of that old photo of Sang: even as a child he'd been forced to play the responsible role. Perhaps he felt that my mother had rebelled where he could not. I started to give way.

But just like that, Sang added, "Why you so proud your mother? She have no *nunchi*."

My mother had no *nunchi*. Same as he thought *I* had no *nunchi* and Emo thought my father had none.

I swallowed. Hard. "I feel like you can't"—I tried to steady my warbling voice—"just love me *for*—"

It was no use. I was losing control. I pressed my hand to my heart, but still it went *pwah!* I could not stop myself from splitting in two.

My uncle flinched from the deluge. He hated tears.

When at last my cries tapered off, Sang said, in a flat, unfeeling voice, "How I'm suppose to control what you feeling? Your feelings *your* feelings."

"Ed *said* you'd say that!"

Shit, shit, *shit*.

"Ed?" I could see the name slowly registering in his head. "Ed . . . you talking about your old lady boss husband? That stupid *babo*?" he said. "That kind of man, he only want easy thing, like fruit about to falling off tree."

"Are you calling me low-hanging fruit?"

Sang did not answer.

"Ever think *you're* the reason I am?"

Then Sang went *chuh!* and shook his head. "So that man teach you nothing but putting the blame on other people?" He stabbed his temple. "You like bearbrain. Nothing going through! What kind of relation you are?"

I didn't answer. His eyes flashed black, like oil spills. "You move back home right now. From now on, you not gonna see him, you not gonna talk to him. You stop everything. Now!"

How stupid I'd been to defend Sang in front of Ed. Stupid! Ed was right. He'd been right all along.

"You can't just order me around however you want and expect me to come running home. Why? So I can be your errand boy at Food?"

"What's wrong Food? You hating coming home that much?" Sang muttered.

"I'm not your daughter!" I shouted. "I wish you'd just leave me alone!"

It was a petulant thing to say; the kind of words that slip out in the heat of an argument. I waited for him to shout back, *So ungrateful! You know how lucky you are?*

But instead Sang's voice grew soft. Almost gentle. "You right, Jane-ah. Uncle not your father," he said. "That what you want, I leave you alone."

There was a dullness to the words, a dullness that matched his eyes, whose angry sheen was quickly fading into a flat, matte brown.

In my heart I knew it: This fight felt different from all our other fights. The dismissiveness reflecting back in Sang's eyes told me he was done with me, that I was no longer his concern. It was what I wanted. And yet I still felt a hollow thud deep in the cavity of my chest.

My uncle and I had broken apart once before, but in the midst of 9/11, Korea, and my grandfather's death we found a way to patch things up again.

If not broke, why you gotta fix? But maybe it was the other way around: What's fixed will always remain broken. Like the door to the walk-in box, the floor tiles at Food. And there were only so many cracks—cracks swelling to fissures, fissures buckling into rifts—that our relationship could endure.

It would take a natural disaster to put us back together again.

Chapter 27

Boeuf Bourguignon

Winter was shedding the last of its chill, and soon it was spring. Ed and I had just finished another of his epic dinners: roasted lamb chops with braised leeks and merguez sausage. Over coffee and slices of a chocolate pecorino torte, Ed said, "I've been doing some thinking. And I think . . . we should have The Talk."

I sat up in my chair. The Talk. Was Ed going to ask me to marry him? We'd only been together—this time around—for a few months. But we loved each other. Maybe it wasn't too soon. Was it?

"Jane, I'd love for you to move in," he said. He looked up at me, gauging my response. When I didn't answer immediately, he went on. "Do you really want to keep shuttling between two apartments? And you have to admit, Jane—my place is a lot nicer than yours." *Not* that *much nicer*, I thought. It was still Queens.

"What's Devon think about it?" I said. "I'm sure she'll just love that."

"Devon's not a child anymore," Ed said. "She's going to have to accept that you're part of my life now."

"And what about Nina?"

"What *about* Nina?" Ed said. "She can find another roommate."

"I feel like I'd be ditching her."

"Not if you give her enough notice," he said impatiently. "Look, if you're worried about rent, you wouldn't have to—"

"It's not about that."

I think Ed expected me to jump at his invitation. But I honestly didn't know what to think. Whatever swells of gratitude I felt at his generosity were tamped down by an unexpected ambivalence. Shouldn't he have proposed to me first? I couldn't shake Sang's comment about the easy, low-hanging fruit.

"Don't you want to be together?" Ed speared his torte with a fork.

I, too, lifted my fork, then lowered it. As usual, I'd stuffed myself at dinner—it was hard not to indulge in such good food. "Of course. I love you, Ed."

"Then what's this really about?" His tone was a little testy. "I'm offering you my *home*."

"I know that, Ed. It's a very generous offer."

On paper it seemed to make sense. I was over at Ed's apartment all the time. And people my age were starting to do that—couple off and move in together. But the thing was, I was just starting out on my new life. Was I ready to put an end to that? I already felt I wasn't seeing much of Nina anymore. When I told Ed that, he relented. There was a shift in his tone, and his voice grew gentle. "Sometimes friends drift apart, sometimes they drift back. You can't fight the course of these things. It just is what it is."

"I don't *want* us to drift apart." Even as I said it, I knew I sounded childish.

"It's not a good or a bad thing, Jane. I've seen it at least a thousand times. I'm sure one day it'll all make sense."

I mulled over Ed's words. "Yeah, but I should still see what she's up to this weekend," I said. "Maybe we should do a girls' night out and catch up."

"Here's what we'll do." Ed began ticking things off on his fingers. "We'll invite her over for dinner here on Saturday. Eat some good food, drink some wine. It'll be a nice and relaxing evening. You guys can catch up. I like Nina—she's a good kid."

I almost said, *We're, like, the same age,* but stopped myself. Sometimes the contrast in the way Ed and I spoke caught me by surprise. I wondered if it sounded as apparent to him as well. But instead of asking, I took a forkful of the torte. A silkiness coated my tongue. His dessert was indeed an unexpected combination—the sharpness of the cheese, the bittersweetness of the chocolate. Ed had been right: The contrasts were what made it all the more delicious.

"Maybe I'll make a boeuf bourguignon," Ed said, taking another bite.

"I've never had it," I admitted. Actually, I'd never even heard of it.

Ed took a deep breath, as if he were about to launch into an explanation. But then he squared his shoulders and said, "It's, like, a drunken beef stew."

* * *

But when I invited Nina over for dinner at Ed's on Saturday, she said she had "a thing."

"What thing?" I asked her. One of her clients was having a housewarming on Saturday. "You mean that guy you have the hots for?" I said. "What's-his-name, Mikhail Gorbachev?"

Nina rolled her eyes. "Mikhail *Gorokhov*."

Mikhail whose last name I could never keep straight worked for a small hedge fund in midtown. Last month Nina had found him a one-bedroom in an elevator doorman building in Murray Hill. She was first struck by (her words) his Superman-ish features—black hair, blue eyes, and "high-rise cheekbones." But it was his organizational skills, and his love of spreadsheets, that had been the real clincher for her. Nina hadn't been this excited about any of the guys she'd dated since Joey Cammareri.

"Why didn't you ask me to go?" I said.

She shrugged. "I figured . . . you know, you and Ed were doing your *own* thing."

"Please. We're not sutured at the hip." Nina loved when I bumbled idiomatic expressions. Sometimes I conflated a Korean proverb with an English one. I did it half on purpose, hamming it up for her to get a laugh.

"But what about dinner?"

"We could do both. The party's not going to start till late, right? And it'd be good for Ed and me to get out of the house for a change."

Nina wrinkled her nose. "You think this is Ed's sort of thing?"

"I'm sure he'd love it."

I actually didn't know if that was the truth, but in that moment I didn't feel like admitting it to her.

"Yeah, no. I'm sure it'll be cool," she said. "But we need to get there *no later* than eleven." Nina had elaborate theories on prime arrival times.

"Totally."

* * *

"Go to one of Nina's parties? In *Murray Hill*? Forget it," Ed said over the phone that afternoon. "We invited *her* to dinner. If she wants to bail, fine. But she's not going to hijack our plans."

"So, um . . . I kind of already said we'd go."

"*Jane.*"

"I'm sorry! I just . . . got caught up in the moment. I thought it'd be fun. Go out, meet new people for once."

"I'll tell you exactly what to expect," Ed said. "A bunch of i-banker kids fresh off their year-end bonuses, bragging about steak houses and strip clubs. They're all drinking Maker's Mark from red Solo cups and getting *totally* hammered." He uttered that last bit in a mocking tone I didn't appreciate. "You're telling me *that* sounds like a good time, when we could just relax at home, enjoy a fantastic meal, and save ourselves the bother?"

Sometimes when Ed spoke like this—I'd once jokingly referred to it as "being teacherly"—I didn't know what to make of it. It was one of Ed's qualities that first drew me in over those late-night heroes. This is not to say that it was condescending; instead he spoke with the weight of personal experience. More often than not, I was able to free-ride on the shorthand of his authority. From an efficiency standpoint alone, it was a good thing; there was no need to reinvent the wheel.

But at times I wondered whether I relied too heavily on Ed's account of things, rather than seeing for myself.

I explained about Nina and Mikhail. "I can't just let her go alone," I said. "Why don't the three of us do dinner? Then after that *I'll* just go with Nina to her thing." *And you can save yourself the bother.*

I could sense a note of suspicion in his tone. "Is that what you'd rather do?"

"I'd *rather* we all go together. But I'm not going to force you."

Ed was silent on the other end of the line. I wondered where his thoughts traveled to—back to his own mid-twenties life? To house parties in Murray Hill, or their equivalent?

Finally he spoke. "Fine, we'll go. But if a single Jell-O shot makes an appearance, you and I are out of there."

* * *

But dinner Saturday night ended up being at our place in Astoria instead of at Ed's. His new oven had blown out; despite Ed's best tinkering, the pilot light failed to engage, and the electrician wouldn't come until Monday. When Ed arrived at our apartment with grocery bags from all over—his brow slick with sweat—he had an air of tension about him.

Nina and I greeted him at the door and relieved him of his bags. As we unpacked the groceries, he rummaged through the cupboards. "So, Ed, what're you making again?" Nina asked.

"Boeuf bour— Beef stew," he said, peering inside a cabinet.

"It's a little hot for stew, don't you think?"

He rifled through. "Where's your thyme?"

Nina and I looked at each other. "We don't have any," I said. "We've got garlic powder?" She held out plastic spice shakers. "And oregano."

Ed shook his head. "Don't you girls ever cook?"

"I *cook*," Nina said defensively. "Just not your fancy stuff." She ate the same three meals every day: granola and yogurt for breakfast, a salad for lunch, and pasta for dinner. Every Sunday night she cooked a batch of bolognese sauce and chopped up her vegetables for the week. When I wasn't with Ed, I ate cornflakes for breakfast, turkey and mustard for lunch, and rice and kimchi for dinner.

"I swear . . ." he muttered to himself.

He waved away Nina's and my offers to help. Back at his apartment, our division of labor was simple: Ed cooked, I did the dishes. I heard the sounds of his bustling about in our kitchen—punctuated by the occasional grousing and opening and slamming shut of drawers.

Nina and I sat at our sawhorse table, each of us catching up on some work. Nina had landed her first big assignment: she was representing the sale of a building, a mixed-use property on the Lower East Side. The seller was a guy from Bay Ridge about our age, someone Nina had met at a happy hour a few months back. He'd inherited the building from his late father and was eager to unload it as quickly as possible. The problem was, this guy was completely at a loss about everything from building repairs to finding tenants, and Nina had to pick up the slack in order to ensure a sale—any sale.

"I'm just supposed to line up the buyer. But in the meantime, David's expecting me to manage the whole property, too," she said. She showed me some quotes she'd gotten from property-management companies, as well as estimated costs for some minor repairs.

"*You* could just do all this," I pointed out. "Then you wouldn't have to outsource any of the repairs." Indeed—over the course of the past few months, Nina had been able to fix more and more of the little things plaguing our apartment as well as the other two units, relying far less on calling a plumber or an outside handyman.

I looked over the statements and sketched some calculations on a napkin. "Let's say you charged him like five percent per unit a month to do the maintenance. You'd still make a decent cut, and you'd be saving him around twenty percent. Plus, it'd make things easier for him, because he'd only have to deal with *you*."

Nina looked over my work. "Jane, you're a genius. I love when you dork out on your numbers."

I shrugged. "It's all there. Just pointing out the obvious."

Ed called from the kitchen, "You ladies have a meat thermometer?"

"No!" we shouted back in unison. The air was filled with the smell of seared meat and sautéed vegetables.

"I'm starving," Nina said. Then she glanced up at the clock. "It's almost nine-thirty! What's *taking* him so long?"

Beth had once said the same thing about Ed's elaborate renovation plans. *I swear, we would've moved in much sooner if Ed hadn't insisted on everything being "just so." It took forever for him to pick out the wood and get the finish just right.* Yet it was something they had in common; Ed cooked the way Beth spoke—with countless digressions and an unrelenting quest for perfection. It was funny: Ed, despite having grown up doing blue-collar work, moved about the kitchen in an unhurried, languid fashion. Sang once had a worker who moved like Ed. By the end of the day, that worker was fired.

"Ed sometimes goes a little *obuh*—I mean, overboard," I said, getting up from the table. "I'll tell him to hurry up."

Perhaps it was because of our rather rudimentary kitchen or the fact that I'd rushed Ed and he'd had to abandon a few key steps, but dinner was a disaster. The stew was supposed to simmer for at least two hours; instead it boiled for thirty minutes. It tasted more like a pot of cooked wine than anything else, and the beef was tough and gamy. The bread was a little raw and yeasty. Ed's meals did not seem to translate outside his own kitchen.

"This *shouldn't* be your first introduction to boeuf bourguignon," Ed said as we took our seats around our table—warped and scratched and streaked with paint primer.

"Hey, better late than never," Nina said graciously as she poured wine into juice glasses. But she snuck another look at the clock; it was after ten.

"Well, in all fairness, I didn't have a lot to work with." Ed held up his glass. "Girls: seriously?"

"What? So we don't own wineglasses," Nina said, less graciously this time. "At least *our* stove was working." She slapped her hands together. "Anyway, let's get this show on the road."

* * *

To make up for lost time, we ended up taking a cab into the city. Which turned out to be a horrible idea, as westbound traffic on the Fifty-ninth Street Bridge was at a standstill; it was, after all, Saturday night, and all of us B&T people were jamming our way into Manhattan.

"Where's this party again?" Ed asked.

"Twenty-eighth and Second."

He rolled his eyes, just like his daughter. I pinched his arm—Nina was the one who'd found Mikhail that apartment.

After we crossed the bridge, we hit more traffic on Second Avenue. "Hey," Ed called out to the cabbie, tapping the Plexiglas partition. "Can you pull over up here?"

I put a hand to his. "Ed, what are you doing?"

"It'll be faster to walk."

"We can't. Our shoes." I was wearing sneakers, but Nina had on strappy heels. She hadn't brought her usual change of flip-flops once we'd decided on a cab.

"Okay, fine," he said as we inched, slowly, down Second Avenue.

By the time we arrived at the party, it was after midnight. The apartment was packed; we were engulfed by tangles of men with cropped, gelled hair and popped collars and women in bright-colored, tight-fitting outfits and matching heels. I understood why Nina had wanted to get there earlier. We could have claimed a spot with easy access to the bar. Nina could have had first-mover advantage with what she called coveted "face time" with Mikhail. Ed took one look around the apartment and said, "I need a drink." He left us to fight his way to the bar.

Nina shrugged as if to say, *Whatever.* Then, suddenly, she grabbed my arm. "That's Mikhail," she whispered.

Nina hadn't lied, exactly, when she said Mikhail's features were Clark Kent-ish. But his black hair was slicked back and gelled to a crunch. His blue eyes looked sharp, like fractured glass, and the pale rosiness of his high cheekbones was delicate, like a porcelain doll's. His tight-fitting black button-down shirt had two too many top buttons undone, revealing a bare, hairless chest that was surprisingly, jarringly, quite tanned. The shirt was tucked into a pair of flared jeans, and his black leather belt had a silver buckle that matched the silver buckles of his shiny black loafers. Nina's taste in men was so predictably B&T. (The only exception to that rule being Joey Cammareri— B&T refurbished as hipster.)

I could only catch glimpses of Mikhail through the throng of redminiskirted women encircling him. "Damn it," Nina said, yanking at the hemline of her black dress. Mikhail lifted his arms, like Moses parting the sea. The red waves of women ebbed away, trickling back into the crowds. He walked—sauntered—toward us; there was an affected hitch in his stride.

"Nina!" he said, draping an arm around her. Then he noticed me. "Hello, Nina's friend! You ladies are having fun at my party?" He had the faint hint of a Russian accent. "Now that *you're* here, we are," Nina said coyly.

"Ah, Nina, you flatter. Now it is my turn." He lifted his arms again and swept them around the apartment. "You are good broker. Tell me, what else you are good at?"

Nina's eyes darted from side to side, the way they did whenever she was given a compliment. Ed, returning with the drinks, rolled his own eyes at me. Obviously he'd just overheard Mikhail. He wedged himself between Nina and me and handed us each a bottle of beer. He himself was drinking scotch. Nina inched away slightly; I knew she was trying to make it absolutely clear that Ed belonged with me.

She jumped in to make introductions. "Mikhail, this is *Jane's* boyfriend, Ed."

Mikhail evaluated Ed, sizing him up and down. "Call me Mike," he said, pumping Ed's hand. "Mikhail works for a *hedge fund*," Nina said. "All kinds of big deals, huh? Movers and shakers?" She shimmied her shoulders for added effect.

"Yes," Mikhail said, "she is right. And tell me, my friend, where do you work?"

"I'm a college professor," Ed said. He did not specify where.

Mikhail mused that Ed must be a "smart man." While the two began to talk, I saw that Nina was staring up at Mikhail with the same unabashed gaze she'd once reserved for Joey Cammareri. It was very unbecoming. Of course, it was only when Nina didn't really give a shit about a guy that she was most sought after. Mikhail did not return her gaze.

Suddenly the tone of Ed and Mikhail's conversation changed. Mikhail said, "It is concerning, yes? To invest in such a path for the future, with so little returns? When there's more money in private sector?"

Ed gave me a look like, *Is this guy for real?*

Mikhail went on. "My friend, you know the average year-end bonuses in my company are—"

"You can't *assign* a quantitative value to the pursuit of knowledge," Ed interrupted.

I ran a hand down his back. His muscles were tense. "Hey, Ed," I interrupted. "Your glass is empty. Let's go get you another—"

Ed handed me his red plastic cup. "Let me put it to you plainly . . ." he said to Mikhail as I stared at his empty cup.

Despite my best efforts to catch her attention, Nina was still locked in her moony-eyed gaze. If she wanted to look like a hanger-on, that was her problem.

I left them, fighting my way to the kitchen. Standing by the fridge, I saw a group of three—two guys and a girl—that seemed set apart from the others. I'd noticed them earlier in the night, because we were the only ones dressed as we were—fitted jeans, T-shirts, and Converse sneakers. I caught a strand of their conversation: ". . . but there're like zero start-up costs."

The three of them were so engaged I couldn't help but be drawn in. Then the guy in the glasses noticed me. "Hey, nice kicks," he said, nodding at my feet.

"Right back at you. All."

We took a moment to admire our matchy-matchy sneakers. (After more than a year of patent-leather heels in Korea, it was a treat to wear comfortable footwear.)

"Sorry, I'll let you guys get back to your thing," I started to say, but the girl shook her head. "We were just talking shop," she said. "I'd tell you more, but—"

"You'd have to kill me?" I said.

"More like I'd put you to sleep."

One of the guys—the one wearing glasses—turned to me. "We run a mobile software start-up. She's our tech guy"—he pointed from the girl to the other guy, in a green T-shirt—"and he's our marketing guy."

"And who's your business guy?" I asked him.

He pointed a thumb at himself. "You're looking at him."

"So if you're wondering how we ended up here," the girl said, "Mikhail's my cousin, and I dragged these poor dudes along."

The guy in the green T-shirt said, "*I* was promised hot guys"—he surveyed the room and wrinkled his nose exaggeratedly—"but turns out it was false advertising."

"Not me, though," the guy in the glasses added quickly.

The girl laughed. "*You* were promised hot girls."

"So, um . . ." I said, changing the subject, "where're you guys based?"

"In Queens. Astoria," the girl said.

"Get out," I said. "I just moved there. But I thought everyone in the hood was—"

"A middle-aged Greek lady?" the glasses guy said. "Then I must hide it well." Which made me laugh.

The guy in the green T-shirt asked, "So, like, where are you originally from?"

When you're a person with an ethnic tinge, you get asked this all the time. After I named my neighborhood, the rounds of inquisitions usually didn't stop until I gave them the answer they wanted to hear: "Korea" or "Asia." (And once an otherwise well-meaning old woman had asked, "The Orient?") And that was how I always used to answer the question, too. Until I went "back there" and learned that that place was not my home.

"I'm from Queens," I said. "I grew up in Flushing."

But this time the line of questions ended there.

"A *native* in our midst!" Green T-shirt cried, and he made an exaggerated gesture of worship—head bowing, arms hailing. He tried to rally the others to do the same. The gesture was so unabashedly corny that I couldn't help but burst out laughing. Beer shot from my mouth and sprayed the glasses guy in the face. "I'm so sorry!" I said as he took off his glasses and began to wipe them with the hem of his shirt.

"Don't worry about it," he said, blinking the beer from his eyelashes.

"*Please*," his friend said. "You just made his day."

"Here—" I held out the napkin wrapped around my beer bottle. "But that's soaked in beer, too. Never mind, I'm not any help . . ."

The glasses guy was taking the napkin from me when Ed approached. "Jane, I thought you were getting us drinks. You left me with Bulgakov over there."

"I got caught up with these guys," I said. "Here, I'll introduce you." I gestured to the group. "I don't actually know your names—"

"It's late. I'm beat." Ed glanced at his watch, not even looking their way. "And I have to be up early tomorrow."

"*I* don't."

"*Jane.*"

"*What.*" Just because he was cranky didn't mean he had to drag us away. He saw that I was having a good time; couldn't he just suck it up? I thought that that was what people did as couples.

Ed turned to face me. It was then that I noticed the lines tracing either side of his mouth, forming ever-so-slight jowls. He looked exhausted. Maybe I should've had the *nunchi* not to have invited him here in the first place.

"Fine," I said, relenting. Ed put his arm around my shoulders; the guy with the glasses looked away. I said good-bye to the group. Just as Ed was steering me from their circle, the girl touched my arm. "Hey. We do this Meetup thing on Saturday mornings at Athens Diner. Just a mix of start-ups and neighborhood folks. You should come by sometime."

Nina was sitting alone on the sofa, arms crossed; we pulled her to her feet. And then we left Mikhail's party.

We shared a cab back to Queens. The three of us were folded in the backseat, the air thick with tension. I could tell that Nina was upset about something; her lips made a tight line. But instead of spitting it out the way she normally did, she just sat there. If she wasn't going to talk, I wasn't going to make her. We dropped her off first, before Ed and I went on to his apartment.

It was almost two when we got home. "I can't believe I had to spend the whole night saving your friend from that nutjob."

I remembered how upset Nina had looked as we left the party. "Maybe she didn't need you to save her—"

"It's not my fault that she's prickly around me lately," he interrupted. "Ever think she's just jealous that you have a boyfriend and she doesn't?"

"That's just ridiculous." But she had said, *Don't you kinda miss the old days?* earlier that evening, while we were waiting for Ed to show up.

"I can't believe I have to be up in a few hours. Queens just renewed my contract for the fall." The fatigue from his voice momentarily lifted. "They ended up assigning me that extra course."

"I'm so happy for you."

"You really sound it," he said. "If this is about leaving early, then I'm sorry, Jane. But I already told you that's not my idea of a good time."

"Well, you just know everything, don't you?" I said. "I met some genuinely cool people back there. I would've introduced you, but you were too busy—"

"I wasn't going to stay and watch some guy flirt with you," Ed said sharply.

"He wasn't *flirting*." (He might have been. But that was beside the point.) "They were telling me about their new start-up. Don't make me feel guilty for wanting to try something new." *For once,* I almost added. "I love you, Ed. And I want you to share these new things with me."

"I can already tell you right now, Jane," he said, pulling back the duvet and sliding under. "It's overrated. All those superficial encounters, they're touch-and-go. I'm just saving you the trouble."

"Ed, would it kill you to make *some* effort?"

The instant the words flew from my mouth, I froze; those were Beth's words, not mine. I could see the recognition sinking in with Ed. His eyebrows were pinched together, the way they used to be whenever he sat across the breakfast table from his wife. His *ex*-wife.

I climbed into bed, curling away from him. But Ed reached his arms out to me. Gently he turned me so that I faced him.

"All I want to do in my time off is to have a nice meal with you and enjoy your company. Jane, I love you. I only want to be with you."

He'd said it to me many times before—*Jane, I only want to be with you.* The words never failed to make me swoon.

But this time I was pretty sure the emphasis was on the "you."

* * *

When I returned home the next day, Nina was poring over one of her DIY manuals at the dining-room table. "You and I need to talk," she said, closing her book. "About last night."

I took the seat across from her. "Yeah. What about it?"

"That *really* wasn't cool of Ed. He was acting like such a douchebag. He totally blew my chances with Mikhail."

"Don't blame that on Ed." My tone was cagey. "From what I heard, it sounds like he bailed you out of that one."

She chuffed. "I don't know what planet *he's* living on."

I told Nina what she didn't want to hear: "If you weren't busy being all moony-eyed with Mikhail, you would've seen how he's kind of a douchebag himself."

Suddenly she fixed her gaze on a stain from last night's dinner on the table's surface. "You have beef with all my guys, don't you?"

"And you shoot down all of mine. First Changhoon. Now Ed."

Nina let out a little laugh. "You have to admit it, Jane. You need to find a balance with your men. One tried way too hard. The other one doesn't even bother."

Ever think she's just jealous? But I wasn't going to give power to Ed's words. I relented. "Look, this is such bullshit. We are *not* going to let a bunch of guys get between us."

"Bros before hos," she said, cracking a smile. We both laughed. It felt good to laugh with her.

Then Nina tilted her head, the way she did when she was about to share bad news. I was immediately on guard. "But, like, you and Ed—" She stopped, started again. "You guys, like, working out okay?"

"*Yeah.* Why."

"It's just . . ." Nina ventured carefully. "I know you blew up Ed Farley back when you were the baby-sitter. But don't you think he's, like, kind of lame?"

"Why? Because he doesn't pop his collars?" I faced Nina. "What's your problem with Ed?"

"It's just . . ." She fiddled with the corner of her book cover. "I just get the sense it's all about what Ed wants. Older guys can sometimes be . . . controlling."

When I didn't say anything, she said, in a light, buoyant tone that I could tell was forced, "Hey, I should know. *I* was with an older man once. Remember? Joey?" Joey Cammareri was only two years older.

I knew she'd said it to try to get me to crack a smile. But I didn't smile back.

"Ed's asked me to move in with him."

Nina struggled to compose her face. "So . . . you going to?"

"I told him I'd think it over."

She got up, came back with two glasses of water, and set them down on our makeshift table.

She drank, we drank. I was still drinking when she took her empty glass to the sink. She washed it. She reached for her bag and shouldered it. I knew she had an open house to work that day. Then she spoke.

"You can be a pretty accommodating person, Jane," she said. She reached for her keys. "Whatever you decide, don't just do it for him. Do it for you."

Chapter 28

Han

I don't know what your beef is with Abba, but you better call it off." Mary's voice rang out through the phone receiver.

"Hello to you, too," I said.

"You haven't been back home in forever." Seven weeks, actually. "And you know Abba's too stubborn to make the first move. You have to be the one to *yangbo* to him."

Yangbo, schmangbo. "Mary, I appreciate your call. But I don't have anything to say to your dad."

"*'Your* dad.' You talk like he's not even related to you." Mary took a deep drag of her cigarette; I could tell by the way she exhaled. "You know what your problem is? You're, like, willfully blind. You think it's only about *you*. You ever hear what they say about me? Like, Umma said she was embarrassed that I was showing off my *defects* to the world. Remember? About those white pants I wore the last time you came home?"

It annoyed me that Mary expected I would remember; it annoyed me even more that I actually *did*.

"I don't think anything." The pants hadn't been as egregious as some of Mary's other fashion choices. "I do think it's good you finally stopped chewing like a cow, though. Last time I was home anyway."

"*Ja-ane!*" Mary said, aghast.

"*Chyap, chyap, chyap,*" I mimicked. "My God, it used to drive me crazy."

"Why didn't you tell me sooner?" she wailed. "Peter"—her on-again, off-again boyfriend who was in his fifth year at SUNY Albany—"said that, too, but I didn't believe him. We got into a huge fight. If my own family doesn't tell me what I need to fix, then who else out there will?"

When Mary said that, I realized that was the internal logic of our family. Tear each other down *before* we stepped outside and faced public humiliation. Like the good friend who points out the spinach wedged in your teeth. But that was the thing, wasn't it? What Sang and Hannah thought were flaws weren't necessarily what other people considered spinach in the teeth. And I was now entirely freed from their particular, critical slant on the world.

"Just come home. Tell him you're sorry. You'll lose one whole excruciating minute of your life." Mary took another drag on her cigarette. "Then everything'll go back to normal again."

But it wouldn't. I had changed, but Sang had stayed the same. And for us to return to "normal," either Sang would have to be willing to change or I'd have to force my eyes shut and become the person he was trying to mold me to be. I told her it wasn't going to happen.

Mary let out another long exhalation. "You're such a *babo*, Jane. You've always been his favorite. And he, like, *misses* you."

"Nice try, Mary."

At that moment the front door buzzed—I couldn't have planned it better. It was probably Ed.

"Gotta go. That's my boyfriend."

Of *course* I felt smug as I said it.

Mary sighed into the receiver. "You're as stubborn as Abba. Goodbye, Jane."

And with those words, she hung up.

As I ran down the stairs to the front door, I thought about what Mary had said. I should have felt liberated now that I no longer had to be subjected to Sang's scrutiny. And yet. Did some part of me miss his picking and prodding, our continual push-and-pull? Was it *jung*? No: I forced the word out of my head.

A slight, black-haired figure was sitting hunched over on our porch.

"Devon?" I said.

She stood up, brushing the dirt from the seat of her pants. "I was in the neighborhood." The thick black eyeliner rimming her eyes was smudged in the summer heat. Her expression was sheepish.

"You're a long way from home," I said.

She toed a stray pebble on the landing. "If now's a bad time, I can just . . ." Maybe she thought I was giving her *nunchi*, because she muttered, "Forget it," and quickly turned on her heel.

"Devon, wait," I said. "It's hot out here. Come inside, we'll talk."

"All right," she said, and we went in, the screen door slamming shut behind us.

As we climbed up the stairs, I asked Devon how she'd found her way here. "We only dropped you off like a thousand times," she said. "I'm not stupid, you know." I thought of that first day I started with Devon's family; it was she who'd navigated the way to and from her school.

"Your mom ever let you redo the map in the primer?"

"There is no more primer," she said. "Yours was the last edition."

Inside, we sat at the kitchen table. I set a glass of ice water before Devon, then rummaged through the cupboard for snacks. All we had were stale pretzels. Technically they were Nina's. I poured them into a bowl and brought them to the table. Devon fingered the water droplets trickling down the side of her glass. I hesitated before getting up to switch on the air conditioner.

"Must be nice having your own place," she mused, looking about the room.

To the objective eye, the shabbiness of Nina's and my apartment was glaringly obvious: the warped wooden table, for one, along with the other foraged pieces from here and there. The floors sloped, tipping to one side as if the house itself were drunk. But it was ours.

"It took a long time to get here," I said.

"I can't wait till I'm old enough to leave that place," Devon said. "Peace out, Brooklyn."

I thought of her empty, cavernous home. One day 646 Thorn would be all hers and hers alone.

"You're welcome to come here whenever you want." I added a hasty disclaimer: "If your mom's okay with it, that is."

"Mom never lets me do *anything*. But whatever." The eyeliner smudged above and below her eyes had hardened into clumps with the cold air-conditioned breeze.

"Is there something you want to talk about?" I asked.

She took a pretzel, only to drop it back into the bowl. "Remember that time? When we went to get moon cakes? And you were telling me about you not fitting in back home?"

"Yeah."

"Well, that's what it's like every single day at school. I feel like a freak!" Devon burst with a sweep of her hand, upsetting the bowl of pretzels. They scattered, dancing softly on the tabletop. With her palms she flattened them to a stop. "It's like, all the white kids assume I hang out with only the Asians, just 'cause *I'm* Asian. But then all the ABCs think I'm such a Twinkie. No, worse. At least if I were a Twinkie, they'd get me. They still wouldn't like me, but they'd *get* me."

She busied herself scooping up the pretzels and returning them to the bowl, where they fell with *ting-ting-tings* against the ceramic.

"And the Korean kids"—she looked up at me in an accusatory way, as if I were a stand-in for every one of them—"they act like they're all that. They're always staring down everyone on the train. I *hate* riding with them. Everyone in that school's so cliquey. Especially Alla."

So that was why Devon had blanched whenever I suggested we get together with Alla and Nina. "What exactly happened between you two?"

"It's not fair. *She's* different, too, but she gets to fit right in."

I remembered that day at Hunter, seeing Alla with the other kids. And I realized that Devon was jealous. Devon had grown up in an altogether different environment, a far cry from the homes of her ABC classmates. Immigrant households did not talk about Derrida or the *New York Review of Books*. Conversation was a luxury, rendered in broken fits and starts.

"No one else gets it. Dad just brushes it off, telling me it's only teenage hormones. Mom's exactly the opposite—she makes a huge deal about everything, like I'm a baby. Can you believe?" Devon cringed. "Mom wants to head up the Chinese-American Parents' Association. She tracked down all the Chinese parents at school and introduced herself as Xiao Nu's mom. And now she's trying to set me up on *play dates*. Like I'm still in the fifth grade! Why can't she just leave me alone?"

"She can't. Your mom"—I swallowed; my throat was dry from the cooled air—"loves you."

"I wish she'd stop. It's so humiliating." She huffed, blowing the bangs from her face. "Today was the last day of school," she said, "and everyone was going off to hang out with their friends. But not me." She traced another tear running down the side of her water glass. "There's no way I'm going back next year. I can't stand five more years of that place."

"Devon, I'm sorry. I never should have pushed Hunter on you."

"You shouldn't be sorry about that," she said. She pushed the bowl of pretzels away. "You should be sorry about pulling a runner on us. On *me*. You broke our promise."

Devon looked up at me, and I expected her eyes to be filled with her usual anger. But they weren't. Instead they were soft and gentle. The same way Emo had stared at my mother in the photo of the two of them that I now had framed on my wall.

"You know," she continued, "it isn't fair. How you left us and went on this big adventure, and now you've got this new life and your own apartment and you're dating my dad. Meanwhile, after you left, my life just went down the drain."

Homewrecker. That word came flooding back to me.

Devon seemed to read my mind. "I know what you did, with my dad."

I stared down at my hands. "I'm sorry, Devon."

"I mean, I didn't know back then—I was just a little kid. But I figured it all out after you left," she said. "I was really mad at you," she said. "I'm *still* mad! I needed someone to talk to, and you weren't there. When Mom and Dad were getting divorced."

My eyes fixed on a warped floorboard. "I couldn't stay. I only would've messed things up more. You don't know how sorry I am."

I'd thought leaving New York had been the right thing to do. But now I realized there was no such thing as the right thing. Someone was always going to end up losing out.

"Jane, does it ever get any better? When will I stop feeling so . . . so . . ." She faltered.

"Honestly, Devon? It's still a struggle," I said. "But you can't keep trying to please everyone else. There comes a time where you just got to be who *you* want to be."

Devon mulled over the words.

I reached for the box of tissues. "Let's wash that junk off your face."

*   *   *

I took Devon on the train back to Brooklyn, once again cutting a right angle through the city. When we arrived at 646 Thorn Street, the house loomed over me, privy to all that I'd done. I was different now. Just as the house, too, was now changed. There were no paper lanterns strung up in the doorway. The door knocker was gone. Instead there were three lit buzzers: B. MAZER, #1. D. CHANGSTEIN, #2. E. BUNKER, #3. The house, once whole, was now subdivided.

I was prepared just to drop Devon off at her door; I had enough sense to know that Beth would not want me roving about in her house. But Devon had asked me to keep her company and assured me that Beth wouldn't be home from work for a few hours yet. She sounded so lonely, her voice etched with pleading, that I consented.

I followed her into the house. Down that same long, dark hallway, but now interspersed among the African masks were Devon's school portraits—the ones that used to hang from the walls upstairs. I'd forgotten what a child she used to be. In the short time since returning from Korea, I had grown accustomed to Devon's older, more mature face. In the photos her cheeks were still chubby and her eyes when she smiled were still bright and shining.

Devon led us to the kitchen. I took my seat at the old solid wood table. It was still unvarnished; the knife cuts etched across its surface had splintered. She poured us Beth's room-temperature barley tea. Devon popped ice into her glass, and the cubes crackled from the shock of the liquid.

We had sat across from each other at this very table through so many meals. Exchanging private glances whenever her mother said something particularly ridiculous. But now Devon and I lapsed into a shy silence. All was still.

The creak of the floorboards cut through that stillness. I remembered the old sounds of the house settling. But then I heard the creaking again, followed by a definitive pounding of footsteps approaching us. I froze; it was Beth in the doorway.

At first she took in only Devon. "Where on *earth* have you been!" she cried. "Do you have *any* idea how late it is? I was worried sick!" Then Beth's eyes alighted on me. "Jane!" she said, startled.

Her clothes were the usual linen and hemp. But her straggling, frizzy hair was now cropped into a neat bob. What was most striking was the transformation to her face—her face! Beth looked *alive*. Her skin was taut and glowing; the sallow tint had faded away, and so had the dark circles that once gathered under her eyes. She looked . . . rested. Like she'd been sleeping well every day for the past year. Her fragrance wafted over to me, and I noticed that it, too, had changed— Beth now smelled of vanilla.

I was so absorbed with studying Beth's changes that I failed to realize the way her eyes grew darker with anger. "Jane. I'll see you out."

You're a babo, *Jane.* How could I have thought it was a good idea to come here in the first place?

Devon jumped to my defense. "Mom, Jane—"

"Devon, go to your room."

"But, Mom—"

"*Now.*"

Devon got up from the table, giving me a sheepish look before disappearing through the door.

Beth glowered. She made a sudden movement, and I flinched. I remembered the way she'd reached for her WNYC tote bag at Food to pay for the fruit. Instead she was reaching for the kitchen door, signaling for me to leave.

"Wait!" I cried. "Can we . . . have a conversation?"

Did she realize I was throwing her own words back at her? She was speechless at first, and then her eyebrows knotted, the way they did when formulating an excuse.

"I'm worried," I continued, before I lost my nerve, "about Devon. She came to see me."

"Devon's no longer your concern." She struggled to maintain her cool. But when she saw I was still frozen beside the kitchen table, she abandoned the door and came toward me. The wooden table bore her weight as she leaned across it. "I don't *ever* want to 'have a conversation' with you about my daughter. I don't want you in her life, *period*." Then Beth's tone erupted. "Do you have any idea how devastated Devon was after you left? And now you're lecturing *me* about how *you're* worried about her? Oh, that is rich, Jane."

I knew she was right.

Beth was shaking her head. "First my h-husband. Now my daughter. I'll admit, Jane, I'm a bit flummoxed by your"—she chose her words pointedly—"unusually robust interest in our family."

Once upon a time, up in Beth's stuffy office, I had listened to her endless lectures on womanhood, motherhood, *wife*hood. She had burdensomely unloaded her unfiltered thoughts onto me, and I had turned around and made fun of her life behind her back. In so many ways, that was a betrayal worse than sleeping with her husband. And now her daughter had come running to me.

Who the fuck was I?

I traced my finger over the raw surface of the table. It had absorbed everything. I looked up at Beth's face. The same pockmarks—fading acne scars—riddled her cheeks. But now her eyes clouded over with hurt. All of her youth and vitality drained away; in that moment she looked like she'd aged twenty years. She had choked up on the word "husband." It was in that moment that I realized: Beth had loved Ed the way I loved Ed. Maybe even more. And now his wife, his "insufferable wife," sat across from me, looking completely, utterly broken.

"I'm sorry," I whispered. But sorry was not enough; it would never be enough.

The other unoccupied chairs around the table looked so empty, so *actively* empty, as though mourning some profound loss.

Beth raised her arm, and that was when I caught a wisp of her familiar scent, cutting through the foreign smell of vanilla: onions. In the past my nose had picked up only its fermented stench, but now its sweetness overpowered me. I blinked, furiously.

"You've done enough damage already." Beth's voice shook with anger. "Now, get the *fuck* out of my house."

I rushed from the kitchen, feeling my way back to the front door like a blind person. When I reached the safety of the street, I let the floodgates burst open and wept. Beth was right. This woman had welcomed me into her home. And I had taken away everything that was hers.

Chapter 29

Jung

As exquisite as New York can be when summer tapers off, with its pleasant whips of warm breeze suffused with the smell of cooling asphalt, at the season's peak the city is utterly punishing. That summer was no exception. The moment you stepped outside, you were assaulted by a thick, merciless humidity. It coated your body like a sticky second skin. The garbage stewing in black trash bags on the hot pavement mingled with whatever fumes were floating up from the sewer grates. Everywhere air conditioners were set to full blast, but the temporary cool offered little reprieve. It was hard not to take heat like that personally; New York seemed to be offering up one big Fuck You.

Perhaps it was the sweltering heat making us irritable, but that summer Nina and I got into a series of escalating fights. Little, piddling things at first. In general, she had a more profligate regard for resources than I did. She'd let the faucet run freely while doing the dishes, even when she was just sponging them with soap. She tore whole sheets from paper-towel rolls instead of quartering them, the way I did. She'd toss out her Ziploc bags after a single use. It was the kind of behavior I teased her about in the beginning, but when she failed to have the *nunchi* to see there was more than half a truth in my jokes, my words turned into sniping, then full-blown arguments.

And of course—she left the air conditioner on throughout the night instead of rationing it in short spurts and just sucking it up miserably hot for the rest of the time, the way we always did back in Flushing. And our Con Ed bill showed it.

I spread it flat on our sawhorse table. "That's one zero too many," I said to Nina, pointing to the total. I went over to the air conditioner and switched it off. When I returned to the table, the backs of my bare legs immediately squelched against the seat of the chair.

"It's like ninety degrees out," she said. "What, you expect me to roast in this apartment?"

"I'm not even *here* half the time. How much A/C does one person need?"

Nina flipped her hair. Damp strands clung to the back of her neck. "That's right. I just sit around throwing wild parties where we blast up the A/C. I'm thinking of upgrading to eighteen thousand BTUs. You don't mind, right? Since you're *never here* half the time."

I didn't respond. After Mikhail's party Nina stopped inviting me as her plus-one to things. So I spent more time with Ed, and her social life marched on without me.

"Look," she said, relenting a little, "the way I figure, we're not spending as much on hot water and gas. I buy fewer groceries. It all comes out in the wash."

But I couldn't shake the bite of her earlier tone. I billowed the thin cotton of my shirt away from my body, and fanned myself with it. Even the smallest of movements felt effortful in the heat. "Quite a balance system you have going on there," I said irritably.

"Okay, I get the hint. I'll just pay the whole bill myself. You happy?" Nina went over and switched the A/C back on.

"That's *not* what I'm saying—"

The heat was making it hard to think. I mumbled something about conserving energy—either learning to do without or asking her uncle to invest in double-paned windows. I stopped fanning myself with my shirt. I waited until the cool waves of air washed over me.

"What do you care? It's not like it's your house." I could just make out her words over the roar of the air conditioner. "Have you decided yet, about moving in with Ed?"

"I'm still thinking it over."

For everyone's sake, I should just have made a choice already: move in with Ed or stay with Nina. I was inconveniencing everyone with my indecision.

"You better decide soon." Nina paused. Then, continuing coolly, "'Cause if you are, I'm gonna start looking for a new roommate."

"Don't worry," I snapped. "I'll be sure to give at least one month's notice."

It felt a far cry from our old nights out.

*   *   *

In the car one day after picking up clothes for the week, Ed said, "All this shuttling back and forth is getting a little ridiculous. Have you had that talk with Nina yet, about moving out?"

"You say it like it's a done deal."

"Well, is it?"

I took in a deep breath. "I've spent a lot of time thinking about it, Ed. And . . . I'm just not ready to move in with you."

"So that's your decision?"

"Ed, it doesn't mean things have to *change* for us."

I hadn't given him the answer he wanted to hear. He said nothing. I don't know whether he was using the silent treatment as a kind of negotiation tactic or what. I fought the urge to break that silence between us.

Ed found a spot across the street from his building. He put the car in park but did not cut the engine. The air conditioner was still on. "Jane," he said, turning to face me, "I'm ready to make a life with you. And you're essentially telling me you're not. How do you expect me to take it?"

I didn't understand why he had to see it as all or nothing. "Why do we have to rush this?" I was only twenty-five. Sometimes it seemed unfair how Ed had already amassed a fortune of life experiences before he ever met me. "It isn't as if my not moving in means we can't be together."

"*It isn't as if,*" he repeated, shaking his head with disbelief. "Look, I know this is all new to you. But it's what people *do* in relationships. Right now this life you're leading—you're straddling two worlds. It isn't working for me anymore."

I thought about all that I was giving up to be with Ed, all the damage I'd already done: With Beth. Devon. Sang. Nina. Changhoon, even. Ed alone stood in the assets column, and the wreck of my other relationships piled up like liabilities in the other. Just as my mother's choosing my father meant sacrificing her family. My whole life people had told me I was like her. But maybe I wasn't.

"Maybe *we're* not working anymore," I said. At first it was one of those things you repeat back to someone on reflex, like I was Ed's echo. But the words, suspended in the thick, recycled air, began to take on a shape of their own.

"Are we seriously having this fight?" he said. When I didn't immediately answer—now it was my turn to be silent—he muttered, "Now you're just being childish." The word made everything snap into place.

"You're always 'been there, done that,' aren't you, Ed? Well, I haven't. Maybe I want to try new things. And I don't want to have to feel guilty or apologize for that either."

"For Christ's sake, Jane!" Ed said. "Is this about that stupid party? Forget about it. What matters is *us*."

He'd once said that some friendships—relationships—run their course and the people drift apart. But when were you supposed to stop investing the time and energy—and hope—in something that's no longer working? When were you supposed to walk away?

"Maybe *we're* like The Thing." After I uttered the words, they felt more true. They felt like relief. "We keep forcing it. But it just doesn't feel right right now. Or maybe . . . maybe not ever."

Ed's cheek was lifting into that crooked half grin of his, a face he made when he was in disbelief. But when he looked again at my face—I was fighting not to cry—his mouth twisted into a frown. Finally he cried out, "Jane! You don't love me, then?"

That cut me. Slowly I turned my face toward his. "I *do* love you, Ed. It's just . . ." I fought for words.

"Jane, we love each other," he insisted again, gently. "A person's lucky if he gets one, maybe two shots at love. And I've found you. Why would I ever let you go?"

Ed's blue eyes grew soft with tenderness. He was staring up at me with that look we've been told our whole lives to hope and wish for from a man, and when that happens, you can't help but go slack and give in. Tears started streaming down my face. I smelled his soap smell—the same scent I'd smelled the first time I'd met him. My mouth, searching, found his.

"No one will ever love you more than I do," Ed murmured, pulling me toward him, kissing my ear.

"What did you just say?" I wiped my eyes with the back of my hand.

"Jane." He was holding my head firmly. He looked at me with his soft eyes, his unwavering gaze. I could feel only the pressure of his palms pressing down on the back of my head. This was suddenly starting to feel constricting, *tap-tap-hae*. "Trust me. It's a lonely world out there."

A certain sadness gripped my heart. Maybe Ed was right. But I was coming to learn that much of your perception of a relationship is shaped by everything else that happens to be going on in your life at the time. When I first met Ed Farley, I had been starved for love. He was the first man I'd ever known to show me kindness. He had taken my loneliness away. And for that I knew I would always be grateful. But being grateful was not enough of a reason to stay with someone.

"You're a beautiful girl. But you're also *young*. You think there'll always be people out there who'll love you?" His voice rose with indignation—it was almost too quick to catch. "Jane, I'm telling you," he said, resuming his earlier gentle tone. "That's not the way the world works."

"Then I have to find out for myself." I pulled back from his embrace, breaking away from Ed. And just like that: *hssst*. All the hot, turbulent air that had filled up inside me was flooding out. I felt light, buoyant. Free.

Reader, I left him. I stepped outside, ignoring Ed's cajoling, then shouting, for me to come back. Immediately the thick humidity felt refreshing compared to the air-conditioned confines of Ed's car. And it was with some satisfaction that I slammed the door behind me.

*   *   *

I might have been the one to end things, but it's not like I was doing cartwheels in the days and weeks that followed our breakup. An inarticulate sadness coated everything, filling the air like particles of dust, burning my lungs, my heart, my inside and outside. In the small hours of the night, I tossed and turned over whether I'd made the right decision. Knowing that Ed was just a phone call or a few miles away made it all the more unbearable. But each time I picked up my phone, I forced myself to stop.

Post-breakup I found my thoughts wandering back to Sang. I remembered Mary's phone call: *He, like, misses you.* But if I reached out to my uncle, what would I say? *You were right, and I was wrong. As usual.* Which would only give him more grounds for thinking how foolish he already thought I was.

Nina, to her credit, was the bigger person when I told her about Ed and me. I felt a little sheepish, in light of all our recent squabbles: *So . . . looks like I'm staying here after all. . . . Hope you haven't found someone to take my place.* She had every reason to lord our breakup over me, but it's a testament to how true a friend she was that she did not. She was the one who went over to Ed's to retrieve my things, and she was the one who forced me out of my room when all I wanted to do when I came home from work was climb into bed and stare up at the ceiling, the way I used to with Ed.

One evening when she set a bowl of pasta in front of me and I picked at it with no appetite, she said, "I know it feels like hell right now, but I think you did the right thing. And when you're ready, you won't be hurting for options. You've got a lot to offer, Jane."

If I were my normal self, I probably would have thanked her in the form of a quip, setting off one of our usual volleys. But for now just her company, and her friendship, was enough.

But then one morning, something felt different. When I rose, my shoulders did not ache with the weight of sadness and guilt. The air tasted fresher, no longer oppressively *tap-tap-hae*. It was flush with life, with possibility.

Nina noticed immediately. "Look who's back with the program."

"This sounds really corny," I said, "but I feel *alive*."

"Yeah, because I left the A/C on all night. Otherwise you'd feel dead and roasted."

"As opposed to alive and roasted?"

"Yeah, yeah, yeah. You can thank me when the next Con Ed bill comes around."

That morning started off like most mornings that August: hot, muggy. Presaging the staggering heat that was to come later that day. That afternoon, at the office, our computer screens suddenly blackened and the lights overhead flicked off. My senses, completely dulled just one night before, were extra-prickly as I blinked in the darkness. My colleagues whispered. *Power outage. Tripped fuse box.* And then what no one had dared utter: *Terrorist attack.* All was quiet panic. The reality of what had happened to our city just two years earlier hung heavily in the thick, humid air.

Back when the fire alarms would go off in school, we always used to ignore them. We took for granted that it was probably just a drill and not an emergency. It felt stupid to be the first one to shoot out of your seat. You didn't want to risk looking like a chump. That was how things used to be. But that was not how things were anymore.

The power did not flicker back on. We checked our cell phones; we could not get through. My colleagues and I reached a quick consensus to evacuate the building. I slipped out of my work shoes and into my commuter sneakers. Led by the light of one colleague's key-chain penlight, we filed down the emergency stairs. It was orderly; no one was jostling to be the first one out. We spilled onto the street, joining the milling crowds. Then I noticed that the traffic lights were out; cars hesitated at the intersections. Under everyone's breath the narrative: *God forbid, God forbid* . . . One car, stalled to the side, had 1010 WINS cranked up at full volume. The news feed streamed out from his rolled-down windows. Citywide power outage. Stretching up the Northeast Corridor into Canada. *Not* an act of terrorism.

You never heard cheers and whoops for a blackout like the ones thundering around me. But my thoughts leaped to the conjoined associations: looting. The store. Sang.

Immediately my body moved east, toward the Fifty-ninth Street Bridge. My whole life the bridge had looked to me like one big industrial eyesore, born from the metal works and steel factories at its base. It had none of the majestic quality of the Brooklyn Bridge, or even the Manhattan Bridge's cool blue-and-white aesthetic.

But as I walked over the bridge, I realized there was a beauty in its perfunctoriness—its interlacing cable work overhead and underfoot, soaring across the East River. It was unglamorous yet sturdy—it was so quintessentially *Queens*.

When I reached the other side of the bridge, I found myself following the same path as the 7 train, bound for Flushing. I traversed neighborhoods I had passed through all my life but never on foot; everywhere were signs of life. Body-shop workers were grilling meat on a portable charcoal grill in front of their garage. Random men off the street jumped into the intersections, transforming themselves into impromptu traffic guards. Perhaps *nunchi* translated into all cultures.

The radio feeds floating from stagnant cars let out minute-by-minute updates in English, Spanish, Chinese, Hindi, Korean. All around me people smiled, as if celebrating the happiest blackout in history. The violet Manhattan skyline fell away behind me, and before me—the vista of Flushing, a glowing wasteland.

Finally I reached Northern Boulevard. I passed Daedong Fish Market, Chosun Dynasty Auto Body, Kumgang Mountain Dry Cleaning—all the familiar storefronts I've known for as long as I can remember. Their corrugated metal gates were pulled down. I braced myself for the worst at Food: Bashed storefronts. Broken windows. Battered uncle.

But when I approached, everything looked intact. The fruit carts

were still out front. Why hadn't Sang rolled them into the safety of
the store? Everything felt strangely calm. I pushed open the auto-
mated door—with the power out, it was heavy and resistant—and
stepped inside.

Food was suffused with a quiet and controlled chaos. Customers
waited on a long but patient line, their arms brimming with gallon
jugs of water, canned beans, cereal boxes. None of them squabbled,
despite the growing darkness, despite the refrigerated air growing
stickier with each swing of the door. Not even Mrs. O'Gall, with her
head of iceberg and her jar of Hellmann's, made so much as a peep.

Sang did not see me at first, but I saw him, lit by the dim glow of
candlelight. He had set up a makeshift table at the front and was
hunched over the change box. The cash register was sealed shut and
abandoned. Beside him flashlights and batteries, candles and condoms
were corralled in a basket on the checkout counter for easier access. He
looked . . . serene. He doled out these supplies in small, gentle exchanges. Hannah stood at his side, handing each person a free pint of
ice cream from a shopping cart. Hwan was nowhere in sight.

Where was their panic? Where was my uncle's metal bat? Sang
was *smiling*. Hannah, too. My eyes darted to the refrigerated section,
teeming with dairy items. My brain computed the tens of thousands
of dollars of merchandise that would spoil overnight.

I grabbed a shopping cart. I swept in milk, cheese, yogurt, eggs on
top. Ran the cart to the back, to the walk-in box, where the insulation
would keep the items refrigerated, even with the power shut off. I
stood in front of the door. Muscle memory told me to grip the handle
and yank it open with all my might—but that was the old door. Instead a gentle click popped it open, and I pushed the cart inside. Then
I ran to the front of the store again.

As I began filling up a second cart, Sang looked up and met my
eyes. I expected his to cloud over in anger. But he looked at me, then
gave a single nod. A nod of gratitude. I nodded back.

When I was done with the dairy products, I moved on to the most
perishable fruits. Gently I eased pints of strawberries, blueberries,

and raspberries into the cart. I surveyed the other fruit, the most expensive: the Asian pears. They could weather this, so I let them be.

After I finished packing the walk-in box to capacity, I returned to the front, where Sang was joined by Mr. Hwang of Daedong Fish Market and Mrs. Kim of Kumgang Mountain Dry Cleaning and Mr. Lee of Chosun Dynasty Auto Body, who had all come in to lend a hand. I bowed to them; when I looked up, their eyes were soft with smiles. *"Lucky you, to have such a good niece,"* they said to Sang.

I was even more surprised to hear his response. *"I know,"* he said quietly.

When the last customer left the store, my uncle took the contents of the change box and locked them in the safe in the basement, while Mr. Hwang and Mr. Lee stood watch by the front doors. When Sang returned, he pressed a box of fruit each on Mr. Hwang and Mrs. Kim and Mr. Lee. He ordered Hannah to walk Mrs. Kim home, but Mr. Hwang offered to drive everybody. We saw them off. Then it was just Sang and me.

The silence between us was thick, the darkness palpable. Then, almost too softly for me to hear, Sang spoke. "I not know."

"About what?"

He hesitated a beat. "About your mother." Then he took up a broom and began making curt, efficient sweeps across the floor.

Reader, I forgave him on the spot. And he forgave me. Maybe he couldn't understand it, but he acknowledged how much that revelation about my parents had meant to me. And that was the last time we talked about my mother—or my father, for that matter.

I reached for the mop and followed my uncle with broad, swirling strokes across the floor. I thought of the painstaking effort we'd taken in laying down each of those floor tiles. The hairline cracks were still there, visible even in the thin wisps of moonlight.

Sang stopped sweeping. "This yours, if you want," he said plainly. When I didn't immediately answer, he said, "The store. Uncle thinking long time. We do this together."

A not-so-long time ago, I would have read the worst in my uncle's

offer. *That's so presumptuous of you. Stop forcing me to keep working here.*
But I didn't see it that way anymore.

"Thank you, Uncle. That's so generous of you," I said. "But I need
to do my own thing."

The moonlight struck his cheekbones at the severest angle. I braced
myself for Sang's reaction. No doubt he would have felt put out—
insulted, even. But it was too dark to make out the expression in his
eyes.

To my surprise he said, "Okay. You do own thing."

He swept and I polished the floors of the store. Our relationship
would always be flawed, but it still worked, in its own jerry-rigged way.
It was guided by a logic that was neither purely Korean nor purely
American, perhaps a bastardized blend of both. But it was *ours*—it
was New York. It took not a natural disaster but a Con Ed one to
bring the two of us together.

When we were done cleaning, he asked, "You gonna come home?"

I nodded. "Yeah. My roommate's gonna worry."

"Okay," he said. "I give you ride your home." He instructed me to
pack some food to take to Nina. When I returned to the front of the
store, he handed me a six-pack of beer.

"Wow, thank you, Uncle."

"Don't be selfish," he ordered. "You suppose to share. Drink while
still cold."

On the walk to the car, I did not mention my breakup with Ed. We
did not talk about the weather, my work, or how I'd navigated my way
from work to Food in the blackout—not even why I'd decided to return. My uncle and I communicated in the bare minimum of prose, our
language reduced to the lowest common denominator.

On the passenger seat, there was a receipt with something scribbled on the back: *"Juan Kim (718) 555-9876."*

"Who's Juan Kim?" I asked my uncle.

Sang's tone grew instantly impatient. "How long you working
Food you still not know Juan?"

Oh. *Hwan.*

"He Korean from Argentina," my uncle explained. "Just like you Korean from America."

This explained why his Korean, though far better than mine, was always shrouded in hesitation. I wondered if it was also why he looked at me frankly, unwaveringly, when most Koreans didn't make much eye contact.

"All this week Juan not show up. Uncle calling, calling that number, nobody pick up. Today again he not show." He tapped the side of his head. "Always Uncle think something not right with Juan. Maybe happen because of immigration. Lot of people, they get broken after. Never they be the same."

"When did Juan come to Ameri—" I started to ask when my uncle interrupted me.

"You know that lady?"

He pointed to a woman whose back was to us, shuffling along Northern Boulevard. One arm was up in the air, trying to flag down a taxi. Yet when a battered sedan—a gypsy cab—slowed down in front of her, she instantly lowered her arm and faced forward, pretending she hadn't seen it. But she wasn't going to find any yellow cabs in this part of Queens. Over one shoulder was draped a cloth tote bag. A WNYC tote bag. After the car in front drove away, she stopped in her tracks and looked behind her—her stricken face gazing not at us but at the forlorn road. It was definitely Beth.

Immediately I scrunched lower in my seat.

"What's wrong you?" my uncle said, slowing down and pulling over to the curb. He honked. Beth jumped with fright and, as if on instinct, waved her hand at us to go away.

But Sang did not drive off. He opened the window—*my* window—and called out over me, to Beth. "You needing ride?"

When Beth recognized our faces, relief flooded her features; but then, when her eyes caught mine, she tightened.

Sang repeated the offer, and she mumbled, "If it's . . . not an inconvenience . . . I'd really appreciate it." She reached for the backseat door handle.

"No!" Sang shouted through the window.

Beth, alarmed, froze. "I'm sorry, I don't have to—"

He ignored her and jerked his head at me. *"Nunchi-do umnya?"*

That was my cue to *yangbo* my seat to Beth. When I stepped out of the car to move to the back, Beth lifted her arm (trembling with hesitation? with exhaustion?) and touched my shoulder. Then, just as quickly, she pulled away.

When Beth stepped inside, the car suddenly felt very small. She had that effect; her presence was all-consuming. From the backseat I could smell her oily, sweaty scalp. I expected, too, for her words to take over. But instead her voice came out in an enervated warble. "Dropped off Devon at Ed's school. Got on the subway, and it stalled. For hours. We had to. . . . climb through the tunnel."

I waited for more of Beth's words, which were never in short supply. I saw roadblocks ahead, the miles of potential spiraling conflict—not conversation—between her and Sang, between her and me. *Shut it down, Jane. Shut it down.*

My uncle gestured for me to give Beth some water—he kept a jug of Poland Spring in the backseat. I poured some into a plastic cup and passed it up to her. "I take you home first," he said to Beth. "You live Thorn and Henry Street, right?"

I remembered it was Sang who had retrieved my things from the house when I was in Korea.

"Good memory," Beth said, revived from the warm water. "But Jane"—she turned around to face me—"lives in Astoria, right? We'll drop her off first, and then you can hop back on the BQE."

"I take you first," he said. "Is okay, we not be inconvenienced."

"No, no. I insist." Her tone was so firm that it made my uncle demur.

We lapsed into silence for maybe half a minute; my uncle was never one for chitchat. When customers at the store would say things, he'd nod wordlessly at them with crescent-moon eyes, a smile forced across his face. If words were required, he'd pull from his repertoire of stock phrases: *So sorry. No problem. Thank you very much. Having nice day.* For the sales vendors and union reps, he reserved his more choice vocabulary: *Is your fault delivery late! You say nine case one case free, but now you trying cheat me?*

But he looked over at Beth and said, "I use to owning fruit-and-vegetable, not far you. So terrible back then, Smith Street!"

I expected Beth to bristle. Beth, the biggest cheerleader for Brooklyn, took the slightest remark about her adopted borough as a personal affront. But I was surprised by her reaction. "Even now you still have to be careful," she said. "I don't let my daughter walk down Smith Street alone at night. I can only *imagine* what things must've been like back then."

"So, Beth," my uncle began. "How is . . . *guh* Chinese girl?" I braced myself for Beth's indignant reaction—*My Chinese girl? How dare you!*—but it never came.

"My daughter, Devon? She's doing . . . good, not great. You know. *Teenagers.*"

Sang shook his head knowingly. "But she must be very smart, too. Chinese people . . ." He paused. In that pause I feared all the possible things that would spill out of his mouth: *Chinese people so cheap. Chinese people not having bathroom. Chinese people like next Mexicans.* Sang went on. "Chinese people," he repeated, "they know how to using this." He tapped his temple.

I breathed a sigh of relief but braced myself for Beth's retort. *I take issue with your comment. You're a culturally insensitive boor.* Beth would lecture him on his sweeping generalizations, his outdated theories of eugenics. She'd quote Stanley Obuheim, Sam Surati, or her own work, to bolster her arguments.

Instead she turned toward Sang, her left cheek lifted by a grin. "You're right, she's very smart." Beth tapped her own head. "She goes to Hunter. Thanks to Jane's help."

"Eh?" went my uncle.

"Jane helped Devon study for the exam. Your niece is a very bright young woman. You're a lucky man, Sang."

I was utterly floored. This woman had no reason to praise me. The last time we saw each other, she'd rightly chased me out of her house.

My uncle waved his hand. "She only okay. She not like Einshtein."

"Well, there's only one Einshtein—I mean, Einstein." They shared a laugh.

It was a little surreal: My uncle and Beth, chattering on like old friends? Never would I ever have imagined them sharing anything— not even the physical space of a car. I watched the trees lining the highway speed by and thought about just how far we'd come to reach this point.

Beth turned around in her seat to face me. "Jane, I never had the chance to say thank you."

I shrugged. "It was my uncle who spotted you first."

"No, I mean . . . for talking, with Devon."

I should have been thanking her. For welcoming me into her home. For showing me a world beyond Flushing. I shrugged again, this time in shyness.

After a little lull, I said, "Beth, I want to say I'm so sorry. What I did, with Ed, it was—"

Beth's eyes darted up at me through the rearview mirror; shooting me *nunchi.* "I was sorry to hear it ended, Jane." Her eyes now glanced over at Sang. I could tell he was pretending not to listen.

"It was for the best," I managed to say.

But my uncle had heard it all. I should have feared his judgment— in the tight confines of his car, no less—but I couldn't keep apologizing to him for who I was.

Then he spoke. "Our Jane not so everyday. But people not always recognize. Should be grateful."

Should be grateful. I don't think I ever had a clearer picture of my uncle before that moment. I could have read his words as *I* should be grateful. Just as I'd spent a lifetime taking each of his rough-hewn words as insults. But perhaps they were simply veiled praises and he lacked the language to make them smooth and polished. I felt one word: *jung.* That warmhearted sensation, rushing over me.

Beth nodded. "Someday someone deserving will."

We turned off the BQE and continued down Thirty-first Street.

Sang and Beth talked on. About Brooklyn. Queens. Baseball, even. Beth commented on the metal bat rolling on the floor by her feet. Sang confessed to being "number one Mets fan" (a fact my uncle never once shared with me). From my perch in the backseat, I found the counterpoint between the two—Sang's blunt, awkward speech, Beth's overabundance of eloquent words—creating a surprising harmony. They still managed to thread their way across that divide.

We pulled up to 917 Helen Street. Nina was perched on an aluminum chair on the porch, fanning herself with a newspaper. When she saw me, she brightened. Sang and Beth waved good-bye before setting off, and I bounded up the steps to our house.

We toasted with Sang's beers. Later we ventured over to the bars, where pints flowed in a free stream—all of us celebrating the fact that it was *only* a blackout. The general tenor of the night was relief, followed by revelry. We all knew it could have been worse—a lot, lot worse. Eventually Nina and I returned to our porch. We talked about our days. We talked about work. We talked about how we each found our way during the blackout. Somewhere, in the distance far behind us, the Manhattan skyline was extinguished, cast in its own violet shadows. The rest of New York glowed in the moonlight.

It was good to be home.

Epilogue

Commuters give the city its tidal restlessness,
natives give it solidity and continuity, but the
settlers give it passion.

—E. B. White, "Here Is New York"

Queens was never supposed to be the plan. I had spent so much of my earlier life riding the 7 *away* from Flushing. I'd stare out the train windows at the city skyline, imagining the life that awaited me there. But even the best-laid plans get rerouted. So here I am, standing on the platform at Queensboro Plaza (wearing a gold-lamé dress, thanks to Eunice Oh), waiting to board the Flushing-bound 7. We're right at the base of the Fifty-ninth Street Bridge, and from the elevated platform you can see the interlaced roads—westbound, eastbound—just as the subway tracks dip up and down, each making way for the other. The Con Edison smokestacks stand tall and proud at the foot of the East River. And though you can't see it from up here, beside the power plant is a bright green baseball field, and I know at this time of day it is filled with picnicking families and men playing soccer. The 7 pulls in, and I step aboard; the train car lets forth its usual creaks and groans with the weight of all us passengers.

Then the train sets off. The city falls away behind us. Flushing blooms ahead.

I never did get that Wall Street job, but I am a CEO, of sorts. Nina and I run our own property-management business, which we officially started not long after the blackout but probably unofficially formed the night of the boeuf bourguignon dinner. The job is exactly that— we help landlords manage their properties. It's an extension of what we've already been doing all these years with Nina's great-uncle's house. I do the financials and act as the liaison between the owner and the tenants. I'm indebted to my early years at Food, which proved to be a good training ground for the now-endless calls and e-mails about late fees, bounced checks, puckering floor tiles, and plumbing problems. (Sometimes, when fielding complaints from the most persnickety of tenants, I think of Mrs. O'Gall shaking a head of iceberg at us. God rest her soul.) Nina drums up new business for us—all those happy-hour connections she made in our early twenties are now paying off—and is also the literal handyman of our operation. The buildings we manage are superless, so Nina is dispatched to the apartment units—tool belt and box in hand. We'd like to think we're younger, nimbler, as well as more tech-savvy (thanks to the influence of our friends in the neighborhood) than our competitors. Being a handy(wo) man is a decidedly unglamorous job, but Nina derives a certain high from it. It always seemed to me that Nina and Eunice shared a fascination with the inner workings of things. I often wondered if it was a trait passed down from their fathers—Mr. Scagliano being an electrician and Dr. Oh a cardiologist. What if Nina had had the same opportunities as Eunice, or vice versa? Maybe Nina would've been the one who'd headed off to MIT, poring over the digital and electrical innards of a computer. Or Eunice poised over how-to manuals, studying wiring and plumbing diagrams.

It's a little uncanny how our neighborhood has taken off. There is an inherent humility in the Queens identity—saying that's where you were from was something you uttered with a disclaimer. Watching these transplants now proudly embrace their adopted borough . . . I can't help but feel it's a little like a negation of everything I come from. Although Nina thinks I should accept this renaissance for what it is (after all, she's witnessed it with her home borough, now overrun with "Beth types"). And she assures me Queens is still plenty scruffy.

Though it looks like she's on her way to becoming an official Queensite: her great-uncle is putting our house on the market. She floated the idea of our going in on the house together. We'd stay on the top floor and continue to rent out the other two units. Eventually, when Nina and I start our own families, we could each take a floor and still have one income-producing unit. We've turned a tidy profit on our business—enough to cover the down payment but not enough for construction. Even though it'd probably be cheaper to do a demo and throw up one of those prefab aluminum-siding houses, Nina wants to keep the integrity of her great-uncle's home. Some things are just worth salvaging. Meanwhile, the inheritance my grandfather left me has been sitting untouched in a bank in Seoul, slowly accruing interest. I've talked it over with Uncle Sang. We ran the numbers, and he thinks I should go for it. It might make a good investment yet.

He is, I think, proud that I've started my own business (I know this because when I showed him our first paycheck, he offered a stiff pat on the back), but I also know he still wishes I were a larger part of Food.

As for my uncle—it turned out he used *his* inheritance to purchase Food's commercial property as well as the building next to it. George, of all people, has taken an interest in the family business. He keeps urging my uncle to tear down the property next door—currently rented to a *jjajangmyun* noodle restaurant—and expand Food. He's become something of a health nut—most recently he's been on a kale-juice kick—and he thinks the store should tap into the organic market. But Uncle Sang likes the predictability of his small-but-manageable margins. "Maybe I'm younger, I be more risky," he says. "But I'm too old now." It's an ongoing debate between the two of them. In truth, business at Food could be better. It's a tight grocery market, with a growing number of larger, fancier supermarkets cropping up all over. But the property value of Food has shot up. Uncle Sang has, however, fared far better than Daedong Fish Market, Kumgang Mountain Dry

Cleaning, Chosun Dynasty Auto Body. None of his friends owned
their own buildings. Their landlords did not renew their leases, and
they've been forced farther up Northern. The Chinese, according to
my uncle, have taken over Flushing.

My uncle has afforded the family a little indulgence, to the surprise
of us all: the purchase of a second home. It's a small cottage on the
North Fork of Long Island. My aunt and uncle drive out there after
they close up shop, and wake to the sunrise. Uncle Sang doesn't say
this, but I know it reminds him of that first home, the one he and my
mother had abandoned long ago in the North. The house that smelled
of wild rice and the Donghae Sea. The house on Long Island smells
like wild wheat and the Sound.

And what, dear reader, of Ed Farley? According to Beth, he's still
adjuncting at Queens College. She worries about his financial state—
he only recently got health insurance, and she suspects he is still living
off his "buyout" of the brownstone. Then, tentatively, she'll add, "He
still asks about you, Jane." Sometimes I think about what would have
happened if Ed and I were still together. But how can I move forward
if I'm consumed with memories of the past? I can only march on.

Devon also sees a lot of us. She comes over to watch Korean dramas with Nina. Those two are *obsessed* with them. They watch everything, from the fluffy soap operas to historical romances to the recent
wave of dark indie thrillers. I walked in on a scene where a guy was
holding a pair of bloodstained scissors to his tongue, and I had to walk
right out. It's probably for the best that Beth's in the dark about this
particular habit.

This summer Beth is taking Devon to China. Beth's had posters
made to tape up in the village square where Devon was abandoned.
The posters have pictures of Devon as a little girl and text in both English and Chinese: *"Dear China Mom, I just want you to know your little
girl is okay. You must have worried all these years about your little one.
We are so blessed. Love, America Mom."* She'd gotten the idea from one
of her adoptive-parenting listserves. Last week Beth proposed something to me: Would I consider coming along on their trip? "Devon

would *really* appreciate the emotional support. And I just know it'll make the transition for her so much easier."

"But I don't speak Chinese," I said. What I really meant was, *But I have no idea what it'll feel like for Devon.* Beth squeezed my hand and said, "You'd know a little better than I would." All week, while mulling over this trip to China, I've been thinking I should also pay my respects to Emo and Big Uncle in Korea. Emo, who wrote to tell me she's getting married. Married! *"What business does an 'Old Miss' like me have getting married?"* she said. Her fiancé is an older man, one of her father's former business associates. He's a divorcé with two grown-up kids. I think of Emo bustling about with wedding plans, cooking chicken ginseng stew. I hope her fiancé makes her happy. I hope he knows how grateful he should be.

Mary, too, lives in Seoul now. She works at my old language school. After graduation she landed a job in the subprime-mortgage market with J.P. Morgan. When things went bust, it threw all kinds of questions up in the air for her. A month after being laid off, she was on a plane to Korea. She tells me she can't quite keep pace with the hurry-hurry nature of things; the second she blinks, "at least three trends have gone by." Which means all references I had from the time I was there are now hopelessly outdated. She also adds, "*Honhyol* celebrities like you are all the rage now. Daewon Hedley, Jason Oh-Smith, Tanya Reese . . . well, maybe Tanya Reese's already on her way out." (It's something Nina keeps telling me, too: "You half-Asian girls are the new California blonds.") "But anyway. You should come back for a visit. You probably wouldn't recognize the place."

Speaking of Korea, I've reconnected with someone else from my time abroad. Not Changhoon, not Monica, but *Rachel.* She's here getting her M.B.A. at Columbia. Once a month we meet on Thirty-second Street for barbecue and *soju.* Rachel's much more relaxed out of the context of Seoul; she's even been known to leave the house barefaced and wearing sneakers. When she first reached out, she brought me news from Korea: Changhoon was married. To *Monica.* "She's *thrilled, of course,*" Rachel said, leaning across the sizzling plate of fatty pork. *"But between you and me, I think he kind of thought, well, she's there, so why not?"* She'd attended their wedding right before she moved to New York, but she hasn't spoken to either of them since. *"It was a little tap-tap-hae being Monica's friend,"* Rachel said. *"That girl's content to be discontent."*

Speaking of weddings, I end this story with one. No, no, not mine. Three months ago Eunice's invitation came in the mail. *Eunice Eunhae Oh and Timothy Gould Mann request your presence in celebrating their matrimony on the twenty-fifth of May. . . .*

And that was when I finally learned Threepio's real name.

Her father, however, will not be walking her down the aisle. Not because he doesn't want to, but because Eunice insists that a host of Stormtroopers escort her instead. I imagined the sadness with which Dr. Oh processed the news, his gentle eyes growing soft and cloudy.

I'm on my way to that wedding now—the ceremony will be at church, the reception in the basement. Eunice asked me to be one of her bridesmaids, which is why I'm wearing this ridiculous dress. (Threepio was pushing for gold bridesmaid bikinis, but that idea was quickly shot down. By me.) Eunice is seating me next to Threepio's best man and frat brother from MIT. "Much in common you and Artoo have," she said. Apparently he, too, runs his own business—a housing Web site where people list their vacant apartments that rent by the day or the week, like an ad hoc B&B. "Hit it off you will." Then Eunice fluttered her fingers at me. *Artoo:* I pictured a dorky Indian guy, most probably a Course VI like Eunice, and shrugged. "Sure, why not," I said. I try to keep an open mind.

The 7 is doing its usual rickety-racket routine. I'll ride this train to its final destination, where Uncle Sang and Aunt Hannah will be waiting for me. My aunt will go tsk-tsk-tsk at me for wearing my dress on the train—a *nunchi*-less move, no doubt. My uncle will be double-parked on the wrong corner of Roosevelt and Main, or *I* will be standing on the wrong corner of Roosevelt and Main, and we'll fight about it the whole ride over to church. It's high time that the MTA invested in some new train cars. But then I'd have to get to know a new train, and I'm certain some part of me would mourn the loss of the old, for all its flaws. After years of riding the 7, I've grown familiar with its herky-jerkiness, learning to accept its particular rhythms instead of fighting against them—or running away. And to realize, despite it all, that it has good intentions. I've begun to feel a comfort in its clumsy rocking. We've weathered so much together these past two-plus decades. You might even say we've developed a kind of *jung*.

ACKNOWLEDGMENTS

Writing a novel is lonely work; I am indebted to so many people whose help and support along the way made this even remotely possible. To Umma and Abba, for teaching me the word *jung* (and for never forcing me to become a doctor, lawyer, and/or concert pianist). To Unnie and Oppa, for the kind of tough love and torment only older siblings can provide. To Richard, Clara, and Gage: your endless giggles and innocence are an inspiration.

To my thesis advisor Xuefei Jin, for guiding this novel through its early drafts, informing so much of its structure, and urging me to "put everything" into this one. To the ever-generous writers Lisa Borders and Michelle Hoover, for whipping this manuscript into shape and taking a ruthless red pen to cliché-ridden (riddled?) sentences like these. To my agents Esmond Harmsworth and Lane Zachary: thank you for your literary counsel and beyond invaluable edits—and for fighting for Eunice (as well as "Poo, Rushing").

To my editor Pam Dorman: I swear you know these characters better than I do!—thank you for pushing them to be fuller, rounder, and subtler in ways I didn't know how. To Seema Mahanian, Clare Ferraro, Kathryn Court, Patrick Nolan, Carolyn Coleburn, Louise Braverman, Kristin Matzen, Andrea Lam, Roseanne Serra, Francesca Belanger, Nancy Sheppard, Sarah Janet, Winnie De Moya, John Fagan, Hal Fessenden, Leigh Butler, Tricia Conley, Kate Griggs, and everyone on the hardcover and paperback sales teams at Penguin Random House: thank you so much for welcoming Jane home.

My gratitude to Fulbright, the Korean-American Educational Commission, and Professor Sung Kyungjun for supporting my novel research in Seoul. I am so grateful for fellowship support from the Center for Fiction in New York, the Jerome Foundation, and the American Association of University Women. To Grub Street in Boston and to all the Novel Incubees, for their careful reads—you guys rock.

A huge thanks to Diana Ahn, for giving this manuscript multiple reads, sharing her real estate and construction expertise, and making a lifetime of slogging on the 7 train all the more bearable. To my Kun-Gomo and my late Kun-Gomobu, for taking such good care of me in Seoul. To Hyemin Yu, for fielding all my stupid questions about modern Korean culture and for her indispensable research skills. To Peter Dimock and Ariana X. Dimock, for their generous reads and insight. To Brett Taylor, for his tireless energy, cartographic prowess, and help fine-tuning the final drafts of this novel. To all my friends and family in New York, Boston, and Korea who have lent their eyes, ears, and patience to this effort.

I am beholden to Charlotte Brontë's *Jane Eyre*.

And to my two great loves: New York City, for inspiring me to become a writer; and Boston, for teaching me how.

APPENDIX: KOREAN FAMILY TERMS

Korean family relations are extremely intricate; below are some commonly used family terms. While it is acceptable to call younger relations by their first name, older relations must be addressed using titles marking that specific relationship. These titles are based not only on your gender and age, but also on the gender and age of the relation you are addressing, as well as whether that relation is on your mother's or father's side. (This is by no means an exhaustive list; e.g., when a Korean marries, he or she will be faced with a whole new set of terms for each in-law member.) Unless otherwise stated, all of these terms are direct addresses.

The Republic of Korea officially uses the Revised Romanization system to romanize Korean words. However, I have departed from the system where I feel other phonetic spellings better represent the pronunciation of the word.

NUCLEAR-FAMILY TERMS

Abuji: Father

Abba: Dad

Umuni: Mother

Umma: Mom

Hyung: Big Brother; what a younger male calls his older brother (or cousin, friend, etc.)

Oppa: Big Brother; what a younger female calls her older brother (or cousin, boyfriend, or older intimate male in her life)

Nuna: Big Sister; what a younger male calls his older sister (or cousin, friend, etc.)

Unnie: Big Sister; what a younger female calls her older sister (or cousin, friend, etc.)

Terms for Grandparents
Harabuji: Grandfather (general term)
Chin-Harabuji: your father's father
Wae-Harabuji: your mother's father
Halmuni: Grandmother (general term)
Chin-Halmuni: your father's mother
Wae-Halmuni: your mother's mother

Terms for Uncle
Kun-Abba: your father's older brother
Jageun-Abba: your father's younger brother
Gomobu: your father's sister's husband
Wae-samchon: your mother's brother (older specified by the prefix *Kun;* younger by the prefix *Jageun;* multiple uncles are often given ordinal numbers in the order of their birth)
Samchon: traditionally your father's bachelor and/or younger brother, but sometimes used as a general term for uncle
Emobu: your mother's sister's husband

Terms for Aunt
Emo: your mother's sister (older specified by the prefix *Kun;* younger by the prefix *Jageun;* multiple aunts are given ordinal numbers)
Gomo: your father's sister (older specified by the prefix *Kun;* younger by the prefix *Jageun;* multiple aunts are given ordinal numbers)
Wae-sugmo: your mother's brother's wife
Kun-Umma: your father's eldest brother's wife
Jageun-Umma: your father's younger brother's wife
Sugmo: another term for your father's younger brother's wife, or the wife of a younger distant male relation of your father